SET *for* DANGER

IN THE PRESIDENT'S SERVICE—
BOOK 15

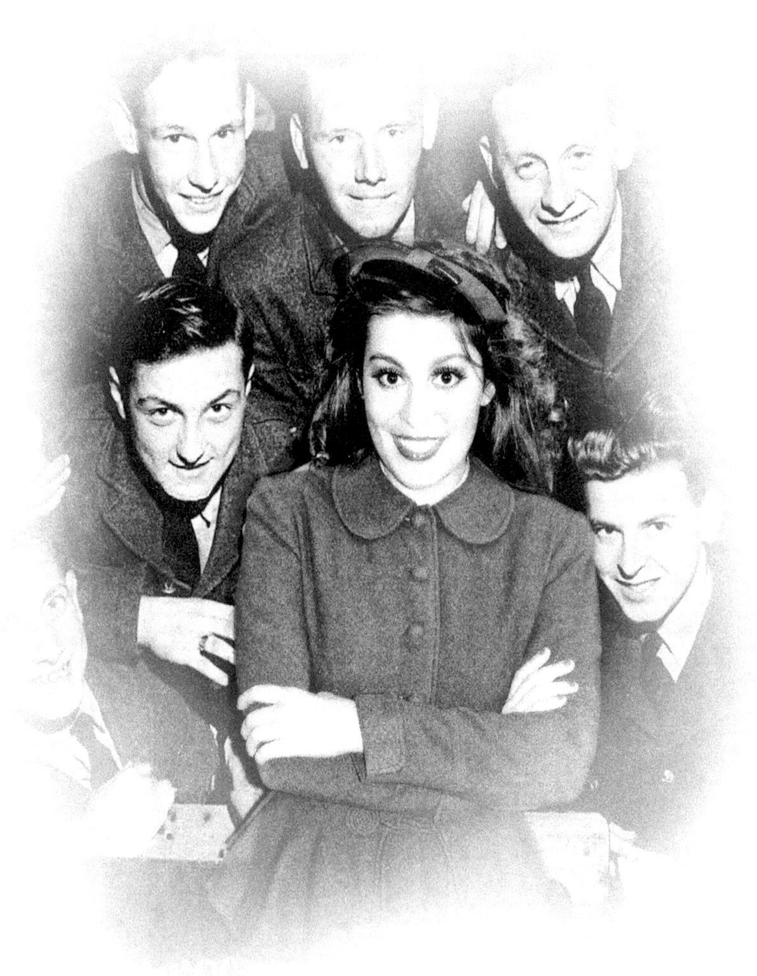

SET *for* DANGER

IN THE PRESIDENT'S SERVICE—
BOOK 15

Ace Collins

Elk Lake
PUBLISHING, INC.

Plymouth, Massachusetts

Copyright Notice

Cover and Interior Design: Derinda Babcock
Editor(s): Tish Martin, Deb Haggerty
Published in Association with Hartline Literary Agency

PUBLISHED BY: Elk Lake Publishing, Inc., 35 Dogwood Dr., Plymouth, MA 02360, 2018

Library Cataloging Data
Names: Collins, Ace (Ace Collins)
Set for Danger: In the President's Service—Book 15 | Ace Collins
406 p. 13.97cm × 21.59cm (5.5 in × 8.5 in.)
Description: Helen Meeker on a USO tour, Teresa Bryant chases Gertrude Root, Napoleon Lancelot tracks down a Hollywood star.
Identifiers: ISBN-13: 978-1-948888-19-6 (trade)
| 978-1-948888-20-2 (POD) | 978-1-948888-21-9 (e-book.)
Key Words: Helen Meeker, Teresa Bryant, WWII, Hollywood Canteen, USO Tours, Murder, Spy Thriller
LCCN: 20182018948423 Fiction

CHAPTER I

Saturday, May 16, 1942
1:42 p.m.
Naval Hospital, Pearl Harbor, Hawaii

What was once paradise but had now become the middle of hell on earth—Honolulu—the center of operations for the Pacific front, was in the middle of a hot, humid day.

After taking out a threadbare handkerchief to mop sweat from his brow, a slightly built balding man, about sixty, wearily walked up two flights of stairs to the entry of a third-floor conference room at Pearl Harbor Navy Hospital. Dr. Cecil Dixon, a man who, up until three months ago, had lived his life in Colorado, had volunteered for medical service in Hawaii to help meet the growing needs of a nation at war. In the language of the day, Dixon was a shrink, and in just ninety days, he'd treated more patients than he had in the last twenty years of private practice in Boulder. And they just kept coming. Most of those he counseled returned to active duty, others were sent home with physical and mental challenges few could comprehend. Was war hell? The doctor didn't know, but he was sure that war opened the door for regular visits from hell, and some of those visits lasted much longer than others. In fact, some never ended.

After pausing at the entry to gather his thoughts, Dixon forced a smile and opened the door to the ten-by-ten-foot room.

The man waiting there, already seated at a small round table, had just returned from a visit to hell and had the scars to prove it. Bathed in the afternoon light pouring from one of the room's two windows, the broad-shouldered captain was obviously a casualty of war—his face was a disaster—his nose crooked, mouth twisted, and a railroad track of scars ran from just over his right eye down his cheek and to his neck. And in his group, he was the lucky one. The others had all died.

"Captain Sharp," the doctor said, stepping into the room and approaching the patient, "I'm Dr. Dixon."

Sharp stood, revealing a six-foot figure that had once been finely sculpted muscle but was now little more than skin and bones. Yet in the man's blue eyes, there was still life, and as they shook hands, Dixon noted unexpected strength in the patient's grip.

"Dr. Dixon, I think you were the first person I saw when they brought me here two months ago."

"I remember that day, young man. When you got off the ship, you could barely stand. In fact, you were more dead than alive. You've come a long way since then. I'd guess you've put on fifteen pounds, and your face is looking much better."

"Well, if you like to study road maps or railroad tracks," Sharp said with irony, "I'm your cup of tea. And on the weight, I'm slowly getting some back. Those darn parasites are hard to get rid of, and they're hungrier than I am."

"Why don't we sit down," Dixon suggested. When his patient was comfortable, the doctor pointed at Sharp's face. "We'll be sending you to Los Angeles to fix that. There's a plastic surgeon in Hollywood who works on the stars, and he has volunteered to make your face look like your Army photo ID."

Sharp laughed. "Can't we go for something a bit better? I'd like to look more like Joel McCrea or Cary Grant."

"Just give him the word," Dixon said before glancing at a file that had been left for him on the table. After leafing through just four paragraphs of handwritten notes, he crossed his arms, leaned back in the chair, and smiled. "You're quite the hero."

"I survived when my friends didn't. That doesn't make me a hero."

"That was on December 8th?"

"Yeah, I was stationed in the Philippines, and the Japs overran us. We didn't retreat fast enough and just got murdered. We fought hard but didn't have a chance. I watched my buddies … my brothers, if you will … go down one by one and I was helpless to stop their pain as they died."

Dixon sadly shook his head. He'd heard this same story more than a dozen times in the past few months. He cleared his throat and continued with his interview. "The notes give me the facts, but no particulars. If you don't mind me asking, how did you survive?"

Sharp tensed. "I didn't run. I'm no coward."

"They don't give medals to cowards. I just thought you might want to share how you managed to get away. As you are surely aware, when the Japanese catch you, then you normally stay caught."

"I didn't get away." The marine's eyes looked toward the ceiling for a few seconds before he shook his head. "I got shot, a mortar exploded, and then I don't remember anything."

"So they thought you were dead?"

"I guess so," Sharp answered with a shrug. "When I woke up there were bodies all around me, but the Japanese had moved on."

"I can't imagine what you must have felt." Dixon's tone indicated great sincerity. He really couldn't grasp what it would be like to wake up and be the only one of twelve to have survived, and to be badly wounded, alone, and confused! Sharp must have been overwhelmed. Maybe that's why he needed to find out what it was in this man that powered him to overcome the odds and survive. "Please tell me more."

The words now tumbled from Sharp's mouth as if they were pouring from a sack. "After discovering I was the only one left, I thought about killing myself. I could hear the Japs and I knew somehow they would find me. Still, I just sat on the grass and waited to be captured. Then, when no one came, I wandered into the jungle."

"How did you survive? Your injuries were severe, and you were all alone."

Sharp took a breath, pushed away from the table, got up, and looked out the window. "A native family found me." He shook his head. "Actually, they didn't find me as much as I crashed into their hut. They took care of me for about a month, and when I gained some strength, they hid me under some fruit in an ox cart and got me to the home of a Filipino preacher. He used his contacts and arranged to have me smuggled out of the area. The trip took several months of relay work, walking a few miles, always at night, and then hiding for as much as a week, but his team of people got me to a small ocean village. Once there, two young men paddled me across miles of ocean to where an Aussie group was entrenched. They put me on the next supply boat back to Australia, and in time, I managed to get to Pearl Harbor."

"And now you'll be getting to go home," Dixon said. He glanced back at the file. "I believe you're from Chicago."

"I guess," Sharp replied, his voice now emotionless. "I mean I grew up in an orphanage there. But I've got no family." He paused, returned to the table, and drummed his fingers while gathering his thoughts. "The guys I served with were the only family I've really known." He ran his hand over his deeply scarred face and frowned. "Besides no one from my past would recognize me now."

"The surgeon in Hollywood will fix that," Dixon assured him. "Captain Sharp, I know how you are physically. You are recovering nicely. But how do you feel emotionally?"

"Emotionally?"

Dixon pointed to his own head. "How is your mind? What are you thinking about? Do you have nightmares?"

"Am I crazy? Is that what you're asking?" Sharp obviously resented the implication.

"No, not crazy, I want to know if you still cared about the things you once cared about. Sometimes, after what you've been though, it's hard to separate the horrors of war from the simple joys of real life. Some can't escape having experienced a nightmare."

"I was raised in an orphanage. My mother was never married and gave me up when I was two. I never really had any simple joys. I just survived from day to day. My life wasn't that much different from this war. I've always been unlucky. The odds were always against me. I always told folks I was born to lose."

"And yet you're here," Dixon pointed out. "As I see it, your life proves you are a survivor."

"I guess."

"And you're much more than what you let on."

Sharp looked concerned. "What do you mean by that?"

"You have a college degree. In fact, according to Army records, you're brilliant."

"I worked hard. ROTC paid for my education, and when I got out, I was paying the country back. And then the war started, and we weren't ready. We were fighting a superior force, and they cut us to pieces. And then, I discovered all that time in school didn't do me one ounce of good."

"You sound bitter."

"I'm not bitter, just a realist. The Germans and Japs are a lot better at war than we are. They have a passion for it. In fact, they welcome it. For them, war's a test of their society's will and a nod to their history. So while they act, the Americans react."

"You sound like you admire them," Dixon noted.

"In some ways, I do," Sharp admitted. "They were prepared and we weren't. I admire folks who look ahead and are ready."

The captain paused and licked his lips. In that instant, Dixon thought he detected a sense of apprehension in the man's deeply scarred face. A second later, the look was gone.

"When can I get back to duty?" Sharp asked. The question was heavy with urgency. "I have some scores to settle."

"In time, but for now you have to get to the States and let them finish the work we started here."

"So, I'll be fit for combat?" Sharp demanded.

"Yes, but with your college degree and your special skill set, I don't think you'll be using a gun in the future."

"What?"

"One of the generals asked me about you yesterday. The brass seems to think a man with your brains and knowledge could likely save more lives by helping to plan this war than by actually putting your life on the line, fighting."

"No!"

Dixon gently smiled. "Captain, isn't it true you were about to be transferred to the Intelligence Department in Washington before the war broke out? There was even a story about the move in your hometown newspaper. The clipping is in your file. Isn't it also true you had agreed to take a post working in DC with a general there—a Jefferson Root? Do remember asking for that assignment?"

"Yes, but that was before I got a real taste of war. That was before my friends were killed in battle. I have something else on my mind now."

Dixon shrugged. While he could identify with Sharp's wishes, he couldn't sympathize with them. Right now, what a man wanted meant little to the military. This was war and it was all about what the country needed. After Sharp's face was operated on, he would be given his orders and expected to do his job. Nothing was going to change that. He wasn't going back to the front lines. In fact, he wouldn't be anywhere near.

"Captain," Dixon explained, "the future will be what it will be. You need to just concentrate on enjoying this day. Tomorrow, you'll be headed to Los Angeles and a few months from now you'll look as good, if not better than, new."

"All I've thought about since December 8th is fighting. That's what kept me going when I was running for my life. I've got to get back to action—"

"Son," Dixon cut in, "I miss my wife and kids. In fact, I have a granddaughter back in Colorado I've never seen. But what I'm doing here, saving the lives of men like you, is far more important than being with my family. If Uncle Sam decides you need to be in Washington, then you go there and do your best. You don't have to shoot a rifle to get revenge. The real revenge is in winning this war so everyone can go home … including me."

Sharp frowned. "But not everyone goes home. Those guys who died with me didn't even get a proper burial."

"You were saved for something," Dixon said, "and you joined the army knowing you have to follow orders. So just serve your country in the best way possible."

"I'm an athlete. I need to be using my gifts where they will do the most good. I rue the day I volunteered for that assignment in Washington."

"Why did you do it?"

"I was bored."

"I think you requested the transfer to intelligence because, Captain, you knew you were the man for the job."

For the first time, Sharp displayed the hint of a smile. Perhaps Dixon had been able to give the recovering solider some perspective.

"Maybe you're right, Doc. Maybe I can help my country best in Washington."

CHAPTER 2

Friday, December 25, 1942
7:50 p.m.
Main Restaurant, Lincoln Hotel, Chicago, Illinois

Just one sentence—the mere mention of a party—opened a door to solving everything that had been buried so deeply in her mind for so long. Thanks to the single sentence, Teresa Bryant now remembered who was behind the attempts on Helen Meeker's life. The answer was so obvious, so why had she taken so long to match a voice with a name? As the illumination set in, Bryant figured Meeker's younger sister, sitting directly across the table, could likely read her face. The young woman was naturally intuitive; surely she must know the mystery had been solved. Yet, if she did, she said nothing.

"Alison," Bryant said, "you finish up your pie." While trying to keep her voice calm, she added, "I've got to get back to the room and call Helen at the Glasglow's."

The young woman didn't question the sudden change in plans. "Okay."

Bryant stood, dropped her napkin on the table, and hurried to the lobby.

A stout, older woman, dressed in a bulky mink coat and oversized hat, stepped in front of her and announced, "I liked you a lot better when you worked for me. I just thought you were seductive then, but now, I realize you're so much more. You're as smart as Einstein and as dangerous as a viper."

"Gertrude Root." Bryant's voice was frigid and her tone sarcastic as she looked at the woman. After fully taking in her adversary's hard, cold features, she said, "Until now I never noticed you have your brother's eyes. If I look deep enough, I can clearly see the pits of hell."

"Flattery will get you nowhere," Root snapped. "Now move toward the front door. We're going to take a ride. You'll like my driver. Meeker met him once in an alley and really fell for him."

"You don't have a gun in your hand," Bryant pointed out, "and even if you did, you wouldn't shoot me here. There are too many witnesses. Even for a power-hungry dame like you, survival trumps everything else. So, I've got the upper hand now. I control *your* fate, and I've got a cop friend who'd love to meet you."

Root seemed unimpressed with Bryant's threats. "Where's your waiter?"

Bryant's brown almost black eyes moved from Root to the dining room.

The man in question standing directly behind Alison now looked a great deal like an assassin. His eyes were dark and menacing, his weak jaw set, and his thin lips revealed a sinister grin. For all practical purposes, he personified death dressed in a red jacket.

Seemingly satisfied Bryant knew the score, Root explained, "Marco has a way of silently ending a life. He can do so quickly and quietly, so sometimes folks don't realize the victim is dead for an hour. I love his technique, and you might admire it too. He uses an ice pick that's sharper than a razor blade. He quickly inserts the pick into a victim's ear, and a second later with just a single thrust, the brain's destroyed. The method is quick, neat, and almost bloodless. So, if you don't go with me now, Meeker's sister dies. What a tragic end to Christmas that would be."

"If I go with you," Bryant whispered, her eyes still locked on the waiter, "how do I know that Marco won't kill Alison anyway?"

"Life is filled with questions," Root replied. "Some of those questions can't be answered until the events play out. Now what's it going to be? Your life or that of the sweet little creature over there?"

Bryant's gaze moved from the waiter to Alison to Root. Obvious to Bryant now was this evil woman had more than her brother's eyes, she also possessed his cold, unfeeling, calculating heart. Her wicked grin proved she didn't have people killed just to further her agenda—she enjoyed it.

"You're sick," Bryant spat, contempt framing both her words and expression.

"Actually, I'm smart. The key was finding out you had reservations for the dining room tonight. Knowing that, I managed to pull some strings and get Marco a job this morning. So, I figured a way to make this play happen."

"That couldn't have been easy—the staff has been here for a long time. There's not much turnover. And tips are much better on holidays. That's why everyone wants to work them."

"Actually," Root explained, "it was very easy. Two of the waiters didn't come in today, and I volunteered one of my men to fill in as a way of helping out the management. They were very appreciative."

Bryant frowned. "I'm sure they were."

"Well, as the wife of a very important general, I feel it's my place to aid the war effort any way I can. I told them as much. I hope you enjoyed your meal."

Bryant looked back at the table and the waiting assassin. "I'd lay odds the two missing waiters will never come back to work."

"A shame how fragile life can be," Root said. "Now, we've wasted enough time. Let's get moving."

Bryant looked down at the much shorter woman and smiled. "I'm not going."

"Meeker's sister dies if you don't," Root hissed.

"But," Bryant pointed out, "by the time Marco punches Alison's ticket, I'll have emptied two bullets into your heart."

"You're bluffing. You're too noble to give up a life you could save. In fact, the only weakness you really have is your Indian morality. You feel that all the innocent lives of this world are sacred."

"Yes," Bryant admitted, "and that's the reason I'm not going with you. The world's at war, and right now, evil has the upper hand. At this moment, Hitler and his minions are killing hundreds of thousands of the innocents I'm trying to protect. Therefore, even on this Christmas night, I have to measure things differently."

"But—"

Bryant cut her off. "Shut up and let me paint a picture for you. Let me explain just how stupid you are. This whole little drama is ego-driven. You wanted to lord over me in a public place to prove how powerful you were, and you used a young woman as a pawn to do so. You likely have been watching us for an hour, relishing the fact that you were going to put me in my place. But you screwed up the math. In this war, all lives aren't equal. There are people who mean more than others. Look at me as an example. My life is much more important than Alison's. You see, I can do things for this country she can't. I love that kid, but she can be easily replaced. I'm not sure I can be."

"I think you're bluffing," Root shot back. "You're not going to allow Meeker's sister to be murdered. I've done my homework. You can easily kill people whom you deem as evil … taking me out might even be something you'd enjoy … but you lose sleep each time you fail to protect those who are weak or helpless."

"Think what you will," Bryant retorted, "but let this sink in. This is much more than philosophy or making a moral judgment. Here is what I'm stating—you kill her, and I kill you. In your mind this is just math … one life plus one life equals two deaths. That math works out well for me. After all, I keep on breathing."

"Quit stalling," Root demanded. "You've wasted too much of my time."

Bryant quietly chuckled. "I'm not stalling. I'm serious. Which life is more important to the war effort—yours or Alison's? Which loss will have the greatest effect?" Bryant leaned closer to Root and whispered, "You see, if I take you out right here and now, then you can't dig through your husband's mind for war plans to sell to Hitler. You would no longer be playing the game of spy with the unaware general supplying you with information. With your death, one of the major sources of government secrets would be shut off from Germany. I'd say your life was therefore far more important than Alison's. I don't want her to die, but my, how this world would be better without you in it. And sometimes some innocents have to give their lives to stop evil."

A stunned Root glanced into the dining room toward Marco, who was just waiting for the sign to step forward. As the older woman considered her options, Bryant dropped her right hand into her purse to grab her gun. A second later, she pushed the barrel into Root's side.

"How's it going to end, Gertrude? Will the final story have three people dead or no one?"

"Three people?" Root questioned.

"Yeah, after I take you out, I'll take out Marco. He'll pay the ultimate price for Alison's death."

Stymied, Root slowly turned back to face Bryant. "I'll still get you and Meeker. If not tonight, I'll get you tomorrow or next week or next month."

Bryant grinned. "How are you going to do that? I know who you are. Within ten minutes, the FBI will have that information. By tomorrow, the Feds will have raided your home and turned everything upside down. If the loot you took from your brother's place is not in your house, they'll find something in the search that will lead them to it. So, I hope you've got a bundle of cash in your purse, because you're never going to be able to get any more."

Root's jaw dropped so low she now had three chins. Her evil eyes had also lost their fire.

"By supplying your demented brother with information," Bryant explained, "you took advantage of a nation's trust and your husband's love. When Bauer died, you moved in and really began to step on people. And you always thought you were so smart. But what killed your brother is now taking you down. Well, your ego is about to take a huge hit. Within twenty-four hours, your picture will be on every newspaper in the country, and you'll be too busy running for life, hiding like a rat, and seeing trouble in the eyes of every person you meet to worry about Helen or me. From this moment forward, we are safe!"

"You—"

Jabbing the gun more deeply into her adversary's ribs, Bryant cut her off. "You can't call me anything I haven't heard, so give up trying."

"Let me get this straight. You're going to let me go?"

"Only to save Alison. She might not mean nearly as much to the war effort as you do, but I don't want to see her die. Besides, if you walk out, you can't make it far."

"How does your plan work? What do I have to do?"

"Gertrude, first that goon, Marco, walks away from the table and disappears. When that happens, I'll let you stroll out the front door to your car. Now, if you value breathing, give him the sign."

"If we walk outside together," Root said, "he has instructions to leave the girl alone and escape through the kitchen."

"If he doesn't," Bryant warned, "if he makes one move toward Alison, you'll find out how heartless I can really be. Now let's go."

Root nodded and took a step toward the exit.

As they moved, Bryant was with her stride for stride. Mirrors disguised several building support columns in the center of the ornate lobby. As she approached the benches set beneath those mirrors, Bryant glanced at the reflection and noted Marco slowly stepping away from the table toward the kitchen. So far so good! She watched the assassin take two more steps and stop.

A sick grin suddenly covered his face as he reached into his pocket and withdrew his weapon of choice. A split second later, he moved back to the table. He was already reaching to steady Alison's head. Marco's right hand, the one holding the icepick, was now moving toward the young woman's ear.

There are moments when time almost stands still. There are others when it speeds up to a blur. This was the latter. The icepick was just a fraction of an inch away from Alison's ear when Bryant turned, raised her hand, and aimed her weapon. No one in the lobby or dining room realized that peace on earth was about to shattered. There was no time to really aim—she could only depend upon years of training and instincts as she squeezed the trigger.

The sound of Bryant's Smith and Wesson woke everyone up. In an instant, voices went quiet and bodies whirled to see what was going on. Shocked faces froze as they realized a beautiful woman had launched a projectile from the lobby into the dining room. The spinning lead found and shattered Marco's wrist, spraying blood on Alison and diners at two other tables.

"Get down," Bryant yelled to stunned diners as she rushed into the dining room.

As people scattered, Marco reached inside his jacket with his left hand and pulled out a revolver. In a move that stunned Bryant, he didn't aim her way. Instead he pointed the weapon at the back of Alison's head. He was still bent on completing his assignment.

A heavyset businessman, about sixty, rushed at Bryant. In his desire to be a hero, he'd confused the good guys for the bad. Lowering his shoulder, as he barreled into her. Bryant brought her elbow to the man's fleshy chin and spun away. Falling to one knee, she regained her focus, spotted Marco's red jacket, aimed, and pulled her trigger three times.

Each of her shots found a place in Marco's chest, knocking him into a table where a group of four horrified guests had been eating their supper. The assassin rolled for a second until his head fell into a bowl of chicken soup.

Sensing things in the dining room were under control, Bryant rose, and turned toward Root. The woman was gone.

"Miss Bryant."

She glanced over at the lobby where Dick Gergin, the Lincoln's assistant manager, stood. His face was paler than the white shirt he wore underneath his black suit.

As the stunned patrons began to push off the floor, Bryant frowned and barked out orders. "Call the police. If possible, have them send Detective Roger Richards to lead the investigation. We need to find the short woman in the mink that just left. She's responsible for this and great deal more."

As Gergin reached for the phone, Bryant slipped her gun back into her purse and hurried to the table where Alison was using a napkin to wipe away the blood on her cheek.

"Are you okay?" Bryant more demanded than asked.

"My motor's still humming on all cylinders! What was that all about?"

"The waiter was about to kill you," Bryant explained as she pointed to the icepick on the floor beside the table. "He was going to stick that thing through your brain."

"What did I do?" Alison asked.

"Nothing. It was a way to hurt your sister, but they failed. And now we know who's behind it, so let's get a hold of Helen. She and I have a trail we have to follow before it grows cold."

"Miss Bryant." She looked back to where Gergin was standing. "The cops are on the way. And that woman you wanted. She's gone! Willie saw her get into a car and speed away. But she left something."

Bryant could see the apprehension in the man's face. "What did Root leave?"

"A large trunk. About thirty minutes ago, she asked me to keep it behind the desk. Someone just called and told me it's a bomb. And, Miss Bryant, the trunk's ticking."

CHAPTER 3

Friday, December 25, 1942
8:40 a.m.
Lincoln Hotel, Chicago, Illinois

As she drove back to the Lincoln Hotel from the Glasglow's, Helen Meeker was on top of the world. This was what Christmas was supposed to be. She'd sung carols, watched three excited kids open gifts, and witnessed a widowed mother's faith restored by a visit from a stranger. And, on top of that, Helen knew thousands of children across the city believed in Santa once more. So thanks in part to the work of Napoleon Lancelot and Teresa Bryant, as well as thousands of volunteers, the jolly old elf seemed very real again. Perhaps the fact the world was at war made this bit of fantasy that much more important.

As she eased her yellow 1937 Packard sedan around the corner toward the entrance to the hotel parking lot, she was greeted by half a dozen police cars, scores of cops, and the main street filled with hundreds of people.

A tall, lanky, gray-headed policeman, likely about sixty, waved toward her and pointed to the curb. "You can't go any further," he said. "We're investigating a crime. We've got the whole place evacuated. So park it or move it along!"

The sudden and dramatic chill ran down Meeker's spine had nothing to do with the below freezing temperatures. Her sister and Teresa Bryant were staying at the hotel, and as there was a person out to inflict as much pain as possible on Meeker, perhaps the crime being investigated dealt with people she dearly loved. The holiday cheer she'd felt only moments before had transformed into a Christmas nightmare.

While attempting to slow her rapidly beating heart, Meeker parked the Packard in the spot pointed out by the beat cop. Stepping into the frigid night air, she inventoried the chaotic scene in attempt to ascertain what might have created this kind of chaos. A child could have easily picked up the panic evident in the eyes of most of the civilians. That alarm stood in stark contrast to the resolve written on the expressions of those in police blue.

"My Lord," a middle-aged woman to Meeker's right said to a man who likely was her husband. "Did you see the way that woman fired that gun?"

"Yeah," he answered as he tilted his hat back on his head. "We're not safe anywhere anymore."

"Who was the shooter?" Meeker asked.

The woman shrugged, "I don't know, but she was an amazing shot."

"Was there an attractive, bubbly, and hip young woman involved?" Meeker demanded.

"Yeah," the man replied, "she was right in the middle of it."

Fear rushed over Meeker like a San Francisco fog. "Was the young woman hurt?"

"I don't know," the woman admitted. "There was blood everywhere."

Meeker sensed she'd gotten as much information as she would from this pair, so she scanned the cops searching for one she knew. About twenty feet to her left, surrounded by who appeared to be hotel staff, she spotted a friend.

Mark O'Malley was in his forties. Since she'd arrived in the Windy City, he'd proved to be one of her greatest allies at the Chicago Police Department. While his light blue eyes usually reflected a child's mischief, his hard-set jaw always signaled his unwavering sense of duty. Tonight, the jaw was tighter than she'd ever seen it.

"O'Malley!" She waved her hand.

"Miss Meeker," O'Malley called over the noise of the crowd and the sound of a fire truck, siren blasting, now turning onto the street. The cop pushed his way through the crowd to her side before continuing, "Richards put out the word you were needed, and I've been looking for you. I searched your room and everywhere in the building. Then someone told us you were out. I guess you heard the news on the radio and want to know about your sister."

His words cut as deep as a butcher knife. Now she was certain Alison was involved. She had to have been the young woman the couple was talking about. Were the cops here because she'd been murdered? After all, somewhere out there was a person who promised that everyone Meeker loved would be killed.

Taking a deep breath, Meeker swallowed hard. "What happened?"

"Someone tried to kill Alison," the cop explained, "but they didn't grasp who they were dealing with. Your partner, the Indian lassie, punched the goon's ticket faster than a twenty-year veteran conductor on the Union Pacific punches a second-class ticket."

"So Alison's okay?"

"Yeah, she's just as tough as you are."

"How long have you been here?"

"I was walking a beat just a block away, and I got here not long after things blew up. In spite of what happened, your sister was as calm as a sleeping cat. Yet, when I asked her what happened, she didn't make a lot of sense. It was like she was speaking a different language. She said something about a trip to the clouds being canceled due to a morning song. I couldn't make heads nor tails of that."

Meeker smiled. If her sister was yapping in slang, she was fine. Yet an attempted murder of one young woman didn't call for all of the cops and an entire hotel's evacuation. Something more had to be in play here.

"What's with the circus, Mark? A failed homicide doesn't call for a parade."

"Some old woman left a trunk at the desk and it isn't a Christmas present. Detective Richards thinks there might be a bomb inside."

Could the attempt on Alison's life and the bomb be tied together? On the surface, it seemed like a long shot, but recently a whole bunch of long shots had paid off. Bryant would have the whole story, and Helen needed to find her.

"O'Malley, where's my partner?"

"Miss Bryant?"

"Yeah."

"She's in the lobby with Detective Richards. They're trying to figure out what to do until a Navy bomb squad gets here."

"Take me to them. Mark, I'll bet you dollars to donuts this has something to do with me."

O'Malley grimly nodded and began pushing his way through the mass of people with Meeker following his every step. At the front entrance, he paused, said something to another cop, and then waited for the door to open.

Meeker stepped through the Lincoln's main entrance and studied the almost completely empty lobby. Compared to the pandemonium outside, this seemed like an evening at the local library. Everyone was speaking in hushed tones, and in spite of the potential danger, no one seemed anxious.

Behind the front desk, Richards and Bryant were calmly studying an old steamer trunk. The huge hunk of antique luggage was about four and half feet tall and two and half feet wide. Twenty feet to their right, Alison stood between two uniformed cops. Just behind the trio was the dining room, where a body sprawled across a table. Based on the evidence she could see, he apparently took his last breath just before the main course was served at a table set for four.

"That's the guy who was going to kill Alison," O'Malley explained, leaning forward. "Your partner's quite a shot."

"Yes, she is," Meeker agreed. Seeing no reason to concern herself with the dead and figuring later would be the time to get the full story from Alison, Meeker marched toward Richards and her partner. "What have you got, Teresa?"

Bryant looked up and frowned. "Based on the ticking coming from inside that box, as well as the slight smell I'm picking up, I'm thinking it's a bomb."

"And if it's packed with explosives," Richards added, "it's big enough to relocate most of the hotel to the south side of town."

The situation was obviously serious, but there was no sense of panic. The guests and staff had been evacuated and the bomb squad called.

"I'm guessing it wasn't Santa who dropped off this present," Meeker joked.

Bryant nodded. "It was Gertrude Root."

Meeker was shocked. "The General's wife? The woman we met on the kidnapping case a few months ago?"

"One and the same, and she also owns the voice I heard on the phone the night you pulled the fuse on Wallace's dealing with the Nazis. It took me a while, but I can now say for sure Root is Bauer's sister. And she almost got Alison tonight."

Meeker glanced at her sister, then to the body of the man spread over the table. "Where's Root?"

"She got away," Richards explained, "but the FBI has been alerted. My department is working it too."

Bryant's eyes never left the trunk. "Helen, Root's hatred for you caused her to misplace her normally sound judgment. Emotions and revenge have now paved the way to hell for her. This seems to a common theme too. I've watched it play out lots of times in my life."

Meeker turned her gaze to the kindly cop who'd escorted her into the lobby. "O'Malley, would you take my sister a long way from this place? If that bomb goes off, I don't want her to be hurt."

Alison frowned. "I'm planted here with you and Teresa."

Meeker glanced back at Alison and smiled. "Mark, if she argues, pick her up and carry her over your shoulder."

"You can't have him do," Alison argued.

"Actually, I can. And for your good and my peace of mind, he's going to."

"O'Malley," Richards added, "once you get the kid out, tell our men to move everyone at least a block away. I want everything around this building completely cleared before the bomb squad gets here."

O'Malley nodded, took Alison's hand, and all but pulled her outside.

As they exited, an Army captain walked in. He was six feet, one-seventy, light blue eyes, square jaw, and about thirty. The ring on his left hand proved he was "rationed," as Alison would say.

"I'm sorry, sir," Richards announced moving from behind the counter and toward the door. "No one can come in here right now. We have a big problem on our hands."

"I just need to get something out of the safe." The captain was polite. "And then I'll leave."

"There's a bomb in that trunk," Richards explained. "That's all that matters right now."

"Your men told me about the bomb, that's why I'm here."

"And that's why you need to walk out now," Richards said.

"Listen," the captain argued, "I shouldn't be telling you this, but earlier today, before I went to a Christmas party, I had the desk clerk place papers vital to the war effort in that safe. I have to get them to the West Coast by tomorrow."

"If the bomb blows up," Bryant said wryly, "the papers will get there on their own."

Richards ignored the woman's sarcasm as he turned his attention to the uninvited visitor. "What's your name?"

"Captain Samuel G. Kelly. Now, for the sake of our country, just open the safe, let me retrieve the papers, and I'll get out of here."

"The people who have the combination have evacuated," Richards explained. "Until we secure this area, they aren't coming back."

"That's not acceptable!"

"That's reality!"

As the two men exchanged unfriendly glares, a uniformed cop pushed through the front. The cop's expression clearly declared he was not the bearer of good news.

"What is it, Harrison?" Richards asked.

"The Navy bomb squad was involved in a wreck. One's dead, and the other's on his way to the hospital."

Richards muttered under his breath, folded his arms over his chest, and frowned. After turning to study the trunk, he snapped his fingers. "Everyone get out."

The two uniformed cops didn't argue—they hit the exit, quickly followed by the cop who had delivered the bad tidings, but the cool and determined army captain hung around.

"I'll wait it out," Kelly announced.

Meeker was impressed. This guy was fearless. With that kind of grit, he didn't need to be a desk jockey stationed in the states; he needed to be on the front line. Yet, that determination didn't impress the homicide detective.

Richards seemed ready to fight the man for daring to defy his orders. With his fists clenched, he stepped forward.

Bryant calmly said, "Kelly, you're too valuable to your country to risk your life unnecessarily. You get going. If I do my work right, you can be the first we let back into the lobby, and you can get your papers then. Roger, why don't you take him out?"

"Okay, ladies, I'll play babysitter to the captain, but you're coming too."

"You, Kelly, and Helen go ahead," Bryant said. "I've defused a few bombs in my life. I'll stick around and see if I can save the hotel and the vital Army papers."

"And I'll stay too," Meeker chimed in. "I actually helped Teresa another time when she deactivated a bomb."

"Helped?" Bryant quipped.

"I made a suggestion or two at that power plant."

"Ladies, we need to leave," an agitated Richards urged.

"No," Meeker said, "you and the captain get out of here. This was all about Teresa and me. We're the reason this bomb is here. Now do your job and make sure everyone stays well away from this building. And keep the captain with you. No one gets back in until we make sure it's safe. We'll signal you."

Richards frowned but didn't argue. After muttering, "Stupid, stubborn dames," he turned, grabbed his guest by the arm and walked out.

Once they were alone in the huge Lincoln Hotel, Meeker joined her partner behind the counter. She studied the trunk. "If that's what you think it is, we have a rather large problem. What do we do first?"

Bryant shrugged and smiled. If she was worried, it didn't show.

"Well," Meeker said, "you're certainly calm. There's no sweat on your brow, your hands are steady, and you don't seem to be in any hurry to stop that thing from ticking."

"Helen, whenever you're dealing with bombs, the only thing that really matters is that what you do first is not the last thing you do."

"That's morbid humor at best."

"Do you want a Coke?" Bryant asked.

"What?"

"Helen, I don't want to do this too quickly. We need to let Richards sweat for a while—he'll be more impressed."

"If," Meeker argued, "it's a time bomb, it could go off any moment."

"That's true," Bryant agreed. "That is, if it's a time bomb."

"Is the trunk locked?"

"I've already picked the lock," Bryant said.

"Then let's open it up and see what we are dealing with."

"And there is the dilemma," Bryant replied.

Her tone and manner was so casual Meeker wondered if her partner had been drinking. Yet, that would have been so unlike Bryant.

"Helen, we have to think about this. How is this bomb fused? Do we need to open the trunk's latches in a specific order? Is there a trip wire we need to find and put out of commission? Does the trunk need to be upright, like it is now, or on its side when we open it up? Tell you what, before we make those decisions, I want you to make a telephone call. While you do that, I'll wander into the kitchen and get a Coke. Do you want one?"

"You want me to make a call?"

"Yes. Get hold of one of your contacts in Washington and get the dope on Captain Samuel G. Kelly."

"Why?"

"Just humor me," Bryant said. "I specifically want to know what he looks like. Now do you want something to drink?"

"Not now! And besides, we just saw him—we know what he looks like."

As Bryant waltzed into the dining room, past the dead man's body and into the kitchen, a perplexed Meeker moved to the phone and rang up a long-distance operator. As she waded through six connections, she watched Bryant return, set a half-empty bottle of Coca-Cola on the trunk's top, and lean against the counter. Obviously, Bryant was still in no real hurry. What was she up to? That question was still unanswered when a person with the needed information finally jumped on the line.

"This is Helen Meeker, my clearance number for Army purposes is E as in Eagle, R as in Ralph, 2-3-9-7-5 Alpha. I need all the information you have on Army Captain Samuel G. Kelly. Yes, I'll wait for you to get the files. He kind of indicated he was with Army intelligence."

As she waited, Meeker grabbed a pencil and beat it against the countertop. When two minutes had passed, she looked over at Bryant. "This might take a while. I hope that something in this room doesn't go off in the meantime."

"We're fine," Bryant assured her.

"Miss Meeker. I've got the information. Are you ready for it?"

"Shoot." She listened to the report, and then called to her partner, "Kelly is forty-four, five-foot-eight, one-hundred sixty. He has brown hair, brown eyes, and is originally from Omaha. He's been in the army for twenty-four years. Do you want anything else?"

"No," Bryant replied. "That's all I need."

"Thank you, Sergeant," Meeker said then hung up. She tossed the pencil on the desk and moved back to where her partner was still casually leaning against the counter. When Bryant didn't offer any explanation, Meeker jabbed, "How are things going?"

"Good."

"Then are you crazy? Do you have a death wish?"

"I'm not crazy," Bryant assured her, "and I have no death wish."

"So you have the bomb figured out?"

"Helen, we'll get to that in a second. First, let's consider another mystery. Why was Gertrude Root in town? She wasn't going to kill us herself. The job had hired help. She didn't have to make this play in person."

"Maybe she wanted her revenge so badly it drove her here. Let's get this bomb defused, and then we can figure that out."

"No hurry. For the moment, I want you to reconsider Root. Her survival skills are too sharp. There has to be more at play here."

"That's only important if we don't get blown up!"

Bryant drained the rest of her Coke, pushed off the counter, and drummed her fingers on the top of the trunk. "Helen, the captain that walked in here tonight. Compare him to the description the Army just gave you."

And at that moment, lighting struck. "The Kelly we met was ten years too young, and last time I checked, grown men don't shrink, and he's three inches too tall to be the real Kelly. His eyes are also the wrong color. He's an imposter. What was your clue, Teresa?" Meeker asked.

"No military intelligence officer would put top secret plans in a hotel safe."

Meeker smiled. The always-cool Bryant was not just thinking of the moment but seeing the entire picture.

"Teresa, I think you're guessing Root dropped off papers for one of her operatives, and that man pretending to be Kelly was to pick them up?"

"What else did you notice about him?" Bryant asked.

Meeker grinned. "He was way too composed and calm. He was worried about the papers but not the bomb."

Bryant nodded and moved toward the safe. She studied the locked cabinet then put her right ear on the cold metal door and left hand on the dial. After spinning it a few times, she smiled, and said, "Helen, the hotel doctor's office is down the right hall. I don't care if you have to break in but get me a stethoscope. I've got a can to crack open."

Meeker hurriedly made her way out of the lobby and down the hall to the room. When the doorknob didn't turn, she broke out the glass with the butt of her Colt. Two minutes of rummaging yielded the needed tool.

"Here you go," Meeker announced as she moved to Bryant's side.

"Thanks."

"You don't think the bomb is live?" a still slightly nervous Meeker asked.

"The fake Kelly wasn't worried about the bomb," Bryant noted, "so why should I?"

Using the stethoscope, a completely relaxed Bryant went to work. Three failed attempts later, she discovered the right combination and pulled the safe door open.

"Should I ask where you learned how to do that?"

Bryant shook her head and turned back to examine the safe's contents. After scanning the few items on the shelves, she pulled out and tossed a leather pouch to Meeker. She then patiently waited to hear what was inside.

"These are locations for hidden plane factories in England," Meeker said. "There appears to be other stuff including the name of one of our agents who is serving in the SS."

"Well, well," Bryant said. "Root must have brought that information here. Likely got it from her husband. The man posing as Kelly indicated he was headed to Los Angeles, so Chicago was where they agreed to make the exchange. I'm betting we'll find money on him that he was supposed to leave in the safe for Root. And as we are in Chicago, and thanks to the stories the press runs on you, everyone in the nation knows that, she probably decided to join her hired hit squad in extracting revenge for her brother's death."

"Not only that," Meeker added, "but because you did hear her voice on the phone, she had to guess that at some point, you'd put two and two together and expose her."

Bryant closed the safe and turned her attention to the trunk. "At first, I thought she might actually be using the bomb to take us out in case her little kidnapping plan didn't work. Then, when the fake captain walked in and was so calm, I began to believe there never was a bomb. If this thing was going to go off, he'd have pressed a lot harder and been a lot more anxious. So I figured the trunk and the call were a ruse to empty the hotel so that the man posing as Kelly could get the papers without being examined too closely. He was sure he could sell his story in the panic, and that no one would actually check to see if he was who he said he was. He probably thought that like the captain of a ship, the manager would be the last one out. And even in this situation, what patriotic person wouldn't open the safe for the good of the war effort." Bryant shook her head and frowned. "But …"

"But what?" Meeker asked.

"If I'm wrong and this bomb is real, we still have a problem."

Meeker smiled. "And I think we can handle this one just like you handled the one on Wallace's yacht. Isn't there a swimming pool in the men's club? And isn't it located in the basement?"

"And there's the hand truck beside the safe," Bryant pointed out. "Let's get to work."

The women pushed the trunk onto the cart and to the elevator. A short ride took them to the basement. Fifty feet later, they were at the door to the men's club.

"Nice place," Meeker observed as she turned on the light. There were billiard and card tables, a full bar, a reading room, a steam chamber, and a pool. After Meeker opened the door to the pool, Bryant wheeled the trunk to the deep end.

"You're leaking," Meeker said.

"What?"

"You're leaving a drop or two of something every six feet." Meeker bent over, rubbed her finger on one of the spots, and examined what she picked up. "Blood!"

"So the trunk's not a trunk, it's a coffin."

"Who's in the box?"

"Maybe the real Kelly," Bryant suggested. "But body or not, there is still an outside chance this thing is rigged to explode. So we need to baptize it."

"Yeah."

With Meeker's help, Bryant pushed the trunk into the water.

The two watched it splash, momentarily float and then slowly sink under ten feet of water. Once the bubbles quit coming to the surface, Bryant flipped off her shoes and dove into the water to swim down to the trunk. After opening the lid, she reached inside and grabbed a man's arm. Pushing off, she brought the body hidden in the trunk to the surface. After breaking the surface, she swam to the edge of the pool and pushed him toward Meeker, who dragged him up onto the concrete. Bryant pulled herself out of the water and studied the victim.

"He's dead," Meeker said.

"Yeah, has been for a while," Bryant agreed. "And even if he's only wearing his underwear, based on his body and face, I'd stay this was the real Kelly."

"No obvious wounds, so how do you think he died?"

Bryant walked to a table, grabbed a towel, and spent a few seconds drying her hair before rejoining Meeker. Leaning close, she turned the man's head to the side and grimly smiled. "Marco."

"Marco?"

"Yeah, the guy I kept from killing your sister seems to have worked his magic on Kelly. The medical examiner will have to confirm, but I think he was murdered by having an ice pick jammed into his brain through his right ear."

Meeker frowned. "Ouch."

"He likely didn't even feel it. By the way, the ticking was made by a large, old fashioned alarm clock. There was no bomb." She looked mournfully at the body again and added, "Sometimes the casualties of war are thousands of miles from the front.

"Teresa, I'd like to pat myself on the back for coming up with the idea of dumping the trunk in the pool. If there had been a bomb, my idea would have saved our lives and prevented a great deal of damage."

"Actually, Helen, I was going to suggest we do that when Kelly walked in. Then I opted to stall, so you could check if that captain was who he said he was. If he was a fake, as

I figured, we needed to get the papers and see what was in them."

"Fine, take all the glory for yourself. By the way, I saw the body in the dining room. So that was Marco?"

"Yep."

"How did you stop him before he killed Alison?"

"Let's just say I did a bit of reflecting and figured out Root's plan. But, there's something you need to consider."

"What's that?"

"Alison should be protected until the war is over. When she goes back to Washington, she doesn't need to go anywhere without someone guarding her every step outside the White House. You need to arrange that. What we are assigned to do shouldn't put her life in danger."

Bryant was right. Meeker had lost enough people she loved without losing her only blood relative. Perhaps FDR would let Alison live in the White House. She'd call and make that suggestion tomorrow.

"Teresa, what about the body in the trunk?"

"We've solved everything else for Richards, why don't we let him puzzle for a while on how the man really died and who he is. He'll be real proud of himself when he tells us about it."

"I can do that," Meeker agreed, "but then we have to tell him we already knew."

"Agreed. Always good to burst his bubbles! Now, as he likely still has the man with him who might shed some answers on what this charade was all about, why don't you go out and let them know everything is clear. Meanwhile, I'm going to go to my room and get out of these wet clothes."

CHAPTER 4

Saturday, December 26, 1942
11:17 a.m.
Monument Studios, Hollywood, California

Abby Force had it all. Standing five-four, tipping the scales at one-hundred fifteen, the young woman's luxurious blonde mane and deep green eyes adorned a face seemingly sculpted by an artist. On top of that, she had charisma and talent, so it was hardly surprising that within six months of being "discovered" while working in a department store, she landed a seven-year contract and positioning as the hottest new star in Hollywood. The Alabama native was twenty-five, and her figure had caused the movie magazines to christen her "The Shape"—a moniker she hated, but the studio publicity department both loved and exploited. Since the start of the war, thousands of GIs had written letters proposing marriage and were displaying her most famous bathing suit photo over their bunks. That pose, in painted form, also graced the noses of four different American B-17 bombers.

On this day after Christmas, Abby was on set, filming a scene with the movie industry's top male heartthrob … Matt Craig. For the past five years, Craig had been box office magic. The wide-shouldered, six-foot actor was called the perfect combination of Clark Gable and Robert Taylor. In appearance he was, but off screen, he was much more like the unassuming Jimmy Stewart. Though everyone wanted Craig at the city's top social gatherings, the thirty-three-year-old bachelor spent more time walking in Griffin Park with his dog or reading a book on his private yacht than he did partying at the Coconut Grove. So except for his occupation, he appeared to be the average Joe, and perhaps why those who worked with the actor not only respected him but also liked him.

Monument Studios spent a quarter of a million dollars to get MGM to loan Craig to them, but studio head David Jacobs wasn't worried about the cost—having Craig and Force in the same movie assured box office magic. Though the magazine hadn't seen a single rush or read the script, *Variety* was already predicting the flick would earn at least two million in ticket sales.

I Spy You was a tense war drama written by award-winning scribe Collin Holden. The script signaled a huge departure from the lightweight romantic comedies Monument usually assigned Force. What everyone wanted to know was whether the glamour queen could pull it off? Could she hold her own with the seasoned Craig? Six weeks into filming, the questions had been answered; she had done all that and more. Yet, even though the studio was thrilled, Force was still nervous and insecure.

During this morning's scene, the actress would be given the task of pulling out a gun and shooting the suave Craig in order to save Britain's new bomber plans from falling into the hands of German officials. Because Force's character, Yvonne, was in love with Craig's character, Jim, this patriotic act was supposed to break her heart. The scene would require her to show a range of emotions she'd never displayed on film. Therefore, she was now as tense as a caged cat, and the coffee she was drinking, her third cup in an hour, was making her even more edgy.

"Five minutes, Miss Force."

The nervous actress looked up from her reflection in the mirror and nodded toward the assistant director. "I'll be there."

This would be the third time in a week she'd worn the same dark suit, hat, and heels. Thankfully, it would be the last. While she found Craig to be gracious and kind, working with a Hollywood icon had been overpowering. He delivered his lines so easily and with such power, she felt like a rank amateur. Whenever Craig was on the set, she simply couldn't relax. Even now, as she studied her face in the mirror, she could read anxiety in her eyes, lips, and jaw.

"You look beautiful."

Mattie Strauss's words were meant to reassure Force, but they made no impact. As Force's body double and personal assistant, Strauss was supposed to be a cheerleader. The only real reason she had landed the job with Force was due to how much the two women resembled each other. Strauss was cute, not devastatingly beautiful like Force, and the stand-in didn't make men smolder like the actress, but both women were the same size and looked enough alike to pass for each other from a distance. Over the past three years, Strauss had even appeared in several scenes, always shown from the back or with her face hidden, in order to give Force a few breaks and save the studio money. Beginning last year, when the actress's fame exploded,

Strauss took on the job of answering the star's fan mail, making appointments, and scheduling interviews. She even lived in Force's mansion.

"I'm glad this is my only scene today," Force announced as she leaned closer to the mirror to study the way she'd been made up.

"There's nothing else on the schedule," Strauss assured her. "When this one is over, you can go home and sleep the day away."

Force frowned at her reflection. "I have no business playing this part. I'm a pinup girl not an actress. This should have gone to Carole Landis or Lana Turner."

"No, the studio made the right choice. Your work has shown that. The crew is raving about how you've made this character real!"

"Wish I felt that way. It seems to me I'm like the high school actress trying to play a major role in minor way."

Strauss placed her hand on Force's shoulder. "Do you have the scene down?"

"I should," Force muttered. "There's not too much to do. I walk into the room, tell him I know who he is and that I want the plans. When he doesn't hand them over, I act as though I'm conflicted. I cry a little then pull the gun from my purse and shoot once. He collapses, I shake my head, drop the gun, turn, and walk out of the room."

Strauss nodded. "They want the shot from three different angles, so it will take a trio of set-ups."

"Yeah, I know. Melvin told me. The way he directs, he'll just use the first one anyway. That's the one that's got to be perfect. Knowing me, I'll drop the gun or trip and fall as I enter the room."

A knock caused both women to turn their heads toward the open dressing room door. Filling the entry was a bulky man holding a large black purse.

"Your bag," prop man Calvin Coggins explained. His expression indicated he didn't feel comfortable holding the feminine accessary and couldn't wait to set it down. "The gun's in it. As we're doing multiple takes, I fully loaded it with blanks. There's no safety, so just pull the Lugar out, squeeze, and fire."

Force stood and took the bag, retrieving the small handgun. Looking at the mirror, she gripped and aimed. Satisfied she could handle the weapon, she dropped the gun into the purse, and after setting the bag on her dressing table, she again looked at her guest. "Tell Melvin I'm on my way." She waited for the man to exit before looking at her stand-in. "Let's get going."

"Just a second," Strauss announced. "You need the necklace. You've always had it on in the scenes where you've worn this outfit—fans will catch the slip if you forget. It's here somewhere. Where did I put it after we shot on Christmas Eve? Ah, here in your make-up case."

The press had dubbed the necklace "Force's good luck charm." A fan had mailed two identical pieces as gifts to Force and Strauss. The actress had first worn hers in the comedy *An Evening at Maud's House*. The necklace then found its way into every film that followed. In October, *Screen Magazine* sponsored a contest offering subscribers a chance to have the chance to win knockoff versions of the necklace. More than forty thousand people entered to win one of the ten prizes. In some ways, the fashion accessory had now become as big a star as Force.

After placing the necklace around her neck and fastening the catch, the actress forced a smile. Now everything was in order, and it was time to go to work.

"Let me adjust it for you," Strauss said as she pulled the necklace up a bit, "and give me a second while I find and put on mine for luck too. As I do that, why don't you run over your lines again."

"Hurry. Melvin doesn't like to be kept waiting."

"It will only take a minute."

In two minutes, Strauss found the necklace partially hidden behind Force's purse. After the assistant put it on, the pair walked down the hall to the set.

On this day and for this scene, Sound Stage 15 had been transformed into an English drawing room. As Force walked onto the set, she noted her costar standing by a walnut desk. As soon as their eyes met, he flashed that devastating smile and just like millions of other women, her knees seemed to grow weak. Once again, a flood of insecurity washed over her like surf on the seashore. She had experienced recurring nightmares that since she'd shot him, she'd be hated by millions of women all over the world.

"Let's get a few stills," publicist Marty Michaels suggested. He directed a photographer to grab shots of the room and close ups of both actors. Once that task was concluded, everyone on the stage seemed to freeze and the set grew as quiet as a church on Friday night.

Just off the set, beside a large, thirty-five millimeter camera, stood Melvin Van Dyke. The balding director was five-foot-five and weighed no more than one hundred and thirty pounds. There was always a cigar in his mouth and a frown on his face. He was bossy and loud. Actors considered him a man's man and loved him, but almost every actress in town fought to keep him from directing their pictures. He had the reputation of disliking women, and his harsh words proved it day after day and film after film.

"Abby, do you have any questions?" Van Dyke growled.

"No, I walk into the room, deliver my lines, shoot Matt, and leave."

"And don't rush it," Van Dyke barked. "Let the emotions build. Let's see the love you feel for him pushing you to want to do the wrong thing. I want those watching the film to actually wonder if you will pull the trigger. And when you do, and he drops, I want them to hurt as much you do. That's not a request, that's the way it has to be."

"I'll do my best."

"Why don't you try to do more than that," the director barked. As his stinging words sank in, he turned back to the crew. "Let's get to shooting. Everyone in their places." Once Van Dyke was satisfied he was in full control, he pointed toward the stage. A second later, the red light came on, the clapboard snapped, and the director called for action.

Pushing her sense of inadequacy from her gut, Force purposefully strolled into the room. Only after her eyes fell on Craig did she pause and sadly shake her head. Remembering Van Dyke's instructions, she took a deep breath, visibly pushing the air from her lungs. "I know who you are and what you've done. I can't let you complete your mission."

Craig, perfectly playing his role of the unprincipled scoundrel, grinned. "I'm a rogue—I've always sold myself to the highest bidder. But I love you, and you love me. Even in war, love trumps everything else."

"Love can't replace my loyalty to Britain," Force insisted. "I'm leaving. Are you coming with me?"

Responding to the cue, the actress reached into her purse and pulled out the gun. As she took aim, she resolutely announced, "I'm not coming with you and you're not leaving. I'm calling Scotland Yard."

The actor laughed. "You won't shoot. Your love for me is too strong. Now put that gun down and let me kiss you. You know you want to."

Now fully into her role, Force dropped her purse and gripped the weapon with both hands. As she did, a tear rolled down her cheek. She allowed that lone teardrop to fall to the floor before firing. The sound of the shot seemed to echo in every corner of the stage.

As the hushed crew looked on, Craig's confident smile was immediately transformed into a look of shock and then, one of agony. He rocked on his heels for several seconds before doubling over and falling forward.

By instinct, Force slowly strolled to the fallen actor, shook her head, dropped the weapon to the floor, turned, and walked out.

A few seconds later, Van Dyke yelled, "Cut! That was perfect! In fact, that was amazing!"

Strolling back through the door, a now-relieved Force looked at the crew. She was completely shocked when they stood as one and gave her an ovation. She had never felt so good. Even the director was applauding her efforts.

The adoration continued for another twenty seconds before the cameraman yelled, "Hey, Matt's still down! He's not moving!"

Dropping his cigar, Van Dyke rushed to the actor.

A dozen others followed in the director's steps.

A stunned Force remained frozen in place. She barely reacted when Strauss rushed to her side.

"What's going on, Abby? Is this a joke?"

"I don't know."

"Get an ambulance," Van Dyke shouted.

"What's wrong?" a grip asked.

"Craig's been shot. I mean really shot! There's blood everywhere!"

"Abby," Strauss whispered. "Did you kill him?"

Force's mouth went dry, and her body grew numb. How had this happened? How had live bullets gotten into the gun?

CHAPTER 5

Tuesday, December 29, 1942
9:17 a.m.
White House, Washington, DC

Even though Meeker had once worked in this hallowed landmark, stepping into the White House for the first time or the thousandth was always an overwhelming experience. And at this moment when a world was at war, this residence represented the heartbeat of liberty. Meeker could almost feel the building pulse as its employees selflessly toiled day and night trying to ward off those bent on destroying freedom around the globe. As a noted author once observed ... these were the best of times and the worst of times ... and nowhere was that more apparent than at 1600 Pennsylvania Avenue.

After showing her credentials at three different checkpoints, Meeker was escorted by her sister to a side room, two doors down from the Oval Office. She paused at the entrance and gave Alison a hug. "Don't know when I'll see you again."

"Sooner than you think," Alison assured her. "Keep your orbs open and your radar working, I might be the blip on your screen at any time."

"Only if I can keep you safe."

"I'm a grown-up doll. It's my job to keep my engine tuned up and to avoid the potholes."

"Okay, but listen to those around you and don't take any chances."

"I'll color within the lines. Now, I need to get to work."

They hugged again and Alison strolled toward her station in another wing of the White House. With her sister officially back at her job in the most secure building on the planet, Meeker felt a bit of comfort. But if she was going to continue her work with the President, the seasoned investigator had to have a promise. She had to know that Alison would be kept safe. If she couldn't get that guarantee, then she was going to resign.

As Mr. Roosevelt was too busy to meet with Meeker, he sent his second-in-command, Vice President Henry Wallace, to give the special agent the rundown on her next assignment. Wallace, an Iowa native, was tall, thin, and blessed with a full head of dark hair. He had switched from the Republican Party to the Democratic side early during the Great Depression. Still, when FDR chose him to be second on the ticket in 1942, a lot of folks were surprised. Some of the party faithful still questioned Wallace's loyalty, yet the President trusted him, and that was enough for Meeker. Though she didn't know him well enough to call him a friend, she had been in rooms with the VP a few times and found him eloquent, down to earth, and principled.

Easing onto an antique, light-blue couch, she crossed her legs and listened to a sound she missed—the White House at work. Voices were coming from everywhere, typewriters were pounding out everything from secret plans to ordinary letters, and a team of hundreds was focused on one mission. The aura was both soothing and overwhelming even to one who had worked there.

"Helen," Wallace said as he entered the room, "it is so good to see you."

Out of both respect and habit, Meeker stood. "Mr. Vice President."

"Sit down, call me Henry, and let's visit."

Meeker eased onto the couch as Wallace took his place on a brown leather wingback chair.

After unbuttoning his suit coat, he brought the fingertips of both hands together in front of his face and stared at the floor as if thinking. After a minute or more of silence, he redirected his gaze to his guest and spoke. "What do you think we need to do with General Root? Jefferson has worked with us for a long time, his record is solid, and no one has ever questioned his loyalty. Yet, with what you and Miss Bryant have exposed, we are faced with a real dilemma. Can we blame the general for his wife?"

Meeker crossed her right leg over her left knee, adjusted the hem of her blue skirt, and placed her folded hands in her lap. As a man's career might depend upon her answer, she chose her words very carefully.

"Mr. Wallace, do you tell your wife everything you hear in the White House? Does she know the confidential information you are given on a daily basis?"

He grimly shook his head. "I trust her with all my body and soul, but if I did that I would have no business serving as the vice president. There are lines that can't be crossed when we are placed in positions of responsibilities."

Meeker cocked an eyebrow. "Then, as cruel as it might sound, you have my answer."

"And it mirrors my thoughts," he admitted. Pushing off the chair, he walked over to a window and stuck his hands in his pockets as if studying the lawn.

Meeker used this chance to make an observation. "I read one of your speeches the other day."

"You must have been very bored," Wallace said.

"What you said," she explained, "made such a deep impression on me that I committed a part of your remarks to heart."

He turned to study his guest. For a few seconds, he seemed as if he was trying to peer through her head and study her mind. Finally, he asked, "What could I have said that made that kind of impact?"

Her response was so immediate and precise, it was as if the newspaper was in front of her and she was reading his words. "It may be shocking to some people in this country to realize that, without meaning to do so, they hold views in common with Hitler when they preach discrimination against other religious, racial, or economic groups."

"I likely shocked some folks with that speech," the vice president admitted with a shrug. "If you are second-in-command, sometimes the only way to actually be noticed is to say something that on the surface seems to be outlandish."

"What you said resonated with me. My two partners are often not treated as equals. There are places they can't go just because of their race. They are as intelligent, talented, and courageous as anyone I've ever met and yet they have to fight for everything they get. Nothing is given; they must earn it all, and even when they do it is often not enough."

"A democracy is a work in progress," Wallace explained. "It's when we stop changing that it ceases to get better." He turned back to the window and folded his arms over his chest. “I'd like to meet your partners sometime.”

“I hope you can, but before that we must find a general's wife.”

“The FBI has a few dozen agents assigned to the case,” Wallace said, “but they haven't found Gertrude Root. The car she was using that night was abandoned in Cicero. As she'd already checked out of her hotel suite before confronting your partner. There was nothing left there that offered any clue as to the direction she was going. We have to believe she has contacts and resources, thus she likely has the money to buy silence.”

“And,” Meeker pointed out, “she has a team. If anyone can find her, Teresa can. She seems to understand Root. She's working on that right now. I can't wait to get back to Chicago and join her.”

Wallace turned to face Meeker. “She'll have to work on her own for a while. We have another assignment for you.”

“But …”

The vice president held up his hand. “What do you know about Matt Craig?”

“The actor?”

“Yes.”

“I've seen him in a few movies. I believe I remember he's from the Midwest. Other than that, I couldn't tell you much. In my mind, he's a competent actor, but it's his appearance that makes him box office.”

Wallace nodded. “Craig's studio-penned biography says he was born and raised in Ames, Iowa, and after studying at Iowa State, he migrated to Los Angeles, was discovered, and MGM developed him into a star. He's in his thirties, he's single, and he's a licensed pilot. His bio also lists his films, his hobbies, and the starlets he has dated. What it doesn't say is that three days ago, he was shot and seriously wounded on the set of a movie."

"Shot?" Meeker repeated. "You mean with a gun?"

"Yeah, by his leading lady too … Abby Force."

"Why would America's Sweetheart gun down the matinee idol of millions?"

"They were playing a scene, and she was supposed to be shooting blanks at Craig. She claims she didn't know there was a real bullet in the weapon, and she's probably telling the truth."

"Why haven't I read about this?" Meeker asked.

"Monument Pictures is keeping the shooting hushed, and the L.A. police department is going along. Neither group wants or needs any bad publicity. The news reports, essentially written by the studio's press agents, just said there was an accident and Craig had been injured. Nevertheless, at this very moment, the man in charge of props is sitting in jail accused of attempted murder. His name is Calvin Coggins. Though no one seems to know the reason, that Coggins didn't like Craig was public knowledge. He'd even threatened him a few times."

"So you're telling me," Meeker cut in, "that Craig's all right?"

"He'll be released from the hospital today. The only thing the injury will really do is delay his joining the U.S. Army. He'd filled out his paperwork and passed his physical about a month ago. He was just putting off entry until the movie he was working on was completed. He was in ROTC in college, spent some time in the National Guard, is a trained pilot, and will go in as an officer and a flyer."

"So," Meeker observed, "if the script has a happy ending, what does this have to do with me?"

"Helen, Hollywood's biography on Craig is as fake as his name. Yes, he spent his childhood in Ames, and yes, he went to college at ISU, but he was born in Germany as Matthew Hoganmeier."

Meeker's eyes lit up. "There's a Hoganmeier who's a general on Hitler's staff."

"That's Craig's father. And though Wilhelm divorced his wife sometime after she left Germany just before the Great War, the boy continued to return each summer to spend two months with his father. In fact, he learned how to fly in Germany. In 1935, when Craig was twenty-five, he met Hitler. He was at the 1936 Berlin Olympics and sat with his father in a box reserved for German military officers. The trips to Germany only ended when Craig landed in the motion picture business in 1937. As we know, within a year, he was a major star."

"Are you worried about whose side Craig is on?"

"We have people planted in the German military and even the SS," Wallace said. "We put them in place years before the war. Who's to say the Nazis haven't done the same thing? If the FBI is worried about Craig, then I am too."

"What does this have to do with me?" Meeker asked.

"We need to know if Craig is really on our side. And with that in mind, we need to know why someone tried to kill him."

"Are you saying you don't think it was the prop man?"

"He claims he didn't," Wallace explained.

Meeker shrugged. "Death row is filled with people who claim they didn't do the deed."

"We just need to be certain. And before he goes into the military on a fulltime basis, we have to know if Craig is a plant or if he's on our side. If the latter's the case, we must then ascertain if he can be compromised because of who his father is. Once you've finished with this matter and solve who shot him and why, you can join your partner in tracking down Gertrude Root."

"Not my first choice," Meeker answered, "but I learned a long time ago my choices usually take a back seat to my Uncle's needs. But know this, I'd rather be working with Teresa. Now what about my sister? Do we have a plan to keep her safe?"

"We do," Wallace assured Meeker. "She'll be moving to an apartment much closer to the White House, and everyone in that complex is with the Secret Service. She'll even carpool with them to work and home each day. If she goes out after hours, someone will shadow her. But we plan to keep her so busy she won't have the time or energy to do much more than go to home and hit the sack."

"Thanks. As I have work to do, I guess I better get to the West Coast. Thank you for your time." Now focused on her mission, Meeker stood, picked up the coat she'd flung over a table, and prepared to leave.

"There's one more thing," Wallace announced. "There's an Army Captain, Michael Sharp, who was so badly injured in the Philippines they had to do some extensive work to give him his face back. He's healthy again and almost ready to return to duty. As his next assignment will be here in Washington with Army Intelligence, we figured you were the person who could best judge if he's mentally competent to return to active service."

"Can't the shrinks tell you that?" Meeker asked as she slipped on her gloves.

"They seem to think he is," the vice president explained, "but as he was the only one of his unit not killed, and he spent months in the jungle working his way back to freedom, we want to have another opinion before we allow him to deal with top secret materials. As your sister would say, he might just be an egg that's easily cracked. So you need to find out if he's stable."

"Do we have someplace to stay in Los Angeles?" Meeker asked. "I'll need a base of operations."

"You'll have rooms at the Roosevelt Hotel. Captain Sharp is already there."

"And the studio and local cops will cooperate?"

"Yes. They have been alerted and will cooperate. The head of Monument, David Jacobs, is a friend of Mrs. Roosevelt. He begged her to use her influence to have you put on the case, and he has promised he'll do anything you want. But beware, no one at the studio or in Hollywood knows about Craig's father. Might be best to keep them in the dark as long as you can. I have to get to a meeting, but before I say goodbye and good luck, do you need anything else?"

"Mr. Wallace … Henry … to get this thing moving along, I'm going to fly directly from DC to LA. But first, I want to call an associate in Chicago. I need him to pack his bags and join me on the West Coast."

"Is he one of the talented and brilliant people you mentioned?"

"Yep."

"Then you can use the phone in this room if you like. And if the hotel gives you any problems about him staying there, have them call me. You have my number."

"Thanks."

CHAPTER 6

Saturday, January 2, 1943
4:17 p.m.
City Jail, Los Angeles, California

Napoleon Lancelot had taken forty hours to get from Chicago to Los Angeles. On the long train trip, he'd been surrounded by sailors, soldiers, flyers, and marines, and evidently, none of them needed sleep. All of them seemed to feel the best way to prepare for duty in the Pacific was to drink, eat, sing, and play poker. As he observed the hijinks, he wondered how many of these boys were heading to their deaths. That solitary thought was so sobering he didn't feel like he had a right to complain about the noise. He was also moved to do something he rarely did. Pray.

Once off the rails and on solid ground, the sleep-deprived and exhausted Lancelot made his way to the hotel. A file on Calvin Coggins was waiting in his room, and while chowing down on a room service lunch, the investigator boned up on the case. What he needed was sleep, but Meeker, who desperately wanted to get on Root's trail, pulled the Go to Jail card and in *Monopoly* lingo, that card urged him to not pass Go but to head directly for jail. So instead of hitting the *oh so inviting* mattress, he showered, shaved, and changed clothes.

An hour later, after surviving a ride in a cab driven by man who had obviously drunk his lunch from a gin bottle, and even after presenting his credentials, he had to go through a half a mile of red tape at the jail before being escorted to a cell where a big man sporting a sour expression sat on a bunk. On the long list of bad days, this one was near the top.

"Coggins, you've got a visitor," a guard announced as he opened the cell door. A few seconds later after Lancelot entered, the door clanked closed, and the guard said, "Call me when you're finished."

The accused had dark, expressionless eyes and a ruddy, pockmarked face. His shoulders were broad, and he possessed hands the size of catchers' mitts. He likely weighed more than two-fifty, but he was as solid as marble sculpture. Yet, even though he was in good shape, he looked five to ten years older than his forty-nine years. Either the evidence file Lancelot had been given was wrong about the age or Coggins had seen some hard times.

The prisoner said nothing as his guest took a seat in the eight-by-eight-foot cell's other bunk. As one minute became two, and as Coggins studied his unexpected guest, his expression soured even more.

"My name's Lancelot."

Coggins shrugged. "About five years ago, I created a sword that was supposed to be yours."

"I saw the film. I think the title was *The White Knight*."

Coggins eyed his guest. "I sense some irony." He let his quip hang for a moment then demanded, "Who are you and why are you here? If you're trying to save my soul, hold the Scripture and swallow the prayers. I don't need Jesus; I need justice."

"I'm not a preacher," Lancelot retorted. "Not even close. For the moment you can think of me as your ticket out of here."

"If that's a joke, I'm not laughing."

"Not as much of a joke as you might think. You see, I work for a woman named Helen Meeker. She's an investigator. She was hired by Monument to prove you're innocent. Seems your boss likes you."

"Jacobs might, but the cops don't. They see this as open and shut. And it's a statement of my real value at Monument that they hire a detective who's as black as the ace of spades." He rolled his eyes. "I'm so unimportant I don't even rate a white private eye."

"Don't go there," Lancelot said. "Right now, this Negro might be the only thing standing between you and a long stretch in prison. And there are a lot of folks in the Windy City that would rather have this black man doing the digging than anyone else. You got that?"

"Just because I heard it doesn't mean I have to believe it."

"Fine. Just like with everyone else, I'll have to prove myself. I've gotten used to doing that. Now, I've got a question for you, and I want you to answer it honestly. Did you put the live round in the gun?"

"No."

"The cops found live bullets on your desk in the prop room. They matched the one they dug out of Craig."

"Yeah, I took those out of the gun when I got it back. You see, the director wanted to use a specific kind of Lugar, and those aren't easy to find right now. Most of them seem to be in the hands of Nazis. As we didn't have any in the prop vault, I had to go on a scavenger hunt. I found one three days before we shot the scene. As soon as I picked it up, I took the live rounds out and put the blanks in."

"How many did your remove?"

"Live rounds?"

"Yes."

"Six."

"There were only five on your desk. Are you sure you didn't leave one in the gun?"

The prop man's glare could have melted the polar ice cap. "No. I took out six. I counted. And then I rechecked the gun twice to make sure there was not another one."

Lancelot nodded. "Let's say you're right."

"I am," Coggins snarled.

"Normally folks might side with you, but you've got a real problem that seems to paint you as a liar. You see everyone on the crew told the cops you had a beef with Matt Craig. Three of them said you threatened to kill him. One even stated you screamed you'd take him apart with your bare hands."

"That was two years ago," Coggins said, "but I didn't follow through then, and I sure didn't the other day." He jabbed his right index finger at Lancelot. "Listen, if I was going to commit a murder, I'd never set myself up to be suspect number one. There are a thousand more discreet ways to punch Craig's ticket that wouldn't point to me."

"True," Lancelot agreed, "but hate causes people to do irrational things. It clouds their judgment. As my mother used to say, hate makes fools out of the wisest people. So tell me this … and tell me straight … do you still hate Craig or did you get over that two years ago?"

"I still hate him," Coggins admitted. "When I heard he'd joined the Army Air Corps, I was thrilled. I thought maybe the Japs could use his plane for target practice. In fact, I'd have prayed for that if I believed in praying."

The raw emotion evident in the prop man's words was numbing. He made no attempt to hide that he hated Craig clear down to the bone. A guilty man usually didn't try to prove his innocence by doing everything in his power to paint himself into a corner. So what was this all about?

"Why?" Lancelot asked. "Why did you dislike him?"

"That's between me and him."

Lancelot rolled his eyes. "Well then, that secret will likely pave your way to wearing stripes and busting rocks. You tell me what drove you to hate a person everyone else in this town loves, or I can't help you."

Coggins stood and menacingly stepped toward his guest. As the veins bulged in his neck, he yelled, "Do you have a daughter?"

Lancelot had always heard the best way to react to respond to an angry bear was to be calm and not move. He fully embraced that tactic. "No."

Perhaps due to Lancelot's subdued reaction, Coggins regained control of his emotions, frowned, and moved back to his bunk. Then, as he studied the bricks on the back wall, he went mute.

Lancelot allowed silence to rule the room for almost five minutes. Only when Coggins once more looked his way, Lancelot, who figured he was treading on dangerous ground, asked "Did Craig do something to your daughter?"

Coggins nodded but surprisingly didn't explode in rage. In fact, his voice barely rose above a whisper.

"Mary was a beautiful girl, and she was smart too. And one day, when she was nineteen, she came to see me at work. I was doing a film, and Craig was just starting out. He was playing a bit part in the movie I was preparing props for. Well, I introduced him to Mary. One thing led to another, and they started seeing each other. Five months to the day I introduced them, she came home in incredible pain. I rushed her to the hospital. They told me she'd had an abortion, and the person who'd performed it didn't know what they were doing." Tears filled his eyes as he looked toward Lancelot. "She almost died that night, and the entire week she was in the hospital, Craig never came to see her. Not once! He knocked my baby up and didn't even care enough to check on her. And when the hospital finally let me take her home, the doctor in charge told me Mary would never be able to have children. Hits you hard when your only kid will never be able to give you a grandchild."

"And no one knows about this other than you, Mary, and Craig?"

He shook his head. "Do you think I'd want to shame my daughter in public? Of course I didn't tell people why I hated Craig."

"Did you confront him back then? Back when you found out?"

"Yes, and that piece of slime claimed he'd never had sex with my girl. He said the baby was someone else's. The only thing he took credit for was giving her the money for the abortion."

"What does she say?" Lancelot gently asked.

"Nothing," he said. "You can't ask the dead questions." He struggled for a moment to find his voice before he finally whispered, "You see, she killed herself just a couple of days after she got out of the hospital."

Lancelot now fully understood why Coggins hated Craig. Any father would. But knowing the truth only compounded the issue of proving the man's innocence. If a jury heard this, and it was sure to come out in a trial, they'd find the prop man guilty after only a few minutes of deliberation. And with what he was about share, the day was about to get much darker.

"Calvin, the case notes state that the bullet they pulled out of Craig had been filed. I guess you know what that means."

The sobbing prisoner nodded. "It increases the chance of inflicting a fatal wound."

Lancelot took a deep breath before admitting, "There's nothing working in your favor. Everyone knows you prepared the weapon that was used; you had the best motive I can imagine; and you had the perfect opportunity. And the woman who actually fired the gun is America's Sweetheart, and no one is going to believe she wanted to murder Craig."

"So it's hopeless," Coggins said. "And if that's case, do you know what's really sad?"

Lancelot shook his head.

"I'm going to go to prison for the rest of my life, and Craig's going to be fit as fiddle in a few weeks. At least if he had died, then my being punished for something I didn't do would be a lot more satisfying."

CHAPTER 7

Saturday January 2, 1943
8:15 pm
Roosevelt Hotel, Los Angeles, California

It had taken Helen Meeker three days to arrange a flight west. After failing a dozen times to get a seat on a regular passenger aircraft, she turned to her government and military contacts. After another day waiting in the commander's office at Fort Meade, she was able to hitch a ride on an Army troop transport plane that was bound for Los Angeles.

For the entire flight, which included a dozen stops in places she'd never heard of, she was the center of attention. As if it were a game, GIs lined up one after another to flirt. Some even asked her to dance as if that were really possible on a C-47, while others begged for hugs or kisses.

On the layovers, the men showered her with donuts, coffee, Cokes, and candy bars. If she moved, they moved. They followed her everywhere but the ladies' room. If these men were any indication, then the enemy better be on guard because the U.S. Army was ready for action. Meeker could assure those in charge the GIs were quick, agile, and focused. In fact, she had seen less hand-to-hand combat during her recent trips behind enemy lines than she had experienced on the flight. On top of that, during those twenty-nine hours, she'd refused a dozen proposals, at least two from married men, and somehow managed to keep her honor intact.

After freshening up and laying out a game plan with Lancelot, Meeker changed into a gray suit, combed her dark auburn hair, applied a new layer of lipstick, and made her way to Roosevelt Hotel's large dining room. While she would have been comfortable wearing this outfit in the White House, when she walked into the dining room, she felt very underdressed.

With its etched grand columns reaching upward from floors covered by imported rugs to a ceiling featuring hand-painted reliefs, the room seemed more a palace than a place to order food. Two rows of several dozen large round tables graced the room's center section with scores of smaller square tables on each side. Each was covered with linen tablecloths, and the Roosevelt's specially designed china was ready for dishes fixed by the greatest chefs on the West Coast.

As Meeker entered, the maître de, a familiar-looking large black man dressed in a tuxedo, looked up and smiled. "Do you have a reservation?"

"Why are we going through this?" Meeker asked.

"Because," Lancelot pointed out, "there might be someone watching."

"And because you're enjoying it."

"That too! But you're the one who said someone needed to keep an eye out for trouble. You're also the one who arranged for me to have this gig tonight. So, I have to stay in character. Now do you have a reservation?"

"Yes."

"And your name?"

"Meeker, and you're way too much into your part."

"Ah, you are on the list. We have a special table set up for you. Just follow me. Mildred will be serving you tonight. At least, I think that's what she said her name was."

After Meeker was seated, her partner strolled back to his station, and an older waitress dressed in a black skirt, white blouse, and red jacket waltzed over.

"Good evening," she said as she handed Meeker a menu. "You might be interested in knowing that you're sitting in the exact spot where Janet Gaynor sat during the first Academy Award presentations. In this very place the actress heard her name called for winning Hollywood's most important award. That was on May 16, 1929."

"Are you sure it was this exact spot?" Meeker asked.

"Well." The woman chuckled. "It was in this room. We're instructed to make everyone feel important."

Meeker grinned. "If I'd been a man, what would you have said?"

"Ah, I would have told you about *Wings* winning for the best picture."

Meeker raised an eyebrow. "You wouldn't have talked about the best actor?"

The woman shrugged. "No one remembers Emil Jannings. Talking about him would have been like showing you a picture of my granddaughter. You wouldn't have cared."

"You seem to know your Hollywood lore."

The slim woman in her early sixties nodded. "I had a few minor roles in silent pictures … nothing that anyone would notice, but working in this town when things were new and fresh was still special. Back then the film business was an experiment, and today it's purely big business."

While the fate of the world hung in the balance, hundreds of diners reflected no worries or concerns. Dressed in their finest, they were ready to party. Meeker glanced toward the bandstand where a small orchestra was playing one of the latest Benny Goodman hits "Someone Else Has Taken My Place."

"Crazy," the waitress said.

Meeker turned her eyes back to the older woman. "What's crazy?"

"That so many people can still forget their cares and whoop it up. But it was that way in the last war too."

"Maybe it's because booze isn't rationed," Meeker suggested.

"We're selling a lot of drinks," the waitress admitted. "Would you like one? Looking into your eyes, you seem to have some worries that need to be numbed."

Was she that obvious? Was the loss and concern she was feeling about everything from her sister's welfare to her own decisions now etched onto her face? That wasn't good.

"You look like a red wine kind of gal," the waitress said.

"No," Meeker answered, "I'll just take a Coke. And by the way, I'm expecting a man."

"Husband or something better?"

"No. He's an Army captain named Sharp. If you spot an officer looking lost, point him in my direction."

"I will, and about our menu, the war has forced us to cut back on several things. That's why a few of our favorites have been marked through, but I still think you can find something that you'll like."

"Do you have potatoes?" Meeker asked.

"Absolutely."

After handing the menu back to the waitress, Meeker said, "Then have the chef bake me the biggest one he can find."

"Will do, and have your Coke in flash."

Meeker shook her head. "Just bring it out with the spud."

As the woman sauntered toward the kitchen, Meeker focused on her assignment. Lancelot seemed positive the prop man wasn't behind the shooting, but her partner had also admitted proving his innocence might be impossible. If Lancelot was right, this could turn out to be a tougher case than she wanted. She needed a one, two, three, and out, so she could get to working on finding Gertrude Root.

"You look frustrated."

Awakened from her thoughts, Meeker looked into the warm, blue eyes of an Army officer. Though his face sported a few light scars around the side of his chin and a larger one at the hairline, he was what Alison would call a "heartthrob." In fact, with his wavy dark hair and easy grin, he could have been a movie star.

"You must be Captain Sharp."

"Call me Michael."

"Have a chair, Michael. And has anyone ever told you that you look like Robert Taylor?"

He sat. "Only in the last few weeks. If you know my story, and I assume you do, then you also know a Hollywood surgeon rebuilt my face. I requested Taylor be the inspiration. I looked much different before I was injured, and I assure you this is an improvement."

"Couldn't they have given you your old face back?" Meeker asked.

"I don't have any family, so I opted to create a new me."

"There's a lot to be said for starting fresh," Meeker admitted. "There are times I wish I could."

He scratched his head and grinned. "The great Helen Meeker … who wouldn't want to be you? You're smart, beautiful, and you've got the ear of perhaps the world's most powerful man. You've lived more adventures than any woman on earth. Lord, you've blown up a mountain and taken out who knows how many enemies of the state."

Suddenly, as she considered the man's observations, Meeker was on edge. His words were both flattering and troubling, and the latter resonated the loudest. When she finally responded, there was an obvious edge in her tone.

"As a soldier, you well know the key to being successful is having a good team around you. I've had the best."

His response seemed intentionally cocky. "And now they've assigned me to be a part of that team."

She ignored his obvious ego as she looked deeply into his eyes. "How do you feel about that?"

"In truth, I'd rather be in DC or on the battlefield, but they didn't give me that option."

"You're only with me on a temporary basis," she assured him. "When the doc clears you for active duty, you'll be where you belong. At least, that's what I was told."

"So you're not the one to make the call? I figured they were using you to test my abilities and my judgment."

His tone seemed to signal a hint of resentment. Was it toward her or the assignment?

"Captain, I'm not a shrink. I'm not going to write up a detailed mental evaluation to share with the Army or anyone else. I'll judge you strictly on how you do your job. Besides, the case I'm working on now is not likely to put anyone in peril. If they wanted to really test your mental state, they would have thrown you into an assignment where there was some real stress ... where lives were really on the line."

"I doubt things will be that easy," Sharp said. "Trouble always follows Helen Meeker." He grinned. "Or maybe Helen Meeker always runs to trouble."

The glint in his eye clearly showed he was enjoying needling her. He was like a cat toying with a mouse, but she was no mouse. And if they were going to be on the same team, now was the time to reverse their roles and put Sharp in his place.

"If I have any trouble with you," she warned, "you'll be the one who gets stung."

"I bet you've stung a lot of men."

"I've done a lot more than break hearts," she snapped. "Now can you work on a team and follow orders, or do I just assign you to doing my laundry and waxing my rented car?"

He leaned forward. "When do I start?" he asked. "And when do I get to be graded by the great Helen Meeker?"

"I'll introduce you to one of my partners tomorrow. He's intelligent, well educated, and his instincts are always spot on. So don't sell him short."

"Why would I?"

"Because he's a Negro." Meeker waited for that reality to set in before adding, "And because of his skin color, most folks have written him off before they see him in action."

"So you're saying he's my equal?" Sharp asked.

"No. I'm saying you'll have to be more extraordinary than you appear to be his equal. He'll give you assignments."

He frowned. "Was that meant to cut me down to size?"

"No, it's just an honest statement of fact. Let's make one thing very clear. You're here because I was assigned to take you under my wing. You remember that! I'm your boss, not your partner. And Lancelot is your superior as well. If you don't treat both of us with the respect we deserve, then I've got the power to keep you off the battlefields and away from Washington."

"Why the threat?" he demanded.

"It's not a threat. I just happen to have that kind of pull—at least concerning you."

"Fine," he grumbled. "I'm ready for work now. In fact, you'll soon discover that I'm better suited for my assignment than anyone you've ever worked with."

"Captain, before I met you I was going to give you a break. I was going to make things easy for you. I was going to let you tag along. I was going to do that because I know soldiers who've been as badly injured as you were and have had the experiences that you have had usually carry scars that no surgeon can find much less fix. But your attitude has changed my philosophy. Now I really hope trouble did follow me to Los Angeles so I can see what you're like under fire."

"I'm fine," he snapped. "My mind and reflexes are as good as ever."

"But what about your judgment? That can only be tested when pressure is applied."

"And you're going to apply it?" he asked.

"You might be a captain in the U.S. Army, but you're a private in my organization. Do you understand that?"

"Yeah, I get it," he snapped.

"Good. Now come up to my room, 405, tomorrow at two. I'll introduce you to my partner. He'll be giving you most of your assignments and orders."

"The Negro?"

"Yeah."

"Do you need anything else from me tonight?"

"Sharp, as you now know the score, I wouldn't blame you a bit if you called your superiors and asked to get another assignment."

"No woman can beat me," he snarled. He then pushed his frown into a smile. "I look forward to working with you."

"Let's hope you feel that way in a week," Meeker replied.

After sizing her up a final time, the captain pushed back from the table and walked toward the lobby. When Sharp was out of the room, Napoleon Lancelot stepped away from his post and strolled to Meeker's table.

"Helen, I almost wish we hadn't bugged the table. Listening to you torch him wasn't fun. You were brutal. I didn't think that was part of the plan. Why did you push him so hard?"

"My gut tells me something's not right. As you no doubt heard, he began by trying to flatter me!"

"That's the ploy every man uses on a woman, especially one that holds his future in her hands."

"That's true, but Nap, he used information even the FBI and Army Intelligence don't know."

Lancelot leaned closer. "What was that?"

"He knew I helped blow up a mountain. How did he find that out? We can't trust him until we learn where he got his information."

CHAPTER 8

Sunday, January 3, 1943
1:15 a.m.
Los Angeles Times, Los Angeles, California

Not wanting to attract undue attention and having no desire to answer any questions on why he was searching for dirt on one of the city's fastest rising stars, Lancelot chose to undertake his first bit of West Coast research when the fewest employees were toiling in the offices of the *Los Angeles Times*. After checking in at the front desk, he took the elevator up to the fifth-floor newspaper morgue.

The library's night attendant, a flighty, thin, dishwater blonde who seemed to be about thirty and evidently bathed in cheap perfume, quickly retrieved the files on Abby Force.

As a matter of courtesy, Lancelot asked why she chose to work the overnight shift. He had no idea that question would start a string of endless explanations coupled to random observations.

"My name's Blanche Prejean. I took this job because no one is here at this time."

"You don't like people?"

"I can take them or leave them. Just too many folks in the daytime don't bathe often enough. I believe cleanliness is next to godliness."

"I took a shower this afternoon," he offered.

"Yeah, you smell fine."

"Good to know," he replied while taking the file from her hands.

"You know," she continued, "you can tell a lot about a person by the way they smell. I would have fallen in love once, but I just couldn't get over the way Mac smelled."

Lancelot knew better, but he asked anyway. "What did he smell like?"

"He worked in tuna factory. I'll let you figure it out."

"So the fish got between you and a ring?"

"I guess you could say that," she admitted. "You know, this is a strange town. Nobody is who they seem to be. That's why smells are so important. You can't hide where you've been from a good nose."

"I'll try to remember that," Lancelot assured her. "Now I need to get to work reading these files."

She shook her head. "Are you looking for something you don't already know?"

"Yeah."

"I wouldn't expect to find it in those stories."

As he studied the two-inch thick folder, he wondered what she meant.

"I noticed when you flashed your identification that you're from Chicago."

"Yeah."

"That likely means you're not hip on the way things are done in this town."

"Is there a specific L.A. method of handling news?"

She sat down at the ten-foot-long library table, and after he'd taken a place across from her, explained what was, at this point, lost to Lancelot. "Everyone out here covers the news just like you do in the Midwest or the East except for one area. When the studios are involved, we print what they give us. Essentially every newspaper is a PR arm of the motion picture industry. So all those stories you're about to read are nothing more than publicity for Abby Force. The truth pretty much begins and ends where she was and whom she was with. And the only reason the studios can't recreate that part of the story is that photographers take pictures. But the why, how, and what in those stories are always carefully crafted to shape the star into an image the studio wants. You see, they retouch a lot more than photographs here and the newspapers fully accept it."

"Thanks."

"No problem," Prejean replied. "Now, if you don't need me, I'm going to the break room and sip on some java. Got to have a lot of that to stay awake in this job."

As the woman pushed away from the table and headed toward the door, Lancelot glanced at his watch and said, "I'm expecting a call in fifteen minutes. The party knows I'll be here. Will the switchboard route the call here to me?"

"Sure. And if I'm not back, just pick up the phone and yap for as long as you like." With a smile and a wave, Prejean sauntered out the door.

Now was the time to dig.

The first twenty clippings proved the woman correct. They were all just puff and fluff. Reading the stories was like looking at an unused coloring book. The profiles were mere lines with little in between. Nothing told him who the real Abby Force was or gave him any reason to suspect she might actually be the one who loaded the live round into the gun that shot Matt Craig. Still he kept reading. He was scanning a story on one of the star's New York publicity trips when the phone on Prejean's desk rang. Pushing away from the table, he ambled over and answered. "Morgue, Napoleon Lancelot."

"That's dismal. In fact, that's a complete downer."

"Alison Meeker, you're right on time, and I hope you dug up and used those Washington sources you have. I need some help. Nothing I'm reading is telling me much about Miss Abby Force—The Sweetheart of the American Cinema."

"I've got something for you," Alison confidently announced. "If she passed first and second, she's now in third grade."

"I'm not following," he admitted.

"She's like eight."

"Most eight-year-olds don't look like she does," Lancelot pointed out.

"So she's the exception, not the rule. And do you know what time it is Washington?"

"Yeah, and I appreciate you getting up to call me in the middle of the night. In truth, this is the first time I've been around a phone for more than a couple of minutes since I got here."

"Well, at least you aren't on a chain."

"Yeah, I understand Helen has restricted your movement."

"Oh, I can move, there're just eyes on me all the time. I'm like a tiger at the zoo. I do a lot of pacing."

Lancelot understood the young woman's frustration but also fully supported Meeker's motivation. As his partner's sister, she did have a target on her back.

"Alison, you were better off when everyone thought Helen was dead, but when the senator dropped the bombshell she was still breathing, and you got put in a tough spot. That's not your sister's fault. Helen let you have a normal life as long as she could, but then reality kicked in. If something happened to you, it would kill her."

"Crazy! A woman who taunts death for a living is scared to let me live."

"I can't solve your problem, so let's get back to Abby Force. What did you mean about her being in third grade?"

"Here's a fact. She wasn't making any waves until 1935. It's like the stork came eight years ago and delivered a fully developed pinup girl."

"Yeah, I realize she's fairly new to the Hollywood scene, but I've done enough homework to know more than that. I've read her bio and learned her parents died in a train wreck when she was six. She was then taken in and raised by a grandmother in Atlanta. Abby was seventeen when Grandma died, and that's when she made the move west. Harlan Marx, the director turned producer, discovered her working as a store clerk. Within a couple of years, she was a star."

"That's nothing more than a three-dollar bill," Alison suggested.

"It's printed everywhere," he argued. "It's her life story. She evidently talks about it all the time."

"It's like Monopoly money," Alison explained. "It's colorful, but you can't spend it. Here's the scoop in language even a square could grasp. Abby Force has no history before eight years ago. About that time, she put on a mask and has been playing an actress ever since. As far as official government records go, she was never even born. There is no record of her in Atlanta or anywhere else."

Lancelot drummed his fingers on the desk and frowned. This reshaped the whole investigation. If the Hollywood story was a complete lie, then who was Force and what was she hiding about her past?

"Want to plunge into even muddier waters?" Alison cut into Lancelot's thoughts.

"Why not?"

"While I can't provide a scoop on where she really came from, I can tell you she's anything but a good luck charm. She always books passage with the Grim Reaper."

"I'm following your lingo," Lancelot acknowledged, "but I need some additional information to make the connection."

"What do Senator William Darby, Congressman Nathan Kelly, industrialist Armstrong Jackson, media mogul Kathryn Street, and General Lee Stewart all have in common?"

Lancelot allowed the names to tumble through his memory. On the surface, they seemed to be unconnected. While they likely might have met from time to time, to his knowledge they'd never made news together. As he tried to establish a link, Alison offered a clue.

"Tombstones."

Lancelot snapped his fingers. "They're all dead."

"And each of them checked out on the day that Abby Force was visiting the same city they were in."

"Murder?"

"No, in each case, the news indicates just bland passings."

"Natural deaths?"

"I like my way of saying it better," Alison said. "In plain English, the Secret Service reports indicate that each of those people was working on something vital for the war effort when they cashed in. None of them were in bad health, either."

"Grim Reaper indeed," he whispered.

"Is that all you need?" she asked.

"Yeah, I'm glad I called and asked you to do some digging. The stuff I'm reading is nothing more than puff and fluff."

"Sounds like the name of a breakfast cereal," Alison said. "On my stuff, the Secret Service already had the information. They just hadn't connected the dots on the deaths and Force's visits. And in truth, they didn't buy the link when I pointed out what I saw. So the U.S. government currently has no interest in Force's background. And by the way, assure my sister I'm safe. In fact, I'm so safe I might as well be in prison. If she continues to keep me this isolated, I'll end up an old maid like she is."

"I don't think I'll tell her that."

"Well, sadly, my life's all level and I like hills."

"I get you."

"Bye."

As he set the phone down, Lancelot glanced back at the file on the table. What Alison had just delivered made the clippings little more than verbal whipped cream—looked good but had no substance. To solve this case, he was going to have to figure out who Abby Force really was.

"Did you find anything?" Prejean asked as she waltzed back into her domain.

Lancelot looked up and nodded. “I discovered you were right about the clippings involving Abby Force, but I’ve got a new direction to follow, and this time, it centers on folks that get real coverage. What do you have on the obituaries of famous Americans?”

“You have names?”

“Five who were tops in their fields and until recently very much alive.”

“Write them down and let’s get started.”

CHAPTER 9

Monday, January 4, 1943
Noon
Farm outside Bloomington, Illinois

Though twenty agents had been working around the clock for almost two weeks to find Gertrude Root, there were no leads. The FBI seemed assured Root was no longer in Chicago, and everyone realized the country's new most wanted criminal was too smart to return to Washington. General Jefferson Root's home and office phones had been tapped, and his wife had not attempted to contact him. In a very real sense, Gertrude had pulled a Houdini—as if the earth had opened up and swallowed her whole.

In this case, the solid information Teresa Bryant had received on Root had not come from the FBI. On Hoover's orders, the agency had completely cut anyone associated with Helen Meeker out of the equation. Roger Richards had been her source. He was also the cop who shared the Bureau's belief Root was likely in Canada or making her way there. Thus, the Royal Mounted Police were now involved, and both the Mounties and the G-Men had a huge problem. The Allied command didn't want to reveal that the wives of one of its generals had been selling information to the Nazis. And there were no wanted posters or press coverage, which meant there was no citizen involvement, and nothing was more important than catching a public enemy than having the public looking for him, or in this case, her.

Bryant was sure years ago Root realized at some point her cover might be blown, so she no doubt had established several different escape routes to use if that happened. In each case, Root would surely have had safe houses stocked with caches of money, clothes, and likely a car. During her years in Washington, Root had always worn designer outfits that made her stand out, but if she dressed down, she would have no problem blending in. Essentially, she'd be invisible among the masses. The men now chasing her were likely still picturing Root as she was in Washington. They weren't looking for an elderly housewife or a scrubwoman. That meant she had so many more ways to hide in plain sight as would a man.

There was another major flaw Bryant saw in the masculine-fueled thinking. The FBI's focus indicated they were using the same tactics as if they were searching for a man. But Root had been successful in a man's world because she had played the game as a woman. Therefore, she wouldn't follow the same course as the agents might expect. And Bryant knew Root well enough to be sure the woman would not panic. She would keep her head and wait for the right moment before making her move. So Root had to be holed up somewhere, but where?

Bryant had spent the past few days studying maps. The FBI was right. Going through Canada offered the easiest route to get to Germany. If the fugitive could make it to the east coast, a U-boat could be dispatched to pick her up off Nova Scotia or Newfoundland. But Bryant questioned that strategy. Why would Hitler want Root now? As her cover was blown, her work for the Nazi cause was finished. Besides, there was nothing new or valuable she could offer them if she did make the Fatherland. Logic dictated Root would be getting no help from Hitler. With that in mind, the best direction to go would not be north in the winter but to instead follow the course set by birds.

If Bryant knew Root as well as she thought she did, then the woman surely had cash in several different banks and under a host of different names. If that were the case, Root could go in a wide variety of directions. But what would be the ultimate goal? Where would she be safe? If she couldn't get back to Germany, there were several countries in South America where she could live well and be protected. Thus, Root likely had a preset escape route that took her through Mexico.

With an almost two-week head start, Root could have already made Argentina, but Bryant was betting that a smart woman fearing the FBI wouldn't immediately rush across the border. Root was crafty and would surely wait until things cooled off before making her way south. So where would she hide out in the meantime? And when considering that location, another old nemesis popped to mind.

Fredrick Bauer had been Gertrude Root's brother. When he'd died, she'd taken control of his world. Perhaps the only place the FBI had not looked that might offer a clue to where Root had gone was Bauer's Central Illinois farm. So Bryant had driven over icy roads to the isolated and now deserted home.

To Bryant, the place looked a great deal different than the last time she and Meeker had visited. Since that time, the FBI had gone over the place with a fine-toothed comb. What they found had proven disappointing. There were no formulas, secret weapons, hidden plans, or cash. When Bauer left, he'd taken everything he needed and destroyed the rest.

On this gray winter day, the fields were covered in five inches of fresh snow, and the barn and home were as cold as an icebox. The scene was bleak and filled with haunting and unsettling memories. Here was where Bauer had almost tapped into Bryant's deepest buried secrets. Here in this place was where she'd almost died. Now devoid of life, the farm was even more foreboding than when the monster had called this place home. The entire area seemed possessed.

Every sound caused her to jump, robbing her of focus. A rabbit running across the snow brought panic. She had not been this unsettled since her days as an orphaned child. Every fiber in her being urged her to rush through this job, but she knew she couldn't. If there were a clue here, she'd need to do a lot of digging.

Three hours of searching the lab proved fruitless. With its beds, empty file cabinets, and tables, it looked like a deserted medical clinic, yet in her mind she could still see what it had been. And what she remembered chilled her to the bone. Scores had died here as a part of a madman's experiments, and their ghosts seemed to be everywhere. What happened in this hidden chamber was almost as numbing as what she'd witnessed the Germans doing to captured Jews inside the mountain during her recent trip behind enemy lines.

She walked from the lab through the snow to the house. In their search, FBI agents had torn the rooms apart, but they'd left the furniture, dishes, appliances, and even the books. Yet, she saw nothing. Hoover's men had looked in every drawer, gone through each book, and searched every closet. Apparently, anything of value had been boxed up and taken back to DC.

Frustrated, Bryant sat behind Bauer's desk. As she eased back in the chair, a single thought played over and over in her mind. No one finds everything. There is always something that's overlooked. So where did she search for what had not been seen? The answer always came back to the fact the FBI team had been all men. After all, J. Edgar didn't have any female agents. So where would a man not look?

Getting up, Bryant made a second tour of the house, this time even searching under furniture and inside rolls of socks. Once again, she found nothing. Pulling her coat around her to close out the cold created by the winter weather and the unheated building, she returned to the office and, although she figured it would be futile, opened each of the desk drawers. About all that was left in the center one was paperclips, pencils, and rubber bands. The three drawers on the right were empty. The top left contained a few bills that would likely never be paid. The bottom file drawer was completely cleaned out. Where had no one looked?

Bryant had been here months ago and knew Bauer had taken the important stuff when he'd deserted the farm. After Meeker informed the FBI about the place, they had swooped in and taken anything the Bureau felt could be used as evidence in a trial. So there were two things left to consider. The first was what Bauer might have forgotten and how the FBI's men might have overlooked it? Where? Where? Where? Why couldn't she figure it out? She just couldn't leave here empty handed.

To slow her heart and refocus, she forced her mind to a different place and a different time. For fifteen minutes, she shuffled through dozens of memories until one jumped out.

As a child in the orphanage, Bryant had one thing she treasured above all else—a beaded bracelet that had been made by her mother. As the staff had been given the task of erasing all her Caddo roots and transforming the little brown orphan into a white girl, they had forbidden her to wear the bauble. When a supervisor discovered Bryant sleeping with the bracelet, it was jerked off her wrist and thrown in the trash. When no one was looking, Bryant dug it out. The hiding place she'd chosen to keep it safe was under the bottom drawer in a wardrobe where she and her roommates kept their clothes.

Opening her eyes and glancing back at the desk, Bryant reached down and yanked the file drawer as far out as it would go. After tilting it slightly downward, she removed it and set it to the side. Falling to her knees she looked into the drawer cavity. A single envelope rested on the floor. She quickly retrieved it, but it was hardly the answer to her prayers. The envelope just contained a bank statement postmarked March 13, 1940, containing about two dozen canceled checks.

With nothing else to go on, she scanned them. The first five had been written to the power company, a grocery, a laboratory supply company, a business store, and Time Magazine. The sixth check captured her interest—four hundred and sixty-five dollars sent to the county clerk in Lake County, Colorado. At the bottom was a notation indicating the check was for taxes on properties 7, 12, 13, and 17 in Gold Cove.

Bryant sat on the floor and leafed through the rest of the documents. When she found nothing but payments for routine bills, she returned her attention to her one glimmer of hope. Was this the answer? She couldn't find it here, so it was time to hit the road. Stuffing the check into her pocket, she hurried from the house and drove to the nearest pay phone. After spending more than five minutes and two dollars in change at a pay phone booth, she was connected to the courthouse in Leadville, Colorado.

"County Tax Office."

"I need to find out about some property in Gold Cove."

"No one's asked about that place in a long time," the woman replied.

"Why's that?" Bryant asked.

"It's a ghost town. When the gold played out, everyone left. An old miner everyone called Lizard Jones hung on for a few decades, but he died more than ten years ago. They say his ghost still roams the empty streets at night."

"So no one's there now?"

"Someone bought the whole town back in 1939. He visited for a few weeks and paid to have the entire area fenced off. From time to time after that, he'd come and go. Sometimes he brought friends. I'd see them in Leadville buying supplies. We all kind of figured they were either hunting or fishing."

"Do you have a name for the owner?"

"Let me look."

As the time passed, Bryant dropped five more quarters into the machine. As she was now down to a few dimes and nickels, she offered a short prayer for the woman to return before she went broke.

A minute that seemed like eternity, the woman's voice popped back on the line. "The owner's name is Bauer. I found a check that was written a month ago for the property taxes that was signed by a Gertrude Root. So maybe she bought the property from him and hasn't requested a deed change yet."

Bryant smiled. At least there might be a chance Root was using the property as a hideout.

"Miss, is there anything left of the town?"

"It's Mrs.—Mrs. Deborah Park—and I've not been there in a long time. It was once a pretty nice town, so I have to figure there might be a few buildings left. It would be kind of socked in by snow right now."

"Thank you."

"You're welcome."

Bryant hung up, stepped out of the booth, and hurried to the car. It would likely be a wasted trip, but she needed to visit Gold Cove. After all, could there be a better place to hide out than in a ghost town during the middle of winter?

CHAPTER 10

Monday, January 4, 1943
4:32 p.m.
1210 Pine Street, Burbank, California

Napoleon Lancelot was unsettled. This affair should have been open and shut, but what he'd found out about Abby Force coupled with his gut telling him Calvin Coggins had been set up had him confounded. Until Helen Meeker visited with Matt Craig, the cloud of confusion was likely to continue to cover the case. On top of all this, he was babysitting a man who obviously found being in Lancelot's presence distasteful, and it had nothing to do with his choice of cologne.

With a disgruntled Captain Michael Sharp in the passenger seat and a mind that kept bouncing from suspect to suspect and scenario to scenario, Lancelot drove his rented Ford across town to 1210 Pine Street. Perhaps in this typical, bungalow-style home setting on a tiny lot reflecting fulfilled middle class dreams, he would discover the whole story behind the weapon that almost cost the city's biggest star his life. Or perhaps, the uncomfortable trip would be just another waste of time.

On the radio Dinah Shore's "Why Don't You Fall In Love with Me" played as Lancelot pushed back in the seat and glanced out the window. With its white stucco and green trim, the house they'd be visiting was hardly fancy, but thanks to shutters and the red tile roof, exuded a modest charm.

As Lancelot eased the black 1937 coupe to a stop by the curb, Sharp spoke for the first time since they'd left the Roosevelt. While Shore's sultry soprano was sweet and light, Sharp's baritone was heavy and filled with deadly venom. "Why am I here?"

Sharp's distaste for being teamed with Lancelot was obvious, and Lancelot was sure he knew the motivation, but there was also no reason to return prejudice with more prejudice. For the moment, the big man would play it cool. He casually reached forward, turned the radio off, killed the engine, glanced over at the passenger, and laid out the facts of life.

"You're here because of your uniform and skin color. You see, some folks won't open the door for a black man, but almost everyone will invite a white military officer into their home."

"Does that bother you?" Sharp asked.

"It's a fact of life, and I've found life's rarely fair. So I deal with it."

"If you don't mind me saying so, you take being thought of as inferior pretty easily. Looks like it just rolls off your back. Kind of makes me wonder if you believe it."

The captain's observation stung. Being marked as having less worth or intelligence was the greatest of all insults, but what could Lancelot do about it? Screaming, yelling, and pouting accomplished nothing. Due to the way the system worked, the only real answer was doing his job so well that he made people think and reconsider their point of view. Yet at this moment, he would have rather dismissed that option, and embraced one that was a bit more physical.

"If you believe you're equal," Sharp taunted, "you should be angry. In fact, rage should drive you to lash out and fight."

"Are you speaking for me or picking a fight between us?"

"Are you asking what I believe?"

"Yeah," Lancelot admitted, "I am."

Sharp had kept his eyes forward the entire trip, as if looking at Lancelot might have made the driver appear human, but now he studied Lancelot's face. Finally, after a dime's worth of awkward seconds, he transferred what was festering in his mind to his mouth. "History seems to prove the white man is superior."

Lancelot raised an eyebrow. "Does it?"

"From my reading of history, yes. Besides, a man who truly believes he's equal would not accept his fate. He would lash out and drive the opponent into the dirt. He'd make him eat his words."

"So, I prove myself by being able to take you apart?"

"If you had the stomach for it," Sharp suggested. "And that's just the point. You don't have enough guts to do that. You're content to play second fiddle. You don't mind having a woman boss you around. Essentially, you take what you are given. No one gets ahead that way. To get to the top, you have to take what others have and make it your own. You have to have fire in your belly to do that. Your race doesn't have any fire."

Every fiber in his body demanded that Lancelot explode, but if he did he would be playing right into the hands of thinking that was so deeply grounded in society. In the case of Sharp these concepts might never be uprooted. Besides, by attacking, he would expose himself as the animal his unwanted companion believed him to be. So he simply turned the page.

"You're here because I need you in the part of the case. That's something I've already explained and something I don't mind admitting. So, for this moment we have to get along. But, when we obtain the needed information, I'll happily drive to Griffin Park and give you a chance to prove your superiority." Lancelot smiled and added, "And after that, I'll drive you to the office of the doctor who fixed your face because he'll have a lot more work to do."

When the obviously stunned Sharp failed to respond, Lancelot shifted into full work mode. As he glanced toward the middle class cottage he brought Sharp up to speed. "The man that lives in this home was employed by the Ford Motor Company for twenty-five years. A couple of weeks back, he sold a gun to a prop man at Monument Studios. We're here to find out the story of that gun."

"Seems like a waste of time," Sharp said.

"Maybe," Lancelot agreed, "but when you work a case you have to cover every angle. I want to know where this guy bought a 1938 Lugar."

"A Lugar? That's a German gun."

"And it's what the studio needed for a scene. But how did Howard Menefee just happen to have one?"

"There could be a thousand reasons," Sharp offered.

"Maybe more like ten, and I have to identify which of those ten is spot on. Now let's put off our previous discussion and get going."

Satisfied that for a few minutes he'd buried the seething racial tension, Lancelot eased out of the coupe with Sharp a step behind, and strolled up the walk to the door. After a single knock, the homeowner answered.

"You Lancelot?" Menefee asked, focusing on Sharp.

"Not him," Lancelot said, redirecting the homeowner's gaze. "I'm the man who called you. Captain Sharp and I are working together on this assignment."

Menefee shrugged. "I guess with so many white boys in uniform they're having to use Negros in new ways now. A dumb cop is a dumb cop."

"This Negro is a college graduate," Lancelot announced. "Now we have some questions. Might we step in? After all, it's a bit brisk in this wind."

"I think I'd rather talk on the porch." Menefee didn't have to explain why he wasn't inviting Lancelot into his home.

"Fine," Lancelot answered. "Let me get right with it. You sold a 1938 Lugar S/42 to Monument Studios a couple of weeks ago.

"Yeah, a man named Coggins was the guy who came by and picked it up. He gave me a more than fair price too."

"How did you come to have it?" Lancelot asked.

"I made four trips to Germany for Henry Ford—the first in '34 and the last in '38. People don't mention it now, but Ford and Hitler were buddies for a while, and Henry was working on deals for car sales in Germany. I was there as an engineer. Things were going pretty well until the Germans decided to start a war, and that was the end of that."

"About the gun?" Lancelot cut in.

"I bought the gun in a shop in Hamburg. Just felt good in my hand when I first picked it up. You know what they say?"

"What's that?"

"When you find the right woman, the one that feels right, it's the only one you need or will ever have."

"What does that have to do with this?"

"Put two and two together. Even you'll figure it out given enough time."

Lancelot ignored the slur and pushed forward. "So you brought the gun home with you, and took it through customs?"

"Why wouldn't I? After all that's the law, and I'm a law-abiding citizen. I pay my taxes every March 15th."

Lancelot paused, letting the reply just hang in the air before posing his next question. "Did you do anything with the Lugar after you got home?"

"I went to the range a few times, but shooting targets got boring. I just tossed it in a drawer. When I saw I had a chance to make a few bills, I answered the ad."

Sharp, who'd been completely mute since the heated discussion in the car, finally got involved in the conversation. "Menefee, you talked about your trips to Germany, how do you feel about the war?"

"The Japs attacked us," Menefee answered, "so we need chase them straight to hell. But I don't have any issues with the Germans. The ones I got to know were nice folks. I even met Hitler once, and he treated me all right. I wish we'd stayed out of Europe. That's the Brits' war not ours."

"Do you still stay in contact with any folks in Germany?" Lancelot asked.

"What right do you have to ask who I associate with?"

"I can't make you answer," Lancelot admitted, "but we can subpoena you to court and you'll to answer there. It's your choice."

"And I thought this was free country," Menefee snapped. "Yeah, I made some friends in Germany. They fed me and entertained me when I was there. When they came to visit our plant in Detroit, I wined and dined them too. When I retired in 1939 and moved out here, a couple of my German friends and their wives came to see Hollywood, and they stayed in my home for a few days. I showed them the town. Up until 1941, we even wrote a lot of letters to each other and exchanged Christmas cards. The war changed all that. Kind of hard to send a letter to Berlin now."

Sharp, now seemingly engaged in the question and answer session, crossed his arms and leaned forward. "So you don't have any issues with Germany?"

"I'm not going to lie to you. I have fewer problems with Germany than I have with England or France. And I like the Nazis a lot more than I do the Russians. In my mind, Hitler better understands who our real enemies are than Roosevelt does. We need to go after the Reds, not be working with them."

Lancelot frowned. While this kind of thinking was no longer as widespread as it had been in 1936, it was still a lot more common that most Americans wanted to believe. Though they hated that Hitler started a war, lots of people still believed he was on point in his thinking on social issues. He wondered if their minds would be changed if they knew about the slave labor Meeker and Bryant had witnessed on their trip behind lines? In this case it didn't matter, but future opinions might just come to define the United States.

"Mr. Menefee," Lancelot asked, "when you got the gun was there anything carved into the wooden grip?"

"Oh that," the man answered with a smile. "I carved the swastika on both sides. Did a good job, too, if I say so myself. I have a woodworking shop in the back."

"Why did you carve a swastika?" Sharp asked.

"It's a German gun. I just thought it needed one. Made the gun seem more impressive when I showed it to my friends."

The captain looked at Lancelot before asking. "Did you carve it before or after we got into the war?"

"I did that back when the Germans took Paris. You see, I never liked the French much. The ones I met on my trips to Europe all seem to think they were better than me."

"So the only reason you sold the gun was for the money?" Lancelot asked.

"Yeah, and the fact I could brag about having my gun in a movie."

"Thank you, sir," Lancelot replied, "I think that's all we need for now."

"Nice to meet you, Captain," Menefee announced with a smile. He didn't even toss a look Lancelot's way. That was hardly a surprise.

After they'd had returned to the car and were both seated, Sharp said, "I now see why I had to be with you. You wouldn't have gotten him to open up without me."

"I'm used to that," Lancelot replied. "Let's talk about something far more important. What did you make of what he said?"

"He's a crusty guy who has some unique views."

"And how far do you think he would go to live out those views? Do you believe he'd kill someone?"

"Hey, I thought this was just about a gun sale," Sharp answered. "He explained where he bought the gun, why he bought it, and why he sold it. If that's what you were after, you got what you needed."

"Yeah, I got what I needed," Lancelot said. "But what I got is not what you think I got."

Sharp frowned. "Is it the racism that gives you problems? I mean there are millions who feel just like him."

"Are you one of them?" Lancelot asked he started the car and pulled out into the street.

"I don't share all that guy's beliefs. Not even close!"

"Just the ones about Negros?" Lancelot asked.

Sharp shrugged. "I've never been around your people. Maybe you'll enlighten me."

"I don't know if I can change your mind on race, but perhaps I can get you to see why this little trip was worth it."

"Well then, change my mind."

"Okay, the gun Menefee sold to the prop man was used to shoot an actor during a scene being filmed at Monument Studios. Somehow a live round found its way into the chamber."

Sharp's expression said everything. He was now off balance, and Lancelot opted to keep him that way.

"And yes, Menefee received cash for his gun but he left something out. He also negotiated a studio pass with the deal. He used that pass on the day after Christmas—the same day the actor caught a piece of lead in his gut."

"So," Sharp replied, excitement in his tone, "if Menefee really is still in contact with friends in Germany, you think he might have been told to find a way to kill this actor?"

"I'm not settling on any theory yet, but a few minutes ago, we were told a lie that lends a bit of credence to that theory. It's also a lie that Menefee has no idea I could trace."

"What's that?"

"If Menefee brought a gun back with him during his trip to Germany, the Customs Department would have noted the weapon. Helen's contacts in Washington have given us copies of the records from all four of his trips. They show things like a watch, bottles of schnapps, glass Christmas ornaments, jewelry, and a clock, but there's no Lugar listed. So either he smuggled it into the country or …"

"Or someone saw the ad placed by the prop man and sent Menefee the gun to sell along with the orders to eliminate this actor. By the way, who is the actor?"

"Helen will make the call on if you can know the actor's name and the other details of his life. All you need now is to know he's alive and going to be fine. Oh, and you can know the bullet they dug out of the guy was filed. So, it was specially prepared for the job."

"You've done your homework!"

"I always do. And if you continue to work with us, you'll be expected to do your homework as well."

Sharp nodded. "What do your friends call you?"

"Nap."

"Hmm, Nap."

"For now, let's just keep it Captain Sharp and Mr. Lancelot. Now, are we going to put on the gloves and duke it out today?"

"No, I think I'd rather fight someone who wasn't as prepared."

"Smart move. I was a Golden Gloves boxer!"

"When were you going to tell me that?" Sharp asked.

Lancelot grinned. "At the same time I took you to visit the plastic surgeon. Time to get back to the hotel. Helen will want to hear what we've found out."

CHAPTER 11

Tuesday, January 5, 1943
10:00 a.m.
9613 Ocean Drive, Malibu, California

In Hollywood the big actresses purchased large homes with palatial grounds, but the single actors usually kept things much simpler. Rather than buy mansions, many opted to rent small homes or apartments. Matt Craig took living on the light side one step further—his bachelor's pad was on the water. According to the gossip rags, Craig took to the sea every free moment he could find, but today his pride and joy was docked at Anchor Harbor.

As the watercraft kept at this marina were owned by the rich and famous, Helen Meeker had to present her identification to a security guard at the end of the long dock.

He checked the ID against the scheduled visitors before pointing to a mahogany vessel. "Mr. Craig's boat is all the way down to the end—slip 91. He's expecting you."

Meeker nodded, pulled her dark blue coat closer to her body to ward off the ocean breeze, adjusted her light blue fedora, and began the two hundred-yard trek. When she arrived at the proper slip, Craig, dressed in dark slacks, white shirt, and captain's hat was waiting on the dock. His yacht was big enough to meet his needs but not so large as to demand constant maintenance.

"You must be Helen," he said, flashing a smile that had won him millions of female fans.

"I am," she replied, extending her hand to his. "This is quite a boat, or should I say, yacht?"

"Actually, it's a speedboat," he explained. "The Hacker Thunderbird was built for cruising in the open water at speeds that most vessels can't match. It's the Duesenberg of marine vessels—fast, sleek, and sexy."

"How long is it?"

"Fifty-five feet, and it's powered by two Kermath five-hundred-fifty horsepower engines. It's as powerful as it is beautiful. When they built this one for me, I had them craft a small bedroom and galley in the nose so I could take it out and stay away from land for days on end. I'll help you get onboard, and I'll show you what makes this gal so special. We'll start with a look at the engines."

While the five-minute tour was impressive, that wasn't why Meeker had made her appointment. She had much bigger fish to fry. They sat at the boat's open stern and the sun's warmth began to soak through her coat. "Did you ever bring Mary Coggins here?"

"How did you know about her?" The shock in his tone indicated this was the last question he figured he'd have to answer.

Meeker removed her coat. "My associate spent some time at the jail visiting with her father. He blames you for her suicide. That would seem to be a motive for his putting a live round in the gun fired by Abby Force."

Craig took off his hat, tossed it onto a table, and ran a hand through his wavy dark hair before leaning back on the bench. He then spent a few moments studying the sky. Just when Meeker was running out of patience and about to ask her a question again, he finally found his voice. "I didn't have the boat then. If I had, I wouldn't have brought her here. She was an innocent kid. She was sweet in a way you don't see out here. You can believe it or not, but I never hugged or kissed her. I just met her a few times at the L.A. Diner and we talked. What I discovered is she wanted to grow up real fast, so I tried to convince her to treasure every moment of her youth. My words fell on deaf ears."

"So," Meeker quietly asked, "you weren't the father?"

"Boy, you must have found out everything," he noted. "I thought only me and the old man knew about the baby." He shrugged. "As I said, I never did anything but shake her hand. She was a pretty girl and was tempting, but she needed someone who had not been around the block as many times as I had. When she told me she was pregnant, and the guy was someone her father wouldn't have approved of, I saw the corner she was in. She asked for some money. I figured out what it was for but acted like I didn't know. And that was the last I saw her."

"So you didn't send her to the person who performed the abortion?"

"No. But since her death, I've often thought about how frightened she must have been going there all alone."

Meeker nodded. "Who was the father?"

He shook his head. "She never told me. Just said her father hated him."

"Coggins admitted to my partner he threatened you a few times."

"Can you blame him?" Craig asked. "In his mind, I was the father and my not standing up and admitting it was the reason she killed herself. If I had been in his shoes, I would have had it in for me too."

"Do you think he was the one who put the live round in the Lugar?"

Craig's eyes found Meeker's. "What does he say?"

"He claims he didn't," she answered.

"Then I'd tend to believe him. Coggins might not have much tact, but based on what I know of him, his word is never to be questioned. If he'd been responsible, he'd have admitted it. In fact, the way he feels about me, he'd have probably bragged about it."

Meeker hadn't seen that answer coming, and for a few seconds, it threw her off track. While she was searching for a new road to travel, her host offered an interesting insight.

"Have you ever been on a movie set?"

"No."

"There are scores of people on a sound stage. There are thousands more on the lot. The day I was shot, anyone could have walked into the prop room and made the substitution."

"But why would they have wanted to kill you?" Meeker demanded. "Why shoot America's Dreamboat?"

"Well, I've been known to keep company with women who were married or engaged. I've also taken some juicy roles from actors who blame me for putting their careers on the skids. And there are likely a few dozen more folks out there who just don't like me as a person. This is a town were almost everyone has goals and agendas and they run over people who get in their way. I've left my footprints on a bunch of them."

"Thanks for narrowing the list of suspects," Meeker quipped.

"My pleasure."

"Mr. Craig—"

"Call me Matt."

"Okay, Matt, aren't you forgetting another reason you might have been targeted?"

This was the moment she'd been waiting for. Now she would see just how open Craig was. Would he acknowledge his father, or would he continue to try to cover it up?

He leaned back and ran his hand over a brass rail. "They almost made a movie about your life."

"I'm glad that didn't happen."

"I'm kind of sad it didn't. I was going to get to play your boyfriend."

"Henry?"

He nodded. "It was a good part too. I liked the chemistry between the two of you. It would have been great stuff on the screen."

"There's a role I'm glad that you didn't play. There was only one Henry."

Craig's eyes caught Meeker's. "That makes it sound as if he's dead."

"Yeah, but he died doing what he loved, and in the process, saved a lot of lives."

"Still must hurt."

"War hurts lots of people every day. I don't get a pass. But this has nothing to do with my question."

"Actually," he suggested, "it does. You're not just a woman and an investigator, you're Helen Meeker. The reason they almost made a movie about you—before the White House knocked the idea down—was because you're Wonder Woman, Nancy Drew, and Lana Turner all wrapped together. You're strong, tough, beautiful, and deadly. You also know things few others do. So you're surely aware of who my father is."

"Yeah, I know about your dad, the general."

"One of Hitler's righthand men," Craig added. "And you want to know if I might have been a target because of my father?"

She nodded. "What do you think?"

"I've thought about it a great deal," he admitted, "but even though I'm going into the Army Air Corps, I can't see the Nazis trying to gun me down. I think my father has enough pull with Hitler to keep me from being targeted."

"Are you sure?"

"Who can predict Hitler? One of his best friends, Ernst Rohm, was the first head of the SS. Hitler trusted him like a brother. But that didn't keep him from having Rohm executed when the man got a bit too powerful. If he'd order the murder of one of his best friends, I can see how I'd be a target. But what would my death mean? Death would make me a martyr. So the Nazis being behind this just doesn't make sense."

Meeker studied Craig's face. She could tell from his pensive expression he still had something on his mind.

"Matt, do you have another theory?"

"How many people know who my father is?"

"Folks in various branches of the intelligence departments," Meeker answered.

"What about Hoover? Does he trust me? Do you think he might be behind a hit to make sure I didn't ever serve in the Army? Maybe he sees me as a Nazi plant."

Meeker considered the theory. Was it possible? Yes! Was it likely? No! If Craig was deemed an enemy plant, then logic deemed J. Edgar would have made sure the actor's request to join the military would have been denied.

"I played in a movie about the Civil War two years ago—a formula picture with two brothers fighting on different sides. In the closing scene, those brothers met in battle. The script had them walking away rather than squaring off. I had them change the ending so that I killed my brother instead. In my mind, loyalty to one's country overruled blood relations. Do you know why I demanded that change?"

"Because of your father?"

"Yeah—my way of proving which side I was really on. While the folks out in here in fantasyland and fans don't know about my relationship with General Wilhelm Hoganmeier, I figured the government did. I wanted to make FDR, J. Edgar, and the rest see where I stood. So, Helen, the bottom line is that I don't know who shot me. The only thing I feel sure about is that it wasn't Coggins."

If that were the case, where did she look next? An almost cold breeze caused her to reach for her coat and put it on. She glanced out to the ocean and noted dark clouds on the horizon. Was this a sign of the direction her life was about to take?

"Helen, would you be bluntly honest if I asked you a question."

"If you want me to, yes."

"What do you think of my acting?"

"I've only seen a few of your movies, but my little sister thinks you are a dreamboat."

"That's not what I asked. I wanted your opinion on my craft."

"I think you're a great-looking man who is calm and assured on the screen."

"You didn't really say anything about my acting."

"In all honesty," Meeker replied, "when you have your looks, you don't need much more. I think you do a great job."

"I'll see if I can get uglier," he replied. "Maybe it will improve my acting. Would you like something to drink? I can brew some coffee or tea? I also have things in the galley that are a bit harder."

"No, I have work to do," she answered.

"Maybe you can come back when you don't," he suggested.

She shook her head and stood. "I'm not sure even the Helen Meeker you described earlier would be safe around you."

Not waiting for Craig to offer his hand, she jumped from the speedboat to the dock and without turning back, headed to her car. It was time to start pulling some strings and get Calvin Coggins his Get Out of Jail free card.

CHAPTER 12

Wednesday, January 6, 1943
8:15 a.m.
White House, Washington, DC

Henry Wallace was in a grim mood. Tradition decreed vice presidents got the bad jobs and most unattractive assignments. For more than a century and a half, those who were second-in-command greeted dignitaries from obscure nations and Boy Scout groups from Middle America. In just the past year, Wallace had done enough of that to fill a scrapbook—a scrapbook that no one outside of his kids would ever read. Yet today, how he wished he had drawn one of those jobs rather than what he'd been assigned. He was being asked to essentially bury a good friend, and that man was not yet dead.

Wallace had known Jefferson Root for more than twenty years. He watched Root move from captain through the ranks to general. He'd been there in 1917 when Congress had honored the World War I veteran for heroic service. Wallace even attended the funeral of Root's first wife as well as the general's second wedding. And the second wife had turned everything upside down for the respected military icon. Bride number two had taken him from the penthouse to the outhouse. That slide was now sadly over. Root could go no deeper than the hole he found himself in at this moment.

As he looked out the windows of the small room just three doors down from the Oval Office, Wallace wondered how much snow was on the ground back in Iowa. Right now, shoveling the white stuff beat wading through the mud soiling an old friend's boots. It was a darn shame!

Hearing a knock, Wallace slowly turned and walked the twelve feet to the door. Opening the entry, the vice president forced a smile, but his ashen complexion and red eyes likely foreshadowed news that was anything but bright.

"Hello, Henry," the guest said, extending his hand. "I would say it was good to see you, but I'm betting it's not."

"Jeff, please come in."

While Root's grip was still firm, the man appeared twenty years older than he had last week. His hair seemed whiter, the uniform looser, his shoulders slumped a bit, and the dark circles under his eyes dropped so low they were approaching his upper lip. Most corpses looked better.

After closing the door, Wallace pointed to a pair of leather wingback chairs. He waited for his guest to sink into the one on the right before taking the other. For the next few minutes, the only noises were muffled sounds from the hallway and the mantel clock.

"Did you know," Wallace finally said, "that the chairs we're sitting in were brought to the White House by Grover Cleveland? They were made in Delaware by a man named Clark. I understand the wood was from trees at Monticello and the leather came from cows raised at Mt. Vernon."

The general ran his right hand over the lion's head carving in the chair's arm. "There's a lot of craftsmanship in this place. A lot of history too. Some of that history is good and some not so much. It appears I've been on both sides, and I can tell you the side I'm on now is darker than midnight. Everyone I've ever worked with or respected has deserted me. I've never felt so lonely."

Wallace sadly nodded. "Jeff, do you remember the first time we met?"

"I think it was 1927. You had a grain company in Iowa, and I spoke in your town. You and your wife had me over to the house for lunch. We ate the pheasant you shot."

"It seems like so long ago," Wallace said.

Root balled his hands together and looked toward the window. His voice cracking with emotion, he announced, "This must be a terrible day for you too."

"How do you mean?"

"It's not what you have to tell me," Root explained. "I mean that won't be a walk in the park, but it goes with the territory. I read that George Washington Carver died yesterday. I know the great man stayed with your family when he was a student at Iowa State. I remember your telling me about the profound impact Carver had on your life as a child."

Wallace sadly answered. "I wished I could have seen him one more time."

"The story didn't say how old he was."

"He was born a slave," Wallace explained, "so he never actually knew his birth date or even the year. He was likely around eighty … maybe a few years older."

"He had about fifteen years on me," Root said.

"He had about thirty on me. You know, George shaped my whole thinking on race. He proved to me that all men are really created equal. I know some of the world's greatest artists and musicians, but he was the most creative people I've ever met and one of the wisest too. It's funny, when I got the call telling me he had died, I got a sudden craving for peanut butter."

"If only all the things we wished for were that easy to get." Root rolled his hands into a ball and squeezed four times before bringing his fingers together in front of his face. "I tried to save you from this job. Last night, I wrote a note to my two children and got out my service revolver, but I just couldn't pull the trigger."

"I'm glad you didn't," Wallace solemnly replied. "Linda and Paul would have had a difficult time dealing with you ending your life like that."

"And my living makes it better for them?" Root asked. "I don't know how much information was passed along to Germany and Japan thanks to my careless talk. How many of our boys died because of me? Everywhere you turn in this town are posters that read, 'Loose Lips Sink Ships,' and the loosest were my own."

"You had no idea who Gertrude was."

"But," Root argued, "just because she was my wife was no reason for me to tell her what I told her. How many of my files did she look through? They often were on my desk when I was out playing golf. And even if I put them in our safe, she had the combination. Do you know how much loot the FBI found in my basement? There was gold, jewels, and artwork."

Wallace nodded. "According to Helen Meeker, your wife's brother was the mastermind. When Helen took him down, Gertrude moved into the top spot. And it wasn't just you that unknowingly provided material to them. They had people in the FBI as well. Who knows where else they are!"

Root buried his right fist into his left palm. "Do they know where Gertrude is?"

"They haven't found her yet, but for the her, the gig is almost up. It's just a matter of time."

"Well, Henry, wherever she is, she cleaned out our checking and savings accounts, so she has some traveling money."

"I'm sorry, but no matter, we will get her." The vice president paused and studied his old friend. How he hated this moment. He was about to drop a bomb that would blow a career into tiny pieces. It was the last thing he wanted to do, but there was no escaping duty. "Jeff, I want you to know that I went to bat for you. Others did as well. The decision the White House and Army made was not a kneejerk reaction to what your wife did."

Root winced. "Just go ahead and tell me."

Wallace shook his head and frowned. "The President and I deeply appreciate the service you've given your country over the past forty years. We really do."

"Get on with it, Henry."

"If you choose to plead innocent, we'll be forced to bring you up on charges of treason. You'll be subject to a court-martial. I think you know the penalty if you're found guilty."

"Death. What if I just plead guilty right now? I figure that would save both the army and the country as much pain and embarrassment as possible."

"You'll be stripped of your stripes and received a dishonorable discharge. You'll likely draw a ten-year stretch in the federal prison. I would think that after we win the war, the President would issue a commutation. You'd probably only be behind bars for three or four years."

"That's probably better than I deserve."

"Is that the way you want it?" Wallace asked.

"It's the way it has to be."

"Promise me something, Jeff."

"What's that?"

"Don't kill yourself. If you do, Gertrude wins."

Though Root seemed to consider the advice, he didn't reply. After slowly pushing out of the chair, he walked across the room slipped his hand around the brass knob, twisted, and opened the door. He paused in the entry and looked back into the room.

"Goodbye, Henry. Thanks for being a good friend."

Wallace mournfully watched the general disappear before standing and moving back to the window. As he once again studied the grounds, he frowned. Some casualties of war never made it to the battlefields.

"Mr. Vice President."

Wallace turned to note a White House page standing in the doorway. The young woman was just over five feet tall and had a wide-eyed look normally seen at a Sinatra concert. She was likely a college student taking a semester break. Thankfully, her innocence prevented her from seeing the dark cloud hovering in the room.

"Yes," Wallace answered.

"There's a group of Girl Scouts here to meet you. You're scheduled to show them around the White House." She looked at a note in her hand. "And your secretary wants to know if you plan to attend Mr. Carver's funeral."

"What's your name?"

"Betty Stagg."

"Where are you from?"

"Iowa. I'm a junior at Iowa State in Ames," she answered proudly.

"Betty, go back and assure the scouts I will be there within five minutes."

"Yes, sir. And about the funeral?"

"I'll need to check my schedule, but I sure hope I can attend."

The page smiled, bowed slightly, and exited. As she did, the vice president turned to the window. It was almost time to move on, but for a few more minutes he wanted to consider the passing of two friends. One was dead, and the other wished he were. It was a very sad day.

CHAPTER 13

Thursday January 7, 1943
6:17 a.m.
Lincoln Hotel, Chicago, Illinois

Teresa Bryant closed the large suitcase. After securing the lock, she glanced around her hotel suite. No matter where she'd lived, no matter what she had done, leaving home was never easy for her. Beginning when her parents were killed and she was taken away from her Caddo village to countless other addresses that were now little more than faded memories, whenever she left a place, she rarely got to return. Though she wouldn't admit it, not even to herself, what she most longed for was a home, but it seemed her wishes would never be granted. She was a nomad in a world where it seemed everyone else had roots.

With her mind on a mission and the death that would likely accompany it, she walked over to the mirror, took a breath, and studied her reflection. Her almost black eyes seemed dull and lifeless, her shoulders slumped, and her skin was a shade paler today.

"What are you fighting for Morning Song?" she whispered.

What indeed? She had been risking her life for a nation that had placed her people on reservations. Even three generations after the Trail of Tears, she and her people were treated not as equals, but rather as second-class members of the human race. There were many places that wouldn't let her kind vote. She was called a squaw, a savage, and a heathen on a regular basis. On top of that, for all her life she'd been urged to erase who she'd been born to be and embrace being like the people who had killed her parents and robbed her of her heritage. And now as she studied her face in the mirror, this spiritual tug of war seemed to be taking a toll. Where were her passion, her drive, and her lust for life? She didn't see them in the reflection. What had happened to them?

A knock on the door yanked her out of self-reflection. After slipping on a long, black coat, she walked to the entry.

"Miss Bryant," the bellboy said, "I was told you had some bags that I needed to take down for you."

She pointed to the two suitcases on her bed.

"It's a cold morning out there. I'm sure glad I'm not the doorman." After retrieving the luggage, the grinning teen asked, "Are you going on a trip?"

She nodded.

"I'd like to go anywhere south," he announced. "I'm so tired of the snow and the wind."

"I've found," she said, "few are ever satisfied with the weather no matter where they are." She wondered if that was also true of life in general.

The bellboy grabbed the bags and walked out the door toward the elevator.

After taking a final look around her room, wondering if she would ever see it again, she closed the door and followed. Three minutes and twelve floors later, they emerged in the lobby. At this time of the day, there was very little activity and it now was almost as empty as during the hotel evacuation when she and Meeker were contemplating what to do with a bomb.

"The desk called for a cab," the boy explained. "If it's not here, it will be soon. Do you want me to go out and check? That way you wouldn't have to go outside and wait in the cold."

"No," Bryant answered, "I'm going where it's even colder, so I might as well get acclimated."

"Colder than here? I didn't know there was any place colder than Chicago."

"There are a few places," she assured him.

As they walked out into the open air, she felt the Windy City in all its glory. The first burst of lake wind chilled her to the bone. With the bellhop at her side, she ducked her head and moved toward the curb. Naturally, there was no taxi waiting.

"Just set the bags down on the curb," Bryant suggested as she reached into her purse and retrieved a half dollar. Handing the bellboy the coin, she said, "You better go inside. You're not dressed for this."

"I'll stay for a few minutes," he replied. "I've got nothing to do this time of the day but wait for people to wake up. And I'll set the bags close to the front door. That way Amos, the doorman, can make sure no one grabs them." After completing that task, he returned to her side and asked, "Where are you going?"

"West to the mountains."

"Skiing?"

"Only if I have to," she replied. "I have someone I have to meet."

"For business?"

"You could say that."

The streets were still dark and Bryant saw the headlights before she noticed the car. It was not a yellow cab, but rather a dark sedan. Its tires squealing, it made the corner doing at least forty.

"Man, that guy's pushing it," the kid said. "He's in an awful hurry to get somewhere."

Bryant casually nodded as she almost absentmindedly studied the approaching vehicle. She recognized that grill—a 1938 Buick. Its long hood covered a powerful straight-eight engine. As it grew nearer, the car picked up speed before slightly veering to the left and heading right toward them. As it drew closer, the driver bumped the passenger tires over the curb and up onto the sidewalk.

"He's crazy!" the bellhop screamed.

Bryant knew better. This was not an act of insanity—it was the sign of a man on a mission. After shoving the boy back toward the hotel, she dove and dove toward the front door. The speeding car came so close, her long hair raked the front fender. By the time she rolled over and jumped up, the sedan had zipped around the corner and was gone.

"You okay?" the boy asked as he brushed off his pants.

"Yeah, I'm fine."

"I'm sorry about that. They were going after me and you got in the way."

A confused Bryant spun to face the bellhop. "What?"

"My dad's a gambler," the kid explained. "He owes a lot of folks. A couple of them told him they'd use his kids to make a point. I guess they just did."

"No harm," Bryant said.

"You saved my life."

She smiled. "I had to push you out of the way so I had a place to land."

"Hey, there's your cab. He's driving up now. I'll get your bags."

The driver got out and rushed around the Packard's nose to the back-passenger door. After Bryant slid in, the bellboy put both her bags beside her.

"Thanks again, lady!"

"You watch your back," Bryant said.

The kid could have been spot on. Perhaps someone was trying to teach his father a lesson, but she doubted it. Root might be on the run, but she still had a team, and far more likely the woman still had hired guns out to get her. Bryant had lived long enough to know that if the money was right, thugs would line up to take anyone down.

"Where to?" the cabbie asked.

Bryant had a seat secured on an American flight to Denver, but now she wondered if that was a wise move. While the airport was busy, it was hardly as packed as train depots. It would be far more difficult for Root's people to follow her if she were on a train.

"Union Station."

"You got it."

If Root was holed up in the ghost town, she would be staying there for a while. So rather than take a direct path to Gold Cove, why not go north first and convince the enemy she was on her way to join the FBI and Mounties in Canada. That would give Bryant time to see if she had a tail. Only when she was convinced there were no eyes following her moves would she turn around and head south. And when she did make that move, she'd be using a different name.

CHAPTER 14

Friday, January 8, 1943
7:16 p.m.
Roosevelt Hotel, Los Angeles

Helen Meeker looked through the outfits she'd brought and frowned. Tonight was a night for a party dress or a gown, and all she had were suits. As she reached for a gray jacket and skirt, she rationalized that no one would really be looking at her. All eyes would be on the stars.

Hearing a knock, she exited her bedroom, waltzed across the suite's living area, and opened the door. On the other side was her partner dressed in a dapper dark blue suit.

"I hope you've had a good day," she said with a smile.

"At least tonight, I'm not going to be with Captain Sharp," he grumbled as he strolled in.

"Not getting along yet?" Meeker asked.

"Not getting along ever. He calls me by my first name. He gives me meager respect, but under it all is a current of loathing."

"You sure you're not imagining that?"

Lancelot shook his head. "No, it's real. The only consolation is he obviously feels the same way about women in positions of authority. Though he doesn't really say it, it seems Sharp believes you and I were put here by God to cater to his needs."

"So he hasn't been any help?" Meeker asked as she eased onto the arm of a couch.

"I give him research, and he digs for me. But no, he hasn't found anything that really helps. To be an intelligence-bound guy, he's sloppy."

"How?"

"I gave him files that I'd already been through on Menefee, and he picked out the obvious but missed the important stuff. In his report, he didn't cite Menefee's meetings with the German brass. In 1938, Menefee had lunch with four Nazi generals in Berlin. Sharp didn't think it was worth noting."

Meeker nodded and folded her arms. "What about Menefee?"

"No one saw him on the set where Craig was shot, but he was on the lot that day. He might have slipped into the prop room when Coggins was out." Lancelot paused, pulled off his fedora and checked the crease before adding, "There's something else that's interesting. Coggins left his prints on all the live shells in the prop room, but the one in the gun was wiped clean."

"The mere fact he left the live rounds he removed from the gun in plain sight," Meeker said, "bothers me a lot. And then there's the issue that Craig doesn't believe Coggins would have done it." She paused, considering the facts. "What does Sharp know about Craig?"

"If you're talking about his father's identity, he knows nothing."

"Let's keep him in the dark."

"You don't trust him?" Lancelot asked as he eased into a chair.

"How I feel is not really that important, but my gut tells me he was assigned to us because Uncle Sam doesn't trust him yet. His injuries were severe, he was isolated for months before getting back to our side, and I think they're wondering if the man who survived all that is ready for duty. If the military doesn't think Sharp is ready to hear secrets, then I don't know either."

"Any word from Teresa?"

Meeker nodded. "She was in Michigan last time she called. She's attempting to lose a tail. She has an idea where Root might be holed up, and wants to make sure she ditches whoever is following her before she heads that direction."

"Let's get this case solved," Lancelot suggested, "and join her for the showdown."

"I'd love to," Meeker assured him. "Now, I guess it's time to tell you we're going clubbing tonight."

The big man frowned. "In case you haven't noticed, Los Angeles is almost as deeply segregated as the South."

"True, but you're welcome at the Hollywood Canteen."

"The club where Hollywood stars serve GIs?"

"Yep. Abby Force is one of the hostesses tonight and we're going along for the ride. I understand Kay Kaiser's band is playing and the Golden Gate Quartet is scheduled to perform. Meet me in the lobby at eight. Force will be picking us up."

CHAPTER 15

Friday, January 8, 1943
8:45 p.m.
Hollywood Canteen, Hollywood, California

Located at 1451 Cahuenga Boulevard, the Hollywood Canteen was the brainchild of Bette Davis and John Garfield. These top Warner Bros. actors first convinced their own boss, Jack Warner, and then the heads of the other studios including MGM's Louis B. Mayer, that to support the war effort, the motion picture industry needed to build a nightclub catering only to GIs. Rallying all the unions to the cause, Davis and Garfield took an old wooden warehouse and transformed it into a huge dancehall and restaurant.

Set crews designed and built the inside of the huge building, the hottest singers and bands in the nation signed up to play each night, studio employees volunteered to make sandwiches and wash dishes, and the biggest stars in business showed up every time the doors opened to wait tables, make small talk, and dance with enlisted men from all branches of the service.

The club opened on October 3, 1942, and by the end of the year, hundreds of thousands of sailors, soldiers, and marines had entered the door. For the military grunts, the best thing about the Canteen was that dancing with Ida Lupino, Marlene Deitrich, Joan Leslie, or Lana Turner and chatting with Humphrey Bogart, Cary Grant, Roy Rogers, and Sidney Greenstreet was free and open to regular enlisted men. Their pass to enter this magical place was their uniform. And there was no reason to be ready with a salute as the club was also off limits to officers. So, in a war too horrible to fathom, the Canteen was an oasis of happiness and wonder for those who bore the real burden of combat.

For Davis, who had a special place in her heart for the common man, this was an outreach of love. Even on the studio lot, she was often closer to the set builders and camera operators than she was the stars. Her best roles were of the world's common women. In the Canteen, she saw serving the men who were risking it all for freedom as her greatest calling. Nothing brought her more joy! And she was there night after night after night.

For Garfield, the Canteen offered a chance to mingle with those who he longed to serve with. The New York born actor had tried to join every branch of the service and been turned down time and time again. One of the screen's most powerful tough guys had a bum ticker. Even the Merchant Marines wouldn't offer him a spot. Thus, beyond playing soldiers in movies, the only way he could really be a part of the war effort was by thanking and honoring servicemen in person. In the first few months of operation, tens of thousands of GIs had not just met Garfield but sensed he was their friend.

The studios rotated staffing the club, and on this night, Warner Bros. was supplying most of the stars and staff. As

Meeker entered the back door with Abby Force, Mattie Strauss, and Napoleon Lancelot, the first person to greet them was Bette Davis.

"The men will be thrilled to dance with you, dear," Davis said as soon as she spotted the movie's latest ingénue. "You all can put your coats in the room to the left."

"It's an honor to be here, Bette," Force answered while taking off her mink and handing it to an attendant. "My other trips to the Canteen have been wonderful. I think you know my assistant, Mattie Strauss. Tonight, I brought along Helen Meeker, a woman I'm sure you've heard of, and one of her partners, Napoleon Lancelot."

"Miss Meeker," Davis said with a smile, "I'm so proud to have someone who has served this nation with us tonight. I've read about some of your exploits and they have awed me, but I'm not sure I was prepared for your beauty. You have the kind of face and figure that will make Lana Turner jealous."

"I doubt that," Meeker replied as she extended her hand.

"Lancelot?" Davis asked.

"Yes, ma'am. That's my real name."

"Welcome to the Canteen. I hope you enjoy yourself. Who's your favorite star?"

"Lena Horne."

"Well, Miss Horne is here tonight—perhaps the two of you can visit."

"I would like that."

"Well, we need to put Abby to work," Davis said, "and I know that in the past Mattie has danced with the boys as well. Miss Meeker, would you like to come with me or would you rather just look around a bit before being jostled around the floor by a few dozen marines?"

"If it's okay, I'll watch from a distance."

"That will be fine."

As Davis escorted Force to the dance floor, Meeker strolled to the side of the stage and looked out on the hundreds filling the club. With Artie Shaw's band pumping out infectious swing music, the Canteen was a hopping place. Everywhere she looked, she saw men and women who had entertained her and millions of others on the screen for years, but what they were doing here was their best work. She soon picked out Joan Crawford in the arms of a soldier on the dance floor, Ann Sheridan signing autographs, and Jimmy Cagney passing out donuts.

"Look at all those faces," Lancelot said as he joined Meeker. "There are men and women of every color here."

"Bette wouldn't have it any other way." Meeker and Lancelot turned to see John Garfield, wearing a mustard stained apron, step beside them. "Hey, I'm Johnny. And Bette told me you are Helen Meeker and her very important partner."

"Guilty," Meeker replied.

"I think Bette told me your name was Napoleon Lancelot," the grinning Garfield said.

"That's right."

Garfield pointed to the dance floor. "Bette made sure the Canteen was fully integrated. She wasn't going to have just white soldiers here. Whoever was in uniform, no matter their color, would be treated equally in this place. Same goes for the folks who entertain or serve. If you look at the far back table you'll see Hattie McDaniel. If we're lucky, she'll sing some blues for us later. Lena Horne seems to already have a full dance card. And I know the Golden Gate Quartet is going to sing a gospel song in a bit. I hope

I can also get them to do 'The General Jumped at Dawn.' Yep, everybody's here, and everybody's treated the same thanks to Bette. Now I've got some sandwiches to make, but if you need anything let me know."

"Amazing," Lancelot whispered.

"No," Meeker argued, "it's the way it should be. By the way, Abby and Mattie look like they are having fun out on the dance floor. I think I might go see if someone will dance with me."

"You go ahead," Lancelot replied. "I see that Hattie McDaniel is headed toward the kitchen. I think I might see if I can meet her."

Forty-five minutes and fifteen dances later, Meeker, Force, and Strauss disappointed a hundred waiting uniformed hoofers by exiting the floor and heading to the break room. There was coffee waiting at a table. Meeker passed on the hot stuff and grabbed a bottle of Coke from a cooler.

As the women caught their wind, Meeker said, "Kind of humbling! Here we are dancing with happy men who in a few weeks or months might well be dead."

Force shrugged. "You never know if the dance you gave them will be their last. I get letters from all over the globe now, and most are from kids just like these guys who seem to think hearing from me or getting a signed photo is the most important thing in the world. None of them realize they're really the ones doing the important stuff." She paused as if to allow that thought to sink in before announcing, "I need a smoke."

As if on cue, Strauss jumped out and headed to the cloakroom.

Lancelot appeared. His smile almost reached to his ears. "She's amazing," he announced as he sat.

"Lena Horne?" Meeker asked.

"Of course she is," Lancelot quickly answered, "but Hattie McDaniel is funny, wise, and what a wit! Boy I have a new respect for her."

"I've met both of them," Force chimed in. "They're great."

Strauss returned with a pack of Lucky Strike Green. After the star took hers, Strauss pulled out one as well.

"I need some matches," Force said, her voice carrying across the room.

A small balding man about forty, who'd been in the room wiping down tables, reached into his pocket, and handed a matchbook to the star.

She opened the cover, which sported the Hollywood Canteen logo, tore off a match, watched it flame, lit her cigarette, and after inhaling, handed the book to Strauss who repeated the exercise.

"I forgot to get Lena Horne's autograph," Lancelot said. Without asking, he grabbed the matchbook from Strauss'a hand, jumped up, and headed to the kitchen.

"I need that book," Strauss argued, but Lancelot paid no attention.

"I'll get you another one," Meeker volunteered.

"You don't have to, ma'am," the man who had given them the first book announced. "I have one more just like that one." He handed the matches to Strauss who casually slipped them into a pocket of her dress.

About that time, a happy Lancelot reappeared. "Look at this!"

Meeker opened the book. On the inside cover, Lena Horne had signed her name and under the autograph was GA36723. Could the actress have given Lancelot her phone number?

"What a night!" Lancelot said with a grin as he retrieved his prize and dropped it into his coat pocket.

"And it's time for us to put a wrap on it," Force announced. "I've got an early morning at the studio tomorrow—a big photo session— and as I've done my dancing, I need to get home and sleep."

"I'll get our coats," Strauss offered.

As the assistant headed to the cloakroom, Meeker's attention was drawn to the man who'd given them the matches. His shift was evidently over, and he was headed out the door. He looked so out of place in a room full of stars, she wondered who he was.

"I hate to leave," Lancelot said as he stood. "It was something being on equal ground today. I've never felt anything like that before."

"Maybe after the war," Meeker suggested as she took her coat from Strauss and slipped into it. "Perhaps when we win, we'll follow Bette's lead and open up the country for everyone." In truth, she didn't believe it would happen, but it was nice to see the possibilities tonight.

The quartet wandered out to the parking lot and through a maze of vehicles until they found Force's Lincoln. They were casually waiting for the star to unlock her car when a shot rang out, bounced off the hood, and struck a Packard sedan parked to the right.

"Get down!" Meeker reached into her purse for her Colt. As she and the other three crouched behind the

Lincoln, the night suddenly grew deathly silent. As time crept, Meeker asked, "Abby, did you get the car unlocked?"

"Yes."

"Then hand me the key. Napoleon, I'll get in, slide over to the driver's seat, and get the car started. While I do that, you reach around the post and unlock the passenger back door. Ladies, I want you to crawl in but don't raise your heads. Nap, when they're secure, climb in the front seat and we'll take off."

After Meeker started the Lincoln's V-12 engine, the trio followed her directions to the letter. Once they were inside, she put the car in reverse, and backed out, keeping her head low. Slipping into first, Meeker pointed the car's alligator hood toward Cahuenga Boulevard. Once she was on the street, she sat up and floored it.

Two blocks later, she took a deep breath and slowed down. For the moment, all that mattered was getting the passengers to safety, and she figured that meant the star and her assistant would be bunking at the Roosevelt Hotel tonight. But there were questions that would haunt Meeker the rest of the night. The first ... who was the shooter gunning for? In the dim light, Force and Strauss would have looked just alike. And, why would someone want one of them dead? Suddenly it seemed as if it was open season on movie stars.

CHAPTER 16

Saturday January 9, 1943
1:15 p.m.
Roosevelt Hotel, Los Angeles, California

Upon Meeker's request, the Los Angeles police searched every inch of Abby Force's Holmby Hills twelve-thousand-square-foot mansion. They found nothing amiss.

When they left, Meeker dispatched Lancelot to conduct another search. With Captain Sharp in tow, Lancelot also determined the palatial white stone house was secure. Still not completely satisfied, Meeker then called the head of Monument Studio security and asked them to post two men at the house and provide twenty-four-hour coverage divided into three eight-hour shifts to make sure whoever attacked last night would not get a second chance. Only when the first team was in place did Meeker allow Force and Strauss to go home.

With nothing more on her plate and no way to pin down a reason for the shooting, the sleep-deprived Meeker was getting ready to finally take a nap when the phone rang. On the end of the line was the man in charge of Monument's publicity—Martin Green.

“The boss tells me you’re out here in our sunny wonderland to protect our assets.”

“If you mean Matt Craig, then you’re right.”

“We have him covered,” Green assured her. “He’s being constantly watched while he recovers on his boat. After last night, it’s Abby we’re worried about.”

“I made sure her house was secure,” Meeker explained.

“So I heard, but because we’re waiting for Matt to heal enough to shoot the final scenes of their movie, we’ve assigned Abby to go out on a USO tour. She’ll be spending time visiting bases in the Pacific. The boss wants you to go as well.”

“How long?”

“Ten days. You’ll be traveling with a standard USO troop and flying from spot to spot. Supposedly the venues are secure, and there will be a half a dozen stars along for the ride. You’ll be doing about three shows a day in different locations—some on land and some on ships. The highlight will be the big show at Guadalcanal. At each stop, Abby will sing a song or two and tell a few jokes. David Jacobs has told the USO that Abby only goes if you go along to protect her.”

“When do we leave?”

“Monday from Edwards.” Green paused. “There’s something else too. We’d prefer you didn’t take your partner. That would complicate things. We’re not set up for feeding and housing someone of a different race.”

Meeker’s face flushed a deep red. She had all she could do not to toss the phone across the room. Yet, what good would pitching a fit do? Nothing would change. She could yell and scream for hours, and she’d still have to make the trip alone. Still, no matter the result, she had to voice her feelings.

"Miss Meeker? Are you still there?"

"I tell you what, Mr. Green, leaving my best man behind is about the worst move you could make."

"It's out of my hands."

"I'm sure it is, but Lancelot is better than any cop or MP you can send on that trip."

"That doesn't matter."

Meeker bit her tongue. At least, she'd made her view clear. If something happened, she could say, "I told you so!" Though she still wanted to pursue bringing Lancelot, now was the time to argue the other insane part of this scenario.

"Mr. Green, due to the fact that someone took a shot at Force last night, I think you have a perfect out for her not going on the trip."

"I'm sorry, she has to go. Those orders come from the top."

"Why?"

"Because we're sending a film crew along to document everything that happens. Having Abby out there doing shows is worth a million dollars in publicity. We'll make a short film for release that will position her as one of the most wonderful and patriotic women in the business. You can't buy this kind of press!"

"So this isn't about the soldiers, sailors, or marines, this is about your studio making a buck."

"A lot more than a buck," Green corrected her. "We're talking hundreds of thousands, if not more. Hey, and seeing Abby will make a lot of men happy. We'll even have a photographer along who'll snap pictures of a few lucky GIs with our star. It's a win-win situation."

"All the more reason we need my partner to provide extra protection. What if I told you I wouldn't go unless Lancelot goes with me?"

"Then my boss will call your boss, and FDR will call you and explain how important this is for everyone. You see, we're going to make sure that the world sees Abby with the famous Helen Meeker. That's great publicity too."

As if things couldn't get any worse. Now Meeker was a part of the reason for the trip.

"If we make a movie about your life," Green explained, "the frontrunner to play you is Miss Force."

"Not my first choice," Meeker snapped.

A knock on the door redirected her focus. She covered the phone receiver and yelled, "Just a minute." She then turned her attention back to the call. "I want a full itinerary by eight tonight. I also want you to secure me enough clothes for the trip. I didn't come out prepared for this. You can have one of your wardrobe people call me for my sizes. And I will not be brought out on stage at any time or pose for any publicity photos with Abby Force. Do you understand that?"

"Yes."

"Fine."

Meeker hung up and marched over to the door in a huff. The face she saw on the other side of the entry didn't improve her mood.

"What do you want?" she snapped.

"Lancelot told me to check with you for an assignment," Captain Michael Sharp answered. "He's run out of things for me to do."

"Pack for a ten-day trip," Meeker barked. "We're going island hopping in the Pacific with the USO."

"Really?"

"Yes, and I want you to keep a close eye on Abby Force."

"That will be a pleasure."

"We leave Monday morning. So get moving, soldier."

Meeker slammed the door before Sharp could reply. Last night at the Canteen, the world seemed to be opening up for everyone, but today the reality of exclusion trumping inclusion was back in the spotlight.

CHAPTER 17

Monday, January 11, 1943
9:45 p.m.
Ames, Iowa

The routine was getting very old. Teresa Bryant hopped on a train, traveled a few hours, got off, checked into a hotel, ate a meal, wandered around town, interviewed local law enforcement, showed them Gertrude Root's picture, and then headed back to her room. The next day, she repeated everything all over again in a new place.

And each day, the man in the brown topcoat and gray hat was always there in the shadows. He never approached or threatened her, but she could never lose him either. He had even stayed with her when she'd changed trains three times in Minneapolis on Saturday.

He had to be Root's boy. There was no other explanation, but why was he not taking the opportunities she'd given him to move in for the kill?

In Bismarck, North Dakota, she had intentionally taken a side trip through a dark alley. That would have been the perfect time for him to make his move. He could have struck and gotten away unnoticed. But he'd done nothing. The same was true two hours ago when she'd walked back from a restaurant on a lonely street in Ames. No one was outside because of the dark and snow.

Strolling to the lobby of the Cyclone Hotel, Bryant stopped at the front desk and asked if she had any messages. As no one knew where she was, there would be no messages, and this was literally nothing more than a ruse meant to kill time and spot her tail. After buying a local paper, she casually strolled up the stairs to the third floor. Once in her room, she turned off the light, quickly crossed to the window, and stepped onto the fire escape. After hurrying down to the alley, she rushed around the building, reentered through the hotel's front door, and made her back up the steps. Peeking around the corner, she spied her friend three doors down from her room. He was leaning against the wall, smoking a cigarette and staring at the door she'd entered three minutes before. Like a cat, she covered the ground between them, and before he could even sense her presence, she jammed the barrel of her gun into his back.

"Do you know what this is?"

"I've got an idea."

"Hands over your head and lead the way to my room. The door's open. Walk slowly over to the bed and keep your hands raised. Any dumb moves and you'll be checking out on this floor and not the lobby. You got that?"

"Sure."

She let him get four steps ahead and then matched his pace. Once they'd both entered her room, she pushed the door shut and locked it. Never once did she take her eyes off the stranger.

"Turn around," she ordered.

He did. He was about six feet tall, with broad shoulders, dark eyes, and a square jaw. His cheekbones were high and skin light caramel. She noted a watch barely visible under his left sleeve, so he was likely right handed.

"Using only your left hand," she ordered, "unbutton and take off that coat. Let it drop on the floor."

He nodded, and with some difficulty, he released the five buttons. He then pushed the garment off his right shoulder before allowing the coat to fall off the other one and puddle on the heavily worn carpet.

"I see by the bulge in your suit jacket you have a gun in a shoulder holster. Lift it out with your thumb and drop it to the floor. If I see your fingers moving, I'll fire. My first bullet will shatter your left knee. If I have to follow up, it will be about eighteen inches higher. And don't think about testing me. I'm a crack shot."

The visitor followed the directions to the T. After the gun hit the floor, he kicked it toward Bryant without even being asked.

"Once again, use only your left and lose your suit coat. After it drops, I want you to slowly turn around. Keep making circles until I tell you to stop."

He nodded, worked the jacket from his shoulders and let it join his topcoat on the carpet. He then made two complete turns. Though she didn't notice any other weapons, there was no reason to take chances.

"Strip down to your socks and underwear. After you get those off you can sit on the bed and we'll talk."

He frowned but still followed her demands. When he stood before her in an undershirt, blue boxers, and dark socks, she noted an ugly scar running around his neck.

"Sit down," Bryant said as she reached over and retrieved the visitor's gun. Only after he was on her bedspread, she asked, "What tribe?"

"Seminole."

"You have a proud heritage. You were the only ones who refused to sign a treaty with Uncle Sam."

"Never trust an uncle who doesn't share your blood," he stoically replied. "Your people made peace and look where it got you."

"No different than you. Just because you're technically in a state of war with the US doesn't change your lot. What's your name?"

"The whites call me Ossie."

"What about your people?"

"Osceola."

"He was a great man and a dynamic chief."

"He was my great, great grandfather."

"Wonder what he'd think of you being humbled by a Caddo woman?"

The man shrugged. "He would likely want to adopt you."

She pointed to his neck. "What's with the scar?"

"I was accused of stealing horses, and they strung me up. The rope snapped, and I fell to the ground. I had passed out, and they left me there all the while thinking I was dead."

"Did you steal the horses?"

"You can't steal what's yours. The ranchers had taken my father's horses, and I'd just tried to get them back. They were the thieves."

Bryant nodded. She had only known one other man who had survived a lynching. Every time she'd seen him after that was like viewing a ghost.

"Osceola, what did you learn from walking so near death?"

He smiled for the first time. "I learned to choose my battles more carefully."

That was not the answer she expected, but it did show the man was wiser than he looked. There were times when victory was far less important than living.

"Why are you following an unimportant Caddo woman?"

"It is a job."

"Who hired you?"

"A man I met in Kansas City. He promised me five thousand."

"For my scalp?" Bryant asked.

"I had to prove you were dead to earn my money," he admitted, "but he didn't demand your hair."

"If what you're saying it true, since you've had plenty of chances, why not take them? A half a dozen times, I set myself up as a target. So why didn't you make your move."

"When I took the job, I didn't get the full story," Osceola admitted. "When they told me your name was Teresa Bryant, I didn't expect you to be ..."

"An Indian?"

"Yeah."

"Does the fact we share a heritage make a difference?"

"I think it does."

"So, why keep tailing me? Why not just walk away?"

"I was trying to figure out what you were doing."

"So you didn't know I was an investigator?"

"No."

"Why did the man want me dead?"

"He said you were going to kill a very important associate."

Bryant smiled. "If his boss is Gertrude Root, he might just be right."

"He gave me no names other than yours."

"Let me ask you a few questions, and I want you to be honest."

The guest in the underwear shrugged. "I swear on the spirit of my ancestors to give you the truth."

"Have you ever killed anyone before?"

"No."

"Then why did they pick you for this job?"

"I volunteered. I told them I was the greatest hunter and killer in Oklahoma. And that's true if I'm going after deer or elk."

"Why did you want to murder someone?"

"I didn't, but there are times when needs overrule morals."

Bryant nodded. "I understand that. And your need was?"

"My wife had cancer and she had to have an operation. At a trading post, a white friend told me about a man who hired folks to kill his enemies. When I heard what he wanted, I measured whose life was more important—a woman I didn't know or my wife. The answer was obvious."

"And you can't kill me because I'm an Indian."

"No," he admitted, "I now have no reason to kill you. My wife died two days ago. When I called a cousin in Oklahoma City, he shared the news. I have no need for the money. Then I became curious as to why someone would want you dead."

"I'm sorry your wife died."

"She was in great pain; perhaps she is at peace now."

She had no doubt she was hearing the truth. She could read his sincerity in his eyes. The only reason to now continue the interrogation was to unmask the man Root was using to target her.

"Osceola, I want you to paint a picture. The man who hired you, what kind person was he?"

"He was a part of the crime scene in Kansas City. Smoked fancy cigars, wore expensive suits, and drove big cars. He has often used our women in his brothels. His hands are bloody, and his thoughts are covered with mud."

"What was his name?"

"Irish Red Mahoney."

Bryant smiled. "And if I was on the road in order to take out Mahoney's trusted associate, what kind of person do you think that would be?"

"Even worse."

"I'm a hunter," Bryant explained. "My prey is the scum of the planet. I don't care what color their skin is or where they live, I just want to stop them from taking advantage of the weak and helpless. The woman I'm after has done things that have led to the deaths of thousands of people. A couple of them were friends of mine. She has also paid a handful of folks to murder my associates. So far, they have failed. I think I know where she's hiding, and I'm going to either take her out or die trying. Everything I've told you in the truth."

"I believe you."

"So the question becomes, will you let me go on my hunt without tracking my every move?"

"If I agree, what happens to me?"

"I'll give you your gun back, let you put on your clothes, and you get to walk away. And I suggest you never go back to Kansas City. At least, not until I have the chance to put Irish Red behind bars. Do we have a deal?"

"Yes."

"Then put on your clothes and get out of here."

Osceola quickly dressed. After he pulled his coat on, Bryant handed him his gun and six hundred dollars in twenties.

"Spend what you need to get back to your family, and the rest can be used for a good horse."

He nodded, walked to the door, and after unlocking and opening it, looked back at Bryant. "Good hunting." He slipped off down the hall.

CHAPTER 18

Thursday, January 14, 1943
7:32 p.m.
Guadalcanal, Pacific Ocean

The initial four days of the trip had been both inspiring and humbling. First at bases in Hawaii, and then on ships at sea, Meeker observed some of Hollywood's lesser stars sing songs and tell jokes to thousands of young men fresh off battlefronts across the Pacific. Even more touching were the hours these entertainers spent in hospital wards.

At each stop, Meeker witnessed Hollywood's finest holding hands and saying prayers with those taking their final breaths. Through tear-filled eyes, she'd listened to grown men asking to hear lullabies or talking about girlfriends back home—girlfriends some would never see again.

She'd also seen the actors and actresses dressed not in gowns and tuxedoes, but in fatigues, sleeping on the ground or in bunks, taking communal showers, eating food from cans, and batting away mosquitoes the size of small birds. And none of them complained. Like the Hollywood Canteen, this tour was the movie business showing its best.

Today, they'd done three shows in different locations for several thousand war-weary marines. The back of a supply truck had been the stage, and rain had fallen throughout each performance. But no one stopped. The songs and jokes kept coming. And when those shows were over, there was a trip to the makeshift field hospital to meet boys who were in limbo between life and death.

"Just keep smiling," a chaplain suggested.

Meeker had heard that for days now. The words were not as much a motto for the tour but a warning. No matter how you felt, no matter how much seeing the real cost of war hurt, you couldn't let your feelings show. You had to put on a smile and keep going.

"I'll Be Seeing You" was the final number performed at each show. As Force sang that song with a voice that was passable, Meeker couldn't decide if the sentimental lyrics were there to comfort or torture. As she watched hundreds of men crying while they listened, Meeker wondered how many of them would ever see those old familiar places again. Did they really need to be reminded of that possibility? Couldn't this be classified as cruel and unusual punishment?

Now, as thousands of men sat on the dirt and looked up at the makeshift stage, Force again told her jokes and drew laughs. But her voice wasn't selling the product today, she was so hoarse after so many performances that she could barely speak above a whisper. What was interesting was the way the GIs looked at her in her halter top dress.

"Helen," orchestra leader Tom Carson called out as the performance wound down, "Abby can't sing the song tonight. I've heard you singing with the group during some of our hospital numbers. Why don't you fill in? The guys will be disappointed if they don't hear someone "'I'll Be Seeing You.'"

"I haven't sung since high school," Meeker countered. "Singing would be painful for me and the men if I went out there."

"That's not true, they'd love you. And in truth, we need you tonight. In fact, they need you tonight. There's a blue evening gown hanging inside the truck the girls are using as a dressing room, and everything you'll need in the way of makeup is there too. For those guys out there, please let us end this performance the way we're supposed to."

"I couldn't."

"But you will," Carson ordered. "Madge, help Helen get dressed. She's going to do the final number."

Suddenly, everything was out of Meeker's hands. One of the back-up singers all but pushed her into the truck and started stripping off Meeker's fatigues. Another member of the troop came in and began to fix her hair and slap on makeup. The gown they slipped on was form-fitting with a plunging neckline. The shoes matched the dress. And in just under ten minutes, the investigator went from drab to stunning. She was then hustled out of the truck to the side of the stage. At that moment, the audience was applauding as Force motioned, bowed, and made her exit. Carson then walked to the microphone and waved for everyone to calm down.

"I know you've heard from your friends who have caught our show that Miss Abby Force normally does our closing number. As you just witnessed, America's Sweetheart has been working so hard she's lost her voice." Carson paused so hundreds of men could groan in unison. "But I've arranged for you to have a good pinch hitter tonight.

Have you all read about the woman who has been called America's real Wonder Woman by the press? Have you seen pictures of Helen Meeker?" The audience broke out in whistles and hollers. "Well, she's here tonight, and you will be mesmerized by her rendition of 'I'll Be Seeing You.'"

At this moment, Meeker would have rather been behind enemy lines in Europe than face that crowd. But she had been given no choice. With little more than a wing and a prayer, she stepped out on stage, and the audience went wild. At this point, the dress—what there was of it—had them hollering, and as the band went into the opening, her voice would be what spelled out if this was a disaster or an inspiration. Her first line was shaky, but when she got to the word *familiar*, she found the confidence that had made her a success in everything she'd ever tried. As her voice filled the night, a hush fell over the crowd. Men's jaws went slack, and the bandleader and orchestra grinned. This was the way the song was supposed to sound. When Meeker closed with the line "I'll be seeing you," the place went nuts. She had to perform the standard two more times before she could leave.

"Great job, Helen," Carson shouted as he followed her off stage.

"Yeah," Force croaked, "seems there's nothing you can't do. Including making me look bad."

"She was saving your skin," Carson snapped. "Now take some honey and whiskey and get some rest so you can take over tomorrow. And cut done on the cigarettes—that's why your throat played out today. Every time I turned around, you were smoking."

"Please get well," Meeker added. "I never want to have to do that again."

After sharing K-rations with some of the officers, the troop broke into small groups and settled in for the night. Meeker, Force, and Strauss had drawn the short straw and been assigned to a tent. Because they had cots and blankets, they had reasons to count their lucky stars. Though he would be spending the night in another location, Captain Sharp was now with them as well.

"You charmed them," Sharp said with a smile as he looked at Force.

In the soft glow of lantern light, Force shrugged. "All I did tonight was whisper some jokes."

"They look at your face and body," Sharp suggested, "and they don't hear anything. How many proposals have you had in the past four days?"

"I have no idea."

As the two continued reflecting on the day, Meeker eased back onto her bunk and closed her eyes. Tonight as she'd sung, she'd heard her share of proposals too. She wondered if the adoration was due to the job she'd done or the fact she was female. She was betting on the latter. But being on stage and the center of attention was a lot more fun than she cared to admit.

"Look at the souvenir one of the guys gave me," Force announced.

Meeker opened her eyes.

The star was holding a pistol.

"That's a Namba-14," Sharp explained. "If you find a Jap with a sidearm, this will almost always be it. Better be careful, if you pull that trigger you could kill someone."

Force shook her head. "I know better than that. I pulled the clip out. Unlike on the studio lot, I'm not going to fire anything that even might be loaded."

The actress ran her hands over the enemy weapon before pointing at Strauss. While the action caused the assistant to grin and put her hands up, the whole thing unnerved Meeker.

"When I pulled the trigger that day on the set," Force said, "I was scared to death. And I didn't even know that I was almost going to kill someone. You see, I was frightened because I thought my career would be over when that scene was shown in movie theaters across the nation. This would be the first time Matt Craig would die in a movie, and it didn't make any difference he was playing a horrible person. So, I figured women would never forgive me. I actually wondered if I was committing career suicide. And when the picture's released, I wonder if it will spell the end of my following with women. The business is fickle."

Force frowned as she laid the gun in her lap.

No longer seeing a need to continue the game, Strauss lowered her arms.

"For every woman who hated you for killing Craig," Sharp mused, "there would be a man who would thank you for it. Husbands don't like to have their wives dreaming about guys like that."

"You sound like someone who speaks from experience," Strauss observed.

"No," Sharp assured her. "I've never been married, but I never liked Craig. There's just something phony about him."

"You have leading man looks," Force said. "You likely know what it's like to have women fall at your feet. With that face and an officer's uniform, you're a magnet."

Meeker glanced over at Sharp. The actress's words had inspired a rare smile.

"Tell me more about my new gun," Force cooed.

"They used to be pretty good," Sharp explained, "but the quality has slowly gone down since the 1930s. If my life depended upon a pistol taken from an enemy soldier, I'd rather have a Lugar. Even when mass-produced for use in battle, the German pride in workmanship is still obvious."

Force again picked up the pistol with her right hand and ran her finger over the barrel. "I wonder how many people were shot by this little piece of hardware? And yet, without the bullets, it's nothing more than a toy."

"It's a lot more than that," Meeker suggested. "You take a uniform off a Nazi soldier, and he's still just as dangerous. That's no movie prop you're holding, it's still an instrument of death."

Force held the Namba-14 up and aimed it at Meeker. After getting her target squared in the sight, she smiled. "Right now, it's a toy. I could pull the trigger a dozen times and nothing would happen." She grinned. "Bang. You're a hero, Helen. I wondered how many times guns have been aimed at you? How many times have you thought your next breath would be your last? How many people have you taken out with a gun something like this one? How many times have you struck this pose and watched someone sweat? How many times have you pulled the trigger? What's it feel like to have that kind of power? What's it like to hold someone's fate in your hand and know that with one pull you end their lives?"

Though seemingly harmless, the scene was also chilling. For thirty seconds, no one moved and not a word was said.

Sharp finally broke the haunting silence. "Abby, when we get tired or our emotions are overloaded, we say and do things that aren't funny."

Force continued to point the gun at Meeker. "You're a killer too, aren't you, Michael. You know what I was talking about. You've ended lives." The actress looked at her assistant. "What about it, Mattie? Have you been nervous having two killers around us all the time?"

Meeker studied Force. Was she cracking up? Had the knowledge she'd shot Craig coupled with the strain of this trip derailed her mind?

"I've spent the last few days," Force continued, "singing to hired guns. That's what we have done to those boys. We've turned them into killers. As I was telling jokes tonight, I began to wonder if they enjoyed taking a life. Do they write in their journals or letters about the pleasure they get killing a Jap?"

"There is no pleasure in ending a life," Meeker said as she studied the gun still aimed in her direction. "Even if that person is your enemy, you know that someone loves them and will miss them. And holding the power of death in your hands doesn't make you feel like a god; it turns your stomach."

"You have to be the best at everything," Force complained. "Tonight, the reaction you got when you wore that gown and sang that song was ten times what I would have gotten. I hated you when I realized your voice was better than mine and that dress fit you better than it did me. I hate everything about you, Helen Meeker!"

"Let me see the gun," Sharp said.

"I want to pull the trigger," Force said. "I want to see how much effort it takes to sign a death warrant."

Tired of watching the actress unravel in front of her eyes, Meeker pushed off the cot, jerked the pistol from the woman's hand and, tossed the gun to Sharp.

"How dare you!"

"Be glad she did," the captain announced. "There's still a round in the chamber. If you'd pulled the trigger, you would have likely killed Helen."

"But I emptied the gun," Force argued.

"Just because you pulled out the clip doesn't mean you cleared the weapon," Sharp explained. After removing the final bullet, he tossed the pistol onto the floor beside Force's cot. "You need some air, Abby. Come with me and let's take a walk."

The actress didn't argue. As if sleepwalking, she took the captain's hand and exited.

"She's been pushed too hard the last year," Strauss said. "There's been too much travel, too much time at the studio, too much work, and no time to relax."

"So you've seen this kind of behavior before?" Meeker asked.

"There have been episodes."

If that were the case, then Force could have been the person who put the live round in gun at the studio, and the actress also might have known there was a live round in the gun she was playing with tonight. That meant Meeker could be sharing a tent with an unstable woman obsessed with murder. Perhaps that was the reason she didn't have a past. Maybe in another life, the actress had been confined to an institution or worse.

CHAPTER 19

Saturday, January 16, 1943
3:25 p.m.
Gold Cove, Colorado

Teresa Bryant should have been dog-tired. She'd made four connections by train from Ames to Denver and then caught a bus that stopped at every wide spot in the road before it reached Leadville. What should have taken a couple of hours took eight. When she arrived in the mining town she was met by heavy snow. Because of drifts making the road impassible, the only way to get to Gold Cove was by horse or on foot. And since no one would rent her a mount, she bought a tired saddle horse for twice what she should have paid and purchased a pack mule for luggage.

After studying a map, she bundled up in a beaver coat and thick gloves and headed out. Relying more on instincts than the snow-covered trail, six hours later, she was looking down on the remnants of what had once been a thriving mining community. Taking out her field glasses and studying the scene below, she noted a solitary hint of life. There was smoke coming from the chimney of what, according the faded sign, was the Nugget Hotel and Café.

Tying up the horse and mule, she retrieved her gun and ammunition and worked her way down the mountainside toward a frozen lake. She carefully picked a route that was hidden from any of the hotel's windows. Once she arrived in what was left of Gold Cove, she paused at a livery stable and took inventory. There were eleven buildings still standing and a dozen more now fully collapsed. Of those still intact, five had lost so many broken windows, they would have been inhabitable. Thus, if Root were here, she would have to be in the brick city jail, the Branch Saloon, Madam Mary's House of Pleasure, the clapboard church, or the hotel.

Choosing a course that took her behind the buildings and away from the snow covered main street, Bryant worked her way through almost waist-high drifts to the jail. She tried the door and found it unlocked. Stepping out of the wind, she strolled through the office and back to the one cell. Except for a few pieces of furniture and a sleeping raccoon, which darted up a set of bunks and out a window when he saw Bryant outfitted in a coat made from his relatives, there was nothing.

The front door would have been in view of the hotel, so Bryant left through the back exit, and made her way to the saloon. Though the door was locked, all she had to do to obtain entry was put her shoulder to the wood. She stepped into the saloon's kitchen, which was still fully equipped for cooking in the last century. There were even cans of beans on the shelves and firewood by the stove. A partially open cabinet revealed dishes and a coffee pot set on a back burner. If you liked cooking 1880s style, this would have been the place to set up shop.

After walking through a swinging door, Bryant entered the saloon's main room. A dozen dust-covered tables complete with ladder-back chairs filled an open area, and to her right was a long bar. Behind the bar was a twelve-by-four-foot mirror and rows of dusty glasses. A dozen decks of cards were stacked by the cash register, but except for a few empties, the booze was gone. If ghosts still roamed this town, they were going to get mighty thirsty.

Retracing her steps, she exited as she had come in and pushed through the snow to Madam Mary's. An unlocked side door opened into a billiard room. Six balls and two cues still rested on the green felt top. The room's only door led to a two-story room filled with velvet-covered furniture. On the wall were a dozen paintings that would have made a sailor blush, and under each was a table holding a partially burned candle in tarnished brass holders. Crossing the room, Bryant made her way to the stairs. The second floor sported five very elaborate bedrooms and two baths. In this case, Bryant was thankful the walls couldn't talk. From the house of sin, she walked to a building that was always open to sinners—the community church.

The house of worship had one room. Eight pews were on the left and eight on the right. At the front of the sanctuary was a pulpit, and on the back wall was an attendance board that still boasted the claim of twenty-nine members. A few feet in front of that sign was an organ. Though no one had likely played there in decades, the organ still appeared to be in good shape. Beside the old instrument was a stack of two dozen hymnbooks and a collection plate. On the back wall was a framed painting of a very European-looking Jesus. As she stepped behind the pulpit, Bryant noticed an open Bible. One verse had been underlined … Exodus 23:22.

> But if thou shalt indeed obey his voice, and do all that I speak, then I will be an enemy unto thine enemies, and an adversary unto thine adversaries.

Sitting down on the front pew, she took a deep breath and considered her options. There was one building left. If Bryant had guessed right then she would literally be meeting her enemy in that hotel, and if Root were there, the doors and windows would be locked. There would be no easy entry. She also had to believe Root wouldn't be alone. Based on the story Osceola told her, the Kansas City mob would be offering protection.

Getting up and strolling over to a side window, Bryant looked toward the Nugget. The light was fading, but she could still see well enough to note the smoke coming from the chimney. Fires didn't continue without being fed, so someone was there. As in this case darkness would truly be a friend, she returned to the pew, closed her eyes, and as she waited, considered what had brought her to this place.

Once, for a very short time, she'd been one of Gertrude Root's girls. She'd been hired for her exotic looks, and she'd been assigned to get information from the men attending the parties. Root was always digging for dirt, and the women she employed were who got the info. What Bryant hadn't known then was that Root was Fredrick Bauer's sister. She also had no idea the man known as Darkness had likely arranged the meeting between Bryant and Root. Yet, now it seemed so obvious.

During that time, Bryant discovered Bauer was not a Nazi but an opportunist—he was looking for a way to gain power and money no matter who won. Yet, the weakness that turned to madness surfaced because Helen Meeker looked so much like a woman Bauer had once loved. That had been the man's undoing.

With her brother's death, Root had gained control of the operation, but even though the group was under new management, one thing didn't change—Gertrude Root's motivation was the same as her brother's. She played both sides again the middle. While not a brilliant scientist like Bauer, Gertrude was better placed to gain access to information that would prove incredibly valuable to Hitler. And she could have stayed under the radar for years if not for her desire to make Meeker pay for killing her brother. Hate and revenge took her eyes off what was far more important. If Bryant could tap into that emotion tonight, Root would be much easier to take down.

On clear cold nights, sound carries in the mountains. Bryant had learned that as a child. Now, if used correctly, perhaps sound could be used as a trap. Perhaps she needed to hold a church service. Moving to the organ, she put her feet on the pedals and pumped. The old instrument still held air. A long time had gone by since she'd been forced to take organ and piano lessons at the orphanage, and perhaps enough of Sister Anne's instruction remained to play a few simple things. Setting her gun on top of the console, she opened a hymnal and thumbed through the pages until she came to "It Is Well With My Soul." After stretching her fingers, she pulled out all the stops and began her recital. After two rousing verses, she grabbed her weapon, hurried toward the window and peeked out.

A man was walking out the hotel's front door. He was dressed in a long coat and held a rifle.

Bryant watched until she was sure he was headed her way, and then moved over behind the door. Two minutes later, the visitor turned the knob and pushed the door open with his rifle.

In the fading sunlight, the room was filled with dancing shadows that made seeing anything in detail impossible. Bryant watched through the door's crack as her guest shifted the weapon to his left arm and dug into his coat. Fishing out a flashlight, he shined its beam toward the organ. Seeing nothing, he opted to take a few steps forward to search the rest of the building. He first looked to his right, which allowed Bryant to moved silently forward and knock the gun out of his arm. As he spun, she stepped back.

"Freeze and lift your hands over your head. If you don't, this moves quickly from a prayer meeting to a funeral."

"Who are you?"

"The ghost of Christmas past," she answered. "Now let's see those hands up."

"If you need food, we have some at the hotel," he muttered.

"I need information."

"What?"

"How many are there with Gertrude Root?"

He went mute, but the look on his face told Bryant all she needed to know. The name meant something, and her trip was anything but wasted.

"Let me explain some things to you," Bryant said. "If I have to use my gun, I'm not worried about being heard. You see, I brought a silencer on this trip. You need to understand this. I'm working for the U.S. Government. Uncle Sam is very interested in Mrs. Root. If you were to help me bring her in, then my uncle would likely reward you. But if you don't supply the information I want, then I will extract it in ways you can't begin to imagine."

"Like what?" he asked.

"Let me put it this way … do you have any heirs? If you don't work with me, then you won't be creating any."

"I don't buy it."

"What do you know about Indians?" she asked. "Let me take a guess. You likely know all about those totem poles. Well, we carve those with knives … very large and sharp knives."

"You're Teresa Bryant. We were warned about you."

"Bright boy. Now I know for sure you're with Gertrude Root. So how many are there in the hotel? And think of what will happen if I find out you're lying to me."

"Counting me, there are four men and Root."

That was about what she'd figured. With this rat already in the cage, that made three demons and the devil left.

"Turn around," she ordered, "and keep your hands up."

The second after he turned, she brought the butt of her gun down on his head. He staggered for a moment then collapsed like a sack of potatoes. She jabbed him with her boot to make sure he was fully out and yanked his coat from his body. After using her knife to cut the garment into strips, she tied and gagged her prisoner. Once she knew he was secure, she dragged him in front of the pulpit and laid him out. Now that she had the bait, it was time to set a second trap.

CHAPTER 20

Saturday, January 16, 1943
7:25 p.m.
Gold Cove, Colorado

Bryant was satisfied she had fully set the scene. The first visitor to her church was bound, gagged, and currently unconscious. By positioning him in front of the pulpit, the church looked ready to hold a funeral, and the only thing missing was the mourners. To signal it was time for visitation, she had made a hurried trip through the snow to Madam Mary's to borrow some candles. She left two burning in the brothel before returning to the church and placing a lit candle in each of the eight windows. She then arranged the last four around the body. After lighting those, she hurried to the organ, found "Rock of Ages" in the hymnal and played one verse. The invitation had been offered, would it be accepted?

Edging to a window, she peeked out. Within a minute, two men exited the hotel and trudged her way through the snow. Each held a rifle. There would be no surprise this time. She figured they'd peek in the windows before entering, and the candlelight would make her an easy target. So, she'd use the pulpit as her hiding place. One minute became two and two became three before the front door slowly opened, signaling it was time for the evening service.

Bryant heard two sets of boots take a pair of steps on wooden floor. They must have paused at the entrance to eyeball what lay ahead.

"Look at Ben," a guff voice announced, "he's tied up like a pig about to be roasted."

"John, don't worry about him now. We have to find the person responsible for the music and all these candles."

"They look to be gone. The only one in the church is Ben."

"Get serious, there has to be someone here. Ben didn't do that to himself and someone played the organ."

"Roger, they're not here now."

"Fine, you check around back. If you see anything, send out a yell."

One set of footsteps proved Roger held his ground as John left. The scout was gone for less than a minute, and during that time the other man didn't move an inch.

"Roger, there're candles burning at Madam Mary's."

"That must be where they went. You go check it out, and I'll see to Ben."

"What do I do if I spot someone?"

"Kill 'em! Within a day, we'll be gone. and no one will likely be up here until spring. So, you'll never be caught."

Heavy footsteps proved John was good at following orders, and Roger closing the door made things warmer. Evidently, the church's only current visitor now wasted no time coming to the front to check on Ben. When footsteps stopped and a board groaned, Bryant silently edged sideways. Roger was too busy untying Ben's gag to sense her movement.

"Go for your gun," she quietly but firmly warned, "and there will be blood on the altar."

Quickly apparent was the man was far better at giving orders than taking them. As he jerked his rifle forward, Bryant reluctantly fired one bullet, which was all that was needed. As the smell of cordite filled the room, Roger fell onto his associate. Now it was time to move to the back of the room and wait for Big Bad John. She'd barely taken her spot when the door swung open.

"Roger, I …"

John froze just two paces beyond the entry.

She could have taken him down easily, but that's not what Bryant wanted. She longed for a powwow. "Drop the rifle," Bryant ordered. "Don't turn around or you'll end up like those two."

He hesitated.

"No more warnings," she added. "I don't want to kill you, but with so much at stake, I will."

The rifle hit the floor.

"Now take off your coat." After it joined the rifle, Bryant gave her next command. "Toss your hat on the pew and turn around and face me."

He was likely about forty—his eyes were green and his hair somewhere between red and blonde. He stood about five-eight and likely didn't weigh more than one-fifty. He was dressed in a flannel shirt and dark blue wool pants.

"Ben gave me the lowdown an hour or so ago," Bryant explained, "but I want to check his facts. So, I'm giving you a test. If I don't like the answers, the result will be permanent passing rather than a failing grade."

"Permanent passing?"

"A time when you breathe no more. Do you understand?"

He nodded.

"Beyond Gertrude Root, how many are left at the hotel?"

"One more."

That matched what she'd heard earlier.

"Describe him."

"He's a big guy, former wrestler; he's from Kansas City. They call him Irish Red. He's Root's ticket to Mexico and then South America."

"Small world."

"I don't understand."

"You don't need to. What kind of guy is Red? Is he a gunman?"

"He doesn't like to get his hands dirty. He came up before the storm to spell out the plans."

"Do you know the plans?"

"If they can get here, a team is coming tomorrow. They'll take the lady to a small private airstrip in Kansas. They have a C-47 that's coming up from Mexico."

"Big plane for one woman," Bryant noted.

"She's taking a couple of truckloads of stuff that's been stored at the hotel."

"Stuff?"

"Paintings, gold, jewelry. That sort of thing."

So she didn't move all her brother's cache to Washington. Figures. Root wasn't the type to put all her eggs into one basket.

"Where're Red and Root now?"

"Waiting for us back at the hotel. They're in a room just off the lobby. There's a good wood stove in there. It's about the only place in this town that's warm."

"John, you're a good man. I think we'll put off your funeral service. Now turn around. I'm going to have to place you on ice for a bit."

"What do you mean by that?"

"Just face the other way."

"You promised not to shoot me," he begged.

"I won't. Just turn around."

Reluctantly, he followed her orders. When he could no longer see her, Bryant flipped the gun around and brought the handle down hard just over his right ear. He was out on his feet for a second, and then sleeping on the floor. Since he was out cold, she had no problem binding and gagging him. Time to blow out the candles and close services for the evening. Her next mission would be to find her two shut-ins and share a visit.

CHAPTER 21

Saturday, January 16, 1943
9:08 p.m.
Gold Cove, Colorado

Bryant traded her raccoon coat for John's long, lined slicker. After turning the collar up, she stuffed her long black hair under his hat and pushed it low onto her head. Shoving her Smith and Wesson pistol into her waistline, she buttoned up the coat, picked up a rifle, and stepped outside. The wind had calmed, and a light snow was falling. That would cloak her march down the main street. After taking a deep breath, she slowly waded through the snow to the hotel. With each step, she tried to look as casual and as masculine as possible. As she stepped on the porch, she brushed snowflakes from her eyes and peeked through a window. Just as forecast, the lobby, lit by three hurricane oil lamps, was empty. There were two doors to the left. She'd have to go inside to figure out the one she needed.

Bryant had faced death many times, but on this occasion, everything felt different. She'd confronted a long list of bad people, but only Gertrude Root and her brother Fredrick Bauer seemed purely evil. Not as if they were harboring demons, but as if they were demons. They seem to value only their own lives and looked at every other human as nothing more than a tool to be used and discarded. Helen Meeker had been ready to confront Bauer, and yet he'd almost killed her. That was a one-on-one battle. In this case, the odds were stacked against Bryant. Would she fare as well as Meeker or would this be the moment when a life somewhat well-lived came to an end? While she wasn't anxious to answer that question, she was too cold to stall any longer.

Keeping her head low, Bryant quietly made her way through the front door and into the lobby. There was a balcony in the back leading to the upstairs rooms. To her right was a check-in desk that displayed a large registration book that likely hadn't been used in decades. The door on her right must have led to what was once a dining room. A hallway on the back wall likely went to more rooms. The lack of wall switches and electric lamps indicated the hotel had never been updated to electricity. Wipe away a bit of dust and spruce up a few things, and the place could have been used as movie set for a western.

Satisfied no one had yet noticed her arrival, Bryant tiptoed over to the side of the room and studied two doors. Behind one, there was likely nothing but cobwebs, but the other hid a prize she'd wanted to claim for some time. She silently reached toward the first door and placed her hand on the flat wood. The door was the same temperature as the room she was in so there was no reason to turn the knob. Five paces took her to the other door. This room passed the hand test. The wood was warm to the touch. Time for the showdown.

There were two ways to make her entrance. She could knock and be given an invitation, and while that initially seemed the wisest choice, Root and Red would likely ask who was there. Bryant's voice would immediately give away that she wasn't one of the men. So this time, entry would be gained by simply twisting the knob and walking in. The fact she was in John's clothing might throw off suspicion just long enough to capture the pair without gunplay.

After taking a deep breath and readying the rifle for action, she tried the knob. Unlocked. Showtime!

Bryant swung the door open and entered with the casual air of someone who belonged. She took only a quick glance around the room before lowering her face so the hat provided the cover she needed.

Root was on a Victorian couch to the right of the stove. She was bundled up in a quilt. Irish Red Mahoney was wearing a dark wool suit and seated on a red-cushioned side chair. His white shirt was unbuttoned at the collar and in his right hand, he held a thirty-eight. An iron pot-bellied stove was nicely warming the room.

Root looked Bryant's way and snapped, "John, what did you guys find?"

Holding the rifle at her side, with the left hand positioned where the barrel met the stock, she moved her right hand down to where her finger was on the trigger. Though the action appeared casual, this simple movement placed Irish Red clearly in the line of fire.

"I asked you a question," an impatient Root grumbled. "What did you guys find?"

Bryant raised her head and smiled. "Indians."

As soon as he saw the uninvited guest's face, the Kansas City thug reacted, and that was unfortunate. If he'd taken just a second to think, he'd have realized there was no way he could raise his weapon up before Bryant had time to fire. Failing to fully consider his limited options cost him his life. As the smoke from the single rifle shot still hung in the air, the head of the KC underworld slumped in his chair.

Bryant didn't notice; she was too busy watching Root. "If I see your hands move under than quilt, I'll punch your ticket too."

"I bet you would," Root replied as she slowly pulled her hands out into the open.

"Stand up," Bryant ordered.

"I'd rather sit."

"And that means you have a gun hidden in the cushions between you and the end of the couch."

"You're a smart one. I knew that the first time we talked."

"I've hidden many a weapon that way," Bryant replied. "Stand up." As Root pushed to her feet, the quilt dropped to the floor and Bryant chuckled. "It has come to this. The Washington society dame is dressed in dungarees and a lumberjack shirt."

"I was saving my formal wear for South America. I guess I won't have much use for it now."

"Perhaps," Bryant said, "they'd let you wear something nice for either the firing squad or electric chair. I'm not sure what they're using for those found guilty of treason."

"I'll send you an invitation," Root answered with a sneer. "I do want you to be aware of this. You can kill me, but you'll never get out of here. In a few hours, an army of my friend's boys will be here, and they'll take you out, and at least I'll die knowing you've dodged your last bullet. That will bring my brother some peace. You know he really did believe you were hundreds of years old."

"And you don't?

"In truth, I don't care. When the boys get here, you'll be dead. How your tombstone reads is no concern of mine."

"Gertrude, I've got a horse and a pack mule. As soon as we're done here, I'll ride out, and I'll strap you onto the jackass. We'll be long gone before your friends get here."

"Will you let me show you something first?" Root asked. "If you see it, you might just change your plans."

"I'll tell you what. You take off your shirt and pants, and I'll let you play show and tell."

"You want me to do what?"

"Strip."

"What kind of sick person are you?"

"I just want to make sure you aren't carrying any heat. Now start shedding. Once I know you'd not playing me for a sucker, you can lead the way to whatever it is you're so proud of." It took less than a minute for the woman to get down to her underwear, and other than the normal bulges created by her body's extra padding due to high living, Root seemed clean. Suddenly her gold necklace with the jade drop seemed so bizarrely out of place with long johns that Bryant chuckled.

"It's surely not that funny. Now do I have to take off the rest?"

Bryant shook her head. "I'll save that pleasure for the FBI. Now lead the way to whatever you feel I need to see."

Rubbing her hands over her arms in attempt to stay warm, Root picked up a flashlight from an end table and exited through the room's one door. After ambling down a hall, she stopped, reached up, and pulled down on a coat hook. A second later, about a four-foot section of the wall sprang open.

"You lead the way," Bryant suggested.

"Please enter King Midas's treasure room," Root replied with the smile of someone filled with pride.

Just as Ben had told Bryant at the church, the room was stacked with paintings, gold, in both bar and coin form, silver, jewels, boxes of cash, and even a few oriental rugs.

"I'm guessing this was payment for betraying your country."

"America's not my country," Root sniped. "And my brother was the man who earned this stuff. He moved it here long before he got out of Illinois. The only thing stored at my home in Washington was out of his house."

"No doubt just a small part of the loot Hitler and the SS have stolen from every corner of Europe."

Root nodded. "Old Adolf has abandoned mines piled high with art. The Nazis have looted some many museums; even Hitler likely doesn't know where it all is. I've been told he doesn't remember where they are hiding the Amber Room. Imagine that!"

Root lit two lanterns and then turned off the flashlight. As the flickering light filled the room, she waved her hand, and announced, "I'll share it with you. I'll leave half for you, and the other part I'll take to South America. You can come back after the war and grab your portion."

Bryant smiled. "If I wanted this, I could just kill you and have it all. So let's cut to the quick; you have no bargaining chips left."

Root took the necklace off, fiddled with the jade drop and sat on an old trunk likely filled with more booty than Bryant could imagine. While this stuff was of great value, it had no soul. Life not wealth and right not wrong had once directed her tribe and still influenced every decision Bryant made.

"Look around you," Root suggested. "There are undiscovered Rembrandts and da Vincis. There are also jewels worn by the crowned heads of Europe and gold looted from the Aztecs and taken from the New World back to Spain on sailing ships."

Bryant shook her head. "How many lives have been lost due to demented, selfish people wanting to possess these things? How many lives have you sacrificed to claim it as your own?"

"I learned a long time ago that the only life that matters is my own."

"Ironic," Bryant said, "because at this moment you can't do anything with it. So for you, it's worthless."

"It was once mine," Root argued.

"But, is having it worth your life? Wouldn't you rather live until you're old rather than dying at fifty? That's what this has cost you."

Root shook her head. "Tell me, is living a long time the formula for happiness? To me, it looks like all you've done is try to find somewhere you can belong. And you still haven't found it. Right now you're working for a government that dismisses you as nothing more than a tamed savage. What kind of life is that?"

"I know who I am," Bryant replied, "and while the government of the United States might not fully appreciate me or my people, this land is my home. I'm fighting for it. It sickens me to have anyone like you spoiling the dirt that holds the bones of my ancestors."

Root shrugged. "Noble words, but even noble words can ring hollow."

"Come on, let's go back and get your clothes. We need to get moving."

Root's jaw suddenly grew tight and she leaned forward as if to catch her breath. A second later, she smiled. "I'm not leaving with you. I'm going to die right here surrounded by the things my brother and I sold our souls to get."

"I'm not shooting you," Bryant explained. "I won't give you that satisfaction."

"I gave myself a last gift," Root answered. "I always keep a dose of cyanide. When you were looking around the room, I took it. I chose the way I lived and the way I will die. We should all be so fortunate." Her breath was now coming in bursts. She had to take a few shallow gulps before whispering, "My only regret is I didn't get to watch you and Meeker die. I would have enjoyed that."

Root fell forward and writhed on the ground for a few seconds before appearing to go into a seizure. After at least a minute of fighting for her breath, she relaxed. Her gruesome death mask indicated the end was anything but pleasant, and Bryant made a mental note to avoid poisons at all cost.

In the flickering light and surrounded by millions of dollars in treasure, Root, dressed in red long johns, looked almost comical—if anything, her death seemed anticlimactic. It also hadn't brought the satisfaction Bryant expected. But what had happened in this room did spell relief. No longer would the woman be a threat to Alison, Napoleon, or Helen. Reaching down, Bryant showed a bit of compassion and closed the dead woman's eyes and only then turned her attention to getting out of Dodge—or in this case, Gold Cove.

Picking up the matchbook Root had employed to light the lanterns, she pulled her coat aside and dropped it into her pocket. Experience told her that in places like this, you could never have too many matches. There were also a few other things she needed as well.

Rushing back down the hall, she reentered the room where the King of the Kansas City underworld was in a state of endless slumber. Like Root, he died completely out of his element and at this moment looked more like a failed gold prospector than a successful hood. Though it hadn't been in her plans, by taking care of Irish Red, she had put to rest a man who could have haunted Osceola. One day she would tell the Seminole who had shown her mercy about the way Irish Red had died. That mission would have to be put off because for the moment the only thing that mattered was setting things in order.

The clock was ticking, and she had several things to accomplish before she could saddle up. The first was to round up the two living members of the game and deposit them in the treasure room for safekeeping. Once she'd figured a way to lock them in, she'd get into the beaver coat, climb back up the mountain to her horse, and head to Leadville. Once in the mining town, she'd make a call to the FBI and tell them where to find Root's body, the hidden hoods, and the treasure. Hopefully J. Edgar's men would get there before the Kansas City mob.

CHAPTER 22

Monday, January 18, 1943
9:22 a.m.
Leadville, Colorado

When she rode out of Gold Cove, the only thing on her mind was getting out to Los Angeles and sharing news of Gertrude Root's death with Helen Meeker. Upon arriving in Leadville, she found there were two obstacles standing between her and accomplishing that goal. The first was Meeker was on a USO tour and there was no way to contact her. Thus, Bryant was only able to give the information to Napoleon Lancelot. He was both relieved and pleased. During their brief call, he updated Bryant on what was happening in Hollywood. His story sounded like a very bad movie script.

Her next call was to the FBI. What Bryant discovered during that conversation turned her world upside down. The Bureau was actually pleased with her actions, however, putting together a team and securing the equipment needed to get to the ghost town would take some time. As they didn't trust local law enforcement, they wanted her to keep an eye on the road to Gold Cove until they arrived. If Irish Red's team arrived, the FBI wanted to know immediately. So, her trip to the West Coast was on hold.

After grabbing a few hours' sleep, she kept an eye on the street from her hotel room. She spotted the outsiders just before midnight. It was quickly apparent they'd come fully prepared for their task. The mob drove into Leadville with two six-wheel drive Dodge WC trunks both of which had snow blades mounted on the front. With this kind of equipment, they were going to be in and out of Gold Cove hours before the Feds arrived.

The same man who'd sold Bryant the horse and mule had a Ford Model A truck equipped with skis on the front and tracks rather than tires on the back. With a vehicle like that, she could follow a few minutes behind the visitors from Kansas City. The problem was that Mort Richardson was mighty proud of his truck. Just to rent it for one day cost two hundred dollars, which was much more than the vehicle was probably worth. As she was now all but out of cash, Bryant was literally forced do some horse trading. After sixty minutes of bartering, she gave Richardson his horse and mule along with five twenties to "borrow" the truck. The time taken to make the deal meant she was now more than an hour behind the hoods. After calling the FBI and giving them her update, she fired up what Richardson called a "snow buggy" and headed back to Gold Cove.

The Dodge WCs had done a great job clearing one lane of the old mountain trail, but the task had not been easy even for the powerful trucks. Thus, an hour into the trip Bryant had to slow down to keep from running up on the Kansas City mob's tail. She stayed well behind until the gang headed down the mountainside leading into town. At that point she parked the buggy and cut through the woods on foot. She was on a hill overlooking Gold Cove when the hoods drove up in front of the hotel. Five men got out and each was carrying a rifle. She figured they also had handguns under their coats.

When she'd alerted the FBI, they'd informed her they'd likely be at Leadville by eleven. That meant, even with the road clear, she wouldn't have a team in place to take on the visitors until sometime after noon. As she was outmanned and outgunned, what she needed to buy was time, and she was running low on funds. As the fake church service wasn't going to work again, she would have to come up with another method of attack. At the moment she was as void of ideas as Gold Cove was of permanent residents.

As Bryant watched, the KC quintet walked into the hotel and disappeared. From her lofty position, Bryant counted the seconds until the men realized that all was not as planned. Three minutes later, two of them flung open the front door and hurried down the street to the church. From there, the duo searched each of town's still erect buildings. Finding nothing but one very cold body, they returned to the hotel.

For fifteen minutes, the world was as quiet as a hotel. Except for the wind and the chirping of birds, the mountains were at peace. That calm was broken when Ben walked out of the church. If the hoods found the guys she'd locked up, then they had also discovered the treasure and Root's body. They were making too much progress in too short a time. Bad news was followed by more bad news as a few minutes later the hoods began carrying the riches out to the truck.

If she'd had a high-powered rifle with a scope, she would have been able to pick them off like ducks in a shooting gallery, but the rifle she had borrowed from John was just a .22. If she could get closer she could use it to create some chaos, but there were no other points other than where she stood that gave her the view she needed. So, to take them on would ultimately mean a street fight, and she would lose. So how could she buy a few hours and keep breathing?

As the loading continued, Bryant backtracked a hundred yards and then, using trees and large boulders for cover, worked her way down to the jail. Though her view was obstructed, she could still see enough to sense how things were progressing. Except for one man, now perched on the hotel roof and serving as a look out, the gang was focused on the task at hand. Once they had carefully packed the first truck, they began placing things into the other. Stepping away from the window, a now frustrated Bryant tried to come up with new plan, but everything she thought of required putting her life on the line. Dying senselessly for a bunch of junk, even it was worth millions, was not the way she wanted to check out of life. Pulling a key ring off a hook on the wall, she sat down in a dusty chair and thought some more. Surely she'd had an experience at someone point that was similar to this one, yet nothing came into her head. Putting the keys down on the desk, she walked back to the window.

A hundred yards away, some of the finest treasures in the world were in the hands of mobsters. But in truth, why did that matter? She'd gone after Root because she was a danger to her friends. That was worth putting her life on the line for, and even though history was littered with the bodies of hundreds or thousands or perhaps millions who had died trying to get their hands on the treasure, Bryant saw the quest as folly. Life had far more value than even a Rembrandt.

The sound of another vehicle pulled Bryant out of her thoughts. Hurrying to the front of the jail, she peeked out the window and watched a third Dodge WC rumble by. There were a pair in the cab. The truck stopped beside the others, and once the driver shut the engine down, the two jumped out. Bryant was close enough to hear what was being said.

"Where's Irish?" the driver asked.

"He's dead," one explained.

"What?"

"According to Ben and John some woman stormed into town a day ago and took him out. She got Roger too."

"A woman?" he asked incredulously. "Are you sure those guys haven't been drinking. If Roger and Irish got it, how did the other two escape?"

"They're in the hotel. They claimed she just captured them with a fake church service and left them bundled up like a Christmas present in the same place the loot was hidden."

"One woman? A church service? What in the blazes …"

"Ben thinks she was an Indian."

"What did she take?" the driver asked.

"Nothing."

"You mean she just roared in here, gunned down the boss and one of our guys, and then left?"

"Yeah. I guess that makes you the boss now."

The big man nodded. "But that was going to be the case all along. I wasn't going to let Irish leave here alive or Root either for that matter. Where is she?"

"She was with them in the treasure room last night and as dead as a possum. We didn't want to look at her, so we moved her to kitchen."

"You sure she was dead?"

"Yeah. She was blue."

"Well, I might not know who the Indian woman was, but I don't mind her doing the job for us. That Root woman scared me. Did everything else work like we'd planned?"

"Yeah, guess it did."

"But with Root out of the way, why are we flying this stuff to Mexico? Why not just keep it?"

"Because we couldn't get rid of it. Except for the cash, this stuff is so well known we wouldn't get a nickel on the dollar for it. But Nazi agents in South America will pay us big bucks to get it back. We get full value and take no chances. And we also get a set of perfect plates."

The money Bryant could understand, but why would these hoods want plates? Sure, there had been some dishes and even gold flatware in the room—she'd seen it—but why keep that?"

As if on cue, one of the hoods piped up and provided the explanation. "Yeah, imagine having real engraving plates for U.S. money and crates of the real paper needed to print it. We'll be making the real thing, and no one will be the wiser."

Now it made sense. While at the FBI, she'd heard that engraving plates for the British pound and American twenties had been stolen. Supposedly, the heist had been a part of a German plan to flood the market with paper money and drive up inflation. But nothing had ever shown up. That must have been because Bauer had the plates and was planning to use them for his personal gain.

"How much longer until we get all the stuff and can move out?" the new boss asked.

"With your truck here, maybe thirty minutes."

"Let's pick up the pace. This town gives me the creeps. And if we figure out who the Indian is, remind me to write her a thank-you note. Jake, get off the roof and help us. We don't need a lookout. This is a ghost town for gosh sakes."

Art was one thing, but real treasury plates were another. Plus, if the FBI were able to meet that plane and take it to Mexico, it would likely provide a vital link to the Nazi machine in South America.

So, Bryant had to find a way to stop these guys. As they were now all inside, she finally had the opportunity to make a move. While her quickly devised plan wasn't clever or smooth, at least it had a small chance of working.

Reaching into her belt, she retrieved her Smith and Wesson, screwed on the silencer, and slipped in a full clip. Moving to the front door, she dashed across the street behind the brothel and to the church. She waited there until the next batch of treasure had been brought out and loaded.

When the men returned inside to get more loot, Bryant ran through the snow to the side of the hotel. Kneeling, she carefully aimed at the front passenger tire of the truck nearest her position. Once she'd knocked a hole it, she fixed her aim on the next front tire. Six shots and an equal number of tires later, she'd accomplished what she wanted. As she could hear footsteps coming through the lobby, she needed to get out of sight. Jogging to the back of the hotel, she noticed something she hadn't seen in the dark. The building had a cellar. Peering through a window, she saw a few old barrels and boxes, but nothing else. She forced the window open, slid in, and dropped to the floor.

The cellar was dark enough she could barely see her hand in front of her face, but thankfully she'd borrowed Root's matchbook. She opened the cover and a single strike later, she could gauge her surroundings. There were no rats or bugs, but the weather was cold. The chamber with its dirt floor was dusty, and based on the lack of tracks, no one had been down here in months, if not years. Whatever had been stored here in the past must have been taken when the hotel closed because now there were only two large boxes were marked nails, two barrels containing salt, and a third barrel whose label read gunpowder. As the match burned out, Bryant grinned. With gunpowder, nails, and matches, she had the material to make some pretty effective bombs. That might take out a few of the hoods but would also destroy the priceless art. Was there a way to accomplish the first part of the equation and avoid the second? Loud voices pulled her concentration away from creating a plan and to the window. Based on the cussing, the men seemed to have discovered their flat tires.

"It's got to be the Indian!"

"You mean to tell me all this havoc could have been done by just one woman?" the boss snapped. "Three of you get out the kits and pumps and fix these tires. There's only one more load of loot inside—you two get that into the truck. The rest of you come with me. We're going to turn this town upside down and find that squaw."

Bryant had gotten a break. The men just assumed she couldn't be in the hotel, so they fanned out looking through the rest of the buildings. Moving to a window at the front of the structure, she wiped away enough dust to watch the street. Within a couple of minutes, the loading team carried out four paintings and two rugs.

"That's it," her old friend Ben announced.

"Then help us fix these tires."

Surprisingly, the hoods weren't amateurs; they knew how to plug holes in tire tubes. They also had an air pump that worked off their engines. Things were now going way too fast. Within twenty minutes, they'd be back on the road, unless she could delay their operation.

Moving back to the barrels and boxes, Bryant cracked open both barrels and dumped their contents on the floor. Opening the nails and gunpowder, she carefully mixed them together in both the empty barrels. She then picked up one of the barrels and carried it up the stairs leading to the first floor and set it down on the top step by the door. The second barrel, she moved under the front porch. With the powder that was left she poured a path leading to the window she'd entered and another to the barrels. She then patiently waited for the boss and his men to return.

Five minutes later, they were standing at the front of the trucks watching the last of the tires being aired up.

"Maybe this really is a ghost town," one said. "We looked everywhere and saw nothing."

"She's supernatural," Ben argued. "She's as quick as a cat and as strong as a bear. I swear I saw fire in her eyes. I think she haunts this town. The sooner we get out the better."

"An Indian squaw ghost," the boss grumbled, "now I've heard it all. But as she saved me the job of taking out Red and Root, I've got no complaints. How much longer on those tires?"

"Five minutes."

While she had no doubt the bombs would explode, because the powder was old, she didn't know how much damage they'd do. Bryant also wondered if she'd be able to get away without being spotted. She figured her best chance was not rolling out the window until a split second before the explosions. If it kicked up enough dust and snow, she'd have some cover.

After reloading her gun, she made her way to window, pulled out Root's matchbook, and retrieved a match. In the sunlight coming through the glass, she saw something she hadn't seen before.

There were two letters and some numbers scribbled on the inside flap. They were only visible when the matchbook was flipped open. Curious! But this was not the time to worry about what that meant.

Striking a match, she lit first the powder trail to the stairs and next, ignited the one leading to the porch. And though every part of her demanded she bail out, she watched the fire slowly do its work. The trail heading toward the porch was moving just a bit faster than the one to the stairs.

When the flame was a foot away from the barrel, Bryant yanked herself up to the window and rolled out.

When the first bomb blew, it felt as though an earthquake had hit the mountain. The building rocked, windows cracked, and the front wall collapsed. A split second later, a second eruption blew through the main part of the lobby. As boards and shingles fell, a cloud of dust and snow fanned out in every direction.

While some men cursed and others screamed, Bryant, using the both the confusion and debris cloud for cover, rushed toward the church. Only after she was inside, did she look back.

Perhaps because the hotel was fragile after years of little maintenance, the bombs had done more damage than she had figured. The front wall had blown away, the porch was gone, and most of the roof had fallen into the lobby.

Five of the hoods were on the ground, and those standing were covered with cuts.

The fronts of the trucks, which had been facing the hotel, were dented, the paint chipped, and the lights smashed. Radiator fluid was pouring out of two of them, and the repaired tires were leaking once more. The back of the vehicles appeared to be in good shape, so the treasure had likely not suffered much damage.

With flames were now creeping up one of the hotel's walls, before long the whole building would erupt. If her body were still in the Nugget, this would be Gertrude Root's funeral pyre, and would likely not be the last time she experienced flames.

The Kansas City thugs were too shocked to notice Bryant open the church door and move back up the side of the hill overlooking the town. Twenty minutes later, she and her snow buggy were headed back to Leadville. She'd just arrived when the FBI showed up. She gave them her report, explained what she knew about the Mexico connection, and sent them on their way. She was tired of playing solo, she wanted to head to Los Angeles and rejoin her group. Four hours later, after a meal, a nap, and a shower, she turned in her rented vehicle and walked toward the bus depot.

"Bryant."

The man standing between her and the Greyhound was about six feet, well built, wearing a tan overcoat and under that a suit. He expression was as dark as his eyes.

Though he didn't flash his identification, she knew he was a G-man. She'd been around so many agents, she could spot them a mile away by the way they stood, their stoic stares, and their haircuts.

"Miss Bryant to you," she answered. "I have a bus to catch, so no time to chat."

"Taylor, FBI, you'll be staying with us. We need to you help close this mission."

"Listen, I wrapped it up for you, all it needed to be a present was a ribbon. Now I've got another mission I need to work on."

"No, we need you for the next leg. You'll be staying with us."

"What?"

"I just got off the phone with Washington, and they demanded we work with you until we have the names of Root's contacts in South America. You're going to Kansas with us to meet that plane. And, where was Root's body?"

"I heard them say they'd moved it to the hotel's kitchen."

"The body wasn't there when we looked in the rubble. Guess it's still buried under all the debris."

"If we're smart," Bryant quipped, "we'll leave it there for the vermin."

CHAPTER 23

Tuesday, January 19, 1943
3:30 p.m.
Five miles north of Sublette, Kansas

The last place Teresa Bryant wanted to be was sitting in a West Kansas barn with the wind chill around zero. The experience was made even worse with the company she was keeping. She didn't mind the two cows. four sheep, and one horse, but the six FBI agents were driving her crazy. In a building where the loft was filled with hay and straw, they were chain smoking. Not smart.

At the front of the barn, standing by a window sipping on a cup of coffee was Thomas Taylor. Taylor was the team's lead investigator, and he made that clear every chance he got. He was likely closing in on forty and single. Unlike the other men who occasionally cracked a joke, he seemed to be in a constant state of discomfort.

Pushing off a John Deere tractor's rear wheel which she'd been using to prop herself up, Bryant strolled across the wood floor to Taylor. She followed his gaze to the window and the long, open field that had the agent's full attention.

"When's the plane due?" she asked.

"Any time. The hood told me they'd planned on getting here midafternoon."

"You still haven't told me why I had to come along."

"The Mexican pilot who's flying in has never seen Gertrude Root. Neither have the South Americans. To sell this we need a woman."

"I'm going to pretend to be Root?"

He nodded. "Yeah, and to make it seem real, we're going to put about half the loot on the plane. If we don't have something to show, they might get spooked."

Bryant looked at the truck parked in the middle of the barn. Not just any truck, but a six-hundred-dollar vehicle loaded with six million in loot. Never had an old Diamond T truck looked so good.

"Did you find the plates?" Bryant asked.

"Yeah, we sent them back to where they belong. We burned the paper."

"Taylor, having someone like me in the role of Gertrude Root might spook the pilot. I hardly look like a general's wife. If you don't believe me, dig up George Custer and asked him."

The agent's expression grew even grimmer than normal. "Bryant, this isn't funny. We need to know who's working with Hitler in places like Brazil and Argentina. We get those names and we can shut down those rings."

"I understand that," she assured him, "but in my opinion, it'd be better to have someone older and whiter to play Root."

"Until you gave us the information on what was going down, we didn't know we needed anyone. You punched your ticket to this party."

Bryant frowned. “So the person who gave you the gang and the treasure and all but wrapped it up into a box is at fault?”

“No,” he said, “what you did was amazing, though in my mind, stupid. No one takes on that many people by herself.”

“I’ll remember that next time,” she shot back. “But how do I pull off being Root?”

“Ben—you remember him, he’s one of the KC mob members you only maimed—says no one knows her. If they asked about your heritage, have a story ready.”

“I can do that, but what’s the plan when we land?”

“Well, that part we will play by ear.”

“That’s not what I need to hear. Why don’t you take the veil off what you found out and put me in the loop.”

“Fine! The pilot’s taking the plane to somewhere in Mexico to meet the South Americans, and there will likely be about a dozen of them. I want at least two of these guys alive so they will be able to lead to the real contacts behind their operation.”

Bryant shook her head. This just didn’t seem to be worth the risk. The Nazis might have some contacts in South America, but they hadn’t convinced anyone to join them in the fight. Why risk a part of the treasure and the team?

“Listen, Taylor, I’ll admit that if you find a link you can likely shut down, but is it worth risking the lives of those men?”

Taylor lowered his voice to a whisper. “As you work with Meeker, I guess I can fill you in on why the mission is so important. Yes, you’re right, none of those countries is going to join Hitler, but there are people in South America who are easily bought and many of those folks hate the United States."

"Can you blame them?" Bryant asked. "We've grabbed their resources, taken advantage of them on business deals, and bully them with our power."

"You've got a point. We've never been that good a neighbor, but the OSS intercepted plans suggesting the Germans are going to send teams of soldiers to stay with the people who've been bought in Brazil, Argentina, and Mexico, along with a couple of Central American nations."

"Why, to blow up the Panama Canal?"

"Could be, but we have that well defended. From what we can gather, the plan is to smuggle a few hundred German soldiers into the US, and then have them stage raids."

"What good would that do? What targets would they hit?"

"Nothing big," Taylor admitted. "That's not the motive. They want to raid a few small towns, blow up a few banks and businesses in America's heartland, and kill a few civilians."

On the surface, that seemed like a futile gesture that would have no impact on the war, but deep down, Bryant sensed something brilliant in the plan. Fear was the greatest motivator of panic. A few coordinated raids in several different states on the same day could completely undo the security American civilians felt. After all, with huge oceans separating them from the actual war, most people thought they would never be threatened by the enemy so no one on the home front believed they would ever come face to face with a German or Japanese soldier.

But four or five raids could create chaos, and people would be seeing Nazis everywhere.

Taylor interrupted her thoughts. "Can you grasp why the FBI needs to get as much information as possible?"

She nodded. "When a force is undermanned then terrorism becomes an instrument in transforming secure people into terrified masses. For those trapped by fear, a raiding party of twenty seems to be an entire brigade. If they can pull this off in a dozen places, people will believe there is a full-scale invasion." She opted not to tell him that she and Meeker had recently employed this same concept behind enemy lines in Germany, and the tactic had worked perfectly.

"So," Taylor announced, "we have to grab the South Americans and take at least a of couple of them while they are still breathing back to DC. Once we identify who the Germans bought, we will spend more money and buy them back to our side."

Sadly, in most cases that would likely work. Those in neutral nations could be bought and sold easily.

"The plane's coming," Taylor announced.

His men immediately put out their cigarettes and got ready for action. The fire hazard was now gone at least.

"What's my job?" Bryant asked.

"When the plane lands, you go out and meet it. If Ben knows what he's talking about, only the pilot, a man named Blanco, will be onboard. He speaks English."

She looked out the window and watched the C-47 float gently down out of the gray sky onto a field that was lightly covered by snow. After taxiing up to the barn, the pilot shut off the engines. A minute later, the door opened, and a heavyset man outfitted in a leather jacket and gloves jumped to the ground.

Bryant pulled up the collar of her raccoon coat and stepped through a side door. She made four steps before stopping and waving.

"Miss Root?" he called out.

"Mr. Blanco?" she answered.

"I trust you have men ready to load the merchandise?"

"Is there anyone with you?"

"No, I am alone as expected."

Bryant turned and nodded. A moment later, double doors opened, and the big Diamond T truck fired up and drove over to the plane. As if they had been trained as longshoremen, the agents quickly began loading the treasure onto the aircraft. Seeing no reason to stand in the wind, Bryant returned to the barn and waited.

CHAPTER 24

Tuesday, January 19, 1943
4:15 p.m.
McDonald's Department Store, Burbank, California

While Force's studio-created bio was likely mostly fiction, Napoleon Lancelot did find one gem that offered a chance to possibly track the actress back to a time before 1936. The woman, now known as American's Sweetheart, first caught the attention of producer Harlan Marx while working as a clerk in a local store. As the man behind the discovery was now overseas serving with the U.S. Navy, the investigator had no choice but to head to McDonald's Department Store in hopes someone would remember Force from her days working behind a counter.

As he eyeballed it, Lancelot determined McDonald's was a typical department store. The four-story building, constructed in the teens, was red brick. A green and white awning covered the main entrance. Four show windows featuring spotlighted merchandise were situated on the front along the walk. Today, they seemed to showcase women's suits.

Lancelot strolled in the front door and stopped at the directory. On the first floor were furniture, appliances, a lunch counter, and offices. The second was devoted solely to women's wear. The next, where the kids congregated, was stocked with toys and youth clothing. The top floor held men's wear and a tailor shop. The store couldn't have been more typical. There were hundreds of retail establishments located across the country that mirrored McDonald's layout right down to the candy department that also served hot nuts.

As he wasn't in the mood to shop, Lancelot walked through the main floor to the offices, where he had no luck getting the receptionist's attention until he flashed his credentials. Then and only then did she lead him down a hall, around a corner and to a door marked "President." She didn't bother knocking but just marched in.

A blonde secretary, about forty-five, raised her head, and her smile was quickly transformed into a look of confusion.

"This is Mr. Lancelot," the receptionist explained between smacks of her gum. "He's a private investigator working with Monument Studios."

"Really?" the woman's tone fully displayed the surprise now etched on her face.

"Yes, really," Lancelot assured her, flashing his credentials. "But if you want to call the studio to confirm that, feel free."

Sensing the need for her services had been completed, the receptionist turned and left. The blonde, whose desk plate said administrative assistant, leaned back in her desk chair, stuck a pencil over her ear and smiled. The expression seemed as forced as the offer that followed. "What can I do for you?"

"I'm here to see your boss."

"Mr. McDonald is very busy. You'll have to come back another time. And please make an appointment."

"Let me put it this way," Lancelot answered. "He needs to see me. This is a matter of a criminal nature, and he will be much better off to deal with the studio directly rather than go through the police. Or to put it another way, we can do this quietly without the press getting involved, or we can plaster it all over the front pages of the Times."

She chewed on the veiled threat for a few seconds before pushing off her chair and knocking on an inner office door. Stepping in, she closed the entry. Now alone, the investigator took a visual inventory.

The room was twenty by twenty with one overhead light. The furnishings were old and well worn. Except for four metal filing cabinets, everything appeared to date back to the store's opening. The pale green walls likely had been painted in the past five years, but the floors urgently needed polish. The Royal typewriter was probably purchased about the same time the wall had been painted. Either the store was not making a great deal of money, or McDonald plowed his cash into things other than his office. Lancelot's eyes were fixed on an adding machine when the door opened, and the blonde reappeared.

"Mr. McDonald will see you."

"Thank you," Lancelot replied.

The owner's office was no fancier than the one he'd just left. The furniture was basic. None of the four wooden chairs were even padded. The owner's desk was large, but unpretentious. Several framed photographs showing various stages of the building's construction hung on the wall. On the desk were three pictures of what was likely McDonald's family.

"Mr. Lancelot?"

McDonald was a large man, a bit over six feet tall, dressed in a dark blue suit. His hair was in full retreat, and his cheeks flapped when he spoke.

"I'm Lancelot, and I won't take much of your time."

"Have a seat."

"Thank you, I will."

"I understand you're an investigator working for Monument."

"Feel free to call the studio and confirm that."

"I already did. They assured me you told Marge the truth. I hope that doesn't offend you. We have a lot of people who use false pretenses to try to get into my office. Now what can I help you with? Marge said this was a criminal matter."

Lancelot nodded. "Something has come up at the studio that the team I'm working with is investigating. To protect Monument's reputation, we are attempting to keep this on the QT."

"So I was told," McDonald answered. "I was also told you worked with Helen Meeker."

"I do."

"Tell Miss Meeker that in exchange for a couple of photos of her visiting our store, we would give her a number of items at no cost."

Lancelot grinned. Helen was being offered a wardrobe, and he was only given a few minutes. Still from a marketing standpoint, the offer made perfect sense.

"I'll tell Helen," Lancelot answered. "But right now, I want to ask you about a woman who worked in your store in 1936."

"That's a long time ago. We have had hundreds of employees come and go since then. Heck, with so many jobs in the war industry open, we sometimes have problems keeping people here long enough to train them."

"I don't doubt that. But the person I need to know about became a major movie star."

"Abby Force."

"That's right."

McDonald smiled and leaned back in his chair. "She worked in our men's department for almost two years. Just having her in the store drew customers. She'd bat those big eyes, flirt a bit, and the cash register would ring. She sold more suits than any sales person before or since."

"I have no doubt," Lancelot replied. "But what can you tell me about her as a person?"

"We loved her. She was dependable, friendly, generous, and respectful of her superiors."

"What about her personal life?"

"No one really knew her in that way. She came to work, did her job and went home. As I recall, she always rode the bus. She didn't allow people to get close to her. She never even went to our company parties."

"Did she use the name Abby Force back then?"

"No," McDonald answered, "we knew her as Gale Hoffman. The studio gave her the new name. In truth, most folks around here called her Sunny. That pretty much defined her attitude. Sweet girl!"

A real name was more than Lancelot had before he entered. If that was all he managed to uncover, the day had been successful. Still, he felt the need to push a bit harder.

"Do you remember where she lived?"

"No," the owner admitted. "Like I said she always took the bus. But we have index cards on all our employees going back to 1917. So Marge could find that information for you. Just ask her when you leave. I hope Sunny's not in any trouble."

"I don't think so," Lancelot replied. "We just have to check out the background of everyone involved in what is likely nothing more than an accident."

"That makes me feel better," McDonald replied. "Besides my family and our farm, this store and its employees mean as much to me as anything. I would love to have a hundred employees like Sunny."

"You have a farm?" Lancelot asked.

"A working farm. I raise cattle." He patted his bulging stomach. "And I'm a really good cook. You should taste my burgers. Many say they are the best in town!"

"And I see from the photo on your desk you have a son in the Navy."

"Had," McDonald correctly him. He then swallowed hard. "He was killed in action in August. The fact he died serving his country doesn't make his death any easier."

"I'm sure. And thank you so much for you time."

McDonald was suddenly too lost in thought to reply. In fact, he didn't seem to notice Lancelot get up and move to the door.

"Did you get what you needed?" Marge asked.

"Almost. Mr. McDonald told me you could find where Gale Hoffman lived when she worked for you."

"The movie star?"

"Yes."

Marge picked up a piece of paper off her desk and handed it to Lancelot. "When you told me you were working with

Monument, there was only one reason to visit us. So while you were talking to Big Mac as we call him, I dug out the file and wrote down the information.

"Thank you, Miss ..."

"Rogers. Oh, and tell Sunny we miss her."

"I will."

Pushing the paper into his pocket, Lancelot walked out the door, down the hall and into the store where he paused and watched a woman purchase some Spanish peanuts for her small boy. As the child grinned, Lancelot thought back to the photo on McDonald's desk. The war always seemed a million miles away until you met someone living a story that showed just how close it was. Shaking his head, the investigator walked out the door and to his car.

CHAPTER 25

Tuesday, January 19, 1943
10:45 p.m.
In the air over New Mexico

While Taylor and the rest of the FBI agents, now posing as member of the Kansas City mob, stayed in the back of the plane, Teresa Bryant plopped into the vacant co-pilot's seat. After a couple of hours of simply watching the United States landscape from the air, she began to quiz the pilot. He was likely shocked when her first question was posed in his language.

"You're a good pilot, why take jobs like this one?"

Blanco glanced from the windshield to his passenger. "You speak Spanish like a Spaniard."

"I learned the language from a man who grew up in the old country," she explained. "I have not spoken it in a long time."

"I feel as if I'm sitting with royalty," he laughed. "Your accent rings with sophistication and culture."

"Hardly royalty, just a woman on the run. Now, why do you take a job like this one?"

After flipping on the autopilot, Blanco leaned back and rubbed his eyes. Reaching inside his coat, he pulled out a pack of cigarettes and offered one to his guest. After Bryant turned him down, the pilot placed one between his lips, returned the remainder to his coat pocket, retrieved a lighter from another pocket, and lit up. Three deep puffs later, he spoke. "I have a family to feed—four girls and a boy and my wife likes new clothes. And so does her mother and her six sisters."

Bryant pointed to the cross the man wore around his neck. "Is that just jewelry or does it mean something?"

"It means something," he assured her.

"Then why take jobs like this. It seems to me you're flying in the face of what that cross stands for."

"I fly planes for a company, that's all. I get an assignment, and I do it. Usually, that means picking up boxes or crates and taking them somewhere. I don't ask what's in the boxes, I just take off and fly to where I'm supposed to go."

"How much do you know about me?" Bryant asked.

"They told me your name was Gertrude Root, and you had items to transport from Kansas to Mexico. They told me where I'd be landing, and they told me, like always, to avoid creating any suspicion."

"So, you don't know who you're dealing with when we land, and you also don't know who I am or who the men with me are?"

Blanco studied the landscape for a few moments. "We're in Mexico now. But who could really tell? The air is the same."

"So do you really know nothing?" Bryant asked again.

"Let me explain something to you," he said, carefully measuring his words. He then paused and licked his lips. When he finally continued, he revealed a philosophy wrapped in a rationalization. "It is always best not to know much when you deal with the people I deal with. When you know nothing, people don't kill you. So, why you are leaving the US is your business not mine. Why you have all these things you loaded into this plane is your business not mine. Who you meet and leave with is your business not mine. My job is simply to go from the lonely spot in Kansas to an even lonelier place in Mexico. What happens after that is not my business nor do I want to know anything about it."

She had no doubt that Blanco was being honest. She could well understand why a good person really didn't want to know when he was involved in bad things. Just not knowing let him pretend what he was doing was just another regular job. By never actually acknowledging what he was, he could sleep with what he had become. She couldn't judge him because there were times she had done the same thing.

"I was warned," Blanco continued, after opening the window and tossing his cigarette out, "that you were ruthless. and I was to be wary. But I don't see that."

Bryant smiled. "I once told a friend that the most dangerous snakes are the most beautiful."

"Is that a warning?" he asked.

"It is," she admitted, "but just file it away for the future. I think you're safe today. How many men are meeting us and have you ever met them before?"

"I don't know them, but I was told there would be six to a dozen, and I'm sure they aren't the kind of hombres you'd want to fool with either."

The odds would certainly be much better than the hoods in the ghost town. The key to capturing a couple alive would be luring them into the plane. Bryant figured that might be easy as they'd surely want to see the loot with their own eyes.

"How am I and my stuff going to get to Argentina? Did they tell you that?"

"There is a system," Blanco explained. "I was told there would be trucks waiting. I've heard they go to the coast and board a ship. I never ask which coast."

Bryant nodded. "And then you gas up and take my men back home."

Blanco shrugged, flipped the autopilot switch off, and turned slightly left. "We will be in Santa Eulalia soon."

"That's where we land?"

"Yes, a few miles outside of town on a private strip."

"What's your first name?" Bryant asked.

"Juan."

"How old are your children?"

"Jose is ten, my youngest girl is two, and the oldest is thirteen. The twins are eight."

"Do you have pictures of them?"

He nodded. "In my billfold."

"Can I see?"

Blanco reached inside his jacket, retrieved his wallet, and flipped it open to reveal a snapshot of his entire family.

Bryant studied it and smiled. "You should be proud, the children are beautiful, and your wife is a rose."

He nodded, closed the billfold, and put it back in his pocket. "I look forward to seeing them tonight. By the time I get home, my children will be in bed, but my wife will wait up for me." He frowned. "Why do you want to know about me? Why ask about my wife and kids?"

"They're important to you, and I thought you'd want to talk about them. A man with a good family should be given the chance to brag a little."

"They're the reason I don't want to know anything about you or the things I do," he explained. There was an obvious sorrow in his tone as he continued. "When I die, I want the priest to say, 'He could have known much but wisely chose to know only what was necessary.' In my world those who know much don't live very long, and for the sake of my children I want to live a long time."

"How long until we land?" Bryant asked.

"Only about twenty minutes."

"I'll go tell my men."

Getting out of her seat and moving to where Taylor sat on the floor, his back against the wall, Bryant leaned close. "We bought a one-way ticket. The pilot told me he's going to be home tonight—that means only one thing."

"We'll be shot, and they'll take the loot."

"Yeah. And in reading between the lines, Root's not going with the gang either. Blanco's tone reminds me of a priest walking a man to his execution."

"Any ideas on how to play this and come out with our skin?"

"A couple," Bryant replied, "but in both of those cases, the plane gets blown up. I need to come up with something where we can get back home with a prisoner and the loot."

CHAPTER 26

Tuesday, January 19, 1943
8:35 p.m. local time
USO Troop over the Pacific

Helen Meeker was dog-tired. The USO troop was now in high gear. They'd do a show, meet the men, visit a hospital, get back on the four-engine flying boat called a Chuck Hawk, and move to another place to repeat the same routine. It was like doing ten two hundred-yard sprints in row, then resting for a few minutes and doing some more. It now seemed there was no time to eat or sleep. The performers grabbed naps when they could and opened cans of K-rations to keep from growing too weak to sing, dance, or joke. Yet for all the pain they endured, the trip was amazing and the people around Helen were as well. They saw this tour as a living thank-you note to those who were giving up their lives for freedom.

Abby Force had not had another episode like she did on Guadalcanal, since that day she'd been very subdued except on stage. Captain Michael Sharp had seemingly become the calming factor she needed. They moved almost as one. With him on duty, Meeker had more time to get to know the rest of those on the tour. She enjoyed hearing how they'd gotten into show business, what they missed about the lives they'd left behind, and their motivation for signing up for one grueling USO tour after another. Meeker had also enjoyed meeting the men who were fighting this war. Talking to them inspired her and leaving them brought a sorrow she couldn't fully understand.

As they flew toward their next gig, the plane's communication's officer tuned into a Honolulu radio station and music played over a makeshift speaker hanging a few feet above Meeker's head. In the past few minutes, she'd heard "Mister Five by Five," "There Are Such Things," and "My Devotion." How could music bring such a sense of peace even in the time of the most destructive war in history?

The Tommy Dorsey Orchestra's version of "It's Starting All Over Again" had just begun when the huge Chuck Hawk seaplane made a sudden swing to the left. A few seconds later, Meeker heard the sound of something she knew too well—machine-gun fire. Seconds later, the music was replaced by the pilot's voice.

"We are under attack. Repeating, we are under attack. Stay calm. Our escorts are taking on the enemy."

Meeker made her way to a window. Two P-47 Thunderbolts were battling four Japanese Zeroes. For the moment, the Thunderbolts were holding their own, but the odds were against them. As six planes swooped and spun, the Chuck Hawk lumbered along. For the moment, their plane was just a spectator, but if the Thunderbolts went down, then the seaplane would become a sitting duck.

"We're leaking fuel," a crewman whispered as he made his way toward the plane's tail. A minute later, he rushed back the cockpit. Yet, even with the somber realization of the fuel leak and the dogfight, the pilot's voice remained calm.

"There's a small island just ahead," he announced. "Return to your seats and get ready for a splashdown. If all goes well, we'll get this thing right up on the beach. As soon as I give the word, let's move quickly but orderly out of the plane and into the trees just beyond the beach."

Meeker glanced across the aisle at Force. The actress and her assistant were remarkably calm. One seat ahead of them, Sharp looked as relaxed as a man sitting in his yard watching the grass grow. The rest of the troop reflected something much more natural—fear!

Outside Meeker's window, a Zero spun wildly downward. Its pilot had parachuted out and was floating toward the ocean. One of the Thunderbolts was on fire, and the flames were spreading too quickly for the flyer to do anything but pray. A second later, the aircraft exploded. The three enemy planes and the one remaining American fighter continued to duel as the Chuck Hawk drifted nearer the water. Up ahead, the small island grew closer.

So far on their tour, the splashdowns had been gentle. This one was anything but. The plane struck the ocean like a falling rock. It bounced three times, pitched to the right with a wing actually touching the water, and then somehow managed to straighten. The island was now less than one hundred yards away, and the pilot was revving the engines to get there more quickly. A Zero broke off from the dogfight and laid down fire just to Meeker's right. Miraculously, none of the rounds hit the plane. Meanwhile, a thousand feet above, the last Thunderbolt was taken out of the show. At the same moment it hit the ocean at several hundred miles an hour, the Chuck Hawk struck the beach and came to an abrupt halt.

"Deplane now!" the pilot demanded. He didn't have to ask a second time.

The passengers raced out through an upper hatch, down the side, and across the wing. Meeker waited and watched through the window as brave crewmen helped troop members off the plane and down to the beach.

"We need to get moving, ma'am," the pilot barked as he appeared in the cabin.

"I need to get my bag," she argued.

"No time."

Meeker nodded, moved forward, and climbed out on the roof. Before sliding down to the wing, she stood there for a moment watching Force, Strauss, and Sharp run for the cover of the trees. Over her head, the trio of Zeroes circled but drew no closer.

The Chuck Hawk's pilot jumped down beside her and studied the dark skies. He appeared completely lost in thought.

"Captain, the moonlight makes us an easy target. Why aren't they coming?"

"Miss Meeker, I don't know."

Meeker had an idea, but she didn't voice it. She had a hunch they might have just jumped out of the frying pan and into the fire. Why waste ammunition if the Japanese already controlled the island?

CHAPTER 27

Friday, January 20, 1943
12:15 a.m.
Five miles outside of Santa Eulalia, Mexico

Taylor decided the only way to prevent a massacre was to create one. He wanted to storm off the plane, guns blazing, and take out as many of the South Americans as possible. He justified his thinking by predicting that at least two of his men would survive and be able to capture and return a wounded man from the other side to provide the needed information on German activities south of the border. He pulled out a piece of paper to sketch out his ideas.

"Was George Custer your grandfather?" Bryant asked after reviewing the G-man's plan.

"What?" Taylor asked.

"You invented a scenario that makes no sense."

"You have a better suggestion?" the agent demanded.

"Well, I advise we make Blanco land somewhere else."

"We have to take back one of those guys to learn what's going on in South America."

"I was afraid you would say that," Bryant replied.

"So we go with my plan," Taylor said.

"Not so fast," Bryant cut in. "I gave you my best plan first, which called for a full retreat, now it's time to listen to my other plan. Taylor, what do you know about Crazy Horse?"

"He wiped out the 7th Cavalry."

"Do you know how he did it?"

"Not really."

"He didn't go chasing Custer, he lured the general into a trap."

"How are we going to do that?"

Bryant smiled. "My pilot friend and I will leave the plane when it lands. I'll explain I felt it wise to come only with the loot and not the guards. I can make up some story about not trusting my own people. They'll buy it. Crooks understand why you can't trust other crooks."

"And then they shoot you and come to the plane," Taylor suggested.

"Not the way I have things planned," Bryant replied. "Do you have a walkie-talkie?"

"An FBI team doesn't go anywhere without them."

"I know that," Bryant assured him, "I was just giving you the chance to tell me. Hand me one of the walkie-talkies. I'll use it to bring the greeting party back onto the plane." One of the agents tossed her the communication devise. As she studied it, she said, "Have your guns ready and find a place to conceal yourselves from the door. I want them in the plane before the action starts. I feel the plane slowing down, so we're about to land. Get hidden and get ready!"

"I don't understand," Taylor complained.

"Obviously," Bryant muttered as she hurried back to the cockpit.

The ground was approaching in a hurry as Blanco guided the plane down between two rows of lit torches onto a dirt strip. To the right was a medium sized wooden barn that likely served as a hanger and to the left were metal fuel tanks. Beside the hanger were two large trucks and a Ford sedan. The men serving as greeters were not in sight.

"Juan, once you're on the ground I want you to taxi to the fuel tanks. Once you've cut off the engines, you and I will both get out. You're going to lead the way to the greeting party."

"Miss Root," the pilot replied, his voice shaking more than the plane, "I'm sorry."

"Sorry for leading me into an ambush?" she asked as she observed him work the plane's wheel, pedals, throttle, and switches. "Or are you sorry for bringing me to a place where I'm scheduled to die?"

"Yes," Blanco admitted. "Both! How did you know? I wasn't supposed to tell you. And, by the way, they promised nothing would happen until after I left."

"So, if you didn't see me gunned down, it wouldn't be real, and you could pretend I was still alive?"

He didn't answer.

As the plane touched down, the pilot eased off the throttle. When the C-47 slowed to a stop, he finally announced, "It's easier not to know."

"I want you to see your family again," Bryant said as she watched the plane turn and head toward the tanks, "but you're not going to unless you play things my way. Here's what you have to do. First, you tell them I'm the only one with you. And remember, I speak Spanish so I'll know what you say and how they reply. Then you explain there's a bomb on the plane."

"What?"

"Just tell them, I'll take it from there."

Once the plane stopped, four men stepped out of the shadows. There was just enough light to see each of them was carrying a handgun. Time to play a bluff that could mean life or death.

"Let's go, Juan, and keep to the script."

Bryant's pistol was in her coat pocket—hidden and ready to fire. In her left hand, she carried the walkie-talkie, the side-sending button pushed all the way down. After Blanco opened the door and jumped out, she followed.

"Amigos, this is Mrs. Root. She's the only one who made the trip. She decided she couldn't trust the men who'd been working with her. But she wanted me to tell you there is a bomb on the plane."

Upon hearing the news, the four stopped and looked at each other. The one on the far right then turned and glanced at one of the trucks.

Seizing on the fact she had their attention, Bryant set her plan in motion. Moving forward until she was only five feet from the South American quartet, she smiled and outlined the situation in Spanish.

"In my left hand is a walkie-talkie. You will note I have the send button pushed all the way down. If I let go of the button, the radio signal triggers a bomb and the whole plane and all the loot blows up. The bomb is large enough that the explosion will also cause the fuel tanks to ignite as well. In other words, I lift my thumb, and all of us die."

"We can easily shoot you," the man closest to Bryant suggested.

"Then my thumb comes off the button, and you die anyway. Unless you play it my way, the local priest is going to be doing a lot of funerals. Do you get me?"

The quartet nodded in unison.

"Okay, the first thing that's going to happen is a couple of you are going to help Juan fuel up this crate. Once it's loaded, two of you will get on this plane with us. We'll take off and fly to where you are to meet the boat."

"What makes you think you won't be killed on the boat?"

"Because," Bryant explained, "the bomb is hidden in a treasure trunk. If that trunk is opened by anyone but me, it will explode, and you will lose all you want to claim as your own as well as your lives. And that will be true for our sea voyage as well. I don't defuse the bomb until I'm safely where I want to be in Argentina. Or, if you don't want to play by my rules, I'll release the button right now. You have three minutes to go back to your friends and discuss your options."

The quartet shuffled to the trucks where two more men got out. As they huddled, Blanco whispered, "You know how to operate. I had no idea there was a bomb."

Bryant, her eyes locked onto the meeting, didn't reply. If this worked, she'd have two hostages and a pilot. If it didn't, she'd be buried under the name of Gertrude Root, and she couldn't think of a worse fate. Finally, the four strolled back to the plane.

"Paulo and Manual will help the pilot with the fuel. Garcia and I will go with you."

"We wait here until the plane's filled. Juan, make sure they fully top off the tanks."

As the pilot and newly minted gas monkeys went to work, the man acting as the leader spoke. This time in English. "They told me you were smart and lethal, but they didn't explain you were beautiful."

"Each quality serves me well," Bryant replied.

"What made you anticipate a double-cross?"

"I always plan for greed to triumph over patriotism," she explained. "Besides, Hitler believes my usefulness is over. He doesn't fully know what additional information I have. If he did, he wouldn't have ordered you to kill me. Once he knows, my skin will be safe."

As the men fueled the plane, the night grew silent and Bryant wondered what Taylor and his men were thinking. As the transmit button was depressed, they could hear the conversation, but except for the last part spoken in English, she wondered if they understood any of it.

"We are finished," Juan announced as he strolled back to where Bryant stood. She watched as the other two moved toward the trucks.

"Okay, gentlemen," Bryant said, "Juan is going to lead the way. He'll get in first. You two will be next, and I'll board last."

The hoods looked at the walkie-talkie and grimly followed the pilot. Neither glanced back as they hopped onto the plane. Blanco was already firing up the engines as Bryant took a final gander at the trucks and the men beside them. After taking a deep breath of the cool night air, she smiled and jumped through the door. Taylor and his men were still hidden under tarps.

"Close and latch the door," Bryant ordered her guests.

Garcia was too mesmerized by the loot to move. The other man took his gaze off the booty just long enough to pull the door closed and lock it. Then his eyes went back to the trunks, paintings, and gold.

"Aren't you glad the bomb didn't go off?" Bryant announced as the plane taxied down the runway. "Think of the waste of blowing all this stuff up. By the way, gentlemen, I have some friends I'd like you to meet. From four different spots, tarps were pushed to the side and the FBI agents, guns drawn appeared.

"What?" Garcia whispered.

"In America, we call them G-men," Bryant explained. "You will be getting to know them real well." She grabbed onto the wall as the plane lifted off. Once they were level, she yelled, "Back to Kansas. You got that Juan?"

"Yes."

As the C-47 turned, Bryant tossed the walkie-talkie to Garcia. His face turned ashen white, and he fell to the floor. He was still buying the charade, but the second man responded much differently, pulling a pistol from his pocket. Before anyone could react, he turned and fired toward the cockpit. The noise of the shot was still echoing in the plane as Taylor and one of his men jumped the guest and quickly subdued him. Yet having him under control only solved a part of the problem. During the struggle, the plane had fallen into a steep dive.

Sensing what must have happened, Bryant pushed past the treasure and the men and scrambled to the cockpit. Hopping into the co-pilot's seat, she pushed an unconscious Blanco off his wheel and grabbed her own, slowly pulling it up. In spite of her efforts, the plane shook and continued to plunge. Yet even as the Mexican landscape grew closer, she didn't panic. Pulling steadily back, Bryant glanced at the gauges. There was too much speed and too little air.

With full tanks, if this crate hit the ground, it would turn night into day. Pulling more, she felt the C-47's nose turn up just a bit, but not enough—the ground was growing closer with each passing second. Not knowing what else to do, she slowly eased back on the wheel a bit more, and the plane seemed to correct itself. She was no more than a few hundred feet over the desert floor. One more pull and the plane leveled out. Taking a breath, she wiped the sweat off her brow and eased back to begin a very slow climb. Several minutes later, when the gauge read 5,000 feet, she leveled off and checked the compass. Slowly banking, she directed the nose toward the north. Everything felt smooth. She reached forward and flipped on the automatic pilot and turned toward Blanco.

The one shot the South American had squeezed off had found the back of the pilot's neck. He'd likely died instantly.

"What you don't know," she whispered to a man who could no longer hear her, "kills you much more often than what you do know."

Taylor stuck his head through the cockpit door and glanced from Bryant to Blanco. "Is he dead?"

"Yeah."

"So you pulled us out?"

"Yeah."

"You never cease to amaze me. I'm sure glad you fly."

"I don't," Bryant admitted. "I observed Blanco on the way down here enough to keep this bird in the air, but landing it is another thing altogether."

"When we get to the States," Taylor calmly replied, "we'll radio for help. Someone can talk you through what you need to do to put this crate on the ground."

"Yeah, that might work," she replied, pointing out the flaw in the agent's plan, "but the bullet that got our pilot ended up putting our radio out of commission. There is a huge hole right through that box."

CHAPTER 28

Wednesday, January 20, 1943
12:17 a.m. local time
Bacon Island, Pacific

The USO landing party escaping from the now grounded Chuck Hawk had no more than gotten into the woods when sniper fire broke out. Though no one was hit, the attack had them penned to the ground. The two marines who'd accompanied the entertainers on the tour, along with the plane's crew and Captain Michael Sharp returned fire, but as they were shooting at targets they couldn't see, they had little to no chance of hitting the enemy.

"We're sitting ducks," Sharp grumbled as he came to Helen Meeker's side. "Oh, we'll survive tonight, but when daylight comes, they can target us at will. I'm going to go and talk to the marines. Maybe we can come up with a plan."

From her place behind a tree, Meeker watched Sharp hug the ground and crawl over to where the marines were huddled behind a large rock. Her Colt was on the plane in her luggage, and without it, she was essentially a spectator. Glancing to her right, she noticed Force and Strauss. Both were sitting on the ground behind two large palms. With

Sharp not covering the pair, Meeker decided to resume the role of babysitter and bodyguard.

She looked back at the place where the Japanese seemed to be located. At the moment there was no activity. Staying low, she jogged toward the actress and her assistant and was halfway to her goal when four shots rang out. All were wide and high. The firing stopped when she reached Force and Strauss. Dropping to her knees in effort to stay out of the line of fire, she studied the women.

Even in the darkness and dressed in fatigues, Force was a beauty. Sweating and mussed, she still looked every bit the star. She must have been too tired or shocked to be scared, and her expression was that of a woman who'd been stood up for a date. With her life hanging in the balance, she looked perturbed.

Strauss was also beautiful, but unlike Force, the assistant had no warmth. Therefore, there was always no charisma. While Force glowed, Strauss simply showed up. Yet to her credit, even in this situation, she was calm and cool.

"Ladies," Meeker whispered, "are you any worse for the wear?"

"If you're asking if we're injured," Strauss answered, "then the answer is no."

"What will they do to us if we're captured?" Force asked. Her tone was surprisingly emotionless. The question was posed as if she was trying to figure out what to order from a menu.

Meeker shrugged. At this point she didn't want to share what she was thinking, but Strauss had no such reservations.

"For the men, it's death or a POW camp. As you and Helen are famous, you'll become their playthings. They'll dangle you out in front of our leaders and taunt them with photos of you behind bars. They'll also use the fact that they have the two of you to try to break morale on the home front."

Force looked at Meeker. "Is that true?"

"We don't know what they would do. We don't even know if they will recognize who we are. To those guys in the woods, Abby Force and Helen Meeker might be complete strangers. They may have never heard of us."

"So don't volunteer any information?" Force asked.

"That would be a good plan."

A cracking of rifle fire broke out and for the next minute, the women hugged the trees and waited for things to cool down. While the bullets that zipped over their heads shredded a few of the large palm leaves, no one in the troop was hit.

"Why do they keep doing that?" Strauss asked.

Meeker grimly smiled. "It's kind of like the neighbor's dog. He'll bark every so often just to keep you awake."

"So," Force demanded, "when does the plan change from tormenting us to attacking us?"

Meeker didn't have an answer. Logic told her they'd start getting serious when daylight gave them clear targets. With the light serving to highlight targets, they'd just hide and shoot. And as the troop had only a handful of guns, resistance wouldn't last long. Rather than sharing her grim forecast, she opted to toss out a bit of hope. "There's a huge factor working in our favor."

"What that's?" Strauss asked.

"The Army knows we came under fire and were shot down. The crew would have radioed that information along with our position. A rescue team is surely on its way.

No further than we are from Hawaii, they will likely be here long before dawn."

A man hiding behind a large coconut tree about thirty feet to the left caught Meeker's attention. Peering through the shadows, she recognized the pilot and that he was waving.

"Ladies, I'll be back in a second."

Hugging the ground, she crawled over to forty-year-old Jim Gleeson. The longtime army vet greeted her with a smile.

"Miss Meeker, this is one screwy night. I'm sorry to put you in this situation."

"In truth, I've had worse. Right now the night doesn't bother me as much as what might come at dawn."

"I want to know something," Gleeson whispered. "Is everything they say about you true?"

"What do they say?"

"The scoop is your instincts are as good as any general, and you can outfight any man. They say you've stared Hitler in the face and didn't even blink."

Meeker had seen Hitler, but she couldn't recall if she'd blinked. Nevertheless, the experience had been one of the most chilling of her life. If she'd gotten out of that mess, surely she could find a way out of this one.

"Jim, you make me sound like that comic book hero."

"My daughter loves Wonder Woman," he replied. He paused and looked toward where Sharp and the marines were talking. "There's something about this that just doesn't feel right."

"War never feels right," Meeker replied. "Your plane got hit by fire, and we had to ditch. I guess we should count our blessings we were close to an island. My guess is that help must be on the way."

"What makes you think that?" Gleeson asked.

"Because you radioed in what was going on."

"I tried, but while our receiver was working, our transmitter was not. We discovered it was out as soon as we got into the air."

Meeker frowned. The odds had just gotten much longer. Sure, when the troop didn't show up at the location for the next scheduled show, a search would be ordered, but without a specific location the Navy would be lucky to find them before the Japs closed in.

"Why do you think there were four Zeros out in the middle of nowhere?" Gleeson asked. "There are no battles around here. We steered far away from any action, and you don't send four planes out on a patrol."

"I don't have an answer for that," Meeker admitted. "My guess would be they were lost."

"Then why didn't they blow us out of the sky?" the pilot asked.

"By hitting our fuel tank, they knocked us down before our fighters drew their attention."

"Actually," Gleeson whispered, "they didn't. Right before the attack, we developed a major fuel leak. Go back and look at our plane—there's not a bullet hole in it anywhere. Either the Jap pilots are the worse shooters in the world, or they had no intention of hitting us."

His words were sobering. If Gleeson's hunch was right, this whole thing was carefully planned, and they'd ditched exactly where the Japanese wanted. Why? Was this whole thing planned so they could get their hands on the movie star?

"Miss Meeker, how many of our people have been hit by sniper fire?"

"None."

That fact was as bizarre as the Chuck Hawk not having been hit. While the shooting had been regular, never once had the spraying lead found a human target. Every shot had been high. The snipers were content with just pinning them down. What was this all about?

"Here comes Captain Sharp," Gleeson whispered.

As Sharp hustled to their position, half a dozen shots rang out. All went several feet over his head.

"That was close," the captain whispered as he sank down to the ground. "I wish I had a cigarette. I left mine on the plane."

Meeker studied Sharp. He appeared just like a man you'd want on your side in combat. He was completely confident and calm. Yet his needing to point out how close the shots had come to him, when they actually hadn't, still revealed his overripe ego.

"Helen, I came over to tell you I'm going to try to get behind the Japs. The two marines will lay down cover for me as I run across that open meadow. Once I get into the jungle, I'll have the cover I need. I've got two pistols and a rifle."

"Captain," Gleeson cut in, "I've figured something out …"

Meeker waved her hand. The pilot got her message and quickly went mute.

"Sharp," Meeker asked, "how do you rate your odds?"

"Long," he admitted, "but we can't stay here doing nothing. If I can get behind them and pick a few off, then it buys us some time."

"But …"

Meeker once again cut Gleeson off by voicing her disapproval for the plan. "I'm not for this."

"For months, while making my escape, I lived in jungles not much different than this. I'm better qualified for this job than anyone else. Besides, I need to prove myself to you so I can get the job I really want."

"And, if you die," Meeker pointed out, "you won't work the job Uncle Sam needs you to work. This is way too risky."

"I'm going, Helen, and you can't stop me. I'm not going to wait until daylight when they can easily pick us all off."

She nodded and watched him hustle back to the marines. He was right in more ways than she cared to admit.

"You didn't let me tell him," Gleeson pointed out.

"He didn't need to know," Meeker answered. "If you'd shared your observations, he might get careless."

"What's this all about?" Gleeson demanded. "None of this makes sense."

"War rarely does."

Meeker's eyes were on Sharp as he readied for his run. Once he'd worked his way to the last palm tree, the marines stood and peppered the other side of the meadow with fire. Running in a zigzag pattern under their lead, Sharp began his one-hundred-yard sprint. The snipers opened up, and scores of shots came from positions in trees and on the ground. For a second, as the captain stumbled and fell face first to the ground, it appeared the Japanese had stopped the officer's bull rush. Yet, Sharp immediately rolled over, rose, and moved forward. Now under even heavier fire, he ceased moving back and forth and charged in a straight line toward the trees. He covered the last four yards airborne, leaping for the cover provided by the jungle like a squirrel diving for a tree. As he faded into the darkness, the night grew so silent Meeker could hear the waves breaking on the shore.

CHAPTER 29

Wednesday, January 20, 1923
4:15 a.m.
Somewhere over New Mexico

Teresa Bryant studied the landscape beneath the C-47. From what she could see in the darkness, it was barren. There were few lights and no landmarks.

"Where are we?" Taylor asked.

"My guess is that we're over New Mexico. So the good news is that we're in the US; the bad news is that at some point, I've got to turn off the autopilot and bring this bird down."

"Can you do it?"

"I wouldn't bet on me," she admitted, "but even if I don't, all we lose is some priceless art."

"And a few lives," the agent pointed out.

"Actually," Bryant replied, "the only life we lose is mine. At the top of the horizon, there are some bright lights. On my last break, I walked back and counted eight parachutes in the back of the plane. You get prisoners in two of them and you and your men in the other six, and when we get close to that town you bail out."

"But ..."

"No buts, Taylor. There's something important those guys know, and your team's mission is to find out what it is. It's the only reason we put our lives on the line and that trumps everything else. As no one likely has any experience skydiving, who knows how many of you will float and how many will dive, but odds are still better than staying on this plane with me."

"You could take one of the chutes," he argued.

"No, I'm the one who has the best opportunity to set this plane down and save the cargo. I was at least sitting in this seat when Blanco landed in Mexico. I watched everything he did."

"Then let me stay with you."

"Taylor, your responsibility is to your men and your job. Now go back and get those chutes on. I'll let you know when it's time to open the door and take a leap of faith."

Bryant had no idea what town she was seeing. It could have been Roswell, Clovis, or even Tucumcari, but whatever it was, this gave Taylor and his men the best chance at living through this adventure. With the autopilot on, she pushed out of the seat and moved to the back of the plane. The eight faces that met her were drawn. None of them really wanted to jump.

"Gentlemen, are you ready?"

"As ready as we can be," Taylor answered.

"Okay, two of the agents need to go first," Bryant suggested, "then shove out a prisoner. After that, an agent and then another prisoner. Then we finish this adventure off with two agents. Line up and let's go out in a hurry. You don't need to be separated."

"I'd still like to stay with you," Taylor announced.

She ignored him as she stepped to the door, unlatched and yanked it open. Cold air rushed into the cabin.

"Now!" Bryant ordered.

In the assigned order, the men stepped to the door and jumped out into the void until only Taylor was left. He was standing at the edge looking down.

"All the chutes opened," the agent announced.

"Except for one," Bryant said.

"I'm staying," came the defiant reply.

"Really?" She took one step forward and put her hand on the agent's chest. As she pushed him out the door, she yelled, "Don't forget to count to three!" She stood in the blowing wind until Taylor's chute opened, then closed and latched the door.

Feeling neither fear nor apprehension, she calmly walked back to the cockpit and settled into her seat. Judging from the gauge, she guessed the crate had six hours of fuel left. The gold and jewels would likely survive a fire, but the paintings would not. The best way to assure all the cargo made it was to just keep flying north until the fuel gave out. If her calculations were correct then with a few course corrections, she'd have a chance to set down on the flat, snow-covered fields of Iowa or Illinois.

CHAPTER 30

Wednesday, January 20, 1943
7:38 a.m. local time
Bacon Island, Pacific

Like the barking dog, the Japanese snipers continued to pepper the stranded USO troop with just enough shots to keep them on edge and unnerved. During this time, Helen Meeker stayed with Force and Strauss, and between visits about everything from food to thoughts of an afterlife, she grabbed catnaps. Now with the sun filtering through the palm leaves, she was on edge.

"So, you think they'll get serious now that's getting light?" Force asked.

"I don't know what to think," Meeker admitted.

"I'd give a week's pay for a scrambled egg," the actress added.

Meeker smiled. "Our pilot told me that we landed on Bacon Island, so I guess you could literally have bacon and eggs."

"Wonder why it's called that?" Strauss asked.

"I asked Gleeson," Meeker said, "and he informed me a hundred years ago there was a shipwreck here. Onboard were a dozen hogs. Until someone came to rescue them, the sailors survived by eating their cargo."

"Wonder if there are any of those pigs' relatives still living here?" Force asked.

Meeker shrugged. "I'm hoping we aren't here long enough to find out."

Without warning, the morning was filled with gunfire. This time was unlike the sniper shots they'd been experiencing. These blasts were constant and sustained. As those around her hit the dirt and prayed, Meeker studied the scene. The marines posted at the big rock were doing nothing, and the reason was quickly obvious. There were no bullets being fired in their direction. The battle was somewhere in the woods.

"What's going on?" Gleeson shouted.

Meeker looked to her left and shrugged. "Sharp or possibly someone else landed on the other side of the island and encountered the Japanese. Whatever is going on, we aren't in the line of fire. So, I look at it as good news."

Meeker's eyes moved toward the seaplane. There was food onboard and also a portable battery-operated radio. While the radio wouldn't transmit, they could pick up broadcasts from Honolulu. As the gunfire in the jungle continued, Meeker rose and raced to the edge of the trees. She hid behind a bent palm for a few moments, attempting to gauge how long she would be running over the open beach until she made the plane. She'd likely take twenty seconds to cover the ground and then another twenty to climb up onto the plane and scramble inside. Was it worth the risk? Logic said no. They weren't starving and listening to a radio really offered nothing but the sounds of home. But there was another reason for wanting to get in that plane. In her luggage were her Colt and ammunition. Both would come in very handy if the Japs made a move toward the troop. She poised, ready to make the sprint when she heard a familiar voice.

"Don't shoot, it's me."

Turning toward the meadow, she watched Captain Michael Sharp emerge from the trees. He had a pack slung over his back and was cradling a rifle. And while his uniform shirt was ripped across the chest, showing signs of having been in a fight, otherwise he looked no worse for the wear. Showing no fear, he ambled across the opening to where the marines waited behind the bolder. Sensing there was nothing to now worry about, Meeker jogged over to the position.

"Surprised to see me?" Sharp asked.

"Nothing surprises me," Meeker answered.

Sharp dropped the pack and the rifle onto the ground before telling them about his mission. "There were five of them. Based on what I found, they were flyers. Likely part of a bomber crew. I'd guess their plane went down somewhere on this island, and they were marooned. Three of them were in trees, so once I got behind them, they were pretty easy to pick off. The others put up a lot more of a fight. One of them worked his way behind me, but his gun jammed. After I got that Jap with my knife, the other guy and I exchanged fire for about ten minutes. I don't think I actually shot him—one of my bullets must have ricocheted off a rock. Either way, he's dead."

"Good job," one of the obviously awed marines announced.

"Yeah, I was lucky. I couldn't have done this if I hadn't spent so much time in the jungle when I escaped the Japs last year. Anyway, you'll find some food and a radio in the pack. I checked the radio out—it works. I'm guessing they didn't call for help because they knew how close they were to Hawaii and were afraid we'd pick up their signal and find them."

"We'll get on the horn and see if we can get a rescue team," the marine said as he reached for the pack.

"Well," Sharp said as he looked at Meeker, "I didn't get killed."

She watched the captain retrieve a pack of Josma cigarettes from his shirt pocket. He casually pulled one out and lit it. After sucking the smoke into his lungs, he smiled. He obviously felt very good about himself.

"Are you sure there were only five?" Meeker asked.

"Oh, yeah," he replied as he exhaled. "I doubled checked before I left."

Meeker looked back toward the jungle. "It takes some kind of soldier to beat five to one odds."

"It helps to be a good athlete," Sharp replied. "And in truth, I was a bit lucky. If a gun hadn't jammed, I'd be drawing flies right now."

"Hey," the marine called out, "I got Pearl. They'll try to send another Chuck Hawk to get us today. They're also going to dispatch a ship to retrieve our plane."

As the USO troop cheered and emerged from the woods to congratulate Sharp, Meeker strolled across the meadow. She'd gone about a dozen steps when the captain caught her.

"Where you going?"

"I thought I'd check out the Japanese camp."

"No reason to," Sharp replied. "I got what we needed and help is on its way."

"I just thought I'd see how they lived. I've never been around the Japanese before. My experience has been with Germans."

He grabbed her elbow. "It's a waste of time. And besides, there are some dangerous animals out there. You're not even armed. Let's go back, get our plane unloaded, and keep an eye on the movie star. Look, the film crew is already digging out their equipment and setting up to shoot. So, you need to stick with Force and make sure she doesn't give away any government secrets." He grinned before adding, "I bet they never thought they'd make a documentary like this one turned out."

Sharp was right on the weapons—she didn't need to go into the jungle without her gun, but she really wanted to see that Japanese camp. She'd fully convinced herself to head back to the plane to retrieve her Colt when another shot rang out.

"Get back in the woods," Sharp ordered.

"Looks like there were six," Meeker said as she ran for cover.

"Yeah," Sharp replied, "guess I should have triple checked."

CHAPTER 31

Wednesday, January 20, 1943
11:48 a.m.
Somewhere Over Iowa

The fuel gauge was hitting the 'E,' so the pilot with no experience needed to start her descent. Below were miles and miles of snow-covered fields. Finding a place to land would be no problem—the only thing Teresa Bryant had to worry about were houses, barns, fences, and cars. If she could avoid those, she might just have a chance to keep on breathing.

Switching off the autopilot, she gripped the wheel and began to consider questions for which she had no answers. How much did she need to decrease speed? How much would be too much? When did she pull the landing gear down? How did she keep the nose up? Easing in the throttle, she pushed the wheel a touch forward and the plane began a slow drop. So far, so good.

For several miles, she gradually worked the plane closer to the ground. The altimeter now assured her she was a thousand feet over the earth, but the ground felt so much closer. Seemingly, she could have put her hand out the window and touched the roofs of silos and barns.

She needed to remember what Blanco had done when he landed in Mexico. She rolled her mind back to yesterday and created a checklist. So far, she had mimicked his moves. But what did he do next? Landing gear? She looked at the myriad of switches, levers, and buttons. Where was it?

Bryant began on the left and went over everything she saw. There was the airspeed indicator, the wiper control, the landing gear pressure gauge, the deicer switch, and finally she spotted the landing gear switch. She pulled the switch and heard the wheels coming down as the plane began to slow even more. With the plane's belly open, there was now a lot more wind noise.

What next?

She looked at the instrument board in front of her and was overwhelmed. What else did she need to do? Why hadn't she watched Blanco more closely?

Looking down at the ground, she studied the landscape for the best place to land. Just ahead, past a farmhouse and barn, were two open fields. Running between them was a road. There was no one on that road, and there were no fences on either side. A tailor-made landing strip for a novice pilot.

Logic dictated she needed slow down. She was about to reach for the throttle when the right engine cut out. She glanced to her left just as the second Pratt and Whitney engine stopped. She'd waited too long—she was out of fuel, and her plane was a glider. Suddenly, the sound of the wind was frightening.

Gathering her wits, Bryant saw she was now not lined up with the road. Remembering her observations of Blanco, she banked a bit to the left and lowered the nose.

Momentarily, she felt as if she were going straight down, so she pulled back a little. The plane fought her for a second, and then the angle adjusted. She had to keep the bird right in the middle of its target.

Pulling her gaze from the world rushing ever closer, she looked at her altimeter—five hundred feet and falling. Glancing back out the glass, her heart sank. The road was going to run out before she hit the ground. With her current rate of descent, she was going to plow into a two-story farmhouse. Even though she was now only two hundred feet above the snow, she said a prayer and banked left.

Ten seconds later, the wing dragged into what had been a cornfield, and the C-47 began to spin like an ice dancer. Though she was buckled into her seat, Bryant felt like the metal ball in an arcade machine and the forces pulling her in a dozen different directions at the same time caused her to black out.

When Bryant came to, she was hanging upside down. As her eyes began to focus and she gathered her thoughts, the first thing that hit her was the cold air. A stiff wind was blowing directly into her face through what had been the windshield. A few more blinks, and she realized she was not looking at where she'd aimed the plane but was instead viewing where she'd been.

Though her head was throbbing, Bryant found the strength to reach for the seat belt's buckle. Jammed. Digging inside her pants, she retrieved a small knife and began sawing. She took almost three minutes cutting through the canvas strap. Unable to catch herself, she fell from the seat and onto what had once been the top of the plane. Landing on her right shoulder, she groaned and passed out again.

The snow blowing in her face demanded Bryant once more acknowledge a world she wished would go away. Finding strength, which she thought she didn't have, she pushed off the glass-covered surface and struggled to her feet. It took more than a minute for the world to stop spinning. Only after the merry-go-round ride was over did she stagger toward the cargo hold. The fact most of the loot had been tied down saved it from being damaged, and while that would please the FBI, at this point she didn't care.

A gaping hole where a wing had once been attached offered the easiest exit. She crawled through the opening. After pushing up on her knees she headed toward the nearest farmhouse.

CHAPTER 32

Thursday, January 21, 1943
10:32 a.m.
Stargate Apartments, Burbank

Napoleon Lancelot chuckled as he pulled up to the Stargate Apartments. In the Los Angeles area even rundown, third-rate housing felt the need to embrace a Hollywood theme. Doubtful though that this dirty stucco, three-story structure had ever been visited by any member of the motion picture community. With its peeling windowpanes, cracked sidewalk, and ill-fitting doors, the building probably should have been condemned.

Getting out of his rented Ford, Lancelot nodded to a couple of elderly women sitting on a wooden bench before making his way to the main entrance where a door almost hung on by one hinge. At one time, there had been a buzzer that visitors pushed to gain access to the main hall, but now only a hole in the wall remained. As the wobbly door was unlocked, he walked into a dark, musty hallway littered with trash. To his left was a bag of trash and on the right was a board listing the names of those occupying the twenty-two units. The manager was in 104.

There were four ceiling fixtures in the narrow hall, but together they hosted only one working light bulb. After kicking aside an empty whiskey bottle and watching it roll against a wall, Lancelot knocked on 104. Though he could hear a radio playing, no one answered. Not willing to give up, he tried again, and a few seconds later, the door creaked open.

"Yeah?"

The woman was maybe five feet tall and likely just as wide. She held a glass in her right hand that could have been tea, but he guessed it wasn't, and a cigarette dangled from the corner of her mouth. Her dress was faded, stained, and clung to her bulges like snow on a mountain. Her eyes were dark and her dirty hair gray. Obviously, the woman had lived a hard life and most of the hardship was probably self-inflicted.

"I'm Napoleon Lancelot," he explained with a smile. "I was hoping to speak to the manager."

"You're speaking to her. Hope you ain't looking for a room; we're all booked up, but if you're looking for a job, that's another story. Now hurry up and spit out what you need. I'm missing my soap opera."

Reaching inside his suit coat, Lancelot pulled out his credentials. Once she saw them, he continued. "I need some information on someone who lived here eight years ago."

"That's a long time."

"I realize that. Were you the manager back then?"

She smiled and took a drink, letting it burn her thoat before grinning and displaying a wide gap where four middle top teeth had once been. "I've been managing this place for ten years. My old man was the manager before that. He was worthless, but I hated it when he died. When he was alive, I didn't have to work. And it takes a lot of energy to keep up a place like this."

Rather than dwell on the irony of her statement, Lancelot plowed ahead. "According the records of the McDonald Department Store, there was a woman who worked there from 1934 until 1936 who lived here. Her name was Gale Hoffman, but people called her Sunny."

"I might remember," she admitted, "but you have to understand my mind's a little foggy sometimes. Do you understand? Sometimes, it takes some prodding to clear away the mist."

Lancelot reached into his pocket and retrieved a five. The woman shrugged and took another swig. A second bill brought a smile and loosened her tongue. After grabbing the pair of greenbacks, she opened up.

"It's getting a lot clearer now. She and her mother lived in 204. The girl was all right, worked hard, paid her bills, but the mother was something else. I never saw a man in their place, so I guess the father must have been dead."

"What do you mean by something else?"

"She was crazy. She talked to herself, wandered the halls, saw things that weren't there, and carried a doll with her everywhere she went. I don't know when she slept, because she was wailing day and night. Sunny had to install locks on the outside of the door and bolt the old woman in when she left for work. Her place was just above this one, and you could hear her pacing back and forth for hours at a time. It was everything I could do not to go up and slap the devil out of her."

"What happened to Mrs. Hoffman?"

"We got so many complaints we had to give Sunny a choice. She either got rid of her mom or moved. So she found a place for the old woman. Some kind of state-run facility for the loonies."

To a certain degree, Lancelot now understood why Gale Hoffman would choose to reinvent herself as Abby Force. Having a mother who was insane was not the formula for finding success in motion pictures or anywhere else for that matter. After all, most folks believed insanity was a family curse that jumped from generation to generation.

"Was the mother always crazy?" Lancelot asked.

"She was when she was here." The manager took a draw on her cigarette before adding, "But I did ask Sunny about that one time. I wish I could remember what she told me."

"Will another five help clear your memory?"

"It might."

Lancelot retrieved another piece of paper decorated with Lincoln's picture. After the manager stuffed the bill into her pocket, she magically remembered what the investigator wanted to know.

"There was another child in the family. He disappeared, and when he never came back, Nina just cracked up. At least that's what Sunny told me."

"She didn't tell you what happened to him?"

"No."

"You said the mother's name was Nina?"

"Yeah?"

"Where did Sunny put her?"

"I told you, in a loony bin."

"Which one?"

She grinned. "Let's just say that it's a place where wildlife lives."

"Would another five help you remember the name?"

"I have my standards. I promised Sunny years ago I wouldn't tell anyone about where she'd taken her mother. I might be a drunk, but I'm not a person who breaks promises. If you can't figure out from what I just told you, then you're not much of a private cop."

Lancelot accepted the brushoff and pushed the conversation back to the former store clerk turned movie star. "So you liked Sunny?"

"I felt sorry for her. Having a mother like that was almost the same as being in prison. And I know a little about that. I was in a government hotel for a couple of years when I was younger. That's where I lost my teeth. There's nothing worse than being locked up. Except I beat up a woman, so I deserved what I got. I don't think Sunny did anything to draw her sentence."

"So, do you know what happened to Sunny?" Lancelot asked.

"No, when she left here, I lost track of her."

"I take it you don't watch the movies or read much."

"Never learned to read," she admitted and holding up her glass, she added, "There are better things to spend money on than picture shows."

Lancelot sadly nodded. "Thanks for your time."

"Thank you for the fifteen dollars."

Lancelot turned, strolled out of the building past the two women and to his car. Now he knew a bit more about Abby Force, but not enough to explain why people died when she was around. Thus, he needed to find out what happened to the mother. Three blocks from the Stargate Apartments, he spotted a phone booth. Parking at the curb, he got out and grabbed the phonebook. Turning to the yellow pages he scanned the listings for sanatoriums. One name fit the clue the old woman had spilled—Woodlands.

CHAPTER 33

Thursday, January 21, 1943
2:17 p.m.
Woodlands Sanatorium, Los Angeles, California

The Woodlands Sanatorium was on the outskirts of the city. The property covered several acres and was surrounded by a tall, chain-link fence. To gain entrance, Lancelot had to show his credentials and explain the reason for his visit. However, only after the main office had called Monument Studios was he allowed to drive down the long, winding lane that led to the large, yellow brick building.

Woodlands could have passed for a college dormitory except for the bars on the window and the guards at the door. The grounds were lush and well-groomed with flowers everywhere. The walks were clean, and a half a dozen benches were placed under century old trees. Yet among the birds and squirrels there was something missing—people.

After getting out of his car, Lancelot walked up six steps. At the door, a guard asked for his name and then checked his notebook.

"I see you were just added. You're supposed to go to Dr. Herman's office. To the left and two doors down the long hall."

"Thank you."

Lancelot was completely alone as he entered a large foyer. A staircase was in the back of the room, and there were halls to the left and right. The floor was wood, and the walls stone and the footsteps made by his size ten, black wingtip shoes echoed as he made his way to Herman's office. The door was solid oak and eight feet tall and when opened revealed a plump, gray-haired receptionist, likely fifty, typing.

She looked over her glasses and smiled. "May I help you?"

"I was told to see Dr. Herman. I'd like to visit a patient."

"We call them residents," the woman explained. "He popped out a couple of minutes ago and told me that when you arrived, you were to go right into his office." She smiled and pointed to a door to the left. Dr. William Herman had been painted in the middle of the frosted glass that made up the top of the entry. Five steps and a twist of the knob gained Lancelot entrance to an unfamiliar world with an even more unexpected host.

Herman was a small man, maybe six inches over five feet. He likely couldn't push the scale to one hundred and thirty after a five-course meal. His skin was dark caramel and his eyes black. He was middle-aged, maybe forty or even fifty, had no hair, and he was a Negro.

"Dr. Herman?"

"William Herman. And you must be Mr. Lancelot." He sized up his guest before adding, "You're not what I was expecting."

"Neither are you, sir."

Herman smiled. "You can be black and get a good job in an insane asylum. Not many doctors want to work in a place like this."

"I see."

"But," Herman added, "there is an expiration date. This environment is tough, and at some point I'll realize I need to walk away." He stood and moved closer to his guest. "I understand you want to talk to Nina Hoffman. May I ask why?"

"She has a daughter, and I'm doing background on her on a criminal matter."

"She's likely who pays the bills for Mrs. Hoffman's care, but I've been here six years, and I've never seen her. In fact, in my time here, you are Mrs. Hoffman's first visitor."

"That's sad," Lancelot said.

"In a facility filled with sad cases, she is one of the saddest. She's far too troubled to be on the streets but is still sane enough to realize the situation she's in. So, if you're looking for answers about anything, you likely aren't going to get them. She rattles on about stuff that makes no sense. My observations indicate she lives most of her days in the world of Mother Goose."

"Mother Goose?"

Herman nodded. "She constantly says things that seem to relate to nursery rhymes. Maybe spending her days with dragons and visiting castles is better than actually confronting her current reality in Woodlands or remembering a horrible past."

As Lancelot considered the verbal picture the doctor had just painted, he walked over to the barred window and looked out on the grounds. What he observed would have made a beautiful park—a place to take a family on a picnic—but there was not a soul on the grass or sitting under the scores of trees.

"We can't let them out," Herman explained. "Several years ago, one of the residents walked down to the pond and drowned. At that point, the owner made rules concerning the grounds. Sometimes a staff member will take a resident out one-on-one on his or her birthday, but that's pretty much it."

"Could there be anything worse," Lancelot asked, "than being surrounded by such beauty and never seeing it?" He turned to face his host and asked, "How do I meet Mrs. Hoffman?"

"I'll take you up to the third flood. She's on the south wing. Just follow me."

With Herman leading the way, the men walked back to the foyer, up two flights of stairs and a sharp right turn. Ten steps later, the doctor retrieved keys from his pocket and unlocked an imposing door. Before he opened the door, he looked back at Lancelot.

"Have you ever been in a place like this?"

"No, sir."

"Then you're in for a shock. The people behind this door have mental illnesses that range from deep psychosis to mental retardation. Some function like babies, some are non-verbal, and others babble all the time. There is constant noise twenty-four hours a day. The only reason you can't hear the din is because this wing is soundproof. When I open the door, the sound will likely seem deafening. Twenty-eight women live beyond this door, and they will likely never get beyond the entry until they die. In other words, the ones we keep here are hopeless cases and are serving a death sentence. Now are you sure you want to visit Mrs. Hoffman?"

"I have to," Lancelot explained.

"Then follow me."

The room was huge, likely sixty by eighty. There were rows of beds to the right and chairs to the left. Four women dressed in white stood in the middle of the room—their eyes constantly following the residents. A tall, thin woman approached Lancelot, studied him, and then began laughing. A young Negro, maybe twenty, was sitting to his left, her knees pulled up to her chest and crying. Half a dozen residents paced back and forth from wall to wall, and others were just sitting in chairs or their beds staring blankly at nothing. A white-haired lady in the back was dancing and screaming at the same time. And beyond her was a rail thin woman with a drawn face, long silver hair, and wild blue eyes, wearing slippers and dressed in a gray sack dress. She walked ten feet, turned, and walked back. All the time, she was muttering to herself. She held an old doll close to her chest.

"You've spotted Mrs. Hoffman," Herman shouted over the din. "She never walks more than six steps before turning around. I'm guessing she must have once lived in a room that only allowed her to take those six steps, which started a pattern that now rules her life."

"What about the doll?"

"It came here with her. Of course back then it had two arms. One of the other residents tore that limb off about three years ago. Why don't I walk you over and let you meet her."

Stepping around five residents who seemingly didn't even notice their presence, the men crossed the room.

When they stood in Hoffman's designated path, she stopped.

"Nina, this is Mr. Lancelot. He would like to talk to you."

The resident's sad eyes went to the guest. She looked him over for a few seconds and shook her head. "My husband would hate you, but he hates almost everyone that doesn't look like he does."

"Why would he hate me?" Lancelot asked.

"Because of the color of your skin."

"What does your husband look like?"

She sadly shook her head. "I haven't seen him in a long time." She paused and caressed the doll's face before glancing up and asking, "What year is it?"

"1943."

She frowned. "I thought it was thirty-four. But if what you say is correct, I haven't seen him for more than twenty years."

Herman nodded to Lancelot as if to say, "You have tapped into something, so keep going."

"Nina, where did you meet your husband?"

She grinned. "Once upon a time, we were in love and lived in a palace. We had servants and hosted parties. It was magical—people danced and laughed."

"Where was this?"

"In Europe. My father was an important man. I met Mr. Hoffman when my family lived in Austria."

"And you got married?" Lancelot asked.

"And we lived happily ever after—" she paused, frowned and pulled the baby closer— "until the war. Then he sent the children and me to America, and the magic was over. There were no balls, gowns, or carriage rides."

"What were your children's names?"

"My boy was John. He was blue-eyed and blond like his father, and our girl was Gale. John and I were close, but Gale was a daddy's girl. She really didn't like me. She fought everything I did. All she wanted to do was please him. She's the one who left me in this place. She couldn't wait to throw me away."

Hoffman pushed Lancelot to the side and began to pace again. As she walked, she constantly stroked the doll's head.

"Look at the floor," Herman suggested.

Obviously, her routine never changed. Over the years, Hoffman's pacing had worn a trail into the wood.

The doctor leaned closer and whispered, "Do you have what you need?"

"I want to ask a couple of more questions."

"Then stand in front of her and force her to stop."

Lancelot waited for Hoffman to make her U-turn and stepped forward. As soon as the woman halted, he spoke.

"What happened to John?"

Hoffman shook her head as tears welled up in her eyes. "Wolf blew down my door, beat me up, and took my boy to a castle to never return. I'll never live happily ever after." She then pushed Lancelot out of the way and began pacing again.

"That's all you're going to get," Herman said. "In fact, if her pattern holds, she won't say anything now for days. I suggest we go."

The two men left the room, the doctor locked the door and the pair walked down the stairs and to the office. Once there, Herman poured two cups of coffee and pointed to a couch and chair on the fair side of the room. Neither man spoke for several minutes. The investigator finally broke the silence.

"That was sobering. I don't think I realized people could be like that. I had an aunt we called crazy, but that was simply because of the way she dressed. She was nothing like those people up there."

"You never get used to it," Herman admitted. "What's sad is that deep inside each of those folks is a sane person trying to get out. If we just could find the keys to unlock those doors."

"What is the key? Do you have any idea?"

"For each of them, the solution would be different. Some of those folks were born with problems, and others had some kind of horrible experience that demanded their retreat from the real world. A few, like Nina Hoffman, suffered an injury that likely led to brain damage."

"An injury?" This news was unexpected.

"Yes," Herman explained. "She has scarring on her scalp. Her files tell us she suffered a serious head injury."

"When?"

"According to the report, in 1923."

"Then her daughter would have been seven or eight. I wonder how old her son was?"

"There is no record of a son," Herman explained. "When we deal with mental issues, we check those things out. We could find no birth records of a John Hoffman. In my opinion, she invented the son and somehow combined him with a favorite nursery rhyme from her youth. Just like her courtship was created in the same way. I would guess she was never married."

Lancelot nodded. If what Herman suggested was true, then Abby Force had several reasons for wanting to bury her past. She was illegitimate, and her mother was crazy. For a star who was now considered the ideal image of the American woman, both of those things might spell disaster. Yet all this bad news did provide the woman a viable alibi. Abby Force would never have intentionally shot Craig for fear of an investigation that would expose her past.

CHAPTER 34

Thursday, January 21, 1943
1:19 a.m.
Bacon Island, Pacific

The initial rush of discovering they were going to be rescued was quickly dashed by the sniper's shot. Then, after the USO troop hid in the trees, more bad news hit. The plane that was supposed to rescue them had engine trouble, and the Navy wouldn't be able to send another one until the next morning. Would they still be alive then? During a time when no one was shooting, the civilians made their way back to the plane where everyone seemed to feel a great deal more secure. In time, the atmosphere turned almost party-like.

Even though a bullet had rushed by her head, which guaranteed at least one sniper was very much alive, Meeker still wanted to go into the jungle and find the camp Sharp had talked about. She wanted to know how the Japanese had gotten this close to Honolulu without being spotted. The marines wanted no part of an expedition. Their job was to guard the USO troop, and they weren't going to desert their duty. Meeker spent most of Wednesday watching the trees. From time to time, she'd see a flash of light, like the sun reflecting off metal, but she never spotted a person, and there was no more gunfire.

In the back of the cabin, the seats were arranged where they faced each other. That's where Sharp, Force, and Strauss huddled, exchanging small talk and laughter. A row up, four band members played cards and shared a bottle. Around the rest of the plane, folks were reading, sleeping, or writing letters. The marines were still on the shore, armed and ready to give their lives if anyone charged from the jungle.

About midnight, when the rain slowed to a shower, one of the band members bummed a cigarette from Sharp. The guitar player took only three draws before snuffing out the smoke while complaining about the strong taste.

"You aren't as tough as you claim," Sharp teased. "If you think that's bad, you should taste a Russian cigarette."

As the wave of security swept through the cabin, the three-man film crew sent to document Force's USO tour got the idea this was a good time to grab some interviews. For a couple of hours, they moved from person to person recording insights and thoughts on everything from the performances to the dogfight that forced the Chuck Hawk down. In time, their focus shifted to Sharp's charge into the jungle. While everyone had great things to say about the captain selfless act, Force sang the loudest praise. She made Sharp sound like the greatest American warrior of all time.

"He's everything a woman could want," she explained. "He has looks, brains, and power. He runs like an Olympic track star and displays the courage of those who win Medals of Honor. He's caring and strong and knows just what to say to calm a frightened woman's heart. He represents the very best of what it is to be an American. I'm looking forward to getting to know him even better."

After Force's testimonial, the crew approached Meeker. As the cameraman set up in front of her chair, the bespectacled director posed the same question he'd asked Force. "How would you describe Captain Sharp's heroism?"

"He did what he was trained to do," Meeker stoically replied.

"Would you like to add anything more?"

"No, I think Miss Force has pretty much taken care of the details."

As the crew wandered off, Force got up from her chair and plopped down in the one next to Meeker. Though she'd been without sleep for a couple of days, the woman still retained the natural beauty that had pushed her to the top of her profession. But as Teresa Bryant had once told Meeker, "The most beautiful snakes are often the most deadly."

"What's the reason for the visit?" Meeker asked.

"Michael told me the plane should be here to pick us up in a couple of hours."

"That's nice."

"And the troop's decided to continue to the next scheduled show. So rather than head directly back to Los Angeles, we're going to entertain for one more day."

"The servicemen will appreciate that."

"What about you?" Force prodded more than asked. "I figured you'd want to go back home."

"I was assigned to go along with you. I'll stick with the job until it's over."

Force leaned closer. "You're not happy, are you?"

"What makes you say that?"

"Well, for starters, Michael's spending all his time with me."

"I don't really care," Meeker answered. "I don't find him interesting."

"Don't you mean that you're threatened by him? Isn't that it?"

Meeker all but swallowed her tongue. The actress had grown so delusional she believed she'd stolen Sharp from Meeker, and for some reason, she now had to lord that over her. While her gut begged her to put Force in her place, Meeker's heart demanded she play it cool.

"Listen, Abby. I'm happy you have found a friend not only because it has made you feel safer during this challenging trip, but because his being with you has made my job a lot easier."

Force chuckled. "What a bunch of baloney. The reason you didn't have anything to say to the film crew is that you're jealous."

"What?" The woman was now coming close to stepping over the line.

"You've always been the most beautiful woman in the room until I came along. And you were always the bravest in the room until Michael entered your world. He stole your glory when he saved us from the Japs, and then he returned to my arms not yours. This trip brought you back down to earth."

Meeker cocked an eyebrow. Why was the actress trying so hard to bruise her ego? What did she hope to gain? Was she that fragile? Strauss had hinted that Force could be unstable—was this another sign? Or maybe she felt in this world women had to compete for everything from screen time to the affections of men. What was her reason?

"Miss Meeker?"

Meeker looked from Force to the plane's pilot.

"Miss Meeker, we got a message on the portable radio. It's for you."

"What did it say?"

"Don't blame me if it doesn't make sense. I swear I made them repeat it three times."

"Just give it to me."

"Morning Song dug the root."

Meeker smiled. At least Bryant had accomplished something.

"Miss Meeker," Gleeson asked, "does that have something to do with a new record?"

"More like an old hit that needed to be broken," she explained. "I now have one less thing to do and one fewer thing to worry about."

"Oh," the man replied. "And the rescue plane will be here in two hours. You'll have a new crew. My men and I are staying here until the boat arrives to take this crate back to Pearl."

"Thanks for saving our neck on the landing," Meeker said.

"No problem," he answered with an informal salute.

As Gleeson walked off, Force asked, "What was that all about?"

"You heard, you figure it out."

"You're a small woman, Helen Meeker. You think you are all that, but you're not. I wouldn't want to play you in a movie. No one likes a film where the heroine doesn't get the man. That spells box office disaster."

"Why am I so under your skin?" Meeker asked. "Was it because I sang one song on the tour, or was it the GIs asked for my autograph and wanted pictures with me too? Surely you're not fragile?"

"Get serious. When it comes to attracting the attention of the GIs, I outscored you there ten to one."

"Okay then, all that's left is you believe I'll find the motive for your purposely shooting Matt Craig."

Force's smug look evaporated and was replaced with one reflecting fear. Suddenly, there were no more caustic words tumbling from her lips and no hate in her eyes. And for a moment, Meeker was almost glad she'd been forced to reveal the elephant that had been invisible throughout this entire trip.

"You can't prove anything," Force finally whispered. "We all know it was the prop man."

"Those who proclaim they have nothing to hide always do." Meeker calmly replied.

Having had her wings clipped, Force pushed out her chair and returned to her spot beside Sharp.

Meeker watched the actress shoot a nervous glance at Strauss before leaning against the plane's wall and closing her eyes. A USO tour, a crash-landing, sniper fire, and two nights on an almost deserted island, and Meeker still didn't know Sharp, Force, and Strauss any better than when the trip began. But at least there was no Gertrude Root around to haunt her anymore.

CHAPTER 35

Saturday, January 23, 1943
7:43 a.m.
Spencer Field, Spencer, Iowa

The DC-3 had once flown for American Airways before being purchased by the military for troop transport. Now, the plane was essentially a C-47 with all the comforts of home. And after days with little sleep, the plane's deeply padded seats most appealed to Teresa Bryant. The crash had left her bruised and sore, and the FBI interrogation had been four hours of frustration. So, no matter what was lying ahead for her in Los Angeles would seem like a vacation compared to the last few days.

A lone woman on a plane filled with more than thirty military officers always created a stir, but when that female possessed exotic beauty combined with an air of confidence, men lined up just to welcome her onto the flight. Only the pilot demanding people get ready for takeoff gave Bryant a break and pushed the passengers into their assigned seats. She dropped into 3A while 3B was filled with a tall, wide-shouldered major with high cheekbones, jet-black hair, and eyes that matched. After the plane was in the air and headed west, he leaned closer and introduced himself.

"I'm Charlie One-Horse."

His voice was deep and possessed a flow that made his words seem to float like clouds in a blue sky. The twinkle in his right eye belied a charm that likely had wowed women in more places than Bryant cared to guess. And his obvious confidence was as intoxicating as any aged liquor.

"Nice to meet you. Major, I'm Teresa Bryant."

"I was expecting something a bit more lyrical," he quipped.

"My Caddo name is Morning Song, but I don't use it much. I'm guessing you're Sioux."

"You have a good eye."

"Not really, my observation was based on the fact the duffle bag you brought on board listed a hometown of Fort Yates, North Dakota. The Great Sioux Reservation is in that area."

"So," One-Horse acknowledged, "You have a scout's eye and a chief's mind. Now, not that I'm complaining, but how did a civilian woman get on a military flight?"

"Let's just say I know the right people."

"We could say that, but that's not an answer."

Bryant shrugged and glanced out the window at the snow-covered landscape below. Flying was a lot more relaxing when you weren't sitting the pilot's chair. Life was also better when you got to be yourself rather than pretending to be the meanest woman in the world.

"Is this your first time to fly?"

Bryant turned back to One-Horse and laughed. "I've logged more flying time in the past few months than most eagles." She was tempted to add that some of that had been in a pilot's seat but opted not to give away too many secrets.

"If that's true then you're likely important enough to grab a seat on this goose. Can I ask what you do?"

"You can ask," she replied.

"But you're not going to tell," he laughed.

She grinned and turned back to look at the world beneath her. Five silent minutes crawled by before she posed her first question.

"What do you do, Major?"

"I'm in intelligence. I'm normally in Washington. I went into the military right out of college."

"What school?"

"None of the obvious choices for Indians—I actually went to the University of Illinois."

"And you assured me you were a Sioux."

A confused look was quickly replaced by a smile. "Morning Song, you're quick! Or should I call you Teresa? Yes, I guess I am a Sioux who became a member of the Illini tribe."

"A good recovery," she said, laughing. "And on my name, let's stick with Miss Bryant."

"Ouch. Are you married?"

"No, hence the Miss."

"It's not nice to make an intelligence officer look dumb," he shot back.

"I've been doing that for years," she assured him. "It's become one of my few hobbies."

"We have several stops," One-Horse said. "Where are you going?"

"Los Angeles. My partners are already there working on a case. I had to close up another matter before I could join them. Enough about me, have you seen any duty at the front?"

His smile evaporated, his body tensed, and his gaze drifted toward the ceiling. "I was in the Pacific for a year. Seemed to spend more time evacuating than fighting. If I was flown to a location, the Japs ran us over. I got shot in Midway. They sent me back to Honolulu and from there to Washington. That's when I got assigned to intelligence."

"Do you miss combat?" Bryant asked.

"No one in their right mind misses combat. I saw too many friends die. I pushed my hands into so many wounds trying to stop the bleeding that I'll never get all the blood washed off."

"There are ghosts that haunt me," she admitted.

He turned to face her. "Really?"

"Yeah."

"I wish I could be more laid back," One-Horse said. "I went through officer's school with a guy who nothing bothered. He played the game of life like he had nothing to lose. And, as he had no family, perhaps he really didn't have anything to lose. He almost died in the Philippines, but somehow he escaped the Japs and made it back to our side. He's supposed come to work in Washington in the next month or so."

"How long did you know him?" Bryant asked.

"Off and on for six or seven years. Not only did we go through basic together, but he and I had a lot of the same assignments before the war."

"So, I'm guessing you're looking forward to seeing him again."

"I'll enjoy talking to him," One-Horse admitted, "but seeing him might not do me much good. He was pretty messed up, and a Hollywood surgeon rebuilt his face. I've heard he doesn't look like he used to. But there are certain things doctors can't change."

"Like what?" Bryant asked.

"He was smart as whip, but clumsy as a lumbering bear. He'd trip over his own feet. If you tossed him a ball, he'd drop it. We used to have football games back at the base, and he was always the last guy picked. But when you played poker with him, he was lethal. It was almost like he could read your mind."

"What's his name?"

"Michael Sharp, but I gave him an Indian handle. I never used his real name."

"What did you hang on him?"

"Dull Knife. He hated that name."

Bryant smiled. She could imagine that a proud American officer would not want to be known for lacking a sharp cutting edge.

"You want some coffee?" One-Horse asked. "They brought some on the plane. It's in the back."

"No, just get some for yourself. I haven't had much sleep in the last few days. I think I'll just ball up like a squirrel and let the world fade away for a while."

"Sweet dreams, Morning Song."

CHAPTER 36

Sunday, January 24, 1943
11:14 a.m.
Second Baptist Church, Los Angeles, California

Feeling a need to focus on something other than the case, Napoleon Lancelot drove his rental car from the Roosevelt Hotel to 1214 Griffin Avenue and the Second Baptist Church. For the first time in what seemed like forever, he walked into a world where he didn't stand out. On this morning, the hundreds surrounding him all shared his heritage.

As he chose a seat in a pew four rows from the back, he studied the inside of the huge brick building. The sanctuary brilliantly reflected traditional black culture and western heritage. The main part of the auditorium had the feel of Los Angeles. With a tall ceiling, the room was bright, and the sun poured through high stained-glass windows creating an atmosphere of California warmth. The pews, while wooden and unpadded, were much more comfortable than the homemade benches Lancelot remembered from childhood.

The hymnals were well worn but hardcover and filled with songs he'd learned as a child. Tindley and Gabriel, two of the pioneers of black gospel music, could be found along with the names of Watts and Luther. Yet the pulpit and choir reflected the church of the south. Situated above the congregation, the area was reset and almost a room to itself. The unique design served to draw eyes toward the pastor and made worship seem much more important and intimate. He could well imagine Sister Rosetta Tharpe raising her voice and filling the room with the sounds of Heaven come down to earth. Though he didn't know a soul who sat in the pews around, he felt so good to be home.

After singing several classic old gospel songs, Lancelot sat down and listened to a new composition by Thomas A. Dorsey. The anthem, "Peace in the Valley," reflected a universal message of man's struggle to find peace in a world troubled by suffering and pain. While the lyrics offered hope, the theme pushed Lancelot into a dark place. At this moment, peace and justice seemed more like myths than things to be hoped or prayed for. The fact was he could never see the lion lying down with the lamb. Perhaps the sermon would be more uplifting.

On this winter Sunday, the pastor had chosen a passage from Galatians about the need to run hard and finish life's race. As the man dug deeply into the Scripture, Lancelot thought back to his visit to the asylum and Nina Hoffman. How sad to be lost in a world where nursery rhymes had become real. As he mourned a woman's pain and suffering, a long-forgotten memory fought its way into the open, and suddenly he was transported to a time and place where he'd met another person seen as crazy by the world.

When Lancelot was a small body, there had been a man who aimlessly walked the city streets pulling a child's wagon. The locals called him Crazy Ralph, but no one knew his real name. They simply hung the handle on him because he seemed so out of touch with reality. Ralph was a big man, with broad shoulders and huge hands, who always wore bib overalls and white shirt, and his life's work seemed to be to sift through trash trying to find something that had value. The treasure could be a broken toy, a busted shovel, or an old tire. He'd place the item onto his wagon and keep walking until he found something else.

The kids were scared of Crazy Ralph, while the adults ignored him. When Lancelot was about ten, he decided to follow the old man and see where he lived. Staying fifty feet behind, the boy mirrored Ralph's steps for five hours. Tired and thirsty, Lancelot was about to give up when the big man made a turn toward the railroad tracks. There he dropped the wagon's handle, stretched and smiled. And there was home—an old boxcar surrounded by piles of the treasure Ralph had claimed out of people's trash. Lancelot was so overwhelmed by the mounds of stuff—some stacked more than ten feet high—that he failed to notice Ralph walking toward him. When the man spoke, the startled boy froze in his tracks.

"You looking for something, kid?"

Too scared to talk, Lancelot just shook his head. At that moment, he was sure he was about to die.

"Well, kid, if you were looking for something, you'd likely find it here. Would you like a cup of water? It's a hot day, and you've been trailing me for a long time."

Though all his instincts told him to run, Lancelot's curiosity begged him to stay, so he followed Ralph through a maze of trash to the boxcar. Old crates that once held car parts had been nailed together as stairs and once inside the relic that had been tossed away by the railroad, the boy was greeted by crudely repaired furniture, an old stove and stacks of newspapers. There was also a sleeping gray cat curled up on a threadbare couch.

"That's Midas," Ralph explained. "He was here when I moved in. So, I guess this is his place not mine." He dipped some water out of a wooden bucket and poured it into a cup. "Drink this before you dry up and blow away."

Napoleon took the dented metal cup and drank. As he did, Ralph sized him up.

"Now that you've found out I don't bite, were you looking for something?"

"No, sir."

"Then you're about the only person I've ever known that wasn't looking for something. That's what a man does—he just starts looking for things that bring him purpose. He keeps right on looking until the day he dies. Mostly, he doesn't find anything that he wants to hold onto. And that's what I do, I just pick up what the people once wanted so badly but grew tired of."

"Why?"

"Goes way back. As a kid, I didn't know my daddy, and my momma didn't want me. She threw me away when I was about your age. The only way I had to live was by finding food in the trash. That's where I found my toys too. And other folks' trash built me every home I've ever had. In time, the kid no one wanted grew into the man no one cared about. But trash has given me more than you can believe."

"How?"

"I learned how to read from the books others threw out. I learned how to fix things and combine stuff in ways that were almost artistic. The things I've collected over the past sixty years have entertained me, taught me, and kept me warm. And nothing in all of this cost me anything but time."

Lancelot shook his head. "They say you're crazy." As soon as the words were out of his mouth, the boy wished he hadn't voiced them. He was about to turn tail and run when the old man laughed.

"Yeah, they probably do. But I know more about the stars than they do. I can build what I need from what others toss away. I have traveled the world in books. And while I don't have a dime, I don't owe a dime to anyone either.

"You see boy, my mother was born a slave. In a very real way, she never shook those chains. She always felt like she wasn't good enough. But look at me. I don't know anyone, white or black, who's as free as I am." He paused and grinned. "Do you have a bicycle?"

"No."

"Every boy needs a bike. You follow me."

Lancelot trailed Ralph out of the boxcar past several piles of old washing machines to a spot where a dozen or more bicycles stood. The fenders didn't match the frames, but all of them appeared to be good working condition.

"Take your pick and ride it home," Ralph suggested.

"Why would you give me a bike?" a confused Lancelot asked.

"For two reasons. The first is that you need to understand that trash, like any person, has value. Something good can be done with what others don't want and there is also something of value in people that others dismiss as strange or even crazy."

"And the second?"

"What's your name?"

"Lancelot."

"That's a good name. Lance, the second is that anyone who shows the interest to come visit a lonely soul needs to be rewarded for that effort. You see, while you don't have a bike, I don't have a friend. Maybe today we both gained something we wanted."

For the next five years, ten months and seven days, Lancelot continued to visit Crazy Ralph. During that time, he learned about the stars, the great works of literature, and the value of trash. Lancelot also brought a lot of his friends to the boxcar and they left with bicycles, wagons, and toys, and also a much different perspective on life.

Ralph wasn't crazy; his life did have purpose. In time, people quit calling him Crazy Ralph and gave him a new handle—the Poor Man's Santa Claus. And when he died, more than five hundred people came to his funeral all because a little boy wanted to know where a crazy man lived.

As the preacher droned on, the old memory faded away, and Lancelot's thoughts turned to the woman he'd recently met. Nina Hoffman seemed to speak in nursery rhymes. Or did she? What if what she told him made sense? What if everything she been telling those at the asylum was real? What if she wasn't crazy but just hard to understand? What if she had her own lingo just like Alison Meeker?

Pulling out a hymnbook, he retrieved a pencil from his suit pocket, grabbed a bulletin and began to rethink his visit. As he put things in a new light, he jotted down some notes.

If Hoffman did travel in Europe as a child, if her father did work over there, then she could have seen castles and might have even been to parties in large homes. She could have met a husband there. Perhaps they had a son while they lived in Europe, and that was why there were no birth records. Maybe the husband did move Nina to Los Angeles for safety during World War I. Abby could have been born here, and maybe the reason folks thought she was illegitimate was because the father was no longer with Nina. Perhaps her husband had come back after the war and beaten her, causing a brain injury. And thanks to male pride, maybe he took her son back to his home. If all of that were true, then her son might still be alive. And if he was, he might just be the key to bringing the woman peace of mind. Perhaps seeing him could restore her sanity.

As the choir began to sing and the congregation stood, Lancelot realized that even if everything he'd just written down was true, he'd have a hard time proving his premise? There was a war raging in Europe, and finding birth and death records would be impossible now. Perhaps this was one mystery that couldn't be solved until the message found in the choir special finally came true. But would Nina Hoffman live long enough for there to be peace in the valley and everywhere else?

CHAPTER 37

Monday, January 25, 1943
9:10 a.m.
Roosevelt Hotel, Los Angeles, California

After checking in at the front desk, a worn-out Teresa Bryant walked up the stairs to the suite the team was using as a base of operations. Though she had been issued a key, she opted to knock. Exactly ten seconds later, Lancelot opened the door.

"Teresa! So good to see you! Do Indians hug?"

"This one does." After the warm embrace, Bryant asked, "Has Helen made it back from the USO tour? I can't wait to hear about that."

"She called from the airport. She's in a cab headed this way right now." Bryant glanced around the suite, and as if reading her mind, Lancelot pointed to a door on her left. "Helen took the room on the right. That one's waiting for you. The captain and I are down the hall."

"Captain?"

"Yeah, we've had a member of the U.S. Army assigned to us. They want Helen to tell them if he's a good fit for the intelligence department. He went on the USO tour with her, and I can't tell you how much I've enjoyed my time away from him."

"Judging from the tone of your voice, you're not fond the captain."

"Teresa, I'm used to racist pigs, but he's taken that attitude further. He walks around as if he is God's gift to the world. Just like he believes everyone should bow down to him. I have to really exert an effort to keep myself from knocking him into tomorrow." Lancelot shrugged and added, "What does that mean anyway? Knocking him into tomorrow? I've said that for years and never thought about what the meaning is."

"If you hit someone hard enough," Bryant explained, "they don't wake up until the next day."

"Okay, now it makes sense. By the way, I read between the lines in your telegram. I'm guessing the phrase about digging up roots meant you found Gertrude."

"Yeah, let me put my bags up and I'll give you the details."

Bryant deposited her luggage on the bed and peeked into the mirror. She immediately wished she hadn't. She looked as if there were black sidewall tires under her eyes. If she didn't start getting some sleep, she was actually going to look her age. She was reaching for some concealer when she heard Meeker's voice. Figuring her partner was likely as tired as she was, she tossed her makeup bag back on the bed and returned to the suite's living area.

"Well, Miss Meeker, how were things on your exotic Pacific junket?"

"Divine," she replied, her sarcastic edge showing. "I can't begin to tell you how overrated frequent baths, hot food, and mattresses are."

"Try taking on a South American gang and hanging out in ghost towns in the Rocky Mountains," Bryant countered.

"But you got Root," Meeker said.

"Actually, I just found her—she got herself. Cyanide's not an easy way to check out of this world."

"You confirmed her death?" Meeker demanded.

"I watched it. Someday, I'll tell you the whole story, but it's too crazy to believe right now. Here's a preview … it involved a German plan to base some forces in South and Central America and have them sneak into the US for guerilla raids."

"And?" Meeker asked.

"Well, the FBI has two guys in custody that should shed some light on that. Oh, and by the way, in my spare time, I took out the Kansas City Mob and learned how to fly at C-47." Bryant grinned. "I didn't learn how to land the plane, but I got pretty good when I was in the air."

"You crashed a plane?" Lancelot asked.

"Yes, the parts are spread over most of Iowa. What did you do? Can you top that?"

"I visited an insane asylum."

"As a patient?" Meeker jabbed.

"No, it's where I found Abby Force's mother. Seems the actress placed Nina Hoffman there before Hollywood came calling."

"Hoffman?" Meeker asked.

"Yeah, back then Abby was Gale Hoffman. The experts think her mother is crazy beyond repair. They see her as being trapped in a fantasy world. I'm not sure I buy into it."

Meeker grimly nodded. "It might the case. I actually saw some signs of her daughter being unstable on the trip. In her defense, the tour was loaded with pressure, and when we were forced down by a quartet of Zeroes on an uncharted island, things got even hotter. Even a combat veteran would have had problems hanging onto reality facing that challenge."

Lancelot pulled a chair away from the table and sat down. "What about our dear captain?"

"He might have saved my life," Meeker admitted, "though that episode was too strange to really figure out. He did perform heroically on the island. He will no doubt be given another medal in the near future."

"Sorry to hear that," Lancelot grumbled. "I can think of a few other things he deserves much more than that."

Meeker frowned. "You're not alone in your dislike for Michael Sharp."

An exhausted Bryant found the entire bent of the conversation uninteresting until her partner mentioned the name Sharp. This had to be the same man One-Horse had been talking about.

"Helen," Bryant cut in, "this Captain Sharp—why are you working with him?"

"I'm evaluating his readiness to serve in Army Intelligence in DC. His whole unit was killed in the Philippines on December 8, 1941, and he managed to escape, hide in the jungle, and worked his way back to us."

"Did he have his face rebuilt?"

"Yeah," Meeker replied, "How did you know?"

"I was on the plane with one of his friends from Officer Training School. He told me all about Sharp. He made him sound like a nice guy."

"He didn't know him very well," Lancelot offered, "or war has changed him a great deal. By the way, something really good did happen to me."

"They didn't keep you in the asylum," Bryant teased.

"No, we went to the Hollywood Canteen and I met Lena Horne and Hattie McDaniel. Lena even autographed a matchbook for me. Want to see it?"

"Sure," Bryant replied with a weary smile.

Lancelot reached into his pocket and retrieved his treasure. Rather than toss the book, he got up, walked over to Bryant and gently placed it in her hand. She studied the front. There was an "HC" printed over stars and stripes on the cover. Flipping to the back, she saw three stars and the words, "Hollywood Canteen" printed in red script. At the bottom was an address … 1451 N. Cahuenga Blvd.

"I don't see an autograph."

"Open it up," Lancelot directed.

At the top was printed "Thinking of You, Kay and Georgia Kyser. Under that, written in blue ink, was "To Nap—Lena Horne."

"Isn't that something?" Lancelot asked.

Without taking her eyes off the matchbook, Bryant nodded. The autograph was nice but what was written down near the fold was what grabbed her interest. There were two letters followed by five numbers.

Bryant walked over and set the still open matchbook on the table before reaching into her pocket and pulling out what had been Gertrude's Root's matchbook. Opening the cover, she read what was written there, "GA 36723." She then looked back to Lancelot's souvenir. "Well, I'll be."

"You'll be what?" Meeker asked.

Bryant shrugged. "The matchbook I'm holding was one that I took from Root after she died. 'GA 36723' had been penciled inside right next to the fold." She looked toward

Lancelot. "Did Miss Horne write these letters and numbers down?"

"No, they were on the book when I handed it to her."

"Napoleon, Helen—not only do the letters and numbers match, but the writing is the same on both. Note the loop in the G and the line through the 7. Where did you get the matchbook?"

"I took it from Force's assistant," Lancelot explained.

"And she got it from a man at the Canteen," Meeker added. "What do you think it means?"

Bryant walked over to a desk and pulled out a phone book. She opened the directory and scanned the exchanges. "In Los Angeles, the GA exchange is short for Garfield. This is likely a phone number."

As Meeker and Lancelot looked on, Bryant picked up the phone and dialed. A woman answered on the fourth ring.

"Hello?"

"Is this Billie Jo?" Bryant asked.

"No, this is Dora Yorkshire."

"So there's no Billie Joe there?"

"No, there never has been. I've lived at 1223 Garfield since I moved out here from Brooklyn in '23. My husband and I have raised three children in this house. There's never been a Yorkshire even visit here."

"Do you know Abby Force?"

"The actress?"

"Yes."

"Of course not. But I met Joan Crawford once."

"I'm sorry, I must have dialed the wrong number."

"That's okay."

Bryant set the phone down.

"Did you get anything?" Meeker asked.

"I have no idea. The woman sounded completely honest. But I think we need to check up on the backgrounds of Dora Yorkshire and her husband and see if we can connect them to Gertrude Root. The fact both of these matchbooks have the same number written by the same hand has to mean something." She looked toward Lancelot. "What do we know about Force's assistant? The one who was given the matchbook."

"Not much," he admitted. "Just the general stuff we got from the studio. Mattie Strauss is a failed actress who looks a lot like Force. When she didn't find any parts, she drifted into work at the studio as Force's double and assistant."

"I can assure you she's cool under fire," Meeker added, "but I can't get a handle on if she's protective of Force or jealous. You rarely see the actress without Strauss—kind of a strange, almost symbiotic relationship."

"Then let's make some calls and do some digging," Bryant suggested. "Maybe Yorkshire can tie this case to the one I just closed.

"Can we wait until tomorrow?" Meeker asked. "I'm exhausted."

"I need to sleep for twenty-four hours," Bryant assured her. "Why don't we call it a night, get some sleep, and then tomorrow, we can exchange notes. Maybe more than just the matchbooks connect in our cases."

"Tell you what," Lancelot suggested, "I'm well rested and I'm hitting brick walls on digging into Nina Hoffman's past, so I'll see what I can find on Strauss."

"Let's meet right here for breakfast," Meeker suggested. "How about nine?"

"I'll be here," Bryant replied.

"As will I," Lancelot added. "By the way, where is Captain Sharp?"

Meeker smiled and cocked her eyebrow. "He's with Force and Strauss. He volunteered to make sure they were safe tonight. So, I'm guessing he will be with them, or should I say Force, all day and all night. And before you ask, I have no idea what that means."

CHAPTER 38

Monday, January 25, 1943
5:15 p.m.
Modern Movie Magazine **Offices, Los Angeles, California**

After striking out at two newspaper morgues, Napoleon Lancelot opted to walk in unannounced to the office of Scoop Melborne, the city's top entertainment reporter. Melborne, a small man with icy blue eyes and wavy red hair, was sitting at his desk so deeply involved in his research he didn't even note the investigator's entrance. Only when Lancelot cleared his throat did the reporter look up.

"Decked out in your blue suit and dapper hat, you look like an intelligent man. That likely means you'll have some advice for me on a problem I'm dealing with." Melborne paused, taking a second look at his unexpected guest. "Let me guess. You're a movie agent representing colored actors or a record plugger for a blues label."

"Actually, I'm an investigator …"

Melborne cut him off before he could finish. "That says it all." The writer waved his hands over a water glass and acted as through he was closely studying the liquid. He continued the ritual for a few seconds before looking up and announcing, "I've looked into the glass, and I see all and know all. The spirits tell me you were named for a famous ruler and a fictional knight and that you possess knowledge far beyond most men."

Lancelot grinned. "I'm impressed. What else do the spirits say?"

"Sit down and let me look back into the magic glass."

After the investigator grabbed a chair in front of the desk and eased onto it, Melborne continued. "You are working on the case of an actor who should be dead but isn't and an actress whose past is as mysterious as the roles she plays on screen."

"You seem to see all," Lancelot noted.

Melborne leaned back in his chair and shrugged. "So, Mr. Lancelot, what brings you to my modest office?"

"Perhaps you could look into your glass one more time and tell me."

"The water is out of magic."

"Seriously, how did you know who I was?"

Melborne leaned forward and put his elbows on the desk. "There's not much that goes on in this town I don't know. I have my spies in every front office at every studio and they keep me informed. Matt Craig was not hurt in an accident, rather Abby Force shot him. The incident was likely an accident, but for the moment a prop man is getting the blame. Seriously, I had no clue as to your identity until you said you were an investigator. The only Negro private eye in L.A. is a part of Helen Meeker's team. So, when you told me what you did, it didn't take a brain surgeon to put two and two together."

"Let's get back to what you said about our case," Lancelot said. "If you know what really happened with the accident then why haven't you written about it? It's a heck of a story."

"Some yarns don't need to be put in the public eye. We don't want to ruin the illusion that is Hollywood." He grinned and added, "Besides, Monument is paying me not to write the story."

"So you're a scribe who can be bought?" Lancelot asked.

"We pretty much all have our price, up to a point. Nothing would hold me back from that story if I thought someone intentionally tried to kill Craig, but if it really was an accident then it helps the business not to share that news with the public. Now let's talk about you."

"There's not much to say."

"Really. From what I've learned, you're a college-educated Negro with more brains and skills than most men, yet you still can't get jobs you deserve because of the color of your skin. That's actually a real crime not an accident."

"It's a fact of life," Lancelot replied. "It's my job to change perceptions and thanks to getting this gig with Helen Meeker, I've been given a chance to surprise a few people."

"Maybe you'll surprise a few more. Now, why did you come into my little world and surprise me? What can a movie gossip spinner do for you?"

Lancelot took a breath and crossed his arms. "I came here with hopes that you'd have information the newspapers don't."

Melborne winked. "Of course, I do."

"Then, Mr. Melborne—"

"Scoop."

"Okay, Scoop, I know a lot about Abby Force and have a file filled with nuggets about Matt Craig. I've talked to the prop man, Calvin Coggins, but I'm drawing blanks on Mattie Strauss."

"Ah, mysterious Mattie." Melborne touched his fingers together in front of his face. "Strauss is a bitter woman. She's like a hundred others who wanted to be in the spotlight, but the only way she's managed to experience that glow is by standing in Abby Force's shadow. Though she says all the right things, she hates everything about this town. She feels she's been treated unfairly, and she honestly thinks she's more talented and beautiful than Force and most of the other actresses in Hollywood. The fact this whole town has rejected her eats at Mattie like a cancer. That's made even worse because on a daily basis, she sees the benefits of stardom and knows she's just borrowing them … the stuff she has is not hers—she didn't earn it—it's all because of Force."

"If she's so unhappy, why doesn't she go home?"

Melborne leaned back in his chair and looked at several signed photos hanging on his wall. "For most people in this business, Hollywood is a drug. Even if they hate what the city does to them and how it treats them, they can't give it up." His eyes returned to his guest. "But for Mattie, it's a bit different. Even if she could give up the drug, even if she found a cure, she has no home to return to.

"Mr. Lancelot, do you know what happens to the women who have no family and come out here hoping for stardom?"

"No," Lancelot admitted. "I've never thought much about it."

"The road is pretty much the same for all of them—just depends upon which fork they take. One leads to suicide, another drug or alcohol addiction, a third takes them to prostitution, and a fourth puts them in menial jobs that pay nothing. Even those that don't take their own lives almost always die young. The cause listed on the death certificate might be an overdose or liver failure, but the real cause is a broken spirit. Except for a select few, this town in a very cruel place."

"You said Strauss had no family—where did she come from?"

"Let me start off by telling you this. You likely haven't been able to dig up any details about her early life because Mattie Strauss is just an invention. The name Strauss likely came from the famous classical composer, and who knows where she grabbed Mattie. The person now known as Mattie Strauss didn't pick up that handle until 1934, before that she was Ruby Hoffman."

Lancelot was shocked. The last name he'd expected to hear was Hoffman. Was that the reason Strauss and Force looked so much alike? Had the boy Nina claimed was taken from her actually been a girl?

"It seems by your expression that news stuns you somehow," Melborne noted.

"In a way, it does. Before we get back to Strauss, what can you tell me about Abby Force?"

"Oh, I take it you already knew that Abby Force was once Gale Hoffman."

"Yeah."

"Well, while each woman has a similar story and the same last name, that's where the connection ends. Force is most likely an illegitimate child born and raised by a woman with serious mental issues—another story I've never printed. It's difficult to track down where Strauss was born. I've heard New York, St. Louis, England, France, and even Germany. Wherever it was, her family was out of the picture real early. Her mother gave her up when she was a toddler, and she was raised in an orphanage in St. Louis, which leads me to believe she was likely born there. When she turned eighteen, she left the home, dropped her real name, and came out West."

"I'm impressed with what you know," Lancelot said. "And I'm even more impressed with how you can remember without notes."

"I have a photographic memory, and I built a file on Strauss just in case she ever became a star. But the effort was a waste of time—I've never written a paragraph on her that didn't include Abby Force."

"And yet," Lancelot said, "she just keeps hanging on."

"Yeah, I know her well enough to realize she's sold on the Hollywood myth. Like hundreds of others, she believes deep down inside her life will have a happy ending."

"Why does she still cling to that?"

"Mr. Lancelot, did you ever see *42nd Street*?"

"No."

"If you'll spare me a bit of time, I'll tell you about it. Warner Bros. made the film about a decade ago, just as talkies were hitting full stride. In that day and time, everyone wanted to see big splashy musicals and Hollywood did what it always does … made so many of them people got tired of seeing them.

"The film I'm telling you about set the mold for all the others that followed. *42nd Street* was also a launching platform for some great stars. Dick Powell and Ginger Rogers were background players who rose to the top after appearing in this flick, and the third lead, George Brent, has gone on to become a solid if bland male lead.

But the two main stars were fading even as the cameras rolled. Bebe Daniels is now out of the business and all but forgotten, and Warner Baxter has fallen so far he's making cheap formula films that play before the main feature. You know, the kind of movies people come in halfway through and don't care.

"Well, *42nd Street*, like so many others, was about Broadway. The female lead in a stage production was a pain, and when she pushes too hard and too far, an unknown kid from the sticks is forced to replace her. Strauss sees herself as that unknown kid and that's why she's a vulture, always circling around Abby Force, hoping and praying that Force dies at the beginning of a major production and the studio has invested too much in the film and the lead's wardrobe to shelve the flick. So Mattie gets called in and finally become a big star! It's a crock but she believes it."

That positioned Strauss with a motive worth investigating, but the Hoffman name was still bugging Lancelot. He had to know more.

"Scoop, did you find out any more about Mattie's parents?"

The writer smiled. "I have contacts in St. Louis who will dig up information for money. As I recall, it only cost ten dollars for me to get a copy of the girl's records from the orphanage. Mattie's mother was Greta Vogel who immigrated to the US from Germany after World War I. Greta didn't share who the father was, and the form says she was not married and never had been, but I'm guessing, as the child's last name was Hoffman, the dad must have carried that name too. And, as I discovered, with so many Germans having settled in the Midwest, it's a very common name."

"Scoop, you mentioned that Strauss was a vulture waiting for Force to screw up. Does Force know that?"

"Everyone in this town realizes there are people standing in line and praying for bad things to happen. Force surely knows Strauss would love to take her place, but Abby also knows that Strauss never will. The woman has no magnetism. Clara Bow was the 'It Girl' because she had 'It.' Force has 'It' but Strauss doesn't. She's as cold as a glacier."

"But could she be capable of …" Lancelot intentionally let the incomplete sentence hang.

"I don't think so. She's calculating, but she's also smart. I think she has a plan, but I'd be shocked if she'd put a bullet in a gun to kill Matt Craig. In my mind, Strauss would want to be the actress that shared the screen with him, not to be the reason he died."

The ringing phone put the conversation on hold. As Lancelot considered what he'd learned, Melborne grabbed the call. After a few hushed sentences, he looked toward his guest.

"Mr. Lancelot, it's for you."

"I left word for Helen and Teresa I'd be here."

"It's not a woman, it's a man named Michael Sharp. And I know nothing about him."

"Sadly, I do. Can I take the call here?"

"Sure," Melborne announced while handing the receiver across the desk.

"This is Lancelot."

"Nap, it's Sharp. You remember the guy we visited who sold the studio the gun?"

"You mean Howard Menefee?"

"Yeah, well, he's dead. I was thinking he knew more than he told us, so I was going over to see him. I knocked and when no one answered, I walked around the side of the house and looked in. He was sitting in a chair. Based on what I could see, he shot himself. There was blood covering his face and a gun was sitting in his lap."

"Did you call the cops?"

"Not yet."

"Where are you now?"

"At a pay phone about a block away."

"Okay, I'll call the police and then drive down. Whatever you do, don't go inside or touch anything."

"Why do you think he knocked himself off?"

"No matter how it looks," Lancelot warned, "don't assume anything yet. I'll be there in half an hour."

After Lancelot handed the phone back to Melborne, the scribe asked, "Something important?"

"Are you really keeping the shooting of Matt Craig out of the press?"

"Yeah, being paid to do so."

"Can I trust you even if I don't shell out some money?"

"Yes. I always pull for underdogs."

"Here it is, Scoop. The man who sold the studio the gun used in the Craig shooting apparently killed himself. Would you like to tag along? I could use a second set of eyes at the crime scene. Plus, as you know the local cops, you might be the only way I get to really look things over."

"Let's go!"

CHAPTER 39

Monday, January 25, 1943
8:05 p.m.
1210 Pine Street, Burbank, California

As Lancelot figured, Scoop Melborne was able to easily talk his way into the home of the now late Howard Menefee. The man's mind was a vault of information and he seemed to be able to withdraw just what he needed at any time. Based on observation, the scribe apparently knew not only every cop at the scene, but also the names of their wives and children.

The detective in charge was a big man, about fifty, with a smile Santa Claus would have coveted. He sported closely cropped black hair, gray slacks, blue coat, white shirt, and a wild, hand-painted red, orange, and blue tie. As he approached the visitors to the crime scene, his hand was extended, and his dark eyes sparkled.

"My name's Chris DiGiovanni, I'm the lead homicide detective on this case and you must be the Chocolate Knight I've heard so much about. It is such a pleasure to meet you."

Melborne leaned close and whispered, "I guess you didn't need me to get in after all."

A shocked Lancelot shook his head before saying, "Chocolate Knight?"

"I hope you don't mind. That's what the boys down at the station have renamed the Negro detective who works with Helen Meeker, and I'm guessing you are that man. Don't worry—it's a compliment. The guys in Chicago told us how good you were. So it's an honor to have you here to observe. And please jump in and point out anything I missed."

"The Chocolate Knight." Sharp laughed. "I've heard everything now."

"Who's the Army officer?" DiGiovanni asked.

"Captain Michael Sharp. You're only meeting part of him."

"What?" the detective replied.

"Yeah, we had to check most of his ego at the door. Not enough room for it and your crime team in this small room."

Sharp shot Lancelot a dirty look, which the investigator didn't acknowledge.

Unfazed but obviously amused, DiGiovanni shook the military officer's hand. "Nice meeting you, Captain. Hey, Scoop, how are you doing?"

"Just chugging along," the writer replied. "How's Helena and the kids?"

"Same as always, spending too much of my money on clothes, food, and Sinatra records. Now, enough chit chat, follow me, boys, and I'll show you the layout of the land."

A dozen steps took the trio from the entry and into a fourteen-by-twelve-foot living room that was obviously rarely used for entertaining. There was stuff piled on chairs, couches, and in corners, as well as enough dust on the bookshelves to plant crops. For the moment, Lancelot put the room observations on the back burner and concentrated on the body. Just as Sharp had reported during his phone call, Howard Menefee was slumped in an overstuffed chair with a gun still resting in his lap. His right hand was six inches from the weapon.

"A .32." Lancelot observed.

"Yeah," DiGiovanni said. "We haven't examined the weapon yet, but I'd guess only one round is missing. He shot himself in the temple just above the left eye, and the slug traveled through the center of his skull before exiting the back of his head and lodging into the far wall."

"You're sure it was suicide?" The unexpected observation caused all the men to turn and see a well-dressed woman wearing a blue fedora standing under the rounded archway separating this room from the entry.

"Meet Helen Meeker," Lancelot announced. "I hope you don't mind, I called and asked her to join us."

"The folks in Chicago speak very highly of you too," DiGiovanni announced with a huge smile. "By the way, I don't mind you horning in on this, but why do you and Lancelot have an interest in a retired guy who knocked himself off?"

"He's tied to case we were called out here to work on," Meeker explained.

"Anything I should know about?" the detective asked.

"I'm kind of on the outside looking in as well," Melborne announced, "so having color added to this black and white picture would be welcomed." He paused and smiled, "So nice to finally meet you, Miss Meeker."

"This is Scoop Melborne," Lancelot explained, "He's the local authority on—"

"Everything," the writer cut in.

"Then you know more than I ever will," Meeker announced.

"It's a shame Jean Harlow died," Melborne pointed out.

"Why's that, and what does that have to do with what's going on here?" a confused Meeker asked.

"She had the fire and spirit needed when the story of your life comes to the big screen. She could have dyed her hair and become Helen Meeker."

Meeker frowned. "Let's hope that never happens. Now, Detective DiGiovanni, back to your question. Is there anything about our case that you should know? Maybe, but for the moment let's just concentrate on what we see here. Keep spilling what you've discovered."

The detective nodded. "It's about as open and shut as any case I've investigated. Here's the note."

Lancelot took the paper and looked it over before passing it to Meeker.

DiGiovanni explained, "What he wrote is pretty cut and dried. He didn't like retirement or California. He also didn't like the way the nation was headed. He writes about his divorce a little and the fact he was estranged from his daughter and then said he was too bitter to go on."

"Did you check it against any other writing samples?" Meeker asked.

"Yeah, he has a journal on the end table beside the chair. The writing's the same. And that journal goes back several years. While the entries are few and far between, it's obvious he hated everyone who didn't look and think just like he did. He certainly didn't like President Roosevelt either."

Lancelot watched as DiGiovanni reached across the dead man's body to the table and retrieved the journal. The detective then strolled back and handed the book to Meeker. As she glanced through the pages, Lancelot stepped out and studied the room.

Beyond the chair holding the victim, there was one chair and a small couch. Except for one place on the couch, just big enough for a single person, they were both covered with newspapers and magazines. There was a desk in the corner that contained stacks of books along with a layer of dust. One set of bookshelves was behind the desk. There were no paintings on the wall or photos of loved ones. On the table where the journal and suicide note had been left was a small Zenith radio and an empty coffee cup.

"You're mentioned in the journal," Meeker said as she handed the book to her partner.

Lancelot read the next to last entry and frowned. The names he'd been called there were nothing like the Chocolate Knight.

"I see by the slant in his writing," Lancelot observed, "Menefee was left-handed."

"Apparently so," DiGiovanni replied.

After handing the journal back to the detective, Lancelot crossed over to the desk and opened a drawer. After sorting through a few bills, he retrieved what must have been a shopping list. He studied the list momentarily before dropping the paper to the desktop. He then opened three more drawers and pulled out a handful of other pieces that had been penned by Menefee. After gathering them up, he walked back across the room, handed them to Meeker and waited. When she grimly nodded, Lancelot turned back to DiGiovanni.

"Will there be an autopsy?" Lancelot asked.

"I doubt it," DiGiovanni answered. "I mean the cause of death is obvious and there is the note."

"It looks like you've got things well covered," Lancelot replied. "And if that's the case, I guess we can go. Scoop, why don't you lead the way? I think it's time we find something to eat."

Lancelot looked at Meeker who nodded. She fully understood what he wanted.

"Come on," Meeker urged, putting her hand on Sharp's shoulder, "there's nothing more to see here. Oh, Napoleon, you'd better put these notes back in the desk where you got them."

"I will," Lancelot assured her as he took them from his boss. Only after Meeker led the men out of the room did the newly christened Chocolate Knight quickly move to DiGiovanni's side. In hushed tones, he announced what he and Meeker had noticed.

"You need to have the coroner request an autopsy."

"Why?"

"There are several things that don't add up. The handwriting in the suicide note and the journal were written by someone who was left-handed, yet these things I found in the desk were penned by a righty."

DiGiovanni glanced at the notes and shook his head. What he didn't realize was that more troubling information was coming.

Lancelot continued. "Also, the journal was supposedly penned when Menefee was in Detroit, Germany, England, France, and Los Angeles, but each entry has the very same shade of ink. When travelling, most people use a pencil or a pen they find in that location. The suicide note is written in the very same ink too."

"My lord, you're right. How did I miss that? I'm a good cop."

"I have no doubt of that, so don't beat yourself up. You had no reason to look beyond the obvious, but Helen and I did."

"What do you mean?"

"Let me hold off on the explanation until I point out one more thing. If Menefee killed himself, and the notes were accurate, he used the wrong hand. The gun appears to have fallen from his right, but you can gather if I'm correct on that theory from the fingerprints you'll take off the handle. You stated, and I observed, the wound was on the left side of the head and traveled at about a forty-five-degree angle through the skull. That's an awkward position for someone who is right-handed to hold a gun."

"Is there anything else I missed?"

"Maybe. There are powder burns on the victim's head and blood on the gun barrel, and that would be fine for a suicide, but if this is murder, that doesn't fit at all. What man would sit still and allow himself to be shot? So, that means there was likely something put in the coffee to knock him out."

"But the cup is empty."

"But there should be evidence in his bloodstream or stomach. So the killer, if you prove there was one, was likely someone Menefee knew and trusted. After all, the newspapers had apparently been pushed aside enough to allow his guest to sit on the far-right side of the couch."

"Do you have more?" DiGiovanni asked.

"When I interviewed him, Menefee alluded that he only needed one woman and one gun, and neither could be replaced. His wife is out of the picture, and he obviously didn't replace her. He sold his Lugar, so where did that gun come from? I don't think the weapon was his."

"Chicago was right about you," DiGiovanni marveled. "You have earned the title of the Chocolate Knight."

"Thanks."

"Mr. Lancelot, you said earlier you were looking beyond the obvious. Why did you do that? What did I miss?"

"What do you know concerning the accident involving Matt Craig around Christmas at Monument Studios?"

"Though we're not talking about the incident," DiGiovanni admitted, "he was shot."

"And," Lancelot said, "the gun that put the bullet in the actor was purchased from the dead man in that chair. That's why I was looking beyond the obvious. Because of knowing that one fact, the obvious for me is that someone wanted or needed to shut Menefee up forever. He knew a lot more than he told me during our meeting."

"So it's no murder of passion."

"No, it's likely a crime of necessity. I think there's a larger plan in the works here, and someone wanted to make sure Menefee didn't expose it."

"Wish I'd known all that going in," DiGiovanni said.

"Wish I'd realized that Menefee might be on a hit list," Lancelot replied. "So don't kick yourself. And don't tell anyone about our request and what I've shared—especially not Sharp or Melborne. Please call me if you find something."

"Better yet," the detective suggested, "you better come see me at the station. You never know who could be listening to a phone call. This is Hollywood and everyone's looking for gossip."

Lancelot nodded. He hadn't thought about that. Possibly their phones at the hotel were being monitored. Time to alert Teresa and Helen to that possibility.

CHAPTER 40

Tuesday, January 26, 1943
10:28 p.m.
1223 Garfield, Los Angeles, California

As Lancelot was doing his research using the phone rather than shoe leather, Teresa Bryant borrowed his rental car for the trip from the Roosevelt Hotel to 1223 Garfield. The bungalow where she hoped to find out more about GA 36723 was likely built around the turn of the century. It was a small one-story structure setting on a postage stamp-sized lot. The green shutters and front door were fading, and the white stucco had turned gray. The front door was placed in the middle of the home with two sets of windows on each side. There was a stoop but no porch.

She had not bothered call ahead but had instead crafted a cover story that hopefully sounded good enough to get through the door. Before knocking, she leaned close to do a bit of audio surveillance. The family radio was turned up and tuned into the highly rated soap opera—*Aunt Jenny's Real Life Stories*. Apparently, the woman of the house fed off of other people's drama.

Bryant knocked twice before the door opened.

Filling the doorway was a woman who looked about sixty. She had dark brown eyes, strawberry red hair cut in a bob, fair skin, and enough freckles to play a long game of connect the dots. She was neither fat nor thin and outfitted in a green housedress that was up to date and stylish. "May I help you?"

"Are you Mrs. Yorkshire?"

"Why, yes, I am." Her voice was clear and hinted of a youth likely spent in the south.

Bryant reached into her purse and retrieved her investigator's badge, quickly flashed it, and announced, "I'm seeking a bit of information for a police investigation."

"My goodness, what?" Yorkshire's eager expression proved she really did feed off of drama. She looked like a hungry dog that had just been offered a piece of steak.

"It was a shooting. Could I step in and ask you a few questions? You might have seen something that you didn't know was important but could lead to us arresting a woman who was involved."

Yorkshire stepped aside. "Certainly, come on in, and I'll shut the radio off. In truth, there's nothing important going on in the show today anyway. Just have a seat on the couch."

Bryant followed directions while the woman hurried over to bathe the room in silence. Then the excited Yorkshire strolled over to a Victorian love seat, smoothed her dress, and sat down.

"Did you say a murder?"

"Actually, a shooting."

"And what was your name again?"

"Bryant."

"Ask me whatever you want, Miss Bryant. How is it the radio cops put it? Oh, yes. I'll shoot straight."

If the woman were involved with Gertrude Root, she would be smart enough not to give it away. So Bryant would have to read expressions as she went through the interrogation.

"Are you married?"

"Oh, yes. Hank and I have been together for over thirty-five years. He works building bombers at a defense plant."

"Always good to meet a family that's helping in the war effort. Now, I'm going to say some names, and I would like you tell me if they mean anything to you. Is that okay?"

"This is so exciting. Nothing like this has ever happened to anyone in our family!"

Bryant nodded. "I'm sure. Now what about Hoffman? Have you ever heard that name? Does it mean anything to you?"

"I knew a family named Hoffman back in Atlanta when I was a child, but I lost track of them years ago. They went to our church. They were good people but very quiet. As I recall, she worked as a librarian, and he was a janitor. Their two children were nice but very homely. I doubt that girl ever found a man."

As her expression indicated she was indeed shooting straight, it was time to move on to the next name. "Mattie Strauss."

"Never known any Strausses, but we call one of our daughters Mattie. She has three children, and they're the cutest things. I have a recent photo if you'd like to see them. My goodness, my granddaughter, Kathryn, is as smart as a whip."

"Maybe you can show me the picture in just a few minutes. For the moment, I'd like to toss out another name and see if it rings a bell. Root?"

Yorkshire paused as if rolling back through years of memories before shaking her head. "No, never knew any Roots, but I do like to garden."

"Okay," Bryant continued, "have you had any strange phone calls recently?"

"I had one the other night. A woman asked for a person named Bobby Jo or Billie Jo or Betty Jo, but that was the only one. Oh, and that local radio quiz show called and asked if I knew today's bonus word. Of course, I hadn't yet read the *Times* so I didn't. But other than that only friends and family have been on the wire."

If Yorkshire was hiding anything, she was a master of deception. Her face and body registered none of the reactions normally associated with surprise or deception. Moving her gaze from her host to an end table she noticed a well-worn Bible.

"I teach a women's Sunday school class," the woman explained. "I read it all the time. My daddy was a preacher. That's why we moved out here to Los Angeles. He was assigned to start a church here. I even met my husband in that church when were both in high school. He's the choir leader now."

"That's nice," Bryant said as she stood. After smoothing her blue skirt, she walked toward the door. Yorkshire followed her step for step. "Thank you for your time."

"But I've told you nothing," Yorkshire replied.

"Oh, yes, you did, and thanks again."

A disappointed Bryant walked out the door and to her car. Once she was behind the wheel, she considered what the clueless woman had spelled out so clearly. The obvious had been too easy and wasn't that always the case? The combination of letters and numbers were most likely not a phone number. At least not one that was in Los Angeles. So what could they be? Time to go back to the suite and find a new place to tie together Gertrude Root and the case Meeker and Lancelot were working on.

CHAPTER 41

Tuesday, January 26, 1943
2:15 p.m.
Roosevelt Hotel, Los Angeles, California

Though she was focused on connecting the dots linking Meeker's case to her apprehension of Root, Teresa Bryant was fighting off something that with each moment was getting harder to ignore. She was hungry. Thus, when she returned to the hotel she went directly to the dining room where she ordered a turkey sandwich and fried potatoes.

While she was waiting on her food she grabbed her notepad and jotted down what she knew. The list of evidence from stolen treasure to the smuggling of Nazi troops through Mexico to the shooting of an actor to a suicide that seemed to be a murder was long, but nothing in that jumbled mountain of information seem to link to GA 36723. And she likely wouldn't be able to discover that link until she figured out what the letters and numbers represented. If it wasn't a phone number what was it?

Bryant was so deep in thought she didn't notice Michael Sharp enter with Abby Force on one arm and Mattie Strauss on the other. They were well across the giant room and completely unaware of her presence as they made their way to table close to the bar. As she looked up to think, Bryant finally spotted the trio whom she only recognized due to photos gathered by Lancelot and Meeker.

At this moment the two women held no fascination for Bryant, but Sharp did. After what Charlie One-Horse had shared on the plane ride west, she relished the chance to learn more about the captain. Now able to spy without being noticed, she studied him as a mountain lion would a deer before sweeping in for the kill.

The man the Sioux intelligence officer had described seemed like military version of the actor Jack Carson. He was a likable but bumbling fool who couldn't walk across a room without tripping.

Yet the man she was looking at now seemed to be like Cary Grant. This guy was smooth, fluid, cool, and those around him appeared to hang on his every word. He appeared very comfortable in his own skin and confident in his every move. When the women looked over the menu, he was also the one who made suggestions. When the waiter came to take the order, Sharp placed that order for both Force and Strauss. As they waited for their food, he performed magic tricks with his napkin. And when their food came, he ate with grace, manners, and polish that would have charmed Emily Post.

Bryant had long believed that deeply hidden facets of a person's personality were revealed as they ate. Strauss was the only left-handed person in the trio. She cut her food and used her glass with only that hand. When she made a point in her conversation she used her left hand only. She appeared to hold her comments until she thought about them. She seemed therefore to be a woman who planned each move very carefully.

Force favored her right as much as Strauss did her left. She ate randomly. She'd nibble on one thing for a while and then move to another and back. She seemed to talk more out of habit than with reason. She also laughed far more than she should.

Sharp was the only one at the table who seemed to be equally comfortable with both hands. He cut his fish by holding the knife in his right hand and then ate what he'd sliced using the fork in his left. He was leading the conversation, evidently sharing jokes that brought smiles and laughter and making points that caused his party to nod their heads in agreement. While Force was fighting for the spotlight, he owned it and wasn't interested in sharing its glow.

"Is there something wrong with your order?"

Bryant brought her eyes from the faraway table to her waiter. "No, it's fine, I just got distracted. I'll get to it, it just might take me a while."

"I see," the waiter answered, "and I understand. Everyone looks at Abby Force when she's in a room. Women and men alike cannot take their eyes off her. My son thinks she is the cat's meow. Have you met her?"

"No," Bryant replied. "I have friends who know her, and they will no doubt introduce me at some point."

"Look at her suit," the waiter suggested. "Clothes hang on most people, but on Abby they hug her body. It's as though everything she wears become an extension of her beauty."

It was obvious the waiter had stars in his eyes. While the dark suit was attractive and obviously tailored, it was not anything that special. Neither was the white, silk blouse. In fact the entire ensemble didn't look much different than something an executive secretary or female lawyer would wear. Yet she was beautiful, and it was the woman's eyes, cheekbones, full lips, and almost sculpted neck that caused Bryant to almost overlook the very link she had been digging for since she discovered the letters and numbers in the matchbook.

"Make sure no one picks up my food," Bryant told the waiter. "I need to go across the room and ask a question."

Moving almost like the lion going in for the kill, she quickly closed the distance from her table to where the Hollywood actress sat. Bryant stood behind the only vacant chair and studied the actress's necklace.

"May I help you?" Strauss asked.

"This is Teresa Bryant," Sharp confidently said before the intruder could speak. As he stood his fork fell from the table to the floor. He ignored it. "She works with Meeker and Lancelot." He then grinned as if proud of his power of observation and said, "I'm right, that's who you are isn't it?"

"Yes, I am Bryant."

"I take it you would like to meet our client?" Sharp asked.

"No introduction is needed," Bryant replied as her eyes remained fixed on Force's necklace. "I just wanted to tell you that if you need anything and you can't find my partners, please give me a call. I'm sharing a suite with Helen."

Then, before anyone could answer, Bryant stooped down and picked up the wayward fork. She tossed it toward Sharp. He effortlessly snapped it out of the air.

"It was so nice meeting you," Bryant announced. She then quickly turned and marched back to her seat. While the numbers still meant nothing, she had a link! The necklace hanging around Force's perfectly formed neck was an exact match to the one Gertrude Root had been wearing the night she took her own life.

CHAPTER 42

Tuesday, January 26, 1943
4:14 pm
Police Morgue, Los Angeles, California

It was an excited Detective Chris DiGiovanni who called Napoleon Lancelot and requested a meeting at the country morgue. The meeting was set up for 4:15, but Lancelot, Meeker, and Bryant arrived a minute early. On a slab was the naked body of Howard Menefee. There had been some carving that had taken place since the last time Lancelot had seen the victim, Menefee was open from stem to stern.

"DiGiovanni," Lancelot announced after the trio entered a place most folks avoided, "You've met Helen Meeker. The other person with us today is the third member of the firm — Teresa Bryant."

"I've heard of you," DiGiovanni replied. "The folks in Chicago described you as Tonto to Meeker's Lone Ranger."

"Who is Tonto?" Bryant asked. "Why does that word keep coming up and what does it mean anyway?"

"Someday I'll explain it," a smiling Meeker assured her partner.

"We have some things to cover," the detective continued, "so I guess we need to get started. Because of the things the Chocolate Knight noticed at the crime scene ..."

"Who's the Chocolate Knight?" Bryant asked.

"That's me!" Lancelot announced with a smile.

"And he's earned that title," DiGiovanni assured Bryant. "He has instincts like no one I've ever known."

"He's the Chocolate Knight and I'm Tonto."

"That's Knight with a 'K,' you know like royalty" Lancelot chimed in.

"Tonto sounds like something you'd name a pet frog," Bryant complained.

"What have you found out?" Meeker asked as she tried to direct the conversation away from nicknames and back to the case.

Before spilling what he'd learned, DiGiovanni faced the body. "As Lancelot expected, an autopsy revealed Menefee had been drugged before he was shot. He had enough Seconal in his system to kill an elephant. It was surely placed in a drink, but not in the coffee that was setting beside his chair. That empty cup showed no traces of the drug and was likely placed there to throw us off. And as Lancelot pointed out, the shot was really on the wrong side of Menefee's head to be self-administered. From the position of the wound, I theorize the killer was likely left-handed."

"Not necessarily," Meeker cut in.

"But by the position of the body," DiGiovanni argued, "the shooter would have been standing to the killer's left and facing him. So the left hand would be the natural hand to use."

"In a struggle yes," Meeker agreed, "but this was staged. It would be easy to reach across with the right hand if Menefee was unconscious."

Bryant stepped over to the table and studied the entry wound. She then turned Menefee's head to look at where the slug exited. When finished with her exam she said, "I'd guess the shooter was right handed."

"Why?" DiGiovanni asked.

"Do you have crime scene photos?" Bryant asked.

"In that file on the desk."

Bryant walked over, opened the folder, and leafed through the eight by tens before pulling one out of the stack and handing it to the detective.

"You'll note the large arms on the chair," Bryant explained. "If this had been a left-handed shooter the angle of the bullet's path would have likely been straight through. Due to the way the chair is made, a southpaw would have had to step to one side, which would have placed them against the lamp stand to achieve the angle of the shot to make it travel the way that it did. A right-handed person could have reached across the arm of the chair and because of the lamp placed the gun in such a way that it created the path we see in Menefee's head."

DiGiovanni studied the print and then walked over to the body before nodding. "I hadn't thought of that." He shot Bryant an admiring glance before adding, "You're a lot more than Tonto. Tonto is just a sidekick, you're not afraid to take the lead."

"Thanks, I guess."

"Anyway," DiGiovanni continued as he placed the photo back into the folder, "there was no break in. So that means Menefee surely knew and trusted the killer. As there were no signs of the victim struggling, I'm also guessing he trusted his guest. There were no fingerprints, nothing stolen that we could find, and the murderer must have been a pro because he or she carefully cleaned up after the crime."

"No one heard the shot?" Lancelot asked.

"No, but it's winter and most folks have their windows closed. If they'd heard anything it would have been muffled and as fuel has been watered down so much during the war, having a car backfire is pretty common these days. So people likely wouldn't have thought anything about a bang even if they heard it."

"The killer used a silencer." Bryant's assertive tone proving she had no doubt.

"What makes you think that?" Lancelot asked.

"If you look at the bruising on Menefee's forehead you'll see the barrel was held directly to the temple when the gun was fired."

"But we found no silencer," DiGiovanni noted.

"Do have the gun here?" Bryant asked.

"Yeah."

"And there are prints on it that need preserved?" Bryant asked.

"No, so you can freely handle it. I'll get it for you."

The big detective opened a box, retrieved the weapon and took it to Bryant. She studied it for a few moments before smiling and handing it back to DiGiovanni.

"You will note," she explained, "you have the blood and flesh you'd expect to see on the gun in every area except for the very end of the barrel. It's perfectly clean. There is also no blood or flesh that leaked inside the barrel. The only answer would be that they employed a silencer."

"How did you guess that?" DiGiovanni demanded.

"The place where the gun was held to Menefee's head has a bruise pattern more like a silencer than a gun barrel. On top of that the crime scene photos revealed the absence of blood and flesh in an area where there should have been both."

The astonished detective looked to Meeker. "Where do you find these people?"

Meeker shrugged. "It most cases they find me. Now that we've confirmed murder and have narrowed the suspects a bit, did you find anything else that might help us?"

"Yeah," DiGiovanni announced with a broad smile, "working on what Lancelot suggested, we dismantled house. On the roof we discovered an antenna that seemed out of place. After all, who needs an antenna to get local radio stations? The wire led through the attic and into the room where Menefee died where it disappeared behind the bookshelves. We moved those and found a radio receiver and transmitter. Beside the equipment was a journal. It appears that through some kind of relay system Menefee was getting messages from friends in Germany."

"He'd traveled there several times before the war," Lancelot explained, "so he did have contacts in that country."

"Well," DiGiovanni continued, "The sentences aren't code, but are fragments. There is no punctuation and no capital letters."

"Can I see it?" Meeker asked.

The detective went back to the evidence box, pulled out the book and gave it to Meeker. She studied it, leafing through each page before handing it to Lancelot. When he was finished he gave it to Bryant who was just beginning her examination when DiGiovanni spoke again.

"This is Menefee's handwriting, we verified that. The suicide note was a sham."

"Nothing seemingly political," Bryant said, "just places and initials." She turned to the final entry and smiled.

"You see something of interest?" DiGiovanni asked.

"So did I," Lancelot chimed in. "The last entry was the same as the letters and numbers in my Hollywood Canteen matchbook."

"And the one I got from Gertrude Root," Bryant added.

"What are you talking about?" DiGiovanni demanded.

"GA 36723," Lancelot explained.

"We figured that was a phone number," the detective explained, "but when we followed up, no one there knew Menefee."

Bryant nodded. "I got that same answer when I did a local search. Do you have good working contacts with police departments across the country?"

"Sure," the detective replied.

"Could you get them to follow up on every GA 36723 in the country and find out if that number can be connected to anyone who might seem like they could be working for organized crime or even an Axis power."

"A spy ring?" DiGiovanni asked.

"It could be," Meeker answered, beating Bryant to the reply.

"It would take a couple of days," the detective explained.

"I don't care if it takes a week, we need it done."

DiGiovanni jotted down the number. "You wait here, and I'll go to my office and get a team of our secretaries on it right now."

As the cop rushed off, Lancelot turned to Bryant. "I guess both of you noticed the writing above the phone number."

Meeker nodded. "Yeah, it's hard to forget that first line on the last page … GR."

"Gertrude Root," Bryant said. "That was followed by RIP GWH."

"The RIP seems obvious," Lancelot observed, "but what does GWH stand for? Any guesses?"

"I'm drawing a blank there," Meeker replied. "The symbol for cash was next, so that indicates a payoff of some kind."

"So," Bryant added, "with the next line reading, 'Package 11/29,' that dollar sign must indicate Menefee was being paid for receiving something in late November. And the only thing that follows is 'GA 36723.' And that number means nothing in Los Angeles."

"So," Meeker concluded, "this likely confirms Gertrude Root is connected to Menefee. What we need to know is why and how and that's tied to GA 36723."

"I met Abby Force earlier today," Bryant added. "She was wearing a really unique necklace."

"The one with the big jewel drop?" Meeker asked.

"Yeah."

"She wore it throughout the USO trip. It's some kind of good luck charm. Strauss has one too."

"So did Gertrude Root," Bryant explained.

"You mean that Root is tied to Menefee as well as Strauss and Force?" Lancelot asked.

"It would seem so," Bryant replied.

As the three tried to weave a pattern into this flood of new information, they each turned back to the body on the slab. If only they knew what had been in the package.

CHAPTER 43

Wednesday, January 27, 1943
10:45 a.m.
Monument Studios, Hollywood, California

Having Bryant again working directly with the team had been the spark that transformed a case stuck in mud to one that was back on the road. Now the problem was that no perceivable connections had morphed into too many. Who was innocent and who was guilty? Who knew it all and who knew nothing? Perhaps a visit to the studios would help sort that out. So Meeker led her team to Monument's back lot in hopes of unmasking someone who was tied to the deadliest sister and brother team since the days of the Egyptian pharaohs.

The studio was a city unto itself. People dressed as everything from Romans to American Indians to Vikings were everywhere the trio looked. On one corner George Washington was visiting with a showgirl and on another Abe Lincoln was playing poker with King George and two Arab sheiks. It was completely surreal.

"There's not one real Indian in that entire group," Bryant pointed out as they passed by a street resembling an Old West town. "This is simply embarrassing."

“Look at that batch of slaves,” Lancelot added, “they’re too well-groomed and too happy to be folks who spend twelve hours a day working under the hot sun.”

“It’s all an illusion,” Meeker pointed out. “Nothing here is real. Even when they shoot the story of someone who actually did walk on this earth, they rewrite history into a story that is grounded in anything but fact. But everything here serves a purpose. The studio provides entertainment for people who are insecure in a time when the world seems to be falling apart. And the movies inspire us to believe that we will win this war and the world will someone find the peace for which it has longed for thousands of years.”

“It’s a nice thought,” Bryant chimed in as she observed four elephants and seven clowns walking down one of the side streets, “but war is reality and peace in an illusion. You can find individual peace but I’m not sure that will ever translate into peace on earth. People naturally want what they don’t have and when those people form groups they attempt to gain what they lust after through social, economic or military war.”

“A bit of philosophy?” Meeker asked as she pointed to a door that read Soundstage 17.

“Experience,” Bryant explained. “Gertrude Root was not a political animal, she was a creature with a lust for power, wealth, and revenge. If we could look far enough into her past we’d likely see one of two things.”

“What’s that?” Lancelot asked.

“A wealthy child who was never disciplined or a poor kid who was constantly beaten down. Something was missing in her youth that drove her to the point where she ended up dying in a room filled with tens of millions of dollars of treasure." Bryant shook her head. "What she possessed ended up possessing her."

Meeker nodded and opened the door. In one brief instant they'd gone from a noisy parade of humanity representing all the ages of time to finding themselves in a huge room with different areas set up to look like various rooms in a contemporary English mansion. Yet except for three people talking in what appeared to be a parlor, the building was void of life.

"The captain and his harem," Bryant noted.

"They bonded during the USO tour," Meeker quietly explained.

"He's a jerk," Lancelot whispered.

"Helen, you've spent time with all of them," Bryant said, "give us your read."

"Force is beautiful but insecure. She possesses knowledge but no real depth. And according to Strauss, she's prone to dips that lead to instability. I saw at least one of those episodes on the USO tour, but I'm not so sure that wasn't more jealousy than mental illness."

"And Strauss?" Bryant asked.

"She's also beautiful but it's a beauty that has no spark. While Force glows, Strauss doesn't even shine."

Lancelot nodded. "She's waiting for a moment that will never come and deep down she knows it. She's the logical pick for who was behind Craig's shooting. If Force had been blamed, she saw herself stepping into the role and becoming a star."

"So she's like a vulture," Bryant observed.

"Explain," Meeker demanded.

"She circles waiting for death, but if death never comes she starves. Now what about Sharp? I've only had one encounter with him. I know that Nap sees him as a racist pig, but Helen what do you see?"

"He's smooth, confident, and, as my sister would say, he's a player. He says the right things and always comes off like a hero, but I don't trust him."

"What's that based on?" Bryant asked.

"Nothing specific I can point to, but when I look at everything all together he makes me feel uneasy. People who go through what he went through develop quirks or twitches. There are things that make them jump or set them off. He displays none of that."

"So," Lancelot asked, "then who in that group talking on the couch is tied to Root? Isn't that what we're all really trying to figure out?"

"It was the last thing on my mind," Meeker admitted, "when we were put on this case, but that telephone number or whatever it is throws me for a loop. Still, even though I'm coming to loath him, logic tells me it's not Sharp because he has had no association with the matchbooks."

"So," Bryant stated the obvious, "If the rooster's in the clear which of the two hens is the fox?"

"I don't have a clue," Meeker admitted, "but we know one thing, those necklaces were custom made. My research shows they aren't being sold in chain stores or being given away in boxes of laundry soap."

"To figure which of the two is the fox," Lancelot suggested, "I think the key is the gun. So what we have to do is find out which of those women is linked to Menefee."

"Would Force's mother know?" Meeker asked.

"I doubt it," Lancelot explained, "Menefee moved to Los Angeles years after she was placed in the institution. And even if she did know something, she talks in riddles and no one seems to be able to crack the code."

"Why don't you give her one more try," Meeker suggested.

Bryant leaned close. "Let me go with him. Perhaps a new face and a woman's point of view can open a door."

"So you're bailing on me?" Meeker asked.

"I'll let you spend the day with the two suspects," Bryant replied, "I'd rather be in a place where I know what's real even if those that live there don't." She looked toward Lancelot and asked, "You think I might be able to help?"

"It couldn't hurt and it would give you a chance to try out a theory I came up with. I can tell you about it as we drive over to Woodlands."

"Let's go," Bryant suggested.

"Have fun." Meeker mournfully watched her team walk out the soundstage door before moving toward the people she had been assigned to watch over. She was already looking for an exit and her job hadn't really begun. Meeker knew that today Force was supposed to give two interviews about her USO trip and take a few hundred publicity photos. While this forecast a day without any danger, it also sounded boring.

As she moved closer, Meeker called out, "I finally made it. When does the fun begin?"

Sharp stood, smiled, and glanced at his watch. "In about ten minutes. They wanted to shoot the photos on this set first."

"Well, this will give me a new experience." After taking a seat in a desk chair, Meeker glanced over to the women. "I notice both of you are wearing the same necklace. It's beautiful and unusual. If you don't mind me asking, where did you get it?"

Strauss won the race to answer. "A fan had them made for us."

"Did you ever meet her?" Meeker quizzed.

This time Force chimed in first. "No, they were delivered to the set with a card that thanked us for our work. We never did find out where they were made or where the fan lived."

"Likely a publicity tool," Strauss explained, "because almost as soon as they arrived Monument put out a press released that was picked up by all the newspapers asking folks to help identify the mystery giver. Nothing ever came of it. So I'm thinking the studio had them made as a way of stirring up coverage for Abby."

Meeker nodded but remained mute. The exclamation would have made sense except that Bryant had spotted a third one on the neck of a woman a thousand miles away. Yet at this point there was no reason to give out with that knowledge. For the moment the more perplexing questions was why? Perhaps, if DiGiovanni could track down where the real GA 36723 was located and who owned that number, things would start to fall into place.

"Helen," Force said, "why don't you and your friends come to the Hollywood Canteen tonight? I'm working the seven-to-nine shift."

"We'll pick you up," Meeker assured her. This would give her the perfect opportunity to search for the balding man who handed out matchbooks.

CHAPTER 44

Wednesday, January 27, 1943
1:07 p.m.
Woodlands Sanitarium, Los Angeles, California

Lancelot convinced Dr. Herman to allow Teresa Bryant to escort Abby Force's mother out of the building for a walk on the grounds. The two men watched from a distance as Bryant led Nina Hoffman to a bench by a small pond.

Unlike Lancelot, Bryant went into this meeting with a lot of knowledge in the bank. She'd heard her partner's theories, knew what he'd heard and observed during his visit. So she felt comfortable dealing with the woman and her issues as long as it was in an environment with few distractions. That's why she had suggested the pond.

Hoffman hugged her doll and watched the ducks and geese glide on the water.

Bryant considered her options. She was sure that over the years the woman had experienced shock treatments, ice baths, and even screaming lectures. She might have been verbally and physically assaulted. So there was no reason to be anything but gentle today. But where was the key to unlocking a door with hinges so rusted by time they might not ever swing free? Now was the time to be patient, sit back and see if the woman would find sanity in a world that offered peace.

"My Gale was like that duck over there," Hoffman announced after almost ten minutes.

Given the opening, Bryant marched through. "How's that?"

"She was ugly."

The answer disappointed Bryant. She'd knew Hoffman always responded in nursery rhymes and it appeared even the new locale would not change that today. This time she seemed to be channeling the story of the swan that thought it was a duck.

"Peace," Hoffman whispered so low Bryant almost missed it.

"Peace?" Bryant asked.

"My husband, Wolfgang, he couldn't ever find peace and so he took war everywhere he went."

Though she had no idea where this story was headed, Bryant prodded for more information. "What was he like?"

Hoffman lightly patted her doll's back and frowned. "He loved uniforms. His boots were always polished and he walked like that big goose over there. Gale so liked it when her father marched."

What the woman was describing fit a lot of classic children's stories, but at this moment Bryant guessed the roots of these images were based on fact. Perhaps being outdoors away from the noise of the institution had opened a window to reality if not a door. It was time to climb into the woman's mind and see if the name Menefee meant anything. Yet before Bryant could act, Hoffman spoke again.

"He hated Pacewalk. They wouldn't let him wear a uniform there. They kept him locked up."

"Pacewalk?" Bryant asked.

She nodded. "It was like it is here; beautiful on the outside but pure hell behind the walls. It was the reason he couldn't stay in Los Angeles. It was the reason he had to go back home."

Bryant was trying to put the pieces together, but the puzzle made no sense. What was a Pacewalk and why did it keep Hoffman from staying with his wife and daughter?

"He was lucky though," Hoffman continued. "He had a friend. You know I have no one here. It was Wolfgang's friend who gave him a place in Germany and let him wear a uniform."

"Does the name Menefee mean anything to you?" Bryant asked.

The old woman shook her head and then continued to reflect on another time. "He did look good in his uniform."

"Your husband?"

"Yes."

"But he had to go back to wear it and I wouldn't go with him."

"And what happened?" Bryant asked.

"He hit me," she whispered. "He hit me again and again and again. And then he took my little John."

"Where did he go?"

"Home to Kassel?"

"To a castle?"

"Not a castle. His town, the place where we lived before the war. The place our son was born. The place where his uniform meant something and got us into the finest parties and balls." She paused and frowned. "He didn't go straight there with our son, Gale got letters from St. Louis and New York first. But only one letter came from Kassel. And after that we never heard anything from him again."

As Hoffman continued to stroke her doll and look at the ducks and geese, Bryant stood and waved to Herman and Lancelot. Pointing to a tree, she met them there, and out of earshot of Hoffman, they huddled.

"I don't think she's been talking in nursery stories," Bryant explained. "I believe Nap was right about that. She has her own language, so let me explain what I think she means."

"If you've broken through," Herman said, "I can't wait to hear what you've found out."

"Here is my guess," Bryant whispered. "What you've been thinking is castle is actually a town in Germany—Kassel. Her husband must have been in World War I on the German side. Sometime during or after the war he went to a place called Pacewalk."

Herman nodded. "That was a German military hospital in World War I. It was used to treat people who had developed mental issues related to the war. Many of those admitted there had shell shock."

Bryant snapped her fingers and looked at Hoffman before posing a question. "Could a disorder like that keep the United States from allowing you to remain in this country and become a citizen?"

"Yeah," Lancelot chimed in. "Forty years ago Teddy Roosevelt signed a bill preventing those with mental disorders from being able to immigrate to the US. I studied that in one of my college history classes."

"Then this all makes sense," Bryant suggested. "Her husband went back to Germany and took their son with him. And someone he met at Pacewalk gave him a job where he could wear a uniform again."

"What makes you say someone at the clinic?" Herman asked.

"Because that's what she told me."

Herman seemed immediately troubled by that news. He frowned, glanced over to Hoffman and ran both his hands over his head.

"Doctor, you look disturbed." Lancelot said.

"I know about Pacewalk because I once studied with a psychiatrist who worked there. His name was Oswald Bumke. He told me about the cases that he treated at Pacewalk and what he learned from them. One of the patients he met at the clinic was Adolf Hitler."

"So Hoffman went back to be Nazi," Bryant suggested.

"That would seem to be sound logic," Herman agreed.

Bryant looked to Lancelot. "Nap, we've got some calls to make. We need to see if there is a Hoffman now serving in the Nazi high command. And we also need to find out if Menefee met with him during his trips to Germany for the Ford Motor Company." She turned to Herman. "Thanks for your time."

"If I might ask," Herman asked. "How did you know bringing Nina to the pond would open up her mind?"

"To my people, water is a source of both peace and strength. Like a drink refreshes you physically, we believe just staring into water awakens memories and puts life into perspective."

Herman smiled. "If, my dear, you ever get tired of doing what you do, please come back and work for me."

Bryant smiled, glanced back to Hoffman and then signaled to Lancelot it was time to get going. The pond had worked its magic!

CHAPTER 45

Wednesday, January 27, 1943
8:07 p.m.
Hollywood Canteen, Los Angeles, California

Teresa Bryant found the Hollywood Canteen to be one of the most refreshing places she'd ever visited. While she was impressed with the multitude of real life stars that were serving coffee and Cokes, making sandwiches, passing out donuts, washing dishes, and dancing with the enlisted men whose uniforms allowed them a free entrance to this unique night club, what she found most fascinating was the fact that men of all races were welcome to this magical place where Hollywood royalty honored real heroes. The scene on the dance floor, at the tables, and beside the counters represented what the United States was supposed to be and, therefore, perhaps foreshadowed a time when the American dream would be open to all people.

On the stage actor Jack Carson was clowning with his friend and often movie co-star Dennis Morgan. On the floor, standing beside the GIs and listening, were Joan Leslie, Ida Lupino, Lana Turner, and countless other actresses who were giving up this night to thank the boys in uniform for all they were doing. And in the light created by the wagon-wheel chandeliers were more smiles than Bryant had seen in years.

As Carson and Morgan left the stage and the swing sounds of Benny Goodman's Orchestra filled the hall, Abby Force, dressed in a bright red suit, walked out and offered to dance with a shocked Marine. Another dozen men immediately lined up behind the leatherneck hoping to be the next.

"Are you impressed?" Helen Meeker asked her partner.

"Yeah, the world owes Bette Davis and John Garfield a great deal for making this place a reality. I'm glad you made me come."

Meeker smiled. "A little later you need to get out on the dance floor and charm some of those men."

"Who said I danced?"

"I thought all Indians danced," Meeker jabbed back.

As she continued to observe from just off the stage, Bryant leaned closer to her partner and asked, "What's on your agenda?"

"I'm looking for the bald guy who passed out the matchbook with the telephone number. He might just be a link we need for our chain of evidence."

"You sound anxious."

"Yeah, with Matt Craig healthy, the studio is planning on filming the scene where Force shoots him tomorrow. I'd like this one to come off a bit differently than the first time."

Bryant nodded before posing a question. "Why didn't Nap come tonight? He said he loved the Canteen the first time he visited this place."

"DiGiovanni called and they were meeting to go over some information. He was also waiting for Alison to give him a ring on some additional materials he needed from the OSS and Secret Service."

"In other words," Bryant said, "he has an angle he doesn't want to share unless it proves out."

"I hope he's onto something. I'd love to have a better idea who was behind the first shooting and the reason for it."

As Meeker went back to her search for the mysterious bald man, Bryant took a deep breath and strolled out to the dance floor. She was immediately surrounded by a dozen men in uniform and for the next hour and a half, a long line of marines, sailors, soldiers, and airmen paraded her all over the dance floor. In the process she had her feet stepped on at least a hundred times, but it all seemed worth it when each man thanked her for making this night special.

When Force bid her goodbyes and headed back to the break room, Bryant broke a few hearts, and joined the actress. They'd no more than arrived backstage when John Garfield approached and asked Force to sing.

"Not tonight John. My voice is played out from just talking and I have an important scene to film tomorrow. Get Helen Meeker to fill my spot. She had no problem singing on the USO tour and the men loved it."

"Really, the private eye is a crooner?"

Not only was this news to Garfield, Bryant was shocked as well. But five minutes later, when the actor pushed Meeker onto stage and told the crowd he had a special treat for them, Bryant would find out that her partner was a woman of many talents.

"This beautiful woman is Helen Meeker," Garfield explained to the crowd. "She is not an entertainer, rather she is one of this nation's best investigators. Now normally she likes to keep a low profile, but tonight she's going to honor us with a tune." He glanced to an obviously displeased Meeker. "I believe the song you sang on the USO tour is one Benny's band doesn't yet know, but everyone knows 'Sweet Dreams, Sweetheart,' so would you warm the hearts of the folks here by sharing that number?"

"Do I have any choice?" Meeker asked.

The applause of the hundreds who had crowded into the Canteen that night answered her question. As Goodman kicked off the song with his clarinet, Bryant edged closer to the stage to watch Meeker.

Dressed in gray suit with her long hair down, Meeker looked like a million dollars and countless GIs were now staring at her as if she were their favorite pinup girl. And as Meeker wrapped her voice around the sentimental love song everyone stopped moving. In the course of one verse she'd broken a thousand hearts. She was not just good; she was great!

"Now you know why I made the suggestion," Force announced to no one and everyone at the same time. "Who'd want to follow that?"

Bryant turned to face the actress. "You sound jealous."

"She's pretty much better than me at everything. She's got the look, maybe not classic Hollywood, but she sure stands out when she walks into a room. She also carries herself with authority. Nothing surprises or rattles her. She'd the kind of woman every woman hates."

"Do you?" Bryant asked.

Force shrugged, turned, and walked back to the break room. As she did Strauss appeared out of the shadows.

"She hates her," Strauss confirmed. "Of course she hates all women. She's sees each female as possible rival. But she hates Meeker even more. Since that night when Helen sang at the USO, Abby has been fit to be tied."

"Does she hate you?" Bryant asked.

Strauss nodded. "We have a mutual understanding. As long as I do my part, I'm fine, but there's a line I can't cross over."

"What happens when you do?"

"Abby goes a little crazy. She throws stuff and does things that you wouldn't expect. In fact, she almost becomes a different person." Strauss paused, as if measuring if she should reveal a secret. "The studio had a lot of people they could have chosen as her double, and after three others failed they picked me because they thought I could better control her when she went over the edge. That's the reason I have real job security and get paid twice what other assistants earn."

"What happened to the three before you?" Bryant asked.

"One walked out, and the other two required the services of a plastic surgeon."

Strauss walked away with no further explanation.

A few seconds later, after experiencing a standing ovation, Meeker strolled off stage. She looked relieved to have gotten that chore behind her.

"Helen you were good," Bryant announced with a smile.

"It doesn't matter to them," Meeker suggested, "They just want to feel someone cares. And it's easy to do that too."

"Did you find your bald guy?"

"No. Do you have anything new?"

"I'm not sure," Bryant admitted, "but I've decided tomorrow I want to be at the studio to watch the final scene filmed."

"Good. I really didn't want to have deal with Sharp, Strauss, and Force all by myself."

"Helen, do you think they could set up a screening of the first time that scene was filmed?"

"We can check. I'll call Jacobs tonight and make the request."

"Good, I want to watch what happened when Craig really got shot."

CHAPTER 46

Wednesday, January 27, 1943
10:07 p.m.
Roosevelt Hotel, Los Angeles

Lancelot looked at the notes he'd spread out across the room's table. At this point there were so many questions but so few answers. In frustration he glanced toward the phone hoping it would ring, but it continued to play dead.

A knock on the door offered relief. Pushing out of his chair he strolled to the entry and put his hand on the knob. Before turning it he raised his voice and asked, "Who's there?"

"DiGiovanni."

Lancelot smiled as he opened the door. Perhaps some good news was in the air. After all, why else would the detective have set up this meeting?

"I can't wait to see what you've brought the Chocolate Knight."

"Do you like that title?"

"I haven't decided yet. Come on in and have a seat."

After the detective sank onto the room's couch, Lancelot pulled one of the table's chairs, spun it round, and mounted it like a horse, folding his arms across the top back.

"What do you have for me?"

"Lancelot …"

"Call me Nap."

"Okay, Nap, we've run the legs off GA 36723. The good news is that in Kentucky they nabbed a bootlegger at that number and in Dallas they closed down a bookie, but there wasn't a single spy, mobster, Klansman or even Axis sympathizer at any of those addresses. In other words, we struck out."

"Teresa was afraid of that," Lancelot admitted. "She has shifted to thinking that it's not a telephone number. But knowing what it's not doesn't give us any clue as to what it is."

"Well," DiGiovanni replied, "while my people were running down the phone numbers, I took a different angle."

"What's that?"

"License plates! In this entire country there are only five cars with GA 36723 and the owners are all clean."

"You're full of good news," Lancelot quipped. He was about to suggest the men break for coffee when the phone rang. "Excuse me." Moving to the table he answered.

"I have a long-distance call from Washington DC for Napoleon Lancelot."

"That's me."

"Go ahead," the operator announced before clicking off.

"Nap, it's Alison."

"I hope you found something out."

"I've mined a few shiny nuggets."

"Let me grab a pen. Okay, shoot."

"The late arrival was a large evil player with the huge teeth was litter mate of the dirty guy's big O."

"Okay, I've jotted that down, keep firing."

"His ticket was punched a month back. No one blew the horn on it though."

After scribbling down the new information, Lancelot said, "Keep plugging."

"His vacation was due to three holes in his schedule."

"Who paid for the trip?"

"A litter mate. This guy's a bill who steers the ship but a pig man at heart whose farm includes a swamp where things often get stuck. He and the large evil player who was dressed like grandma had a turf war."

After studying each word he'd been given, a confused Lancelot asked, "Did the boss take sides?"

"The boss seems to favor bacon. At least that what the king thought."

"Are things calm now?"

"Storm warnings are in affect throughout the litter."

Lancelot scratched his head and shrugged. "Did you get the mini-fees?"

"The payment arrived. Seems the man who issued the check gave both men a present as a way thanking them for meeting him at Club 38."

Though he refused to admit it, Lancelot had never been this lost. Still he plowed on by trying to talk in the same style as the woman on the other end.

"Have you ordered any icing for the cake?"

"Not going to have any dessert this time."

"Thanks, I'll tell the other side of your family's coin you sent greetings."

"Ask for parole." With that the line went dead.

"You got something that might help us clear up this mess?" DiGiovanni asked.

"I have no idea," Lancelot replied. "The call was from Helen's sister and I don't really understand the code." He tossed the pad over to the detective.

DiGiovanni took a long first look and then a second before scratching his head. "It's all Greek to me."

"Alison talks in the college lingo of the day. As I was afraid the line might be bugged, I didn't ask her to translate, but rather just attempted to feel my way along. Knowing I might get lost, I jotted it all down. Teresa is really good at turning phrases like this into English."

"I'd like to see her perform that trick." The detective's reply came just as the door opened, and Meeker and Bryant strolled in.

"Nap, you should have come," Meeker announced, "each time I see what they're doing there gives me more faith in the American spirit."

"And you missed a chance to hear our esteem leader warble," Bryant added as she closed the door. Turning toward the guest she asked, "How are you Mr. DiGiovanni and what do we owe the pleasure of your company?"

"Bad news I'm afraid. There are no suspicious people at GA 36723 anywhere in the US. And I also ran the license plates with that number and came up empty."

"What about your hunches?" Meeker asked Lancelot.

"I might have something, but I can't break the code. It's your sister's words, so I wrote them down for Teresa."

He retrieved the legal pad from the detective and gave it to Bryant. She glanced at it before asking, "What did you ask her to find out?"

"I was looking for background on Nina Hoffman's former husband."

With Meeker looking over her shoulder, Bryant went to work on the first couple of lines. "The first part of this information is gold. It clearly tells us that Hoffman was part of Hitler's inner circle, hence the Big O, and the litter reference is for family, so that likely means he was a general. After all, the generals make up most of Hitler's inner circle or, as Alison said, Big O." She studied the line again. "Now I understand something else Nina told me. She kept calling her husband by a name that naturally sounded like it came out of a Mother Goose story, but she was actually giving me his real name. When Alison told you about the large evil player who dressed like grandma it has to be the Big Bad Wolf. After all, to Alison's friends a guy who's always chasing skirts is a wolf. Hoffman's first name therefore has to be Wolf, as Nina called him, or more likely Wolfgang. The next part is also obvious. He was shot three times and the fact the horn didn't blow means that the death has never been publicized. I'm guessing the SS contacts in Germany must have given our side the word on his death."

"I'm impressed," DiGiovanni said.

"What about the part where I asked who paid for his last trip?" Lancelot asked.

"Now that I know the question it helps me some," Bryant explained. "The litter mate would mean the killer or perhaps the man who order the execution was another general in Hitler's inner circle. Let me chew on the rest for a second." As the other three anxiously waited, Bryant studied the transcription. "Okay, I think I have it. The man who steers the ship is at the helm. The German name for Bill is Will, so the General's first name is Wilhelm. A big pig is a hog, and a swamp where things get stuck could be a bog."

"Hog bog doesn't make any sense," Lancelot suggested.

Meeker snapped her fingers. "But if you get stuck you are mired down."

"Yeah," Bryant chimed in, "I'm betting the general who was behind the execution is Wilhelm Hogmeier."

"Hoganmeier," Meeker corrected her. "Wilhelm Hoganmeier is the father of Matt Craig."

"So," Lancelot whispered, "within the last months Abby Force's father was gunned down by Matt Craig's dad. That's bizarre."

"I'm lost," DiGiovanni said.

"Let's look at the rest of the note," Bryant suggested. "The turf war likely means the two were jockeying for position with Hitler. The 'boss favors bacon' surely means that Hitler must have sided with Hoganmeier and ordered the SS to eliminate Hoffman. And storm warnings likely mean the matter has not been put to rest yet. More folks on the inside might be taken down."

Bryant scanned the remainder of the message before looking to Lancelot. "What did you ask next?"

"I was looking for a connection between either of those litter mates and Menefee."

"Okay, that's pretty clear. Menefee met with them in 1938." Bryant glanced toward DiGiovanni. "And remember the radio log you found behind the bookshelves. There was a line that read RIP GWH. That has to mean that General Hoffman was killed."

"Wow," the cop whispered, "the Lone Ranger would have actually been your sidekick."

Bryant frowned and looked back at the notes. "Next Alison said there was no icing on the cake. That means the OSS had no more information."

"So," Lancelot noted, "Nina Hoffman told me that her daughter was always a daddy's girl. Perhaps she got word that Craig's father had rubbed out her dad and figured the best way to settle the score was by staging the accident on the movie set."

"How does she get the word?" Bryant asked.

"Maybe through Gertrude Root?" Meeker suggested. "Maybe GA 36723 is a code for the hit. After all cops use numbers to identify different kinds of crimes."

"But," Bryant argued, "she got the matchbook after the accident at the studio."

"It could be," Lancelot suggested, that even after the failure the hit was still on and she was to find a way to do it again."

"Why don't we just grab Force now?" DiGiovanni asked.

"It's all circumstantial," Meeker explained. "Nothing we have here will hold up."

"Nap," Bryant said, "at Woodlands I learned that when Hoffman beat up Nina and grabbed their son he headed east. But he didn't immediately make it back to Germany. He stopped in St. Louis for a while."

"Yeah," Lancelot replied, "that's where Strauss might have been born and, according to Scoop Melborne, when she was taken to the orphanage her mother gave the child's name was Ruby Hoffman. Maybe Strauss looks enough like Force to be her sister because she is actually her half-sister."

Bryant nodded. "I'll bet Abby Force doesn't even know. So the question now becomes, which one of Willie Hoffman's daughters wants revenge for her father's death?"

"We have two suspects," Meeker observed.

"Strauss has more motives," Lancelot suggested. "She gets rid of the man who killed her father and also frames the sister, which gets her crack at stardom. For her it's not just revenge; it's reward."

"But what could GA stand for?" Bryant asked the group.

"Garfield, gate, gal…" DiGiovanni suggested, "and that's just a start."

"What's Force's real first name?" Bryant asked.

"Gale," Lancelot replied.

Bryant walked over to the telephone, picked up the receiver and studied the dial. She then retrieved a pencil and paper and began to scribble.

"There's no number that works," the detective said.

"It's not the number," Bryant said. "Though we only use them to identify a prefix, each number on a phone represents three letters. If I look it that way 36723 translates to FORCE."

"Gale Force," Meeker said.

Bryant smiled. "A strong wind that is capable of great damage."

"But what's it mean?" Lancelot asked. "Why spell out Abby's real first name and couple it to her movie star last name?"

"When the weather service issues gale force wind alerts," Bryant concluded, "it's a serious warning. Abby might not be the shooter; she might well be the target."

"But why?" the detective asked.

"That's what we have to figure before they reshoot the murder scene tomorrow," Meeker said.

CHAPTER 47

Thursday, January 28, 1943
3:14 p.m.
Monument Studios, Hollywood, California

While Meeker and Lancelot kept close tabs on Strauss and Force, and therefore also shadowed their constant companion, Captain Michael Sharp, Teresa Bryant spent the time leading up to the final scene reshoot doing some digging on her own. Initially she went to the screening room and watched the film from when Craig was shot. After rerunning it for an hour, she walked to the photo lab. There she reviewed every publicity picture taken on the *I Spy You* set. Next came the prop room where Calvin Coggins was examining the Lugar that once was and would soon be again the pivotal player in this bit of Hollywood drama.

"Do you mind if I take a look?" Bryant asked.

Coggins gazed toward the door and frowned. "Who are you?"

"My name's Bryant, I work with the man who's really responsible for you not being in jail."

"Lancelot?"

"Yeah."

"Okay then I don't mind you looking. I've checked it a hundred times and found nothing wrong. I can fully guarantee the only thing in this weapon are blanks."

Bryant crossed the room and took the German made handgun. After carefully studying everything from the chamber to each of the fake rounds, she set it on a workbench. "Mr. Coggins, did you go through the same procedure a month ago that you did today?"

"No," he admitted. "I only checked it twice then. Today I've gone over more than twenty times."

"Where does the gun go from here?"

"I'll give it to Abby Force who'll place it in the purse she's carrying during the scene."

"When do you do that?" Bryant asked.

"I need to do it now."

Bryant heard footsteps made by a man wearing leather soled dress shoes. So she paused her interrogation and looked toward the open door.

"How are you doing, Cecil?"

Coggins turned as studio head David Jacobs casually strolled into the room. "I'm fine sir. Thanks for having faith in me."

"I take it you're Teresa Bryant," Jacobs said, framing his observation in a smile. "Meeker told me you'd be here today and that you would be a beautiful American Indian. You are that!"

Bryant ignored the compliment and nodded. "I've carefully inspected the Lugar. The way it is right now it couldn't harm anyone unless they used it as hammer. In order to make sure Mr. Coggins stays in the clear, I'd like your permission to take possession of the gun. I want to be the one to place it into the purse."

Jacobs nodded. "That sounds wise to me."

With both men watching, Bryant picked up the Lugar and a screwdriver from the workbench and set to work making a deep gash in the swastika Menefee had cared into the wood handle. When finished, she admired her work.

The studio head asked, "What are you doing?"

"When this scene was shot was the first time," Bryant explained, "Coggins placed a Lugar he'd purchased from Menefee into the purse. We know Matt Craig was shot with a Lugar containing a real bullet. The police held onto the Lugar until the studio convinced the district attorney this whole thing had been an accident. Then this gun was returned to the studio. Is that correct?"

"It is," Jacobs answered.

"But are you sure this is the same gun?" Bryant asked.

"It has to be," Coggins assured her.

Bryant shrugged. "Did you write down any specific information that could prove that?"

"Are you suggesting," Jacobs demanded, "this Lugar is not the same gun Calvin bought?"

Bryant didn't answer, but instead posed a question of her own. "Who demanded that this specific type, model, and manufacture be used for this scene?"

"Melvin Van Dyke," Coggins explained.

"No doubt," Jacobs agreed, "Melvin's a stickler for details and it often costs me a fortune. But he wouldn't do anything to harm Craig or anyone else. The man is a teddy bear."

"But," Bryant pointed out, "how many people knew the director had asked that this type of weapon be used in that scene?"

"We put out the word across the whole studio," Jacobs explained, "just in case there was someone on the lot that might have had one at home."

Bryant smiled. "So switching out the gun with the blanks for an identical one with live rounds would have been easy. Simply put, there would have been no way of proving which was which."

"So," Coggins suggested, "with that mark now there is actual proof if there is a switch made. But do you and Meeker actually believe the guns were switched?"

"I don't know," Bryant admitted, "but this is one way to find out if a switch will be made this time." She slipped the Lugar into her purse. "I need two blanks just like the ones in this gun."

"Why?" Coggins asked.

"Your work is good," Bryant explained. "I take it you make your own blanks."

"Yes."

"And at a quick glance, they look real," she noted.

"They have to," he explained. "There are times when a camera grabs a shot of the rounds being loaded into a weapon."

"Did you make up more blanks that you needed for this scene?"

"Yes. With Melvin directing we often shoot the same scene a half a dozen times. So I always make enough to cover extra shots."

"Then give me two of them. They might just be the key to saving the next scene from becoming fatal." With Jacobs looking on, a confused Coggins opened a drawer, pulled out two blanks, and handed them to Bryant, who dropped them into her jacket pocket. "Now," she said, "before the call for action, I have some work to do."

Bryant's next stop was Force's dressing room. She stood in the open doorway and inventoried what she saw. Strauss was standing in the far corner studying Force as the actress checked her makeup. On the other side Meeker and Lancelot were leaning against a wall carefully following everything happening in front of them. Hovering over Force's shoulder was Sharp.

"How do I look?" the actress asked.

"Beautiful as always," Strauss answered as if on cue.

Force looked at a color photograph taped to the mirror. It appeared to be one taken the day when the accidental shooting almost killed Matt Craig.

Choosing this moment to move forward, Bryant walked over to the dressing table and glanced from the photo to the actress. "It appears you're ready. Where's the purse you'll be carrying? I have the Lugar."

"On the table."

Bryant walked over, put the weapon into the handbag, and handed it to the actress. "I think it's time you get on the set." Bryant silently watched the star, the captain, and the assistant leave. When she was alone with her partners she said, "Nap, make sure that no one touches that purse until I join you."

"What's going on?" Meeker asked.

"A theory," Bryant explained. "You go on out. I'll catch up after I do a quick search of the room."

CHAPTER 48

Thursday, January 28, 1943
5:01 p.m.
Monument Studios, Hollywood, California

Helen Meeker watched as Melvin Van Dyke took charge of the scene. The director was just about to make a speech when Teresa Bryant walked around the set and joined Meeker about fifteen feet from where the parlor had been constructed.

"Abby, do you have any questions?" Van Dyke asked. "I know this can't be comfortable for any of us, but are you okay?"

"I'm fine," the actress assured him.

"So what do you do?"

"I walk into the room, deliver my lines, shoot Matt, and leave. But why couldn't we just use the stuff we shot back in December?"

"We might cut in parts of that film, but the cameras are set up for different angles today."

"Okay. Same scene but shot a different way."

"And don't rush it," Van Dyke begged. "I want to see how doing this hurts you. You have to sell it."

"I'll try."

"How do you feel about this, Matt?" Van Dyke asked.

"I just want to get it over with."

"In truth," the director announced, "what happened last time might just give us the edge we need to really make this one of the best scenes I've ever directed."

Even Meeker felt the apprehension that blanketed the room as she settled into a chair to watch action. Everyone was on edge, well almost everyone. Glancing to her left she noted Bryant smiling. What did her partner know that she didn't?

"Let's get to shooting," Van Dyke announced. "Everyone in their places." He took a final look at the staging area immediately grew quiet. Now satisfied everything was ready, he sat in his chair, a red light came on, the clapboard snapped, and there was the call for action.

As written in the script, Force purposefully strolled into the room. Only after her eyes fell on Craig did she pause and sadly shake her head. Taking a deep breath, she visibly pushed the air from her lungs, before announcing, "I know who you are and what's you've done. I can't let you complete your mission."

"Hold it," Van Dyke screamed. "Cut." He glared at the actress. "Where's that necklace you're supposed to have on? You had it back in December. The editors have to have everything be the same!"

Force glanced down and frowned. "I must have left it on my dressing table."

"Get it," the director demanded. "If we shoot without it a million fans will be writing letters demanding to know why you had it on in the last scene and not this one."

As the crew grumbled, Force glared at Strauss before the two of them rushed off the set. After they'd departed, Meeker noticed Bryant was still grinning.

"Teresa, what's so funny?"

"It's all about details, Helen. Van Dyke is like us, he never misses a thing. That's what makes him so predictable and so good."

Meeker was puzzling over what her partner meant when Force and Strauss reappeared. This time the necklace was in place.

"Okay," Van Dyke barked, venting some of his obvious frustration, "let's really do it this time. From the top."

When 'Action' was called Force walked through the door and onto the set. Again taking a deep breath, she announced, "I know who you are and what you've done. I can't let you complete your mission."

Craig grinned. "I'm a rogue, I've always sold myself to the highest bidder. But I love you and you love me. Even in war love trumps everything else."

"It can't replace loyalty to Britain," Force answered.

"I'm leaving. Are you coming with me?"

Responding to the cue, the actress reached into her purse and pulled out the Lugar. After she aimed she announced, "I'm not coming with you and you're not leaving. I'm calling Scotland Yard."

The actor laughed. "You won't shoot. Your love for me is too strong. Now put that gun down and let me kiss you. You know you want to."

There was an edge in the room that even Meeker could feel. The last time this action had led to a man almost dying. What would happen now?

With all eyes on her, Force dropped the purse and gripped the weapon with both hands. As she did, a tear rolled down her cheek. She allowed that lone teardrop to fall before firing. The sound of the shot seemed to echo in every corner of the sound stage. As the hushed crew looked on, Craig's confident smile turned to a look of pain. He rocked on his heals before falling forward. Force then approached the fallen actor, shook her head, dropped the weapon, turned, and walked out.

A few seconds later Van Dyke yelled, "Cut!" Then his and everyone else's eyes turned to Craig.

The actor remained still for a moment before rolling over and pushing off the floor. Once on his feet, he smiled, glanced to the crew, and triumphantly announced, "Not a scratch!"

As applause broke out, Meeker shifted her gaze to Bryant. Her partner was intently focused on first Force and then Strauss. Neither was smiling. In fact, both appeared to be a state of shock.

A relieved David Jacobs moved between where Meeker sat and Bryant stood. He smiled and said, "I guess I brought you out here for nothing. It was all just a bizarre mistake."

"It's Hollywood," Bryant replied, her eyes still locked onto the actress and her assistant, "Nothing is as it appears to be."

Meeker knew that now was not the time or the place to ask her partner about what seemed to be a cryptic observation. When Bryant was ready, she'd share what she knew.

"Helen," Force announced as she moved off the set, "because this came off so well, I'm having a party at my house tomorrow night. I was hoping you and your team could come. Michael will be there, and Matt will surely join us as well."

Meeker looked toward a smiling Bryant before saying, "We'll be there."

As a satisfied Force walked back to Strauss, Bryant strolled onto the set and picked up the Lugar. She then walked over and showed the gun to Jacobs.

He took it, examined the handle, and then walked across the room to hand it to Calvin Coggins.

CHAPTER 49

Friday, January 29, 1943
8:00 p.m.
Holmby Hills, Los Angeles, California

"Teresa, you've been awfully quiet the past twenty-four hours," Meeker observed as she pulled the rented Ford up to the front door of Abby Force's thirty-room, stone house.

"I second that," Lancelot added from the backseat. "I mean I'm glad you convinced Jacobs the shooting was an accident, but it still casts Coggins in a bad light. I mean he once again looks like the guy who almost made a fatal mistake."

"He made no mistake," Bryant answered, "and Lucas knows that. The movie mogul just wants this whole mess to disappear, so he's willing to pay us to go away. And Nap, don't be too concerned with my holding things back. I have a feeling you and Helen have cards you don't want to reveal until the time is right."

As Meeker reached for the car's door handle she quipped, "But will our cards come together to make a winning hand?"

"Let's go in and find out," Bryant suggested. "And let's not wait for the action to come to us. When you get a chance to lead with anything that will call into question the character of those in this room, take it. I know I will."

Strauss, wearing a burgundy evening gown and carrying a matching purse, greeted them, took their coats, and pointed to an open door leading into a living room. The furniture was white, as were the curtains and the carpet. A full bar set off to the left, a stone fireplace, crackling with a wood fire, was to the right. On the far wall hung a six-foot tall painting of Abby Force dressed, naturally, in a form fitting white gown.

"Good evening," Force announced from the center of the grand room. She was wearing the same dress as was displayed in the painting—a number that appeared almost liquid in the way it moved. After waving her arms to make sure she had everyone's attention, the actress added, "I'm so glad you agreed to come. If you want a drink, feel free to fix it, there are cigarettes and cigars on the coffee table and Mattie had the cook drum up some wonderful angel food cake. The pieces are cut and ready."

Leaning on the bar, Jacobs and Craig, both in suits, were sipping what appeared to be brandy. Sitting in an oversized chair, a uniformed Sharp had a glass half filled with whiskey in this right hand and held a cigarette between his thumb and index finger of his left. Strauss, looking peeved, moved past the officer and gracefully eased down onto the couch.

"I think we're fine on the drinks," Meeker announced for her team. "We had a late supper."

"We're here to celebrate," Force explained. Her smile, though radiant, didn't appear to be sincere. She swept across the room to the fireplace where she seemed to pose before adding, "Helen, your team cleared me of the shooting and that's something of which I'm very thankful.

And tonight we also salute Matt Craig as he heads off to fly for the Army Air Corps." She then looked toward Jacobs and said, "Oh, and if I may add, we also are here to kick off the biggest film of the year—*I Spy You*."

"I guess Hollywood does guarantee happy endings," Strauss cracked as she nursed her drink.

"Most times the movies do end on a happy note," Meeker agreed, "but that's not always the case in our business. Some crimes are never solved. They remain open like a festering wound and they continue to seep pain for years." Meeker looked to her partners as if warning them she was about to tell a fib, before continuing, "Right before we were called to help on this case, Teresa and I dumped a bomb into a swimming pool. The bomb would have killed hundreds, but it was meant to guarantee my team died. There was no concern about innocent lives; it was all about revenge."

"What does that have to do with tonight?" Jacobs asked. "Though if we make a movie about your life it would be a great scene."

Meeker walked across the room to face the mogul. "Why did you call Mrs. Roosevelt and ask her to put my team on this case?"

Jacobs shrugged. "I was told you were the best in the business and that you could get to the bottom of this mess. I had to be assured that what happened was an accident. And if it wasn't that, I had known why someone would want to murder the biggest star in Hollywood."

"Who told you that I was that good?" Meeker demanded.

His response was immediate. "Abby."

Meeker turned to face the actress. "Is that true?"

"Well, yes. We almost made a movie about your life. I'd read the screenplay and realized you could get to this bottom of this mess. So I pushed Mr. Jacobs to get you to clear my name. After all, my whole career was on the line."

"So Mattie," Meeker said, "what did you think of having outsiders come in?"

The woman took another gulp of her drink and shrugged. "I'm not paid to think. My business is to be a stand-in, answer fan mail, and make sure Abby gets to where she needs to be. But, as my paycheck depends upon doing those things, sure I wanted her name cleared. So yes, I told her you'd be a good person to have on our side. I may have even reminded Abby about reading that screenplay."

Lancelot waved and stepped forward. "But Mattie, Scoop Melborne told me that you wanted nothing worse than to replace Abby. In fact, he suggested you were secretly doing everything you could to convince the studio that she was unstable."

"What else did that gossip monger say?"

Meeker nodded and moved to the side as Lancelot took over. "Mattie, you were born Ruby Hoffman and raised in an orphanage in St. Louis."

"Your name was Hoffman?" an apparently shocked Force asked. As she was an actress Meeker had no idea if what she was reading in the woman's face was real or just fabricated for the audience.

"Why does that surprise you?" Lancelot asked. "Perhaps it's because your real last name is also Hoffman. Your mother Nina is currently at the Woodlands Sanitarium."

A stunned Force found the couch and sat down. As the color drained from her face, she appeared as white as her dress. Now everyone in the room was locked in on Lancelot waiting to see what bombshell would fall next.

"Miss Force," Lancelot asked, "where's your father?"

"He's dead."

"Nap," Meeker suggested, "let's leave it there for a moment." She turned and moved to where everyone in the room could easily see her. "At first I resented being called in on this case because it took me off one that I viewed as being far more important. I now understand that there were two reasons for getting my team to Los Angeles. The first was to give the person who'd tried to murder us time to get away. The second was set us as targets here and finish the job that failed back in Chicago. This wasn't really about the murder case."

"You're talking nonsense," Jacobs suggested.

"Let me connect the dots," Bryant said as she moved to the fireplace. "Hoffman is a name shared by Strauss and Force." She turned to the assistant and posed a question. "How much younger are you than Abby?"

"Three years."

Bryant nodded. "That's about what I figured. When Abby's father left Los Angeles, after beating up his wife and taking their son, he was headed back to Germany. But he couldn't go directly back home. First he needed money. He landed in St. Louis where he worked for about a year and met another woman. They had a child whom the mother named Ruby."

"You mean . . . ?" Jacobs whispered.

"Yes," Bryant explained, "Mattie and Abby are half-sisters. That's the reason they look so much alike."

"That can't be true," Force snapped.

"And," Lancelot announced, "The father of these two women is Wolfgang Hoffman. Wolf, as he wife called him, once met a man in a mental hospital where both were being treated for shellshock. That man convinced Hoffman to return to Germany and help him start a new political movement. Thanks to the OSS we know that Hoffman would become a part of Hitler's inner circle and rise to the rank of general. As he just loved uniforms that must have made him very happy!"

Jacobs gulped the remainder of his drink. "Are you telling me that Abby's father is a Nazi leader?"

"Was," Bryant cut in. "In a power play led by another general named Wilhelm Hoganmeier, Hoffman was executed within the last few months. And that's where it gets really interesting."

Meeker looked over to Craig. "Do you want to share something with us?"

The actor grimly nodded. "My father is General Wilhelm Hoganmeier. He's second in command of the German Luftwaffe."

Jacobs slapped the top of his head. As the color drained from his face he hurried behind the bar to refresh his drink. After gulping it down he moaned, "My Lord, I have two Nazi offspring starring in my unreleased picture. This will ruin me."

"Well," Bryant suggested, "look at the bright side."

"What bright side?"

"If you had known that you wouldn't have asked Helen, Nap, and me to investigate. So that means you're in the clear when it comes to criminal activity. You might go broke, but you won't have to do any prison time."

"But there are others in this very room," Meeker explained, "who aren't so innocent. In fact, there's a murderer in our midst."

The room grew deathly silent as Meeker looked back to Bryant.

"Helen's right, but before we expose the identity, let's look at one murder than was avoided; the killing of Matt Craig." Bryant turned toward the actor. "Matt, you were lucky when the first accident on the set didn't kill you. You would have likely died yesterday but the bullet that was placed in your prop gun by the would-be killer was a blank."

"They were all blanks," Jacobs argued. "You proved that in the prop room. And the gun used was the same as the one Abby dropped to the floor at the end of the scene. I saw the scratch you made for identification. You showed it to me!"

Bryant nodded. "And I searched Force's dressing room for a second gun, and there wasn't one. But there was a live round in the hidden compartment in the necklace. And the only reason I knew to look there was because another woman, Gertrude Root, had one just like it where she kept a cyanide pill. The killer couldn't put the live round in the Lugar before the scene because there were too many eyes on her. Yet she knew Van Dyke's passion for detail and she was sure when Abby wasn't wearing the necklace, the director would spot it, thus giving that someone the needed opportunity to insert the live round."

"I didn't do it," Force insisted.

"You had to," Strauss argued.

"How can you prove who did it?" Sharp asked. "They both went back to the dressing room to get the necklace."

"Murders can be very well-planned," Bryant explained, "but when unexpected events mess up the timing of the murder, things get overlooked. I'd removed the live rounds that were in both Mattie's and Abby's lookalike necklaces and replaced them with blanks. I wiped both clean and used gloves when making that change. The wannabe assassin didn't think about that when she hurriedly took what she thought was the live round out of the necklace and placed it into the Lugar."

Strauss quietly reached into her purse and pulled out a small pistol. "I never get a break," she barked. "In all my life I've always been the one who was cheated. If Abby had been any kind of shot, she'd have killed him the first time. But no, she couldn't do any better in that job than when she tried to sing on the USO tour. Alley cats sound better than the great star. But this time, I have the upper hand. I'm the one with the gun, and I made sure there were no blanks in this baby. Get ready for a performance of a lifetime!"

"How did you know Gertrude Root?" Meeker demanded. "You might as well tell me, you've got nothing to lose."

"I never met her," Strauss admitted, "at least not face to face. But my father told me if Root or her brother ever needed anything, I was to do what they wanted."

"How could your father mean anything to you?" Lancelot asked. "After all, he deserted you and your mother."

"He kept in touch, he sent me money, and he was the one person who was always loyal to me. He'd have brought me to Germany if he could. And when he died…"

"Who told you he was dead?" Meeker asked.

"Herman Menefee. My father met him about ten years ago and they stayed in touch. Menefee also told me back in October who was responsible for killing him. I promised at that point I'd get even."

"Thus, the motive was revenge," Bryant stated, "not a political assassination."

"Exactly! And when Van Dyke demanded a Lugar be used, Menefee contacted people back in Germany and they smuggled my father's personal gun here to make sure it was used in the scene."

"That was the package Menefee received," Lancelot cut in. "Now almost everything makes sense. But did you kill Senator William Darby, Congressman Nathan Kelly, industrialist Armstrong Jackson, media mogul Kathryn Street, and General Lee Stewart when you were on publicity trips with Abby?"

"No," Strauss shot back. "I got the money through Menefee and he told me it came through a man he called Darkness. I was told who to give the cash to, but I didn't really know why until I started reading the newspapers and realized that well-known people had died on the day before each payoff. Then I realized I was likely funding hits."

"So you were being used," Lancelot noted.

"Yes, I was, but that was all right. Menefee assured me that what I was doing was helping my father."

"Enough talk," Meeker said. "You might as well drop the gun, there are too many of us and there's no escape route. So you can't get away."

"But I can do one thing before you bring me down," she argued. "I can avenge my father's death and settle the score with his killer's family. An eye for an eye and a tooth for a tooth."

Strauss turned toward Craig and smiled. Yet just as she was about to pull the trigger, a shot rang out. As he was just out of her range of vision, Strauss likely never saw Sharp pull a small gun from his boot. The captain's lead was instantly lethal and as blood seeped from her chest and stained her dress, Strauss fell to the floor without as much as a whimper.

"You saved my life," Craig whispered even before the smoke cleared.

"I did what any soldier does," Sharp replied, "and perhaps now I've proven to Helen that I belong in DC"

Meeker grimly smiled. "You have proven a great deal. The first is you're a very good shot. The second is that you know far more than you should."

"I don't understand."

"When we first met you talked about my team blowing up a mountain behind enemy lines. How did you find out about that?"

"I heard it from Army Intelligence."

"They don't know that and neither does the FBI. Except for those who figured things out in Berlin, no one but a few folks at the OSS know that bit of information. The bottom line is that you're a plant. The real Michael Sharp must have been killed and discovered by the Japanese."

"That's ridiculous. I fought my way back to our lines. I was so badly injured my face was even destroyed."

"And," Meeker said, "that was the key to making the charade work.

"I met a man who knew the real Sharp," Bryant added, "I found out he was nothing like you. Oh, you are the same height, build, have the same eye and hair color, but he was clumsy. He couldn't walk across the room without tripping. And he wasn't a lady's man. You might have known all about Sharp's past and each detail of her life, but you didn't move like him. Maybe it's that your ego was too large to allow you to appear like anything other than the perfect Aryan male. On top of that, when I watched you eat a meal, you made a big mistake. Most folks wouldn't have noticed, but I did. Your table manners are impeccable. You have obviously been trained how to properly hold a fork and even how to chew. But I noticed that when you ate your fish you cut it with your knife in your right hand and then used your fork, which you kept in your left hand, to spear the fish and bring it to your mouth. Only Europeans do that. Americans set their knives down and switch hands with their fork before spearing their meat."

Meeker took a step toward Sharp.

"Don't come any closer," he warned. "I'm not going to put this down until you stop trying to frame me. After all, I just saved Matt's life. I even saved yours back in the jungle. A Nazi plant wouldn't have done that."

"They would," Meeker pointed out, "if it meant they could get inside our intelligence department. Saving me was a small price to pay for that. Now, if you want more proof that I can see through your mask, let me shell it out. You needed a cigarette at Bacon Island. When you came back from the jungle after supposedly saving us you had a pack and even offered others a smoke."

"So," Sharp snapped, "I got them off the dead Jap."

Meeker shook her head. "When you bummed a cigarette on the set while we were shooting the final scene I suddenly remembered that pack you had at Bacon Island. The brand you brought back from your mission was Josma. There isn't one of those within several thousand miles of Japan. That's a German brand. And when you smoke you hold your cigarette between your thumb and index finger, Americans always placed their smokes between the index and middle finger."

"Hmm," Lancelot quipped, "it seems smoking is bad for your health. Perhaps it's a habit you should have given up before you met Helen."

"I'm just different," Sharp argued. "I was raised in an orphanage, I just picked up habits because I wasn't taught the proper way to do things. You've proved nothing."

What does the term 'dull knife' mean to you?" Bryant asked.

"It's obvious," Sharp countered, "it means your blade is not sharp."

"Nothing else?"

He shook his head, "If you're trying to trap me, that won't work."

"Actually," Bryant explained, "the trap worked fine. 'Dull Knife' is what Charlie One-Horse nicknamed you. Now what's the matter, John? Have you run out of explanations? Is the rope we've tossed around your neck growing too tight?"

"John," Force whispered. "That was my brother's name."

Meeker moved one step closer to the now sweating Sharp. "The Japanese were likely told by the Germans to look over the bodies of all dead Americans. Sharp's was an almost a perfect match in size and build to the man you see standing before us now. When the Nazis discovered Sharp had no family then that made the switch ever more perfect. But the key that surely convinced them to work with the Japanese and create this mission was discovering that Sharp was about to transferred to intelligence. That had to come from Washington. My guess is that a certain general told his wife and she got the information back to Germany."

"You think you have it all figured out," Sharp snarled.

"Yes I do," Meeker agreed. "You already spoke English and could easily pass as the real Sharp, that is, if you had a different face. It must have been a great sacrifice to let them carve you up, but it was only because of that sacrifice that you almost got a ticket to DC. And don't act so shocked that we figured it out. We have several plants inside Germany who have essentially used the same method to go undercover."

"Are you my brother?" Force asked.

He glanced her way and smiled. "We share the same parents, but I was raised by the one who wasn't crazy."

"You killed your own sister," a now angry Force said.

"She was the bastard daughter of my father and a Jewish prostitute, and she was not fit to carry our name."

The reunited sibling squabble gave Matt Craig the opening he'd been looking for. He bound two steps forward, leaped over the couch, and hit Sharp like a linebacker taking down a halfback. As the rest of the room watched, the men wrestled. The pair was rolling in front of the fireplace when a single, muffled shot rang out.

With her Colt now out of her purse and in her hand, Meeker watched Craig roll off and stand up. Under him, the man posing as Sharp fought for breath.

Sensing his time was short, Meeker and Bryant moved closer and bent down over the now unmasked John Hoffman. He looked into Meeker's blue eyes and grinned.

"I should have killed you," he whispered. "If my cover was ever blown they told me I needed to get you before I tried to make my way back home." After the admission, he took a shallow breath and his head rolled to the side.

As a stunned Force collapsed on the couch, Jacobs walked back to the bar to pour another drink and a mute Craig stared into the unseeing eyes of the man he'd just killed. Needing to tie up loose ends, Meeker signaled for her team to follow her into foyer.

"I guess we played our cards right," Meeker said when the trio was out of earshot of those in the living room.

"The information came together in a hurry," Lancelot added. "Did you know he was Strauss and Force's brother?"

"I guessed," Bryant said, "but I thought it was a long shot. I simply said the name to see if he reacted. He didn't but evidently it triggered an old memory for Force. What I want I want to know is who killed Menefee?"

"If my reading of the evidence is correct," Lancelot suggested, "it wasn't Strauss. She was left-handed."

"But why would the man pretending to be Sharp need to take him out?"

"Perhaps," Meeker suggested, "because he knew too much. And as the two of you had been to Menefee's home, it makes sense that Menefee would have invited him in upon a return visit. Still there is no real proof. So I guess there are some things we'll never know. Let's call DiGiovanni and turn this mess over to him. And Nap, use your influence as the Chocolate Knight to bury anything that indicates there is any Nazi presence in this. This needs to be seen as nothing more than another homicide."

"The detective and I will dream something up," Lancelot assured her, "perhaps Jacobs can help us with the scripting."

"Helen," Bryant said, "let's go back to the hotel and pack. I'm ready to go home."

CHAPTER 50

Friday, February 4, 1943
7:44 p.m.
Overlook Restaurant, Ventura, California

After dropping Napoleon Lancelot off at the airport, Helen Meeker and Teresa Bryant headed north along Highway 101 to meet Matt Craig and Abby Force at a rural restaurant just outside of Ventura. The Overlook was named because its view of the Pacific, but as it was already after sunset it was now nothing more than a dark. After Meeker parked the car, the two women made their way inside.

"May I help you?" a tall man in a dark suit asked.

"We're meeting a couple," Meeker explained, "and we're about fifteen minutes late, so they're likely already here."

"The movie stars?"

"Yes."

"At his request, I gave them one of our most private areas. Just make your way down the back wall and past the conference room. Then take a left at the hall and you will see three tables. As per Mr. Craig's instructions, the other two will remain unused tonight. He paid me well to make sure of that."

"Thank you," Meeker replied.

The Overlook was only about half full on this night and most of the diners were far too intent on their meals to notice the women make their way to the wall and toward the back of the building. As Meeker passed the conference room the door opened and the waiter emerged. The entry stayed open just long enough for her to glance inside.

"Did you see that?" Bryant whispered as they continued walking toward their table.

"Yep, a senator, two members of the house, and a general. There are another dozen folks in there I didn't know. Must be some kind of big meeting going on. And based on the fact it's happening in a closed room, no one's supposed to ever find out about it."

Though her normal curiosity would have demanded she learn more, this was not a normal night. On this Friday evening Meeker simply wanted to have a final meeting with Craig and then get back to Chicago. It might be a lot colder in the Windy City, but she was tired of being in a place where the unreal and real were so hard to distinguish. As the women rounded the corner, Craig, dressed in a dark suit, stood.

"Good evening ladies, dining with three beautiful women must make me the most fortunate man in this state."

"We were surprised that you invited us," Meeker replied.

"Yes," Bryant added, "we understood that you will be joining the Army tomorrow."

He smiled. "And please sit down, because tonight we're celebrating that fact. We are also celebrating that Abby's and my father will never be known. So thanks to you and the studio, our movie will likely be a big success."

“That was mostly the studio,” Meeker assured him.

As soon as they took their seats, a waitress appeared and stood, pencil in hand, as they looked at the menu. Because of rationing a number of the most appealing items were crossed through.

“I’ve eaten here so many times that this back room is all but mine,” Craig explained. “Abby and I’ve already given our order in and based on what available tonight, I’d suggest the smoked chicken and boiled potatoes.”

“Put a Coke with that and I take it,” Meeker announced.

“Ditto,” Bryant added.

The teenage waitress jotted down the requests and hurried off. Within a minute she was back with the drinks and left.

A single candle set in the middle of the table created a sense of calm that was rarely know in today’s world. “I needed this night away from town,” Force explained. “This week has been nothing but a funeral and false news stories. I don’t understand why we couldn’t have just told the world about what really happened that night. Why did we reinvent the nightmare as nothing more than an accidental gas leak that killed Mattie? And why was there no mention of Sharp? Unlike Matt, I’m tied of living lies. I kind of want to be just simple Sunny Hoffman, a cute kid who sells men’s suits.”

Meeker looked to Bryant to take the lead and she did. “There was no mention of Sharp because we felt it best to keep the Nazis off balance. If they think he’s alive and working in Washington, it might work to our advantage.”

“So there will be a man named Michael Sharp working in Army Intelligence?” Craig asked.

"That's classified and likely hasn't been decided yet," Bryant explained.

"What a family I have," Force moaned. "My half sister tried to kill an American hero, my brother was a Nazi spy, my father was a German general, and my mother's just plain crazy."

"Actually," Bryant cut in, "your mother was the key to figuring most of this out. She made enough sense to move us in the right direction. In fact, without her, Matt might not be here tonight. Without her, you'd likely be in jail, charged with murder, and Matt would be dead. On top of that, Strauss would be trying to move into your spot on the studio lot and the fake Sharp would be on his way to Washington. In a real sense your mother is a hero!"

Force shook her head. "Whoever said fact is stranger than fiction was spot on."

"And," Meeker said, "though none of us will ever forget it, it's water under the bridge now. You've got your entire career in front of you."

"And," Bryant added, "Helen will never be stealing your spotlight again."

As those at the table chuckled, Meeker thought she heard a car backfire, but when that was followed by forty more bursts and the sound of boots rushing into the building, she knew better.

The restaurant was under attack!

She quickly looked at Bryant; her partner was already reaching into her purse for a gun. Five seconds later, when her Colt in her hand, Meeker peaked around the corner. What she saw all but stopped her heart. There were more than two-dozen Nazi storm troopers killing everyone in the dining room and the conference room. Even the teenage waitress was on the floor, bleeding from at least three wounds.

"We've got no chance," Bryant whispered.

"What's going on?" Craig asked.

"Carnage," Meeker answered as she turned to face him. "Is there a back way out of this place?" Craig pointed toward an exit to their right leading to a patio overlooking the ocean. Meeker nodded. "There's nothing we can do to help, so let's get moving."

With Craig holding the door Bryant and Meeker hustled out onto the deck. After quickly studying her options, Meeker pointed to some large boulders close to the shore. "We can use them for cover and then work our way back to the highway."

"Let's get going," Craig said as he burst out the door.

With Bryant leading the way, they made their way fifty yards down a hillside to the rocks. Only when they were out of view of the restaurant did Bryant stop, look back and make a sobering observation.

"Where's Abby?"

"She didn't make it," a breathless Craig answered. "She was shot before we could get out of the room."

A stunned Meeker glanced toward the Overlook. "The invaders are getting into two trucks and taking off." As she turned she lowered her gun and asked, "What was that all about?"

"It had to be a plan," Bryant explained, "and Root was a part of it. I heard about it when I was on her trail. Raids like this were supposed to stir up panic, but tonight, based on who was in that room, this one did a lot more. They took out some very important people."

"Including America's Sweetheart," Craig said.

As that sobering thought sank in, a burst of fire followed by a deafening explosion shook the entire area. Pieces of wood and brick were tossed through the air like confetti. The explosion was so powerful some of the debris landed in the Pacific.

"There went the evidence," Bryant suggested.

"Yeah, but if no one saw the Nazis, then it can likely be sold as just a freak gas explosion. That'll keep the whole West Coast from panicking."

"Helen," Bryant asked, "were the storm troopers headed our way?"

Meeker shook her head. "They were interested in getting the folks in the dining room and conference area. They didn't even look in our direction when I was watching."

"Then how did Abby get shot?"

The women looked at each other before quickly turning to Craig. He held two guns, and each was targeting one of them.

"Stupid fools." He laughed. "You got so close but you never figured it all out. Now drop your guns to the ground and start walking toward the beach."

After pitching her Colt, Meeker turned and dejectedly marched across a sandy beach now covered with debris. Bryant repeated the actions and followed. When they were both at the water's edge, Craig announced, "You may stop and turn around."

"What's this all about?" Meeker demanded. "If you're going to kill us, at least let us know why."

"It sounds like Teresa already has it figured out."

"You're a part of the mission Root was going to South American to help organize."

"I knew about it," he admitted, "but it had been in the works three years. So the plans were made before the US even entered the war. Germany has to buy time until Europe is defeated. The best way is to keep Americans frightened on the home front is to pull raids like this. My father calls it terrorism."

"The invaders never came into our area," Bryant stated, "so that means you must have killed Force? I can understand why you'd want to take out Helen and me, but why did Abby have to die?"

"That's simple. My father told me her family had to pay for the crimes of their father. It seemed her dad headed up a plot to assassinate Hitler. I was given the word to make sure everyone with any ties to Hoffman died."

Meeker nodded. "So you killed Menefee."

"I really didn't want to," Craig admitted. "Herman was a good man and I'd worked with him for years. He delivered messages between my father and me. But then he chose sides and he picked the wrong one."

"What's your part in all of this?" Bryant asked.

"As you will be dead in a matter of minutes, it won't hurt you to know. The explosion was cover. The cops will never be able to identify all the bodies, but a few minutes before you arrived, Scoop Melborne was at the Overlook. I gave him an exclusive story and allowed him to take some photographs of my last night as a civilian. During the interview I even mentioned that I thought I smelled gas. Then he raced off to report it on his weekly radio show. Thanks to him, and the ring and wallet I left behind, everyone will know that I'm dead and that frees me up to lead Operation Gale Force. Tonight was the debut of our special forces raids. From this point forward I will be directing the operations. We will appear out of nowhere, inflict damage, and kill specialized targets and disappear into thin air. Without the uniforms my men will look just like every other American man and we'll have the paperwork to back it up."

"You won't do that much damage," Bryant said.

"The key is not the amount of damage, the key is the panic our attacks on American soil will create. We just need to shake up the civilians enough to force your government to seek a truce."

"There's something in all this that doesn't add up," Meeker surmised.

"What's that?" Craig asked.

"Why did Root pass along the information to Strauss and Force about Operation Gale Force in those matchbooks?

Craig shook his head, "I don't know anything about matchbooks."

"What does GA 36723 mean to you?" Bryant asked.

Craig laughed. "It's the registration number on my boat. So the matchbooks must have been their signal to kill me. You see, Root's brother didn't trust my father so that likely meant his sister didn't either. She must have passed that information along to Hoffman. Hoffman gave it to his contacts in a way where they didn't have to use my birth or stage name to order the hit. Now, as the authorities will soon be here, and I have to disappear, it's time for me to get rid of the two of you. Say your prayers if you have any to say."

Meeker frowned and looked to her left. "You want to tell me how old you are?"

"No reason to," Bryant answered, her eyes looking straight ahead. "We'll talk about it at another time and in another place."

"I've always admired your optimism," Meeker replied with a grin, "or is this all about looking at the afterlife? You've never been straight with me about what you really believe about that."

Bryant laughed. "We'll have lots of time for that discussion. Movie stars never really kill people. When the director says, 'Cut,' everyone always gets back up."

"I'll guess I'll shoot you first," Craig announced as he smiled at Bryant. "You know, I've never seen a person so calm and relaxed. How can you joke at a time like this? It's almost like you want to die."

A second later a single shot rang out and as it did a shocked look was suddenly etched onto Craig's face. He staggered for a moment and then turned. Abby Force, her dress soaked with blood was holding the gun Meeker had dropped on the ground. Meeker shook her head, she'd seen this same scene play out before, but this time the dialogue had been rewritten.

"I killed you," Craig whispered.

"You shot me," Force corrected him. "Not everyone dies when they're shot. You should know that."

Craig's arm dropped to his side as he fell to his knees. He then studied the actress for a few seconds before falling forward. A split second later a satisfied Force also dropped to the ground.

After kicking the gun away from Craig, Meeker hurried to the actress. There was no pulse.

"She finished her mission," Bryant sadly said, "and settled a family score. I'll guess we'll never know if she was a part of what happened at the studio."

"No matter what, her final performance was her best," Meeker added. She looked back at her partner and frowned. "Did you see this coming?"

"No, Craig was the one person in all of this I didn't doubt. This is also the first time I can remember where maybe everyone was the bad guy. It appears not a single person we dealt with was clean."

"Let's call the FBI," Meeker suggested. "They have some men dressed in German uniforms to round up and we'll let them and DiGiovanni deal with the press."

Bryant studied the two bodies before glancing up to the decimated restaurant and wearily shaking her head. "I haven't been this tired in a hundred years."

The sounds of sirens prevented Meeker from digging into that cryptic observation. For the moment it was time to try to explain the unexplainable to a group of cops that were ill prepared to deal with what Craig had called terrorism. Maybe on the flight back to Chicago Meeker could dive into what Bryant had really meant. After all, as her partner had pointed out, they had lots of time.

ABOUT THE AUTHOR

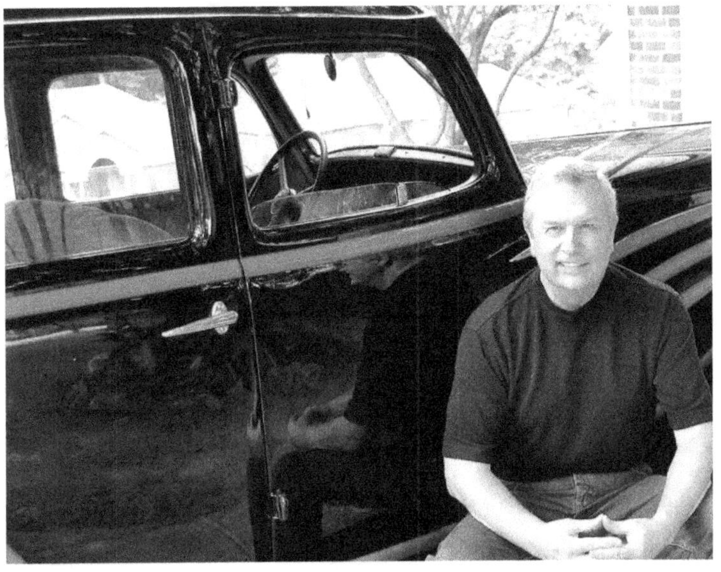

Ace Collins is the prolific author of more than 80 books including *The Stories Behind the Best-Loved Songs of Christmas, Lassie: A Dog's Life, The Color of Justice*, and *Service Tails*, and the fifteen-book (so far) series, *In the President's Service* for Elk Lake Publishing Inc.

Ace and his wife, Kathy, live in Arkadelphia, AR, where he happily writes, fixes up old cars, and plays his vintage Fender guitar.

ACE COLLINS—
IN THE PRESIDENT'S SERVICE

In the President's Service: Episodes 1-3
In the President's Service: Episodes 4-6

Prequel: The Yellow Packard

1. A Date With Death
2. The Dark Pool
3. Blood Brothers
4. Fatal Addiction
5. The Devil's Eyes
6. The Dead Can Talk
7. Bottled Madness
8. Shadows in the Moonlight
9. Evilution
10. Uneasy Alliance
11. The 13th Floor
12. The White Rose
13. The Cat's Eye
14. The Red Suit Case
15. Set for Danger

THE COLLECTION

www.ingramcontent.com/pod-product-compliance
Lightning Source LLC
Chambersburg PA
CBHW070354260626
47161CB00001B/139

9781948888202